THE
ANGEL OF
INNISFREE

PATRICK F. ROONEY

ALSO BY PATRICK F. ROONEY:
THE ACHERON DECEPTION

ISBN-10: 0-9907436-2-4
ISBN-13: 978-0-9907436-2-0

DEDICATION

To Anne and Bill White,
and to my parents,
for having the courage to
build a new life for themselves in America.

ACKNOWLEDGMENTS

To my brother-in-law, Bill White, for igniting my interest in Civil War history, as well as Ireland's Neolithic archeology.

To Dominic Rooney in Galway, Ireland, for his book entitled *The life and times of Sir Frederick Hamilton, 1590 – 1647*. His fascinating account of the life of Frederick Hamilton contains a vivid description of the setting used in the early chapters of the book. I'd also like to thank Dominic for sharing his Irish history expertise with me and for lending me a copy of Prin Duignan's booklet entitled *North Leitrim in Famine Times, 1840 – 50*.

To Tom Wheeler, whose book entitled *Mr. Lincoln's T-Mails: How Abraham Lincoln Used the Telegraph to Win the Civil War*, described the important role the telegraph played during Lincoln's presidency.

To Tyler Anbinder, whose book entitled *Five Points*, describes New York City during the 19th century.

To James McPherson, whose book entitled *Battle Cry of Freedom*, contains a superbly written history of the American Civil War.

To Melissa Lowe, for her valuable "beta-reader" feedback and encouragement.

To my friend and Irish Solicitor, Conor Maguire of Manorhamilton, Ireland, for his judicious observations and advice.

To my editor, Tammy Salyer, for her sharp-eyed proofreading skills and copyediting suggestions.

And to Patti Roberts of Paradox Book Designs, for her wonderful cover art and formatting assistance.

The Lake Isle of Innisfree

I will arise and go now, and go to Innisfree,
And a small cabin build there, of clay and wattles made;
Nine bean rows will I have there, a hive for the honey bee,
And live alone in the bee loud glade.

And I shall have some peace there, for peace comes dropping slow,
Dropping from the veils of the morning to where the cricket sings;
There midnight's all a glimmer, and noon a purple glow,
And evening full of the linnet's wings.

I will arise and go now, for always night and day
I hear lake water lapping with low sounds by the shore;
While I stand on the roadway, or on the pavements grey,
I hear it in the deep heart's core.

– W. B. Yeats (1888)

1. BRIAN O'ROURKE

Creevelea Abbey. Dromahair, Ireland. September 4, 1848.

THE SHAKESPEARE PLAY Brother Bernard is reading aloud to me, *As You Like It,* is making me laugh. The antics of noblemen living with peasants in the forest and a woman that disguises herself as a man so she can spy on her beloved are hilarious.

It feels good to laugh again—something I haven't done much lately. It's hard to be cheerful when I watch people starve to death every day.

My attention strays to the rain as I listen to Brother Bernard. It's been drizzling all afternoon, making the sloped roof of his small, canvas wedge tent sag down almost to our heads.

Three elderly women wander onto the grass in front of us—sisters by the looks of them. Their bare feet, sopping wet dresses, and tousled hair give them the appearance of walking scarecrows. They meander among the abbey's roofless walls for a moment before they walk toward us. We often get vagrants seeking shelter here in the tent, especially when it rains.

Brother Bernard stops reading and picks up a sharp stick as they approach. One of the women stoops down and tries to enter.

"Move along now," he says, poking her leg. "There's no room for you here. The Viking meadow is on the north side of the lake. Cross the footbridge and go left on the trail and you'll find it."

"The devil be with you!" she snarls as she turns away.

Her sisters follow her through the tall grass toward the footbridge.

Brother Bernard repeats the previous line he read, and continues from where he left off. We share a few more laughs, and then he finishes the play, and closes his book.

The rain has dissipated to a fine mist now.

"So Brian," he says, "what did you like most about Shakespeare's *As You Like It?*"

I shift my legs and lean back against the tent, which butts up against one of the abbey's thick exterior rock walls. I'm not sure what to say. The gray and black ruins stare back at me impassively when I search them for a response.

I wonder if the monks who used to live here ever read Shakespeare.

My gaze returns to Brother Bernard. "I liked the lines that said 'all the world's a stage, and all the men and women merely players. They have their exits and their entrances, and one man in his time plays many parts.'"

He nods at me as he smiles. "Why do you like that passage?"

"I don't know... maybe because it's true."

"What do you mean?"

"I've watched hundreds of people die in the meadow—children, farmers, old people, shopkeepers, even teenagers like me—and everyone goes stiff in the end. The roles they played in their lives don't seem to matter when death takes them. It's as if they're leaving the stage at the end of a play. The earth still rotates. The seasons still change."

The brown-robed, fifty-three-year-old Frenchman—his hair cut short in a tonsure style, with a shaved patch on the crown—purses his lips as he studies me. "Do you really believe that the roles we play don't matter?"

Another difficult question. "I guess I'm not sure."

The sun emerges from behind a cloud, prompting the dark gray walls of the dilapidated ruins to sparkle with reflecting light. A gentle breeze urges the thick scent of ozone into my nostrils.

I feel sad as I look at Brother Bernard. I'm going to miss him.

"I've enjoyed having you as my mentor," I say. "Studying French, Latin, mathematics, and literature has been enlightening, but most of all, I loved playing the violin with you."

"I enjoyed our time together too, my son. You have an inquisitive mind... and you're quite mature for a sixteen-year-old."

He steps out of the tent and stretches his arms up toward the sky. I follow him. It feels good to stand up after sitting for so long.

"Let's play some music before I go," he says, "after we put the tent away. It looks like the weather is clearing."

We yank the stakes out of the muddy grass, coil the ropes, and fold the tent into a rectangle. Brother Bernard lays the tent dry-side-up on the wall, and we sit down next to each other. He takes his violin out of its leather case, as I grab mine from my burlap backpack.

Several misty banks of fog hover around us, drifting like cotton-robed ghosts along the ground.

"I'd like to play Vivaldi's Summer Concerto," he says. "Do you want to try the solo part this time?"

"I'd love to."

He sets his music on a rock in front of us, and we brace our violins beneath our chins.

"Imagine the notes to be like raindrops in a storm," he says. "Let the musical tension build with each repetition of the theme, like a brook that becomes a stream that flows into a river."

He watches me closely as I raise my bow. I nod, and we release the first subtle melody—a gentle hint of the storm to follow. Vivaldi's Summer Concerto is always challenging, especially the solo part, but I've memorized the notes, so all I need to do is channel the music through the strings.

The intensity builds slowly. Sweet at first, then cogent, insistent, demanding, until we're flailing our bows releasing an ocean of sound that echoes off the rock walls. We queue each other with nods as the piece ebbs and flows, forceful, then relaxed, strident, then calm—and in what seems like a moment, the eleven-minute concerto is over, and we round our bows with a flourish at the end.

The final notes reverberate around the abbey's roofless partitions for several seconds—walls that witnessed celibate monks singing Gregorian chants for centuries before the religious wars came. The gurgling chortle of the Bonet River below the abbey returns as the music fades away. The river, flowing west toward Lough Gill, is boisterous after the recent rainstorms.

Brother Bernard grins. "I don't think there's much more I can teach you, my son."

"Thanks. I've learned a lot from you these past two years."

"I hope you get to perform with an orchestra someday. It's like a rainbow for the ears when all the instruments harmonize together."

"I hope I do too."

He places his violin in its leather case, while I store mine in my burlap backpack.

"I'm looking forward to resuming my role as a teacher at the Conservatoire de Paris," he says, as he shoves his case into his backpack. "One of my fondest memories is playing with the Conservatoire's orchestra during the debut of Hector Berlioz's *Symphonie Fantastique* in 1830."

A misty rain begins, prodding the dark green hills around us to emit an earthy, pungent redolence. The rain then stops as quickly as it began.

I grab a burlap pouch out of my backpack and hand it to Brother Bernard. "Da said to tell you he appreciates the schooling you've given Mary and me. He's sorry he can't pay you anything more than this bit of oatmeal."

"Tell your father that I appreciate his generosity. He's a good man. He was very kind to share his home with me during those bone-chilling nights last winter. I enjoyed playing music and swapping stories with your family around the fire pit."

"We enjoyed having you, Brother Bernard."

He opens the pouch, pours some oats into my hand, and some into his own, and we gobble down the precious grains. I lick my fingers when I'm done to get every morsel. The snack does little to quench the hunger gnawing at my gut.

He stows the pouch in his backpack.

"Why didn't your brothers take advantage of my lessons while I was here?" he says.

"Patrick and James say that book learning is a waste of time when you're fighting to stay alive."

The monk shakes his head. "Your brothers should pay attention to history. The Anglo-Irish government authorities prohibited Catholics from attending school for centuries after the Protestant plantations. Keeping a population ignorant and hungry makes them easy to subjugate."

I nod my agreement. "Mary said she's sorry she couldn't say goodbye. Da took her to Manorhamilton to find her a husband this morning."

"Your sister's a clever girl. I've noticed that women are just as smart as men when they have the opportunity to study."

"Indeed."

A double rainbow appears above the arched walls. We gaze at it for a moment in silence.

"I'm glad we met here for our lessons," he says. "This Franciscan friary, which was built in 1508 by your ancestor, Owen O'Rourke, was a center for learning and spiritual meditation in the Kingdom of Breifne, before Oliver Cromwell's troops destroyed it in 1649. He built the friary on a site that St. Patrick used as a church in the fifth century. Several generations of my ancestors came here from France to study."

I wonder if my ancestors are looking down at us, I muse, as I stare at the rainbows. I feel their spirits here sometimes—or at least *I think* I do.

"Where'd you get that oatmeal?" he says.

I survey the hills to make sure no one is listening. "Da and my brothers and their Ribbonmen friends flipped over a grain wagon outside Manorhamilton yesterday. The English were bringing the grain to Sligo for export to England. More than two hundred people converged on the site and scooped up every morsel. My brothers filled a couple of bags for our family."

He nods. "It's hard to understand the lack of compassion shown by your Protestant overlords. There's more than enough livestock and grain produced in Ireland to feed everyone, yet they continue to export dozens of shiploads of Irish produce every day, while thousands of people here are starving to death."

"What caused our potatoes to turn into black slime again, Brother Bernard? It's the third year in a row. Is God punishing us?"

His gaze veers to a fog bank floating toward us. "It's impossible to know God's plan."

The fog shrouds us as it passes, leaving a delicate mist in its wake.

"Where will you go when you leave here today?"

He stands, pulls a map canister out of his backpack, extracts a map of Western Europe, and unfurls it on top of the thick rock wall. I'm six inches taller than he is when I stand up next to him.

He points at Sligo on the map, which is eight miles west of us, on the other side of Lough Gill. "I'll board a ship here tomorrow morning," he says. He traces a path with his finger along the western and southern coasts of Ireland. "And from there I'll sail to Galway and Kinsale. I'll then board a steamer in Kinsale." His finger moves from Kinsale to France. "And cross the Celtic Sea to Brittany, where I was born. After a brief visit with my sister, I'll return to Paris, and resume my teaching position at the Conservatoire."

He turns and looks at me with a concerned stare. "I think you'll need to leave Ireland soon if you want to survive. Things are going to get very ugly here this winter."

"Why do you say that?"

"The Crown is sending more troops to Ireland to squash subversive groups such as the Ribbonmen and the Molly Maguire's, after the Young Irelander Rebellion in Tipperary last July. The English Parliament is determined to rid the country of rebels, as well as tenants that can't pay their rent. You'll see mass evictions and starvation if you stay... even worse than what you've witnessed the past two years."

"That explains why I've seen so many soldiers on the roads recently."

"I saw English troops patrolling all the routes to the ports when I travelled across Ireland this past summer. Tell your brothers to be careful. The Crown will hang them, or sentence them to life in prison, for stealing that much grain."

A shiver jolts my spine. The damp air is cooling as the sun drops toward the horizon.

"Personally, I'd prefer the gallows," he says. "I spent a week in Dublin's Kilmainham Gaol last year. The prison cells are freezing, damp, and crawling with rats. The guards made us break rocks with sledgehammers from dawn to dusk, to make gravel for the roads. I couldn't imagine a more dismal hell on earth."

"Why were you in prison?"

"The Irish Constabulary in Dublin arrested me for sleeping in St. Stephen's Green."

"That seems like a harsh punishment for such a minor infraction."

"Yes, it was, but it's typical with the Protestant warden, since I'm obviously Catholic."

"What's going to happen to the leaders of the Young Irelander Rebellion? I heard they've been imprisoned."

"They'll probably be hanged, or sent to the penal colony on Van Diemen's Land."

The monk pulls a world map out of his canister and unfurls it on the wall. He points at Ireland. "Here we are." He moves his finger along the west coast of Africa and across the Indian Ocean to an island south of Australia. "And here's Van Diemen's Land."

"That's really far."

"Yes, it is, and the voyage is dangerous. It takes two-and-a-half to three months, depending on the weather." He points at North America. "It only takes three to six weeks to reach Canada or the United States from here. That's where I'd go if I were you."

He rolls up his maps and shoves them into the canister in his backpack.

A large black and white magpie lands on a stone arch across from us as we sit down. It's Maggie. I recognize her by the tiny white spot beneath her black beak. I rescued her after she fell from her nest when she was a fledgling, and fed her worms until she was strong enough to fly.

She greets me with a warbling screech when we lock eyes.

"I have some going-away presents for you," the monk says.

He digs deep into his backpack, pulls out a pair of used leather boots, and hands them to me. "Try these on." He chuckles. "They should fit you. I have large feet, even though I'm short."

I push my bare feet into the boots, lace them, stand up, and walk around in a circle. "These are grand, Brother Bernard. I've never worn shoes before."

"I wish I had some socks to give you. You'll get blisters until your feet get used to them."

"I won't mind. My feet are pretty tough already."

"I have something else for you."

He slides a bundle wrapped in a blanket out of his backpack. He removes the blanket, and hands me six wooden sticks with flags attached.

"These are your country's new tricolor flags," he says. "One of your Young Irelander leaders, a fellow named Thomas Meagher, brought them back from Paris earlier this year, after he met with the rebels that overthrew the French monarchy. The green and orange stripes on the outside represent the Catholics and Protestants of Ireland, and the white stripe in the middle symbolizes hopes for peace between them."

I wave one of the flags above my head. "This is grand. Thank you."

"Would you like to learn how to use flags to send messages,

something I learned when I fought at the Battle of Waterloo, in 1815?"

"I didn't know you were in the military."

He raises his eyebrows. "I had no choice. Napoleon conscripted me into the French army when I was twenty."

He pulls a sheet of paper out of his backpack and places it on the wall. The paper has drawings of stickmen holding flags in each hand.

"Those are the flag signals," he says. "Each position represents a letter, a number, or a message control command. Stand in front of me, and I'll show you how to use flags to make an optical telegraph."

I hand him two flags, keep two, and lay the other two on the wall.

"You begin each new word with both flags down," he says, as I face him. "Move your right hand forty-five degrees for the letter *A*."

I look at the drawing and emulate his movements.

"Good," he says. "Raise your right hand to ninety degrees for the letter *B*."

I move my right hand another forty-five degrees. "I get it." I look at the paper and move another forty-five degrees. "And this is the letter *C*."

"That's right."

We practice each letter, number, and command for several minutes. Brother Bernard then pulls a Leitrim and a Sligo county map out of his canister, and unfurls them on the wall.

"You should take these with you," he says. "Your father's Ribbonmen could use flags to send messages to each other from these hilltops." He points at locations marked in red on the maps. "This might help them intercept shipments that are on their way to the ports."

"Won't Clements's soldiers see our messages too?"

He chuckles. "That's very insightful, Brian. Yes, the enemy will see them too. That's why it's a good idea to use coded messages. Your brilliant Irish field marshal, the Duke of Wellington—who was born in Dublin by the way—decoded our messages during the battle of Waterloo. Having information about our pending troop movements helped him defeat Napoleon. We didn't realize what he was doing until it was too late."

"How do you send a coded message?"

"First you create a cipher. For example, add the number three to each code." He chuckles. "I use the number three, because it reminds me of the holy trinity. You represent the letter *A* by sending the flag signal for the letter *D*. *E* is used to represent the letter *B*, and so forth."

"I see. That's very clever."

The monk gazes at me with a serious stare. "There *is* a danger, though."

"What's that?"

"The Crown may view your spying activities as an act of war, and they'll certainly retaliate if you steal their grain shipments."

I shrug my shoulders. "Things can't get much worse than they already are."

He nods. "That's true, which is why I gave you these flags. Norah Gallagher, a seamstress in Manorhamilton, made these for me, in exchange for some French lessons I gave her children. I'm sure she'll make more if you ask her."

"I need to show these flags and maps to Da first, to see if he approves."

I shove the flags, maps, and flag signal paper into my backpack. We then sit down next to each other on the wall. He pulls a tobacco pipe out of a pocket in his cloak, lights it, and exhales a lungful of smoke.

"What was it like," I say, "being a soldier in Napoleon's army?"

He puffs on his pipe before he responds. "It was horrible. I'll never forget the look in that English soldier's eye when I gutted him with my knife. His blood and excrement gushed over me as we wrestled, and then he died in my arms. That's why I became a monk. I shut myself away from the world after the war."

"That must have been awful. I've seen a lot of people die, but I've never caused it myself."

He sucks on his pipe and exhales. "You should go to America, Brian. You can make a good life for yourself there."

"I don't want to die on a coffin ship. I've heard that sharks follow the ships, waiting for the dead bodies the sailors throw overboard. Besides, my father wouldn't let me. He says this is our land, and these are our people, and it's our responsibility to take care of them. We're the last of the ruling O'Rourke clan in Leitrim."

"Be careful of catching diseases on a ship if you do go," he says. "I witnessed a terrible outbreak of cholera in Liverpool. The boarding houses near the docks were crowded with refugees—sometimes twenty to a room. I noticed that everyone in the house succumbed to the same illness after one person got sick. The doctors say that miasma, what they call *evil air*, causes the disease, but I'm not so sure. The entire city would have gotten sick if it was evil air."

He puffs on his pipe. "Most people believe that disease is God's providence... that there's nothing that can be done about it—but I think the sick were contaminating each other. Cramming people into close quarters on a ship is another good way to spread disease. Try to sleep alone if you can, and stay away from anyone that gets sick."

"How can we leave? Da says our clan has been here for over a thousand years."

"You'll have to if you want to survive. Over half a million people have died of starvation and related diseases the past two years, and another half million could die this year. The English estate owners want their Irish property cleared of tenants, so they can use their land for livestock production. Sheep and cattle farming are more lucrative than grain production, now that they've abolished the Corn Laws, and it takes one-tenth as many farmers. The Crown is also levying a tax on landlords, when their indigent tenants go to the workhouses, so it's cheaper to just evict them."

My mind strays to the gurgling babble of the river beyond the meadow... flowing ever onward to the ocean—the ocean that could bring me to America. "Da says our clan ruled these lands for seven hundred years, before the English came. He named me after our ancestral leader—Brian O'Rourke. He says it's my responsibility to take care of our people."

The monk dismisses the hills with his hand. "You won't be able to help anyone if you're dead. You'll starve to death... or end up in prison. Besides, do you really want to raise a family in a country governed by tyrants that have no regard for their own people?"

"How can we buy tickets for a famine ship? Da doesn't have any money."

"Use your brain. You're a smart boy. You can always earn a shilling by warming a man's heart with a song. You also know how to read and write, you can speak French and Latin, and you're brilliant with mathematics. You learned Euclid's *Elements* much quicker than I did."

"The formulas and equations just seemed like puzzles to me."

"You can have the violin music we played together if you'd like."

I point at my temple. "Thanks, but I've already memorized the violin parts."

He chuckles. "That's what I mean, son. You have special gifts. God has blessed you with a sharp mind, and a voracious capacity to learn. Always remember, though, that knowledge and wisdom aren't the same thing."

"What do you mean?"

"Wisdom is being able to see the world for what it is, rather than what you want it to be."

This seems important, but I'm not sure why. I'll have to think about it later.

"I pray that you don't let your precious gifts go to waste," he goes on. "That's why I read you the Shakespeare play. I think it's saying that our lives belong to us... to do with as we like."

The gleam in his eye awakens something inside me. Maybe I *can* go to America someday.

"Ma says I have special gifts too," I say. "She says she saw it in my eyes when I was born."

He chuckles. "Is that so?"

"I never know what having special gifts means, until someone points them out to me—things I take for granted, like learning languages quickly, or memorizing melodies on my violin after I hear them once."

He nods. "I wish *I* had those abilities."

"I used to think that my dark eyes and black hair were the reason for my special gifts. As you know, my brothers and sister have reddish-blond hair and blue eyes." I chuckle. "I thought my dark eyes meant that I had something different growing inside me when I was a child, like some kind of animal that would die, if I didn't feed it. I know that was silly now that I'm sixteen."

He laughs, and takes a long puff on his pipe.

My two older brothers, nineteen-year-old Patrick and eighteen-year-old James, like to tease me about how different I look, but they're the first to defend me when someone implies that Ma wasn't faithful to Da. They also taught me how to fight so I can stand up for myself—bare-knuckled boxing that draws blood when you aim for the nose—and how to throw knives. Mary, our seventeen-year-old sister, is the best when it comes to spiking a target with a dagger, though.

"I've been wondering about a few things," I say. "I guess I should ask you *now*, since you'll be leaving soon."

"What are your questions, my son?"

I'm reluctant to ask him this, but I'm also curious to hear what he'll say. "Is murder a sin if you're in combat, like when you were conscripted into the army?"

He stares at the ruins for a moment before he answers. "I don't really know. I guess I'll find out after I die."

"I also want to know why God punishes us with starvation, disease, and war."

The monk studies me with a steady gaze. "That's another good question, my son... another one I can't answer. At some point, I think it just comes down to faith."

"Faith?"

"Yes. Faith—that there's a higher power, something to lean on, that's bigger than all of us."

I feel ignorant about God—what he, *or it*—really is. Relying on faith seems vague.

His eyebrows rise. "Can I trust you with a secret? Maybe this will help you understand the world a little better."

"Of course."

He stares deep into my eyes. "Although I'm a monk, and a teacher, I'm also a vassal of the state. I work for the French government. I use my spiritual avocation as a disguise."

"What do you do for them?"

He looks around furtively. "My government sent me here at the request of the Holy See. I'm one of several agents in Ireland keeping an eye on things. Unfortunately, my government has been in turmoil since the February Revolution, so they've called us all home now."

"The Holy See... do you mean the Vatican... the pope?"

"That's right. You'll recall from our history discussions that Catholicism has been under siege in Britain for centuries, ever since Henry the Eighth divorced Catherine of Aragon, so he could marry Anne Boleyn. We've been keeping a close watch on Britain's rulers ever since."

"Is the pope going to help us?"

He shakes his head. "No. Although the Catholic Church is very wealthy, they don't have an army of their own. They rely on countries like France and Spain to fight their battles. However, neither country wants to start a war with England right now."

"Why did you come *here,* to Dromahair?"

"I like staying here when I'm not travelling around Ireland. The monks at Creevelea Abbey educated several generations of my ancestors. My clan is from Brittany, in northwest France. We traded with your O'Rourke clan for centuries, before the British came. That's why I learned your native language so easily. We share the same Celtic tongue."

"I see."

The monk taps his pipe against the wall and empties the ashes. He then stows it in his cloak.

"I have one more thing to give you before I leave," he says. "Follow me."

We walk to the abbey's covered water well. There's a wooden bucket tied to a thick rope attached to a crankshaft, beneath the circular roof.

He pulls a four-inch stone key out of his cloak. "I'm entrusting this key to you," he says. "You should only use it if you need a place to hide. It opens a secret chamber beneath the abbey."

He drops the key into the well. It disappears with a *plop* beneath the dark water.

"How deep is that?" I say.

"About ten feet below the water line. You can swim, can't you?"

"Yes."

I stare into the moss-walled cylinder. I can swim, but I hope I never have to jump in there. I'm sure the water is freezing, and I'd have to climb up the slippery rope to reach the edge.

We walk back to the wall. He squeezes the folded tent into his backpack, lifts it, and I help him secure the belts around his waist and shoulders.

He hugs me for a few seconds, and steps back holding my shoulders. "I wish you luck, my son. You'll be in my prayers."

"You'll be in mine too, Brother Bernard. Have a safe journey."

I watch him as he trudges west on a trail that leads to the southern edge of Lough Gill. He turns and waves at the top of the hill, and vanishes on the other side.

I secure my backpack around my shoulders, cross the footbridge over the Bonet River, and turn left on a footpath that leads to the north side of Lough Gill. I zigzag along the jagged shoreline for a mile past the inlet, veer north at a fork in the trail, cross a dirt road, and ascend the hill to our home.

Wisps of smoke from a peat fire are wafting out of our crooked chimney when I arrive ten minutes later. I hide the six tricolor flags in a crevice beneath two large rocks. I'll show them to Da tomorrow morning when the light is better.

The clatter of galloping hooves pulls my gaze down to Parke's Castle, on the north side of the lake. A covered carriage pulled by two white stallions enters the castle gate, followed by four English soldiers on horses.

Hmm. The castle must have important guests for Solicitor Reilly's eviction brigade to accompany them.

Most of the five-mile-wide lake is visible below me. Da says our location here is a good vantage point to observe our lands. Parke's Castle—currently occupied by Viscount Clements's eviction solicitor, Charles Reilly—stands on land our O'Rourke clan governed for centuries, when we ruled the Kingdom of Breifne.

Ma emerges from our mud and stone hut and stands next to me. "I'm glad you're home," she says, hugging me sideways. "Did Brother Bernard leave today?"

"Yes, he did. I'm going to miss him."

"I'm sure you will. He was very kind to tutor you without asking for anything in return."

"Indeed." I point at my leather boots. "Look what he gave me."

"That was nice of him. Your brothers will be envious. Maybe I'll knit you some wool socks for Christmas."

"That would be wonderful, Ma."

The setting sun casts a silver iridescent glow across the lake.

"Our castle sure looks grand in the evening," she says.

"Is it really ours? Brother Bernard told me the castle was built by the Protestants."

"That's partially true. Your father's ancestors built the original castle. The Crown confiscated it after Queen Elizabeth executed Brian

O'Rourke for treason in 1591, for giving shelter to soldiers from the Spanish Armada. The Crown then gave the castle and all the land around it to English noblemen, during the Protestant plantations in 1620. An Englishman then built his own castle, using materials from the original O'Rourke castle."

She stoops down and enters our one-room stone hut. I follow her inside, and stow my backpack in the corner.

Ma shoves a peat brick into the fire pit. "Your brothers went with Da and Mary to Manorhamilton this morning. They should be back soon."

She stirs a pot of oatmeal next to the fire. "I hope we get some good news tonight. Mary's a pretty girl, but a bag of oatmeal isn't much to offer as a dowry."

Ma casts her gaze at Mildred, our pig, who is lounging on the hay of our family bed. "Mildred would be an enticing dowry," she says, "but Da wants to keep her for food this winter."

"Mary's only seventeen. Why does she need to be betrothed now?"

"Finding her a husband with money will ensure she doesn't starve to death this winter. All the potatoes we planted on the hillside are rotten."

"Brother Bernard said it's the same all across Ireland. He thinks a half-million people could starve to death this winter. Maybe it's time to immigrate to America."

Ma shakes her head. "Your father will never leave his land."

I contemplate the smoldering coals in the fire pit.

Ma pulls a comb from her pocket. "Sit down next to me so I can fix your hair. You need to look proper... when you usher the dying into eternity."

I sit down cross-legged with my back to her, and she starts to unsnarl my tangles.

"My beautiful Black Irishman," she says. "You look a lot like your grandfather. He had black hair and dark eyes too."

"Why do you call me Black Irish? I'm not black."

She chuckles. "I know. It's just a saying, because of the Spanish blood in your veins. Some of the Spanish Armada soldiers stayed in Ireland and started families with O'Rourke women. That's where your Spanish blood came from."

I stare at the oatmeal. "May I eat before I go down to the meadow?

I'm hungry."

"We can't eat until Da returns. Don't worry. I'll save some for you."

"Do I really need to keep going to the meadow? It's depressing... watching people die every night, especially the children."

"Your father will be disappointed if you don't comfort them."

She finishes combing my hair. "There. You look very handsome."

"Thanks, Ma."

I stand up, sling my backpack over my shoulder, and we duck our heads as we exit. The lake shimmers with an orange radiance as the sun kisses the horizon.

"There are a lot of people in the meadow tonight," she says. "A family trudged up our trail to beg me for oatmeal today. They must have heard about the grain wagon. I had to turn the poor souls away. We only have one bag left for ourselves. We won't have any if Mary is betrothed."

I hug her. "Goodbye, Ma."

I turn and trudge down the trail. A star appears above me as I reach the meadow.

I climb to the top of the Viking rock, and pull out my violin. Da says that our ancestors placed the stone here over a thousand years ago, when this was an important meeting place.

There are at least three dozen people lying on the grass below me. Some of them are moaning, huddled in fetal positions, holding their stomachs. Many have green teeth and leaves tangled in their unkempt hair. Others are already stiff, lifeless. Several emaciated children gripped by the dysentery that accompanies cholera are lying in fetid pools of diarrhea. They'll be dead soon—a welcome escape from their tortured lives, I presume. The three sisters I saw earlier are here too.

Several tinkers are milling about in the woods. They'll descend like vultures to steal the clothes and shoes from the dead after I leave.

I raise my violin to my shoulder, and begin the same way I do every night, playing the melody from Chopin's "Funeral March."

2. ELIZABETH REILLY

Parke's Castle. Newtown, Ireland.

THE LAST CHORD echoes around the rock-walled parlor for several seconds before it fades away. I pull my hands off the piano keyboard and open my eyes.

Abigail Hughes, my portly forty-five-year-old governess, stirs from her sleep in the rocking chair next to the fireplace.

"That was nice, Elizabeth," she says, as she covers a yawn with her hand.

"Thank you, Miss Hughes. That's the first time I've played Bach's 4th invention in D minor from memory without looking at the music. The piano Father borrowed sounds marvelous, don't you think?"

"It certainly does."

I turn and survey the room. Flames from the fireplace are casting a warm glow over the dark Victorian furniture and Indian rugs on the stone floor.

"It feels good to be home after so many years away," I say.

"How long has it been since your mother died?"

"Nine years. I was seven when Father sent me to live with Aunt Bess in London."

Miss Hughes stands up and lays her half-finished needlepoint handkerchief in the seat. "It was nice of Viscount Clements to let your father borrow the piano so you can practice."

"It was indeed. I love the way the bass notes rumble around the rock walls in here."

"I'm going to the kitchen for some tea. Shall I send the maid up with some for you?"

"No thanks. I'm fine."

Harold Mayberry, Father's butler, steps into the parlor. He's wearing a high-collared white shirt with a white bowtie and a black jacket cropped squarely at the back.

He offers me a large envelope on a silver tray. "This arrived by post for you this afternoon, Miss Reilly."

"Oh good." I look at the sender's address. "It's from Aunt Bess. This is probably Robert Schumann's *Scenes from Childhood* book of piano songs she ordered for me. They're very popular in London right now."

I tear the side of the envelope and pull out the contents. "Yes, it is!"

Mayberry smiles when I place the envelope on his tray. "I'm glad you're pleased, Miss Reilly."

"I'll be back in a few minutes," Miss Hughes says.

Mayberry waits for her to pass him, and then he follows her out of the parlor.

I place the music on the keyboard stand and open the book to the first song, "Of Foreign Lands and Peoples." I then sight-read the piece without stopping. *That was very nice.*

I page through the book until I reach a song called "Träumerei," which means *dreaming* in English. I take a few deep breaths, and play the melancholy piece to the end, which brings tears to my eyes. I wipe them away with a handkerchief as I look around the room. I feel sad. Perhaps it's because I'm tired. It was a long journey from England... or maybe it's because I'm remembering Mother being here.

I rise from the piano bench and walk across the colorful Indian rugs to the fireplace. Father reminded me when we toured the castle this evening that the rugs were a wedding present to him and Mother from Uncle John—his brother—who's a soldier of fortune with the British East India Company in Madras.

I sit down in the rocking chair. I'm glad Father kept this. It reminds me of her. Mother used to sit here by the fire, coughing and coughing, until the night she died of consumption.

The room feels stuffy. I unbutton the top of my high-collared white shirt. Miss Hughes will be annoyed—she always wants me to look prim and proper—but I don't care.

I walk across the room, push aside the lace curtains, and open a window. Miss Hughes told me not to open the windows, but I love the sweet aroma of the peat bricks the peasant's burn in their fireplaces. Mother always loved that smell too. She said it reminded her of her childhood in Donegal.

The surface of the lake bordering Parke's Castle looks silver beneath the moonlight. I see the silhouette of a tiny island on the other side. I think mother called it Innisfree.

It's faint… the sound: a violin, weeping a forlorn, enchanting melody. I lean out the window to hear more clearly. The melody is mesmerizing, almost gypsy-like, laced with a theme I know I've heard somewhere before.

Miss Hughes enters the parlor. "What are you doing?"

She marches across the room, closes the window, and pulls the lace curtains shut. "I told you not to open the windows. Now it stinks like the peat logs the Irish use."

"But I wanted to look at the moon."

Miss Hughes puts her hands on her hips. "It's time for bed. I'll send your father up to say good night in a few minutes."

I sulk out of the parlor and scurry up the stone steps to my third-floor bedroom.

I'm lying in bed reading next to an oil lamp when Father arrives. He remains standing at the doorway. I wish he'd sit down next to me… or hug me. He never showed me much affection when I was a child either. I guess being away for nine years hasn't changed that.

"Hello, Father."

"Hello, Elizabeth. It'll be nice to have you here for a few weeks. How was your voyage?"

"I was seasick for the first two days, until I got used to the swell of the waves."

"How do you like London?"

"It's nice. Aunt Bess has been very good to me."

Father stares at me for several seconds, as if he's searching for something to say. "I'm glad we'll have some time together before you get married. We'll need to find you a husband next year. You'll be seventeen in February after all. Aunt Bess, with Viscount Clements and my brother John as your sponsors, will present you to Queen Victoria next spring. You'll have a busy social life afterward, attending parties and such to catch a young man's eye."

I'm not sure how to respond, so I say nothing. I have no interest in "catching a man's eye." I'm going to be a concert pianist.

Father folds his arms across his chest. "Viscount Clements will introduce you to the sons of some of his business associates when we visit him at Lough Rynn in a few days."

"Thank you for borrowing the piano from him. It has a marvelous tone."

"You're welcome. We'll bring it back with us to Lough Rynn. I told Clements you'd play a concert for his guests while we're there. I hope that's all right."

"I'd like that. I need more experience playing in public if I'm going to be a concert pianist."

Father presses his lips together but doesn't say anything.

I sit up and lean back against the headboard. "Things have changed a lot since I left here nine years ago. I saw peasants dressed in rags sleeping on the quays when we arrived in Sligo this afternoon. Our ship captain said they're waiting for famine ships to take them to Canada or America. I also saw hundreds of people lying in ditches along the roads. They looked awful... as thin as skeletons. Some of them were naked, with green teeth."

Father shakes his head. "The Irish potato crop has failed for the third year in a row. Thousands of people are starving all over the country. People's teeth turn green when their desperation compels them to eat grass, which has no real nutritional value for humans. They're probably naked because they sold their clothing to buy food."

"Why does the potato crop keep failing?"

"I don't know. The politicians in Parliament say the famine is God's providence."

"Providence?"

"Yes. Providence is God's way of manifesting his will, through nature and the markets. Irish land is more profitable for livestock production now that Parliament has repealed the Corn Laws. The politicians say that famine is God's way of purging the land of people who aren't needed."

"That sounds very cruel... and cold-hearted."

He nods. "Charles Trevelyan, the British treasurer in charge of relief efforts in Ireland, says that famine is God's way of punishing Irish Catholics for their profligate ways."

"What do you mean?"

"It's their punishment for being lazy. Irish Catholics love to get drunk and fight, and they never save money. Most of them can't even read or write... and they're licentious, the way they breed children like dogs, and they constantly disparage Queen Victoria. Did you hear about the Young Ireland Rebellion near Tipperary this past July? They surrounded a brigade of English troops and threatened to kill them."

"I read about that in the newspaper. The article said that the Young Ireland rebels have Protestant members too."

He frowns. "Well, *most* of them are Catholic."

"The London newspapers depict Irish Catholics as low-browed baboons in their satirical cartoons, as if they're nothing more than animals. It doesn't seem right... letting people starve to death as punishment for their sins."

"The plantation owners are in a precarious situation. The Crown passed a law that requires landlords to pay taxes for their tenants that receive assistance in the workhouses, and bankers are refusing to refinance their debts. Many landowners have already defaulted on their loans."

"My mother was Catholic. Would you have let *her* starve to death if she were still alive?"

"Your mother wasn't Catholic when she died. She discarded the papacy when we got married in the Church of England."

He pulls a folded sheet of paper from his pocket, walks across the room, and hands it to me. "Look at this."

The paper has a drawing of a coffin in the middle surrounded by handguns. A scribble beneath the picture says, "*Solicitor Reilly—stop your evictions and Protestant tithe collections, or you will face the consequences!*"

"The Ribbonmen are leaving me death threats because I handle the paperwork for Lord Leitrim's evictions," Father says.

I hand it back to him. "Are we in danger?"

"No. The Irish Constabulary and British soldiers in the barracks next door will protect us."

"I had no idea things were so dangerous here when I kept pestering Aunt Bess to let me come home for a visit."

He nods. "Try not to worry. Just stay close to the castle walls and you'll be safe. I'm pleased that you came, Elizabeth. I see a lot of your mother in you now that you're older."

"How am I like her?"

"Well... she had a slim figure, blue eyes, and long blond hair just like you. She was a very talented dancer too. I'm sure she'd be proud of you if she were still alive. Perhaps she *is* proud of you—looking down from heaven."

"Heaven? Which version of heaven do you believe in, Father?"

He smiles, turns, and walks to the doorway. "Good night," he says.

I hear the hard soles of his boots echoing in the stairwell as he descends the stone steps.

3. BRIAN O'ROURKE

The O'Rourke Hut. The next morning.

MARY IS COOKING hard rolls next to the fire pit. "Breakfast is ready," she says.

Da gets up from his log and places another peat brick in the fire. He sits back down and puts his hands together to say grace.

We fold our hands and bow our heads. "Bless us, oh Lord, and these thy gifts," we utter, "which we are about to receive, from thy bounty, through Jesus Christ our Lord. Amen."

Mary separates the freshly baked hard rolls with her knife and hands one to each of us. We dip our rolls into tin cups filled with thin black tea to soften them. No one complains about the insipid blandness. We're just grateful to have something to eat.

"I have something to show everyone," I say after we finish.

I duck through the doorway and they follow me outside.

I retrieve the Irish flags from beneath the rocks, and pull the Sligo and Leitrim maps and flag-signal paper out of my pocket. "Brother Bernard gave me these before he left yesterday."

I wave one of the flags above my head. "This is Ireland's new flag. The Young Ireland leaders brought it back from France earlier this year. Brother Bernard taught me how to use these flags to send messages from hilltops."

I face Da. "Sending messages could be useful when you're trying to intercept grain or livestock shipments heading to the port in Sligo."

"How can you use flags to send messages?" he says.

I place the paper with the stickman drawings on the ground, keep two of the flags, and hand the rest to Da.

"This is called an *optical telegraph*," I say. "Each stickman drawing represents a letter, a number, or a control word. Watch me and I'll demonstrate."

I point both flags at the ground. "You begin each word with both flags down."

I raise my right hand to a forty-five-degree angle. "This is the signal for the letter *A*."

I move the flag up forty-five degrees. "And this is *B*."

I raise my hand another forty-five degrees. "This is the letter *C*."

Da chuckles. "That's very clever."

I face my brothers. "I can teach you how to do this if you'd like."

Da hands each of them two flags. We then practice the signals until we've gone through all the letters of the alphabet, the numbers from zero to nine, and each of the message control words.

"You'll need to memorize these flag signals to send messages quickly," I say. "But think about it. Men standing on hilltops can relay messages much quicker than a horse can run."

Da strokes his chin with his hand. "I see what you're saying, son. We could also use this optical telegraph to keep track of Reilly's eviction brigade soldiers as they move along the roads."

I kneel down and spread the Sligo and Leitrim maps out on the ground. Everyone kneels beside me.

"Brother Bernard marked all the hilltops," I say, as I point at the red circles on the map. "I figure we could watch all the roads from Dromahair to Sligo with six Ribbonmen."

Da smiles. "Good idea. These hills will be our training ground. Can you make some more copies of the coded signal sheets? Everybody will need one."

"Yes, sir."

"I'm sure we'll get the hang of it with a bit of practice," James says.

Da nods. "Hold on a moment," he says as he stands up.

He enters the stone hut and returns a moment later. "Stand up, son," he says to me.

I stand. So does everyone else. At six feet tall, I'm three inches shorter than Da and my brothers.

Da wraps a short green ribbon around a button on my shirt. "This is the secret symbol of the Ribbonmen. You're one of us now."

I beam with pride. I didn't expect this. "Thanks, Da."

"You're welcome."

He looks at Patrick, James, and me. "I want you to practice these signals until you have them memorized. We'll move to the nearby hilltops this afternoon to demonstrate the telegraph to our men. We're going to need a lot more flags."

"Norah Gallagher in Manorhamilton made these for Brother Bernard," I say. "She'll probably make more if we ask her."

"I know Norah," Ma says. "I'll walk over to Manorhamilton this morning and help her sew some flags, assuming she's willing."

"I want to help," Mary says. "I may as well be a soldier, since no one wants me for their wife." She stares at us with a stern gaze. "And I can fight. You know I can."

James points at a bruise on his shoulder. "She has a fierce right hook when she's angry."

Everyone chuckles.

Da nods. "You could hide the flags beneath your dress when you deliver them to our troops. Do you think you could teach them how to use the flag signals?"

She smiles. "Certainly."

Da chuckles. "Perhaps you'll be a famous warrior like Queen Medb one day—the Irish Queen of Connacht. She had many husbands during her reign."

Ma nudges him. "Aye there, Paddy. Don't go puttin' ideas in the girl's head. One husband is more than enough for any woman to manage."

We all laugh.

Da grins. "You're right about that, Deirdre." He faces Mary. "The bards say that Queen Medb was buried standing upright in her cairn on Knocknarea west of Sligo, so she could face her enemies in Ulster even after her death."

He pulls another strand of ribbon from his pocket, kneels down in front of Mary, and wraps it around a button on her dress. "You're one of us now too."

"Thanks, Da. I won't disappoint you."

"I'm sure you won't, my dear."

Mary smiles as we congratulate her with hugs.

Ma faces Da. "When do you think Solicitor Reilly will come to evict us?" she says. "The beggars that came here yesterday told me that Viscount Clements cleared all the tenants from his land in Rossinver. They said he's evicting most of his tenants in the county."

Da shakes his head. "I've never trusted Reilly. His O'Reilly clan in County Cavan dropped the *O* from their name and sold their souls to the devil when they fled to England."

Ma smirks. "That was over a hundred years ago, Paddy, and that's not the whole story. They joined the Church of England so they could feed their children. What would you have done?"

Da focuses his gaze on us. "I would have entered heaven with a clear conscience."

Ma frowns and ducks into the hut without responding.

4. ELIZABETH REILLY

Parke's Castle. That night.

MISS HUGHES DOESN'T accompany me to the parlor after dinner. She's probably bored after listening to me practice the same pieces all day.

I play Beethoven's *Moonlight Sonata* from the beginning to the end without hesitation. I then stand up, push aside the lace curtains, and open the window that faces Lough Gill.

The sweet smell of peat smoke fills my nostrils. The rain has stopped and the fog has lifted, leaving the island of Innisfree clearly visible on the other side of the lake. I take a deep breath of the cool night air, and return to the piano, where I play Schumann's "Träumerei."

A distant violin outside the window echoes the melody back to me after I finish. I rush to the window and lean my head out. The music has stopped.

I hear the violin farther away a few minutes later, playing the melody to Chopin's "Funeral March."

I close the parlor window and walk to the dining room, where I find Father and Miss Hughes sitting at the table playing cards. "I'm tired," I say. "I'm going to bed early tonight."

"Good night," they say in unison.

I hustle up the stairs to my bedroom. The violinist is still playing when I open my window. I recognize most of the melodies as I listen for the next hour. The music stops abruptly when the rain begins.

I rise early and go to the dining room to eat breakfast the next morning. I then return to my bedroom, pull on some tight-fitting Jodhpur riding breeches and high paddock boots, and walk outside to the stable. The groom places a sidesaddle on a black mare named Raven, and I climb up on the horse.

"Stay close to the walls," Miss Hughes calls out to me as the groom opens the gate. "Your father says it's dangerous to ride in the forests. There are lots of criminals about."

"I'll be fine."

I pass beyond Miss Hughes's view, steer the horse to a trail that borders Lough Gill, and head east toward where I heard the violin music last night. I hear voices after a quarter of a mile, so I stop, dismount, and tie Raven's reins to a tree limb. I hide behind bushes with my head down as I make my way toward the voices, until I see six soldiers in a large meadow next to the lake.

I recognize them, even though they have scarves tied across their faces. They live in the barracks inside our castle walls. Four of them escorted us to Parke's Castle from Sligo. The big man in his mid-fifties is Sergeant Milton—the garrison troop leader. He makes me feel uneasy. I hate the way he undressed me with his eyes when he met us at the harbor. He made me feel like I was a piece of meat he couldn't wait to devour. Miss Hughes thinks he's handsome—but he wasn't looking at her!

I crawl closer to the edge of the meadow for a better look. I cover my mouth with my hand to stifle a scream. At least twenty rigor-mortised bodies are lying stiff on the ground. Most are naked, or clothed only in undergarments. Some of the dead are embracing each other.

The soldiers are prying the corpses apart with iron crowbars. Working in pairs, they then grab the cadavers' wrists and ankles, swing them once, and toss them up into the back of a wagon harnessed behind four horses.

I squeeze my nose with my fingers to block the awful stench when the breeze changes direction. It doesn't help.

Sergeant Milton yanks a four-year-old boy out of its dead mother's arms. "Hey, look at this," he says, holding the frail boy above his head. "It looks like we caught ourselves a live one."

The other soldiers stop to watch.

Sergeant Milton tries to make the boy's skeleton-thin body stand up, as if it's a puppet. He laughs each time the boy collapses to the ground. He lifts the boy and puts his ear to the boy's mouth, pretending to listen.

Milton drops the boy on the ground. "He's talking Irish gibberish," he says. "He told me to put him out of his misery."

He raises his crowbar and swings down hard, crushing the boy's

28

skull with one blow.

My God! I almost scream.

Milton tosses the boy onto the heap of bodies in the back of the wagon, and the other soldiers go back to work.

I crawl into the bushes behind me and throw up.

The wagon is full when I return. There are still a dozen bodies lying in the grass.

I follow at a distance as the soldiers steer the wagon to a nearby field, where several men are digging a hole with shovels. Milton and his men climb into the back of the wagon and throw the bodies into the trench. The men on the ground then shovel dirt over the corpses. There are no priests or vicars to send them to eternity.

I return through the forest to Raven, and ride back to the castle.

Practicing piano the rest of the day is a good escape from the horror that I witnessed. I'm too upset to eat dinner afterwards, so I tell Father that I'm tired, and go to bed early.

The violinist starts playing after dark.

I wait until the castle has quieted, tiptoe down the stairs, and leave the castle through an ancient stairwell next to the lake. Be careful, I tell myself, as I survey the calm water. Miss Hughes and Father will get very angry if they catch you sneaking out.

The half-moon provides plenty of light as I walk east along the trail. I hide behind a bush at the edge of the meadow, watching at least forty people lying huddled together on the grass. A teenage boy about my age is sitting on top of a tall rectangular stone playing the violin. I remember Mother telling me once that the Vikings placed the stone here a thousand years ago.

A family drifts down from the road north of the meadow. They can barely hold each other up as they trudge forward, as if every step takes all their strength. No one speaks to them as they collapse at the edge of the congregation.

The moans of the dying and the halfhearted cry of a baby provide a chilling accompaniment to the boy's violin music. Some of his melodies are from Beethoven, Shubert, and Mozart pieces I heard when I went to concerts with Aunt Bess.

A man in front of me shakes violently. With a deep-throated gasp, he goes still.

A shiver of fear rolls down my spine.

An hour passes, as the moon moves higher in the sky. The boy packs his violin in a cloth bag, slings it over his shoulder, and jumps down from the rock. The insistent wail of a baby punctures the darkness as he walks away.

I follow him as he crosses a dirt road and heads up the hill. The boy's long, curly hair bobs up and down in the moonlight ahead of me. He approaches a straw-roofed hut and goes inside. The crooked hovel, leaning against the side of a hill, looks like a drunkard hanging on to a friend.

I hide behind a large boulder near the entrance. I see five people sitting around a fire pit inside the single-room hut. A young woman is playing a wooden flute. Two full-grown teenage boys are playing tambourines. An older couple sits next to them on a log. The woman is singing a Gaelic folk song I've heard before. Her voice is pure and sweet. There's a pig sleeping on a straw bed in the corner.

The boy scoops something that I guess to be oatmeal from a pot into a small bowl. He then sits on the ground and starts to eat, shoveling the cereal into his mouth with his fingers.

I recognize this place. I've been here before. This is the O'Rourke hut. Father called it that when I was a child.

The song ends, and everyone looks at the boy.

"How many souls did you comfort tonight?" the older woman asks.

I recognize her voice—Deirdre, I think her name is.

"A few more tonight," the boy answers. "Forty… or forty-five."

The boy slurps the last of the oatmeal into his mouth and licks his fingers. "Do I really need to keep doing this, Da? It's very depressing to watch people die every night."

The older man picks up a peat brick and places it into the fire pit. "These are our people… your people, Brian Boru O'Rourke."

The man moves the coals around with a wooden stick. "The comfort of your music is all we can give them now, as they enter death's door."

Everyone is silent, contemplating the flames.

The firelight colors Brian's face with an amber glow. He has long, curly black hair and eyes that sparkle in the reflecting light. My pelvis jolts with a contraction that startles me. I've never felt *that* before. I feel my skin flush as I watch him. *My God… he's beautiful.*

I remember now. Mother used to visit Deirdre here. We only came here when Father was away on business, though. It was our secret.

Deirdre used to call Brian her Black Irish son. "It's the Spanish Armada," she'd say.

The women would laugh then, and make a toast to the Spanish with their teacups.

My history teacher in London told us about the Spanish ships that crashed on the western shore of Ireland in 1588. It happened during a ferocious storm, while they were sailing southwest from Scotland to attack the British fleet during the war with Queen Elizabeth—the woman father named me after.

Brian is the youngest—the same age as me. He has two older brothers and an older sister. They have similar physical traits… but with light-colored hair.

The oldest boy stands up and starts prancing around the hut with his head held high. "Tell me who this is," he says.

They chuckle.

"I give up," his sister says. "Who is it?"

"I'm Viscount Clements." He continues to prance around the room. "I took another virgin today. I walk like this because I own all the virgins in Leitrim and Donegal."

His father and siblings laugh.

"Stop that nonsense, Patrick," his mother says, admonishing him with a scolding voice.

Patrick sits down.

"It's disgraceful," she says, "what Clements is doing to our young women."

Brian looks at his sister. "So Mary, did you get any marriage proposals today?"

She stares into the fire pit with a vacant gaze. "Nobody wants me."

She starts to cry, shielding her eyes with her hands.

Deirdre hugs her and rubs her back. "Try not to worry, my dear," she says. "I'm sure we'll find you a husband."

Her father stands up and starts pacing around the room.

I remember him now. Everyone calls him "Big Paddy," because he's so tall and muscular.

Brian pulls his violin out of his backpack and starts to play a song.

His brothers join in on tambourine and melodeon, and Mary picks up her flute.

Big Paddy sits back down on the log and lights a tobacco pipe.

There's so much affection here. I can feel it, even though they're poor.

I scoot quietly down the trail and walk back to the castle, taking the road to avoid the meadow.

The smell of bacon cooking awakens me the next morning. I enter the dining room and sit down. The table has two plates of fruit, a loaf of freshly baked bread, a plate filled with sausage and bacon, and a large bowl of scrambled eggs.

I eat an apple with some toast and sip black tea with milk.

Miss Hughes isn't as reticent. She consumes three helpings to satiate her corpulent belly.

You ate enough to feed a starving family, I almost blurt out, but I don't want to be rude.

"We'll be going to Lough Rynn tomorrow," Father says, from behind the business section of his newspaper. "I have a meeting there with William Sydney Clements. He's managing his elderly father's landholdings now."

"I'm looking forward to going," Miss Hughes says. "I've heard his castle is beautiful."

Father lowers his newspaper and looks at me. "Be sure to pack some nice clothes. Some of Viscount Clements's business associates from Belfast, London, and Dublin will be attending your recital. It'll be a good opportunity for you to practice your manners with some wealthy young men. Perhaps I'll arrange a marriage with one of them during the season next summer."

I don't want a marriage—arranged, or otherwise.

"Do we really have to go?" I say. "I hear the roads are dangerous."

Father sips his tea. "Sergeant Milton and his soldiers will accompany us. He'll ensure we're safe from the Ribbonmen."

His gaze returns to the newspaper.

"But what if I don't want to get married?" I say. "I want to study piano with Chopin. He's living in London now. Aunt Bess told me he's looking for students. I attended his concert at Lord Falmouth's house in St. James's Square in July. He was magnificent."

Father continues to read without responding.

Arghhh! This is so frustrating. He isn't listening to a word I say.

"Chopin followed the French royal family to England," Miss Hughes says. "They had to flee during the February Revolution earlier this year. It seems like every country has subversive rebels these days... except for England, of course."

"Um-hmm," Father says, from behind his newspaper.

"Why do we need protection from the Ribbonmen?" I say to Father.

"They're criminals." He lowers his newspaper and stares at me. "They overturned a wagon filled with oats on the road outside Manorhamilton last week."

"Maybe they were hungry."

He scowls. "That's no excuse for violence. A masked man with a handgun chased the driver away, and then a bunch of men wearing masks turned over the wagon. The people in Manorhamilton stole every ounce of grain before my men arrived. I'm sure Viscount Clements is furious. It was his grain shipment."

Father's gaze returns to the newspaper. "Don't worry," he says. "Sergeant Milton will take care of any hoodlums we encounter."

"I think the sergeant is very handsome," Miss Hughes says to my father. "I can tell from his accent that he's originally from London. Has he ever been married?"

"You'll have to talk with him about that."

I stare at Miss Hughes. Should I tell her how cruel the sergeant is, the way he killed that little boy yesterday without a second of hesitation?

No. Miss Hughes would probably like him *even more* if she knew. She loves to laugh at the cartoons that depict Irish Catholics as moronic baboons.

We have a long day of travel ahead of us tomorrow, so I go to bed after dinner. I push the lace curtains aside and open my window. Dark clouds are shielding the moon.

I hear Brian's violin music as I lie in bed. I imagine Brian there, sitting on the Viking rock, ushering the dead into the afterlife. He stops playing when the rain begins.

The raindrops drum a slow symphony on the roof, lulling me to sleep. I sleep fitfully, awakened several times by ghostly visions of corpses rising up from the meadow in my nightmares.

Miss Hughes enters my room early the next morning. "Your father wants to leave soon," she says. "Lough Rynn is forty miles away at the southern end of Clements's ninety thousand acres. You should eat quickly and get ready."

I rub the sleep out of my eyes. "What about the piano?"

"The soldiers are loading it into a coach."

"I'll be down in a few minutes."

We leave Parke's Castle thirty minutes later. I'm riding in the front carriage with Father and Miss Hughes. A second covered coach behind us carries the piano. There are six soldiers riding on horses with us.

I peer out the window as we pass the Creevelea ruins near Dromahair. I see two young men on hilltops waving orange, white, and green flags in each hand.

"What are those men doing?" I ask Father.

He drops his newspaper into his lap and sticks his head out the window. He stares at the men for a moment, and then motions for Sergeant Milton to come up alongside the coach.

"Why are those boys waving flags?" Father bellows.

"I've seen three of them since we left," Milton replies. "I think they're spying on us… sending messages to each other."

Father studies one of the teenagers as we approach another hill. "That looks like one of Paddy O'Rourke's boys."

"It is," Milton says. "I spotted another one on a hilltop near the abbey. Do you want us to take care of them?"

"Not now. I need to talk with Viscount Clements first."

We round a bend and continue on a level road for two miles. I don't see any more flag wavers as we head south toward Lough Rynn.

I'll tell Brian that he and his brothers are in danger when we return, I promise myself.

A steady rain begins after we've traveled ten miles. It continues for the rest of our journey. The temperature dives after the sun sets. I'm shivering beneath my overcoat and blanket when we finally arrive at Lough Rynn at 10 p.m.

Sergeant Milton and his soldiers accompany the piano coach to the back of the castle while we disembark in the front. Clements's footman greets us at the door. He helps us remove our boots in the foyer, and we pull on clean shoes. He then ushers us into the study, where Viscount

William Sydney Clements, the bearded forty-two-year-old son of the eighty-year-old Earl of Leitrim, is sitting in front of an oversized rent ledger.

Clements stands and shakes Father's hand when we enter. "I trust your journey went well."

"It did, my lord," Father says, "except for a bit of rain along the way."

Clements sits down. "I'm busy now. We'll talk in the morning." His attention returns to his accounts, ignoring us.

The housekeeper enters. "I'll show you to your rooms," she says, and we follow her up the stairs.

I sneeze repeatedly as I get ready for bed. "I think I'm getting a cold," I say to Miss Hughes.

"I'll let you sleep late tomorrow," she says. "That will fix you up."

"How long do we have to stay here?"

"Just a few days."

Miss Hughes awakens me at 9:00 a.m. the next morning. "Your father is having breakfast with Viscount Clements," she says. "We should join them."

I sit up and blow my nose. "I'm not feeling well."

Miss Hughes frowns. "It's time to get dressed. I'll come back for you in ten minutes."

Father is sitting next to Viscount Clements when I enter the dining room. Clements stands and takes my hand.

"You've become quite a beautiful young woman," he says. "I believe you were seven years old the last time I saw you."

"Thank you, my lord."

I release his hand, and sit down at a table large enough to seat twenty people. Miss Hughes sits next to Clements.

"Elizabeth has become quite an accomplished piano player, my lord," Miss Hughes says.

"I'm looking forward to your concert this afternoon," Clements replies. "The piano tuner will be here later this morning. It probably needs to be tuned after your journey yesterday."

"Thank you, my lord," I say. "The music always sounds better when it's in tune."

He chuckles. "It does indeed."

Miss Hughes and I take a stroll on the outdoor footpaths after breakfast. There's a serene lake next to the stately castle. I blow my nose into my handkerchief several times as we walk.

We hurry back when the rain begins.

"I have a cold," I say to Miss Hughes. "I need to take a nap before I play."

"That's fine, dear. I'll wake you up in time to fix your hair."

Miss Hughes wakes me an hour before the concert. She feels my forehead. "You're warm."

I blow my nose twice.

"I wish I didn't have to play," I say, in a nasally voice.

"Just get through your recital, and you can come back to bed. I'll ask the kitchen staff to bring you up some chicken soup for dinner."

Miss Hughes helps me attach my cane-stiffened petticoat below my waist. I then pull on a shoulder-less blue silk evening dress garlanded with white silk flowers at the bottom. She brushes my hair, twists it, and pins it in a bun at the back of my head.

"You look lovely, my dear," she says.

"Thank you, Miss Hughes."

Father, Viscount Clements, and three men stand up when we enter the yellow-wallpapered parlor. Each man is wearing a black waistcoat and high-collared white shirt with a black cravat.

"This is Albert Campbell, from Belfast," Viscount Clements says, introducing me to the first young man. "His family is in the linen manufacturing business."

The thirty-year-old Campbell bows as he takes my hand. "How do you do, Miss Reilly?"

"Very well, thank you."

He's attractive... and he has good manners, but he's too old for me.

Viscount Clements points at the next man. "This is Herbert Mason, my banker from London."

The middle-aged Englishman nods at me from across the room.

"And this young man is Stephen Cunningham," Clements continues. "He's taking a break from his studies at Trinity College to help his father in the wool trade."

The twenty-one-year-old Cunningham takes my hand and bows slightly. "I've heard a lot about you, Miss Reilly. You are *indeed,* a very lovely girl."

He sports mutton-chop sideburns, a look popular in London now with men wanting to look like Prince Albert, Queen Victoria's consort.

"Thank you, sir," I say.

He continues to hold my hand after his greeting.

I feel uncomfortable, so I pull my hand away.

"I hear you're living in London," he says. "I often stay with friends there near the Strand. Perhaps we can meet for tea sometime."

Cunningham turns and takes Miss Hughes's hand. "Of course, you can bring your lovely chaperone with you if you'd like."

Miss Hughes smiles demurely. "Thank you, Mr. Cunningham. We can meet you next month after we return to London."

I walk to the piano bench and sit down. The piano is set up sideways so that everyone can see my hands while I play.

Miss Hughes sits next to Father on the sofa, while Clements, Mason, Campbell, and Cunningham settle into padded armchairs. All of the Victorian-style furniture looks new.

The housekeepers, butler, cooks, and footmen are standing in the adjacent dining room, watching through a doublewide doorway.

I open my sheet music. I've memorized the piece, but I want the music handy just in case.

"I'm going to warm up with a Bach Invention," I say, more hesitantly than I'd planned. I glance at the audience. "I hope that's acceptable to everyone."

Everyone chuckles.

"I'm sure that will be fine, my dear," Father says.

Calm down! I tell myself.

I blow my nose, take a sip of water, place my hands over the keyboard, and start to play.

Everyone claps enthusiastically when I finish.

Thank God, I say to myself as I take a bow. I didn't make any mistakes.

I blow my nose while a footman refills the men's brandy glasses.

A gentle rain is pattering against a wall of windows that looks out at the lake next to the piano. It's a perfect backdrop for Beethoven's melancholy arpeggios as I begin the *Moonlight Sonata*.

I'm perspiring when I finish the turbulent third movement a quarter of an hour later.

Everyone stands and gives me a raucous ovation. Mr. Cunningham shouts several "Bravos."

They sit down and the footman refills their glasses.

"I apologize for cutting my concert short today, my lord," I say to Viscount Clements, "but I'm feeling a bit under the weather. My last piece will be Chopin's Nocturne, opus 9 number 2."

Clements nods. "That's fine, my dear."

Everyone applauds when I finish.

I take a bow and smile—partially because I played well, but mostly because I'm relieved that it's over.

The men retire to the billiards room while Miss Hughes accompanies me upstairs.

"You sounded marvelous," Miss Hughes says. "Mr. Cunningham seems quite smitten by you. His father is very wealthy, you know. They live in a beautiful home across from Merrion Square in Dublin."

I pull off my dress and remove my petticoat with Miss Hughes's help.

"I'm not coming to dinner," I say. "Please give my regrets to Lord Clements and his guests."

"I will, dear. I'll ask the servants to bring you up some soup later this evening."

5. SOLICITOR CHARLES REILLY

Lough Rynn Castle.

THE BUTLER REFILLS our brandy glasses and leaves the oak-walled billiard room, closing the door behind him.

Viscount Clements unfurls several Irish county maps on his billiard table. His ninety thousand acres in Donegal, Leitrim, Kildare, and Galway are clearly marked on each map.

Cunningham waves his hand over Clements's landholdings. "Are these the properties my father will be leasing for sheep production, my lord?"

"That's right," Clements says.

"My father told me to remind you that the tenants must be cleared off the land before he'll sign a lease agreement. He also wants a clause in the contract stating that you'll indemnify him for taxes he gets stuck with if any of your tenants go to the workhouses."

"Don't worry," Clements says. "Eight thousand have already left, and the rest will be gone by the end of May. Remind your father that my pastures have many advantages. My tenants' ancestors subdivided the land with rock walls when they split their farms among their sons over the centuries. Those stone partitions are useful when you need to separate ewes and rams for breeding and shearing."

Clements turns to me. "I want you to issue *Notice to Vacate* letters to the rest of my tenants in North Leitrim and Donegal, Solicitor Reilly." He points at his landholdings in those counties on the map. "I don't care if they're Protestant or Catholic. I want my lands cleared. I'm giving the same instructions to all of my solicitors. Make sure your eviction brigade soldiers burn the timbers and straw the peasants use for roofs after they demolish the tenant's homes. I'm tired of seeing vagrants sleeping in ditches under piles of straw along the roads. It's unsightly, and having shelter encourages them to stay in Ireland longer."

"I understand, my lord," I reply.

Mason faces Clements. "The sooner you get rid of your tenants, the sooner your welfare taxes will stop, my lord. You've been a judicious manager of your father's landholdings up to this point. However, the Crown's mandate requiring landlords to pay for their tenants that go to the workhouses could break you if you don't get rid of them soon. We're getting reports from across the country that the potato crop has failed again. There's only room for five percent of the destitute in the overcrowded workhouses, and the Crown is refusing to build any more."

Clements scowls. "I know. The Crown is ignoring our problems. All I hear when I write to members of Parliament about the rampant starvation in Ireland is laissez-faire—that it's not the government's responsibility to get involved."

Mason nods. "You're better off than many landlords, though. Your prudent financial practices have given you a cushion. Many property owners that leveraged their land with debt are going into foreclosure. My bank has repossessed tens of thousands of acres. You can purchase those properties for a pittance once you clear the peasants from your land and secure long-term leases for livestock production."

Mason turns to Campbell. "Tell your father I'll provide the financing for him to build another garment factory in Belfast if he agrees to purchase Cunningham's wool."

Campbell smiles. "I'm sure Father will be pleased to hear that."

Clements hands me a stack of papers. "Here's the list of tenants I want you to evict," he says.

I look quickly through the papers. Each page has rows of leaseholder names, addresses, and property descriptions. "There are at least four hundred names here, my lord. I'll need more eviction brigades."

"I wrote to the prime minister about the Ribbonmen attack on our grain shipment outside Manorhamilton. He agreed to send me another company of soldiers in two weeks. You can use the platoon stationed at the Manorhamilton Court House if you need extra help for your evictions until they get here."

Viscount Clements hands me a sheet of paper with four names and addresses. "Make sure you exclude these families from your evictions."

Cunningham chuckles. "Are those the families with young women you've taken an interest in? I hear you're not shy about using your *droit du seigneur* privileges with the women on your lands."

Clements flashes a sardonic smile. "You shouldn't believe everything you hear."

Everyone laughs but me.

I place the papers in my leather briefcase. "Evicting Paddy O'Rourke's is going to be troublesome, my lord," I say. "He still believes he owns the land his forefathers possessed. His ancestors ruled the Kingdom of Breifne for seven hundred years before the British came."

Clements scowls. "That's ridiculous."

"I saw two of O'Rourke's sons on hilltops waving flags yesterday. I think they were spying on us... using flags to send messages to each other."

Clements pounds the table with his fist. "My Ribbonmen informant told me that those boys were responsible for the grain theft in Manorhamilton last week. The O'Rourke clan has been a thorn in the side of the Crown for centuries. My ancestors in Cromwell's army fought against them when we tried to rid Ireland of the papacy in 1649—yet they're still here! I told you to evict the O'Rourke's from their hut on the side of the hill last year. Why haven't you taken action?"

I look at the floor to avoid his menacing stare. I can't tell him I postponed the O'Rourke eviction because of Claire. She was friends with Deirdre O'Rourke.

I hope you're proud of me, Claire, I say to myself, if you're looking down from heaven. The raindrops pounding the window seem to grow louder as everyone waits for me to respond.

Clements leans forward with his hands on the table. "Well, I'm taking care of it myself," he says. "Sergeant Milton told me about the O'Rourke spies this morning. That's an act of war, as far as I'm concerned. I told Sergeant Milton I'd give him twenty pounds sterling for each O'Rourke male he captures. I'll pay him next month when I come to Parke's Castle to check on your progress with the evictions."

"How will you know that Sergeant Milton captured them, my lord? We have nowhere to imprison the O'Rourke's within our castle walls."

"I'm sure Sergeant Milton will figure something out."

The butler knocks on the door and enters the room. "Dinner is served, my lord."

My gaze veers back to Clements. "Can we talk in private?"

"We'll join you in a moment," Clements says to the other men.

Mason, Cunningham, and Campbell follow the butler to the dining room, and Clements closes the door.

"What is it?" he says, annoyed.

"What are your plans for me, my lord? I doubt that you'll need a solicitor to manage your evictions and Church of Ireland tithe collections after most of your tenants are gone."

"You're correct. I was going to talk with you about that after dinner. My barrister in London will be drawing up my contracts with Cunningham's father, so I won't need you for that. I'm terminating your employment next spring after we finish the evictions. You'll need to vacate the castle by the end of May. I'll be leasing it from Lane-Fox beginning in June. I want to use it as one of my residences when I travel up north from now on."

"I see."

Damn! I suspected this might happen.

I feel queasy as I summon the courage for my next inquiry. "As you know," I say tentatively, "I've been sending most of my earnings to my sister to support Elizabeth these past nine years. Can I count on your help finding a new position when I return to London next summer?"

Clements folds his hands behind his back. "I'll write a letter of recommendation for you—*if* you handle the evictions as I've instructed. Otherwise, I'll make sure you never work again."

He glares at me. "Although you've been good at handling contracts and other legal matters, you're the worst agent I have when it comes to tithe collections and evictions."

I stare at the floor. I know he's right, but I still feel angry.

"I have another project for you," Clements says.

I look him in the eye. "What's that, my lord?"

"I want you to hire Mary O'Rourke to work as a maid at Parke's Castle before you evict her family. I saw her walking along the road last summer. She's become quite an alluring young woman. I'll need some privacy with her when I come to the castle next month."

I stare at Clements without responding.

He smirks, opens the door, and enters the dining room. I follow him in, sit down at the table, unfold my serviette, and place it in my lap.

The butler is carving a crisply baked duck, placing each slice on a silver serving tray.

A footman wearing black tails and a white bow tie picks up the tray when the butler is finished. He moves around the table and presents the tray to Miss Hughes.

"This looks marvelous, my lord," Miss Hughes says, as she shovels several slices onto her plate.

The first footman moves to the Viscount with the tray. A second footman offers Miss Hughes a large bowl of blackberry sauce to complement the duck, and she indulges herself generously.

"I'm sorry Elizabeth can't join us," I say. "She's not feeling well."

"That's too bad," Cunningham says. "I was hoping we could get to know each other."

"Me too," Campbell says.

"Perhaps I'll take her to a concert at Exeter Hall when we're back in London next month," Cunningham says.

Miss Hughes nods. "I'm sure she'd like that. Elizabeth attended a lecture at Exeter with her Aunt Bess last summer. Prince Albert was addressing the British and Foreign Anti-Slavery Society, discussing the need to abolish slavery in America. Her aunt said the prince was very handsome."

"I don't see how the colonies can make do without their slaves," Mason interjects.

"I agree," Campbell says. "The price of cotton would quadruple. We'd have to raise our linen prices substantially to compensate."

The footmen circle the table several more times presenting trays filled with boiled carrots, roasted potatoes, baked tomatoes, and dark brown bread with butter. Viscount Clements starts to eat after we've filled our plates, and we follow his lead.

"Let's go into the billiard room for cigars and brandy," Clements says after dinner.

"I'm going to retire early tonight, my lord," I say.

Clements walks toward the billiards room without responding.

I certainly won't miss him, I muse, as I walk to my room. I just need to persevere long enough to get Elizabeth married off to an appropriate suitor.

6. ELIZABETH REILLY

Elizabeth's bedroom. Later that night.

A TAPPING—barely audible—melts into my dream. Brian is sitting on the Viking rock playing his violin. He grows larger as the translucent apparitions rise from the meadow and disappear into the ether, and then I'm soaring above him like an eagle, watching everything.

He plays beautifully... as beautifully as he is handsome.

An erotic rush consumes me... foreign... pleasant. Brian... is caressing my breasts... his fingertips... on my stomach... under my nightgown... between my legs.

"Ahhh!" I scream.

I jump up against the headboard.

Cunningham's hand covers my mouth. "Shh!"

I slap him hard, across the face.

"Damn it," he yells. "What'd you do that for?"

His words are slurred. He's drunk.

"Get out of here!"

Miss Hughes bursts through the door carrying an oil lamp in her hand. "What are you doing here, Mr. Cunningham?" she says.

I pull the bedcovers up over my nightgown.

"He fondled me in my bed," I yell.

Cunningham stands up. "I did not," he says haughtily. "She invited me here."

Father enters behind Miss Hughes. "What's going on?"

I glare at Cunningham. "Nothing, Father. I had a nightmare. Can you stay with me, Miss Hughes?"

"Certainly, my dear."

Father frowns as Cunningham slithers by him through the doorway.

"We're leaving in the morning," Father says.

"I thought we were staying for a few days," Miss Hughes says.

Father walks away without explaining.

7. SOLICITOR CHARLES REILLY

Solicitor Reilly's bedroom. The next morning.

I'M EXHAUSTED after wrestling with sleep all night. Cunningham's intrusion into Elizabeth's bedroom is infuriating. I'm getting angrier the more I think about it, especially since I'm not sure what I should do.

The morning twilight is creeping across the eastern skyline when I push the lace curtains aside. A few wispy clouds dot the sky. The rain has vanished.

I know I should confront Cunningham about his impropriety. Perhaps I should challenge him to a duel, to restore Elizabeth's honor.

No. His father would most certainly have me arrested if I kill his son. He's one of the most powerful men in Dublin—in Britain, for that matter.

I'll aim away from him during the duel. That way we can both save our honor.

No. That wouldn't work either. The brash young man would certainly aim to kill. I see that in his nature. I'll have to aim for his heart and pull the trigger first, but then where would we be? Would we have to flee to America to escape the wrath of his father?

That's probably why Elizabeth said nothing happened. She knows the consequences. I'd need to defend her honor if she exposed his indiscretion.

Unable to sleep, I rise from my bed and get dressed. I'm anxious to get home anyway.

The ground is muddy when we begin our journey back to Parke's Castle. I'm sitting next to Miss Hughes so that Elizabeth can lie down across from us. Her cold is worse than it was yesterday. Sergeant Milton and his soldiers are riding behind us.

Our progress improves considerably when the roads dry out by midday. We reach Dromahair an hour after sunset.

I call out to our driver to stop the carriage a mile from our castle. I motion with my hand for Sergeant Milton as I step down to the road.

"Please accompany Elizabeth and Miss Hughes to the castle," I say to him. "I'll walk the rest of the way. I need to loosen up my legs after the long journey."

Sergeant Milton nods. "Yes, sir."

"The Crown is sending additional troops in two weeks to help with our evictions. You'll need to prepare accommodations for more soldiers in your barracks."

"I will, sir. I heard that from Viscount Clements too."

"Come see me in the morning. Viscount Clements has a special mission I need to discuss with you... involving the O'Rourke's."

Milton smiles. "Clements told me about the reward. I'm going to track them down tomorrow."

I face Elizabeth through the carriage window. "Get some sleep, my dear. I'll check on you when I get home."

She pokes her head out from beneath the blanket. "Thank you, Father."

I watch the soldiers escort the carriage until they disappear beyond a bend in the road. The clouds are gone, leaving the sky filled with stars.

The waxing gibbous moon peeks over the eastern horizon as I begin my hike up the trail to the O'Rourke's hut. The glow of a fire inside indicates they're home.

I stop to listen to the music they're playing. They sound wonderful.

Their lives are going to change drastically after tonight. I hope they accept my help.

I wait until they finish their song, and then I say, "Big Paddy," from beyond the doorway.

Paddy stoops down and steps outside. "What do you want, O'Reilly?"

"I need to talk with you. It's important."

"Come inside and warm yourself."

I bend down and follow him into the hut. Deirdre moves off the log and sits down in the dirt next to her children.

Big Paddy points at the log. "Have a seat," he says, as he joins Deirdre on the ground.

I sit on the log to acknowledge his hospitality, and rub my hands together above the fire pit. Everyone is studying me warily, especially the teenage boys.

The pig rises from its slumber on the hay in the corner and waddles over to us. It smells my leg, snorts, and plops down next to me.

Everyone chuckles.

"It looks like you've made yourself a new friend," Big Paddy says.

I pull a folded piece of paper from my coat pocket. "I'm sorry to bring you bad news. The Earl of Leitrim's son—Viscount Clements—is clearing most of his tenants from his land… and you haven't paid your rent for over two years. This is your eviction notice."

I hand him the paper.

Paddy reads it and scowls. "I'm not paying this rack rent. Clements is even charging me extra for having a chimney."

He crumbles the paper into a ball and throws it into the fire pit. "Besides, we've been here for over a thousand years. It'll take more than a piece of paper to chase us off our land."

I look at Mary. "Clements wants to offer you a job as a maid at Parke's Castle. He'll be using it himself after I move out at the end of May."

Mary shoots a fearful gaze at her father.

"He just wants to steal her virginity," one of the teenage boys says.

I stare down at the orange coals smoldering in the fire pit.

Big Paddy's stare swings from Mary to me. "She's not interested."

"I understand."

I pull ten pounds sterling in coins from my pocket and offer them to Big Paddy. "You can purchase three ship fares to New York with this. You can earn enough to buy food for your journey and a couple of more fares, if you sell your pig."

Paddy looks at the money in my hand. "Why are you doing this, O'Reilly?"

I look at Deirdre. "You were kind to Claire. I know she visited you here when I was away. I'm sure she'd want me to help you if she were still alive."

"You can keep your money, O'Reilly," Paddy says. "I'm not sending my children to ocean graves on a famine ship. Besides, this is our land. My boys will inherit it when I'm gone."

I pull my hand back. "It won't go well for you when Clements's soldiers come. He's put a bounty on your heads for your Ribbonmen activities—twenty pounds sterling for each of you."

Paddy stands up. "You've said what you needed to say, O'Reilly."

I leave the money on the log when I stand.

I look at Deirdre. "I'm sorry I can't do more to help you."

"Thanks for coming," she says. "I do miss Claire. She was very sweet."

I acknowledge her with a nod, stoop down, and exit through the doorway.

"Wait," Big Paddy says.

He follows me out and hands me the ten pounds sterling. "We don't take charity."

I shove the money into my pocket, and plod back down the trail.

8. BRIAN O'ROURKE

O'Rourke's hut. The next morning.

WE RISE AT sunrise from our straw bed. Da throws a peat brick into the fire pit and stirs the coals to bring the flames to life.

"It's Brian's turn to empty the chamber pot," Mary says to Ma.

"No it isn't," I say. "I emptied it yesterday."

No one wants to empty the chamber pot, so we challenge each other every morning to see who has to do it. Ma is the arbiter.

"Brian's right," Ma says. "It's your turn."

Mary picks up the pot, clamps her fingers over her nose, and leaves the hut. She places the pot in the corner when she returns.

We huddle around the coals, taking small sips of black tea. No one mentions food. We ate the last of our oats last night.

"Should I go to Manorhamilton to pick up the flags Norah Gallagher made?" I say to Da. "I can teach our soldiers there how to use flags to send messages."

"Good idea," he says. "We have six Ribbonmen in Manorhamilton, including Norah's son. We'll be able to watch all the roads between Manorhamilton and Dromahair once they're trained."

Da turns to Patrick and James. "We'll have to kill Mildred if we don't find something to eat soon. Get the men out on the hilltops first thing this morning. Take the burlap bags in case you spot a grain wagon. I need to stay here... to see if O'Reilly's eviction brigade shows up."

"Yes, sir," they say.

"Are you sure you don't want me to stay?" I say.

"No, Brian. We'll be fine."

I lift my backpack and tighten the straps around my shoulders. I always keep it with me. My violin is the only thing I own other than the clothes I'm wearing. James and Patrick pick up the Irish flags, and we trudge down the hill together.

9. SERGEANT MILTON

The road below O'Rourke's hut.

MY SIX-PERSON demolition squad arrives at the trail below the O'Rourke's hut late in the afternoon. We dismount in a field next to the road, and tie our horses' reins to tree branches.

This will be our fourth eviction and demolition today. The first three went smoothly, with no armed resistance, just the typical anguish of crying children, wailing mothers, and men glaring at us with hatred in their eyes.

It's exasperating to have to dislodge families from their homes. The peasants never concede that we're actually doing them a favor. They'll die a slow, miserable death by starvation or disease this winter if they stay. The smart ones will immigrate to a country that needs them. There's no place for them here in Ireland now, and the landlords need to reclaim their land, which is their right under the law.

I never thought I'd be doing something like this when I joined Wellington's army to fight Napoleon in 1815. However, this is my mission now, and I will perform it with the zeal and enthusiasm expected of me by the Crown. Besides, performing evictions does have its rewards. The money I'm making will allow me to purchase a small farm in the English countryside after I retire next year.

"Bring the burlap bag and your sword," I say to Corporal Wilcox.

"Yes... yes, Uncle George," he stammers. "I mean... yes, Sergeant."

The rest of us remove our rifles and crowbars from our saddles, and then we fan out in a horizontal assault formation on the hill. It's always wise to approach the peasants cautiously. Although most of them don't have weapons, other than perhaps a pitchfork or an ax, we occasionally confront someone that has a firearm.

I understand why they'd want to defend their home. I'd do the same thing, unless I realized it was futile, and it *is* futile, since they don't own the land.

Mary—Paddy O'Rourke's strikingly attractive teenage daughter—is sitting on a boulder near the entrance to their mud-and-rock-walled hut when we arrive. I've seen her walking along the road several times the past few months. Tall and thin like her brothers, with reddish-blond hair and a shapely figure, she gets more beautiful every time I see her.

"Da," she bellows, "the soldiers are here."

Her parents exit the hut and face us. Big Paddy has a hand behind his back.

I point my rifle at his chest, and my men do the same.

"Get off my land," Big Paddy yells.

Huh! What a joke. The arrogant pauper thinks this is *his* land, even though he hasn't paid his rent for over two years.

"Solicitor Reilly gave you a *Notice to Vacate*," I say. "I'm pleased to see you're still here, though. It'll make my job easier."

I nod at my nephew. "Show them why, Corporal Wilcox."

Wilcox unties the rope at the top of his burlap bag and dumps out the contents. James's and Patrick's blood-spattered heads roll across the dirt and stop at Deirdre's feet.

Deirdre and Mary scream. Deirdre drops to her knees, shrieking and squealing.

Mary jumps down from the boulder and kneels next to her mother.

Big Paddy pulls a handgun from behind his back.

We shoot before he aims. Our bullets stagger him backward. Blood spews from his mouth as he crumples to the ground.

Deirdre crawls over to him and lifts his head. He's trying to say something when his gaze freezes, and then he's staring at her with vacant eyes.

Mary rushes to me. "Murderer!" she screams, hammering her fists on my chest.

I conk her on the side of the head with the butt of my rifle.

She topples to the dirt, unconscious.

"Tie the women up," I yell. "And gag their mouths."

Deirdre takes off running up the side of the hill. Two of my soldiers run after her. She's a strong runner, even in a long skirt. The slimy remains of rotten potato plants slow my men down as they climb. They tackle her after twenty yards, and drag her back down the hill.

She screams and squirms as we bind her legs and arms to her body with a rope. I force her teeth apart with a stick, shove a rag into her mouth, and secure it with a rope tied around her head.

"Tie her to the top of that boulder," I say. "We'll let the buzzards finish her off."

My men lift her onto the boulder and secure her so she can't escape.

Mary remains unconscious as we bind her arms and legs. The side of her head is bleeding.

"Give me your sword," I say to Wilcox.

He pulls it from the scabbard on his belt and hands it to me.

It takes six hacking blows to chop through the thick tendons and vertebrae of Big Paddy's neck. I wipe the blood off the sword on Big Paddy's shirt, and hand it back to my nephew.

"Put the heads in the bag," I say to him.

Wilcox scoops the heads into his burlap bag and ties a rope across the top.

I'll show the heads to Viscount Clements to claim my reward when he visits Parke's Castle next month. It's easier this way. Otherwise, I'd have to assign soldiers to guard the O'Rourke's in a jail cell until Clements arrives, and I'm already short of men.

I pry the Dragoon pistol out of Big Paddy's hand, aim it at the ground, cock the hammer, and pull the trigger. There's no report.

"The gun was empty," I say. I turn my gaze to Paddy's torso. "He should have known better than to point an empty gun at someone. That's a guaranteed road to the grave."

I hand the weapon to Corporal Wilcox. "You can keep this as a souvenir, Henry."

"I'd... I'd... I'd like that, Uncle George... I mean, Sergeant Wilcox."

He sticks the pistol beneath his belt at the front of his trousers.

I nod and smile. The boy doesn't have much going on upstairs, but he's obedient, which is the most important trait for a soldier. Most importantly, my sister is happy that I found him a job. She was worried that she'd have to take care of him for the rest of his life.

I walk over to Deirdre and remove the gag from her mouth. "Where's your other son? I know there's another one around here somewhere."

She stares at me defiantly. "You'll burn in hell for what you've done!" she screams.

I pry her teeth apart with the stick and re-insert the gag.

I walk over to Mary. "She sure is a pretty young thing. I think we should keep her for ourselves."

Several of my men chuckle as they nod their agreement.

I turn to Wilcox. "Take the pig to the castle. It's a good day for a pig roast. Talk to Solicitor Reilly's cook. He'll know how to prepare it for the spit."

My men smile.

"Leave your horse," I say to Wilcox. "I'll bring it back after I take Mary to the cave."

"Yes... yes... yes, sir."

Wilcox ties a rope around the pig's neck, and she follows him willingly down the trail.

I face my men. "Demolish the house and throw the rocks down the side of the hill. I don't want squatters up here trying to rebuild. Then burn the straw and anything else you find."

They stare at me with expressions of bewilderment, or contempt— I'm not sure which. I know they don't want to leave Mrs. O'Rourke tied to a rock, but they'll follow my orders.

"I'll be back in a couple of hours," I say.

"Yes, sir," my men reply.

I hoist Mary over my shoulder and shuffle down the trail. Even though she's tall, she's slender, so she's easy to carry.

I drape her over the saddle of Wilcox's horse, and bind her feet and arms together with a rope beneath the horse's belly. The wound on her head has stopped bleeding. She'll be fine.

I stuff my handkerchief into her mouth and secure it around her head with a rope to gag her. I don't want to listen to her scream if she wakes up before we get there. I tie a rope to my saddle, and attach the other end to the halter on Wilcox's horse so I can lead it behind me.

I mount my saddle, ride east a quarter of a mile, and veer north on a trail that leads into the hills. The cave I've used to detain other women will be perfect for Mary too.

10. BRIAN O'ROURKE

Manorhamilton, Ireland.

NORAH GALLAGHER and a woman I've never met are stitching orange, white, and green strips of cloth together to make Irish flags when we enter the kitchen.

"I'm going to give Brian some tea before he goes home," Sean Gallagher says to his mother.

"That's fine, dear," Norah says. "I just heated up a fresh kettle."

Sean picks up two teacups from a shelf and places them in front of us as we sit down. Norah takes the teapot off the stove and fills our cups with black tea. I add a spoonful of sugar to mine after she puts the bowl in front of me.

"This is Evelyn Maguire," Norah says. "She volunteered to make flags with me."

I reach across the table and shake Evelyn's hand. "That's very kind of you," I say.

"It's for a good cause," she says, "and I like the symbolic meaning of the colors."

"How did your Ribbonmen training go?" Norah says to me.

"Great. Our soldiers are fast learners."

"We'll start monitoring the roads between Manorhamilton and Dromahair tomorrow morning," Sean says. "Brian taught us how to send secure messages using a cipher code."

We chat for a few minutes, and then I gulp down the rest of my tea and stand up. "I should head back. I need to play my violin in the Viking meadow after the sun sets."

"That's a noble thing you're doing for those poor starving souls," Norah says.

"Thank you, ma'am. It's the least we can do for them."

It's late when I start running west on the road that leads back to Lough Gill. The setting sun is painting the clouds with vibrant swaths of orange and purple as I approach Dromahair.

Maggie dives at me as I reach the eastern end of Lough Gill.

That's odd. She's never done that before.

She screeches and dives at me again.

I stop running and bend over, panting, trying to catch my breath.

Maggie lands on a tree branch and starts warbling and screeching frantically.

"What's wrong, Maggie?" I say aloud to her.

Her agitated cries continue.

"What are you trying to tell me?"

I scan the hills—my senses on high alert. There's no obvious danger I can see.

I start walking cautiously down the footpath that borders the lake. Maggie stays near me, screeching, flying, and landing on tree branches.

The clouds turn slate gray as daylight drains from the sky. It looks like it will rain soon.

I smell smoke as I approach the road near our home. A murder of crows is circling high above the hills.

"Is there a fire somewhere?" I say to Maggie. "Is that what you're trying to tell me?"

I stop abruptly. Several soldiers are mounting horses. I hide behind a bush as I watch them ride west toward the castle. I wait until they disappear, and then I run across the road and vault up the trail hurtling as fast as my legs will take me.

I see Ma tied to the boulder.

"Oh God!" I yell.

There's straw burning on the ground where our house used to be.

Seeing Pa's decapitated body makes me wretch. I drop to my knees and puke in the dirt.

I look away from him as I remove the gag from Ma's mouth. She starts to cry as I untie her.

I feel dizzy. This can't be real! "What happened, Ma?"

She continues to cry without answering. I help her down from the boulder. She drops to her knees, wailing, hugging Pa's bloody chest.

Mary's tin whistle flute is beside the embers. I pick it up and stuff it into my backpack.

"Come on, Ma," I say as I lift her to her feet. "We need to get out of here."

She hangs on to me, looking down at Da, wailing inconsolably.

I lift her, cradle her in my arms, and plod down the trail. A frigid rain begins as I reach the north side of Lough Gill. I run two miles to Creevelea Abbey without stopping. We're sopping wet when we arrive.

I lay her down beneath an image of St. Francis carved into a stone pillar. She withers into a fetal position and continues to wail, rocking side to side.

I scan the ruins as the freezing deluge pours down on us. Something terrible happened—just as Reilly predicted. The soldiers are probably looking for me too. We need to hide.

The stone key!

"I'll be back in a couple of minutes, Ma."

I walk to the well and remove my boots. I'm not a good swimmer, but I have no choice. I must find the key.

I unwind the rope until the wooden bucket hits the water with a splash. I slither over the side and grab the rope. It's slimy with moss, so I slip down rapidly.

"Ahhh!" I cry out, when I hit the freezing water.

I flail around for a moment, trying to recover from the shock. I take a deep breath, bend headfirst into the water, and propel myself to the bottom, which seems to take forever.

There's six inches of slimy moss on the floor of the well. I find nothing with my hand, so I swim back to the surface.

I inhale several deep breaths while I hold on to the rope to stay afloat.

The key has to be there! No one but Brother Bernard would take it.

I inhale deeply, and dive to the bottom. There's no key, only handfuls of muck.

I'm trembling violently as I float back to the surface. I can barely hold the slick rope.

I must try again. Ma's life depends on it. We have to find shelter.

I dive again, and force myself to stay down, searching the cylindrical cavity methodically with my hand. I feel something hard in the sludge. It feels like a rock. No. *It's the key!*

I grab it, turn upright, and propel myself to the surface. My left hand clings to the rope as I shiver. I tread water as I shove the skinny end of the key into the right pocket of my trousers.

The slimy rope is difficult to grasp as I climb. I plunge back into the water after a few feet. I go farther the next time. It takes several attempts to reach the top. I swing my legs over the edge, and flop over the side.

Torrents of rain pour down on me as I lie in the grass, gasping for air.

"Thank you, Lord," I say aloud. "Thank you... for delivering me."

I pull on my wet leather boots, clutch the stone key in my hand, and walk back to Ma. She's shaking, rolled up in a ball.

I examine the cross-shaped key. *Damn*! I should have asked Brother Bernard where the chamber was before he left.

I begin my quest at the south transept. I search the floor with my hands, since I can't see in the dark. My fingers start to bleed when I cut them on the sharp-edged rocks.

The cloister and nave yield no openings. The rain is still pouring down hard.

There are some loose stones where an altar once stood in the chancel. I move the rocks, and find an opening the same shape as the key. *Yes!*

I insert the key and twist hard. Nothing.

Something gives way when I twist the other direction. Metal gnashes against stone as I rotate the key ninety degrees. A small opening appears in the floor. There's enough space for me to slip my hand in.

The stone covering the metal plate is loose. I pick it up and move it to the side. I jostle the plate in different directions, until it slides into a crevice beneath the stone floor.

I can't see, so I feel the opening with my hand. It feels like a step.

I stick my foot into the opening, take another step, and continue down a steep stairway that descends in a spiral. The musty smell of mold greets me when I reach the bottom.

My hand finds three candles and a package of phosphorus matches on a ledge. I light two candles. A narrow chamber appears in front of me. I duck my head down and step forward, holding a candle in each hand.

I jump back when I see a skeleton. It's standing upright.

After a few deep breaths, I continue forward, passing several skeletons hanging from wires tied to the rock walls. Some have deteriorating robes. A malodorous stench pervades the claustrophobic cavity. I find a straw bed with blankets on the floor beyond the skeletons.

This must be a hypogeum—an underground burial crypt for the monks. Brother Bernard must have slept here.

I leave the candles burning near the staircase and return to Ma.

"I found a place for us to stay," I say to her.

She doesn't respond.

I lift her and carry her to the top of the stairs. "We need to go down into the crypt. It's dry down there. Do you want me to carry you?"

"No. I can step down myself."

"I'll go in first so I can guide you."

I descend four steps and reach up to her, and we step carefully down to the floor.

"This is a crypt for the monks that used to live in the abbey," I say, as I hand her a candle.

I climb the steps and pull the iron grate closed over the entrance. It fits perfectly, preventing water from seeping in.

We walk past a dozen skeletons standing upright on each side of the chamber. There are two cloaks hanging on hooks on the wall next to the straw bed.

"It looks like Brother Bernard left some cloaks here," I say.

We remove our wet clothes and dry ourselves with the cloaks.

Ma is shaking as she lies down on the hay beneath a blanket.

"I'll bury Da once the rain stops," I tell her. "We can't leave him like that."

I leave one candle lit while I watch her. She eventually falls into a fitful sleep.

The rain stops an hour later. I pull one of the cloaks over my head, and leave the crypt.

I return after several hours, carrying a bundle of wet clothes. Ma awakens when I shake her.

"I took these clothes from the dead bodies in the meadow," I say. "I rinsed them in the lake after I buried Da. No one had coats... so we'll have to wear multiple layers to stay warm."

She stares at me without speaking. I hang the wet clothes on the skeletons, and lie down next to her, and soon we're both asleep.

A thunderous quake awakens us the next morning. The rain is pounding the rock ceiling above our heads. Humidity leaching through the mildewed walls saturates the foul air.

"They'll... kill you," Ma says, "and behead you, if they find you... like they did with Patrick, and James, and your father. Sergeant Milton took Mary. You have to find her!"

I light a candle. The slack-jawed gapes on the skeletons' skulls sends a shiver down my spine.

I remove one of the dresses I hung on a skeleton, and bring it to Ma. "Put this on. It's almost dry."

"What is this place?" she says, as she pulls on the damp garment.

I told her last night. She must not have been listening.

"It's a burial chamber for the monks. Brother Bernard gave me a key for it before he left. I think he must have slept here. We'll need to stay hidden during the day since they're hunting for me. I'll search for Mary tonight."

She drops to her knees on the stone floor and starts murmuring a Hail Mary. I kneel down beside her, and we pray for several hours, until we fall asleep again.

The rain has stopped when I awaken. The hunger gnawing my belly is making my stomach hurt.

It's dark outside when I move the iron plate at the top of the staircase. "I'm going to look for Mary," I say. "I'll bring back some water and food if I can."

Ma doesn't respond.

I return three hours later, light a candle, and raise her head with my hand. "Drink this," I say, holding a cup to her lips. "It's water from the river. I couldn't find any food."

She drinks a few sips and drops back to the hay.

"Look what I found on the hill below our home."

A smile touches her lips. "Our chamber pot," she says. "How lovely."

"I need to be careful." I show her a piece of paper. "Sergeant Milton nailed wanted posters like this to trees along the road. He's offering five pounds to anyone that tells him where I'm hiding. That's a tempting reward for someone who's starving."

11. ELIZABETH REILLY

Parke's Castle. September 14, 1848.

FATHER AND MISS Hughes are sitting next to each other when I walk into the dining room.

"I'm glad you're feeling better," Father says.

I sit down at the table. "I'm going to try to eat something," I say.

"You look good," Miss Hughes says. "I guess the chicken soup we kept bringing you finally did the trick."

I think about Brian as I spoon boiled potatoes and carrots onto my plate. I need to warn him about the danger his family faces. My feverish dreams kept reminding me, but I was too sick to leave my room.

I hope it's not too late. I opened my window hoping to hear his violin last night, but I didn't hear anything.

"What happened to those boys who were waving flags when we were on our way to Viscount Clements's castle?" I say to Father.

He exchanges glances with Miss Hughes, as if they're sharing a secret, and then he turns his gaze toward me. "We don't need to worry about them spying on us any longer," he says.

Miss Hughes, who's never been shy about disparaging the Irish, is ominously quiet, which has me concerned.

Something terrible must have happened. I feel it in their silence.

I wait until everyone's gone to bed, before I sneak down the stairs and leave the castle. An almost full moon hangs over the horizon as I make my way through the woods to the meadow. There are only a few people lying in the grass tonight.

Maybe they've stopped coming because Brian isn't around.

I walk to the road and hike up the hill to Brian's house.

It's gone. The moonlight illuminates some rocks on the ground arranged in the shape of a cross, over a mound of dirt that looks like a gravesite. There's a flag planted at one end of the grave—the same flag I saw the boys waving on the hilltops.

I see a wanted poster tacked to a tree as I return to the castle. Sergeant Milton is offering a reward for information about Brian's whereabouts.

Thank God! That must mean he's still alive. I need to find him.

I dress in riding clothes and mount Raven's saddle after breakfast the next morning.

Father yells, "Stop!" as I canter the horse toward the gate.

"I don't want you out there on you own," he says. "It's too dangerous."

"I'll be fine."

"No you won't. Sergeant Milton will need to accompany you if you go out."

"Never mind."

I return to the barn and dismount, and the groom removes Raven's saddle.

Dark clouds are blocking the moon when I sneak out of the castle after everyone has gone to bed. I begin my search in the meadow to ensure Brian isn't among the dying. There are only five people here tonight. Perhaps everyone knows that Brian won't be coming here to play his violin anymore. Someone would probably turn him in for the reward if he did.

I hike the trails around Lough Gill for three hours, before I return home. I then clean the mud off my boots, and sneak back up the stairs to my room.

I search for him every night for the next week and a half. There's no sign of him anywhere.

We're sitting by the fireplace in the parlor after dinner when Father says, "Don't you think it's time for you to resume your studies in London?"

Miss Hughes is in the rocking chair, crocheting a shawl.

"I'm not ready to go back yet," I say.

"Are you sure? I thought you'd be missing Aunt Bess by now."

"It's been good to get to know you again, Father, and I *do* enjoy the castle. I have fond memories of my childhood here. I'd like to stay for a little while longer, if that's all right."

He smiles. "It has been nice having you here. I see a lot of your mother in you."

"Thank you, Father. I still miss her after all these years. Do you?"

A flicker of grief flashes across his eyes. "Yes... I do miss her. I miss her every day."

"Everything seemed so much easier here when I was younger. Mother and I would explore the countryside and have picnics next to the lake. We didn't have soldiers everywhere... and people starving to death, like there is now."

"I miss those times too."

"How did you meet her, Father?"

A smile forms on his lips. "Claire was step dancing at a hotel in Donegal Town the first time I saw her. She was the prettiest dancer I'd ever seen. Her father, your grandfather, Peter McNeil, was playing the fiddle while she danced. He was one of the best fiddle players in Ireland."

"What happened to him?"

Father's smile fades away. "Your grandfather refused to talk with Claire after we got married. He was furious that she changed religions. She never saw her family after that."

There it is again: religious differences, thrusting thorns of discontent into people's lives.

"What happened to them?" I say.

"Someone from Donegal told me that Claire's family died of starvation two years ago."

Father looks at Miss Hughes. "Could you excuse us?" he says. "I need to talk with Elizabeth alone for a few minutes."

"Certainly, Mr. Reilly." She rises from her chair. "It's bedtime for me anyhow."

We say "good night," as she leaves the room.

Father stands up and walks over to the fireplace. He turns to face me with his hands behind his back.

"I'll be returning to London in June," he says. "I say returning, because London was my boyhood home. My great-grandfather moved our family to London from County Cavan a hundred years ago."

"Really? So both sides of our family are Irish?"

"We're part English and part Irish. Unfortunately, I'll be looking for work when I return. Viscount Clements won't need my services after I finish filing the paperwork for his evictions next spring. He wants me to vacate the castle by the end of May."

"I thought this was *our* castle."

"No. It actually belongs to the Lane-Fox family. I've been leasing it since before you were born. I'm getting it for a very low rate because Clements is friends with George Lane-Fox, the High Sherriff of Leitrim."

Father turns around and stares at the logs burning in the fireplace. "My lack of employment is going to change our financial situation until I find another position. It's important that we arrange a marriage for you next summer, while we're still in Clements's good graces. He has deep connections in London, political as well as financial."

"How did Clements get so wealthy?"

"Several generations of his family served as military officers for the Crown. The English kings gave them Irish land over the centuries as a reward for their services. Clements's ancestors also expanded their estates by purchasing large tracks of land themselves."

"What if I don't want to get married? I want to become a concert pianist."

He turns and faces me. "I won't be able to afford that."

I didn't realize we had money issues. There must be a way for me to follow my dreams. "I can always teach piano lessons to support myself, until I'm good enough to play concerts."

"The seas will get rough once winter sets in. You shouldn't wait too long to return."

"Thank you for being honest with me about our financial situation, Father." I stand up. "I think I'll retire for the evening."

"Good night, my dear."

I walk up the stairs to my bedroom, after I use the privy.

It's almost inaudible, the sound, drifting through my open bedroom window as I lie in bed. I jump up and listen. I recognize the melody. It's the second movement of Beethoven's Symphony no. 7—the sad one. The faint violin notes stop in the middle of a phrase.

I dress quickly and hurry down the stairs to the back exit. Then I hesitate. I sneak back to the kitchen, shove an apple into my pocket, and return to the bottom of the stairwell, where I pull on my boots and exit to the trail next to the lake.

The waning crescent moon provides just enough light to guide me to the meadow. Brian is there, lying in the grass, hugging his mother. His violin and bow are beside him.

There are four bodies next to them. Everyone is still.

I probe beneath Brian's jaw with my fingertips. He has a faint pulse.

I check Deirdre's pulse. Nothing. I shake her. There's no response. She's gone.

I bite off a chunk of apple, and place it into Brian's mouth.

His teeth don't chew. I push his jaw up and down. The apple falls out.

I bite off another chunk and chew it into mush. I then fasten my mouth to his lips, and squeeze the pulp out with my tongue. He swallows with an unconscious reflex. I feed him the rest of the apple the same way, chewing the fruit, and feeding him with a kiss.

His eyes blink open for a second and close after I finish.

He won't last long if I don't do something. *Think!*

I could hide him in the castle. No. That wouldn't be safe.

My gaze settles on a tiny island on the other side of the lake—Innisfree.

12. BRIAN O'ROURKE

The Viking Meadow.

MY DEATH DREAM returns as the angel glides away. *Will I meet God in this cold purgatory, more angels, or are there devils here too?*

The angel returns and lifts me up. She drapes my arm over her shoulder, and we float in stumbles through the fog to a boat, where she lays me down and covers me with a blanket.

The angel's long blond hair flows down past her shoulders. Her oars extend like wings into the water rotating in undulating circles, lifting and pulling, dropping and rolling, lifting and pulling, dropping and rolling. A sliver of moon paints a halo around her head in the misty haze.

The angel stops rowing after a while, carries me on her shoulder again, and lays me down on the grass. Her lips bestow a gentle kiss on my forehead. She covers me with a blanket, and I drift into a dream.

The chattering song of a magpie awakens me the next morning. It's hot. I push the blanket aside and lean upright on my elbow.

The sun is painting slow-moving shadows on the hills below the clouds. Maggie greets me with a warble from her perch on a tree limb.

My burlap backpack is beside me. I find my violin inside, next to several apples, and a loaf of bread. I break off a corner of the bread and shove it into my mouth. It doesn't dissolve. I crawl through the thick brush down to the edge of the lake, take a drink, and the bread slithers down my throat.

Parke's Castle is shimmering golden-orange on the other side of the lake. After looking around, I realize that I'm on the tiny island of Innisfree. I crawl back to the blanket, pull it over my head, and fall asleep.

Night has come when the angel shakes my shoulder. I feel dizzy, as if I'm watching myself from outside my body as I stare up at her.

"You must eat to gain your strength," she says.

She lifts me upright and places a cup to my lips, and I drink. It's water.

"Are you… are you… my guardian angel?" I say.

She giggles. "Yes, Brian O'Rourke. I'll be your guardian angel—if that's what you want."

She hands me an apple. "The soldiers are looking for you everywhere."

I take a bite, chew it into a pulp, and swallow.

"I thought you weren't going to make it for a while," she says.

"Where's Ma?"

She shakes her head. "I'm sorry, Brian. Your mother had already passed when I found you in the meadow last night."

My tears flow, and I brush them away.

She takes my hand, brings it to her lips, and kisses it.

"What's your name?" I say.

"Elizabeth. Elizabeth Reilly. I'm visiting my father at Parke's Castle."

"Where's Mary? Have you seen Mary… my sister?"

"Mary?"

"Sergeant Milton kidnapped her. I searched for her everywhere. I need my monk's cloak to hide from the soldiers. They're hunting for me."

"I'll watch Sergeant Milton closely tomorrow to see where he goes."

"Solicitor Reilly—the man who evicts people… is he your father?"

She looks down at the grass. "Yes. He handles the paperwork for Viscount Clements's evictions. The viscount asked Sergeant Milton to capture the men in your family because of your Ribbonmen deeds."

I study her while I chew another bite of the apple. "Your father came to our house," I say after I swallow. "He warned us about the soldiers."

Her eyes widen. "He did?"

"He offered us money for fares on a famine ship... but my father refused."

Her gaze moves across the lake to Parke's Castle, which is barely visible behind the fog.

"Why did you take me here?" I say. "Why did you save my life?"

"I figured this would be a safe place for you to hide while you recuperate."

She retrieves a package from the rowboat and hands it to me. "I took this army tent from the soldier's barracks. The soldiers are looking for you, so you should hide this in the trees when you set it up. I need to get back to the castle before someone notices the boat is missing. I'll be back tomorrow night with more food."

I stand up. "Thank you, Elizabeth… for saving my life."

She smiles. "You're welcome, Brian O'Rourke."

We walk to the rowboat together. She steps in, sits down, and picks up the oars. I push the bow of the boat backward into the water to get her started. We stare at each other as she rows away, until she evanesces and disappears in the fog.

I set up the tent in the center of the island behind a thicket of trees, and fall asleep inside.

A thick haze surrounds Innisfree when I awaken the next morning. The effluvium in the trees slowly dissolves as the sun rises higher in the sky.

I've seen Innisfree from our home on the side of the hill for years, but I've never explored the island. A gaggle of geese swims away from the south side as I approach them.

I hear bees droning as I return to the tent. Their whirring buzz leads me to an overturned tree trunk, where I find a beehive hidden beneath the roots. I dislodge the hive with a stick, and run away fast to escape the ire of the queen's attendants.

Harvesting the honey is messy. I break away a piece of the hive with a long stick, and squeeze the honey out of the wax. It tastes wonderful on the bread Elizabeth brought me.

"Thank you, God," I say aloud, as I look up at the sky. "Thank you for this food... and thank you for Elizabeth!"

I notice a hole in the dirt beneath the tree trunk where I dislodged the beehive. It looks like the entrance to a cave.

I kick the hole with my boot to widen it, and then I slither into the opening. The cavern gets larger as I crawl farther inside. I stop when my hand touches a bone.

Yikes!

I scurry backward through the entrance.

I calm myself, and then I crawl back in again—more slowly this time, letting my eyes adjust to the darkness. There's a human skeleton lying face down in the dirt. Its bony fingers are clutching a metal box to its chest. A jewel-hilted dagger has fallen away from a decomposing sheath next to its hip.

I lift the weapon out of the dust, crawl backward out of the cave, and scrutinize the dagger in the sunlight. There's a Celtic design in the hilt—our O'Rourke coat of arms! The grip behind the cross guard fits my hand perfectly.

The narrow six-inch tempered-steel blade is sharp on my fingertip. I slice the bark off a slender sapling to test the edges. Both sides cut like razors.

I crawl back into the cave and stare at the bony fingers clutching the metal box. "Hello, ancient one," I say aloud. "It's good to meet you. I think we're related; or maybe you died here when you were hiding from Queen Elizabeth's soldiers. I hope you don't mind if I take your box."

I push the skeleton onto its side.

The skull shifts sideways and stares at me, sending a wave of fear through my spine.

I grab the metal box and pull. The hands clutching the box snap back to its chest like a spring. I break off a bony finger phalange, wiggle the box out of its grip, and sidle backward out of the cave.

I pry the top open with the tip of the dagger. There's a six-inch cross inside, with eleven bright red rubies embedded in the metal to symbolize Jesus. The outer edges are speckled with clear gems that sparkle in the sunlight.

Are those diamonds? I'm not sure. I've never seen a diamond before.

I look through the opening and contemplate the skeleton. *What secrets do you hold... ancient one? This cross must have been important to you.*

I place the cross and dagger on a log. I then crawl back into the cave, and wait for my eyes to adjust. There's a patch of dark, curly hair pasted to the skeleton's skull. It's the same color as mine. There's a rusted suit of armor stacked next to the wall on the other side of the skeleton.

"I'm sorry I disturbed you," I say aloud.

I sidle back out of the cave, and wrestle the overturned tree stump into the opening to protect the gravesite.

The moon is high when Elizabeth returns. She brings me six slices of ham, and a bottle of wine, and we sit down next to each other outside the tent. She opens the wine bottle with a corkscrew, takes a drink, and hands it to me.

I take a sip. "This is good. It's much better than the drop of wine the priest in Dromahair gives us at Christmas."

I hand the bottle back to her.

Several frogs are croaking at each other in a nearby marsh. Their rhythmic dialogue seems to grow louder as we contemplate the sallow outline of the new moon.

"It's very peaceful here," she says. "It would be nice to live on a tranquil island like this someday."

"Indeed. It's been a good place to recuperate while I regain my strength—a slice of heaven... amid the hell that Ireland has become."

She nods, drinks, and hands me the bottle.

I take a mouthful, and savor the fruity flavor before I swallow. "This is very nice." I chuckle. "The more I drink, the better it tastes."

She laughs, which makes me feel warm inside. Her laughter is like music to my soul.

"I took it from the pantry," she says. "I hope I'm back in London before Father misses it."

"You're going to England?"

"Yes. I live there with my aunt. I'm just visiting my father here. It's the first time I've seen him in nine years."

Her gaze finds the castle on the other side of the lake. "I was sent away to London after my mother died... when I was seven."

"I'm sorry for your loss."

She nods. "Thanks. I don't know my Father very well. He always seems rather emotionless to me. I was surprised when you told me that he offered your father money to escape."

Yeah, I ruminate—but Da was too proud to take the money... *and now they're all dead, except for Mary!*

I swallow another mouthful, and pass the bottle back to her.

"I'll be returning to London soon, now that I've found you," she says. "I wanted to make sure you were safe before I left."

"That was very thoughtful of you."

Her face looks lovely. She does look like an angel in her flowing white dress. I think she's the most beautiful woman I've ever met, and we're both the same age.

"I have some information about Mary," she says. "I followed Sergeant Milton when he left the barracks this evening. One of the grooms told me that Milton leaves every night, and he doesn't return until morning. I lost him on the trail that leads north into the hills. I'll hide there tomorrow evening to see where he goes."

"Thank you, Elizabeth. I hope she's all right. It's been weeks since Milton kidnapped her."

Elizabeth gently squeezes my wrist. "Don't worry. We'll find her."

She lifts the bottle to her lips, drinks a mouthful, and hands it to me.

I take another sip.

"I think what's happening here in Ireland is terrible," she says, "the starvation, and the brutality of the soldiers. I could never live here now. London's a lot more civilized."

"I always thought I'd live here forever... I don't feel that way anymore."

"That's understandable."

I hand the bottle back to her. "Could you help me with a few things? I'd like to leave Innisfree tomorrow night to search for Mary."

"What do you need?"

"Can you get me a good pair of trousers, some buttons, and a needle with some strong thread? I want to sew two pairs of trousers together so I can stay warm during my voyage across the ocean. I've decided to go to America after I find Mary. There's nothing here for us now."

"That's a good idea. I should be able to get some trousers from the wardrobe in my father's room. I'll bring those with the other things you asked for when I return tomorrow."

"I don't want to be a bother, but could you bring them back here tonight? That way I can sew during the day, so I'll be ready to leave tomorrow night."

She stares at the water. "I'll have to sneak into my father's room to get the trousers. I'll try to get some money for you too. Father will be angry when he finds it missing, but I'll tell him I needed it to do some shopping. By the way, I went into Sligo today. I saw an advertisement for a famine ship named the *Dromahair* that's leaving for New York in two days. The captain's name is Mr. Pyne. I checked around. People say he has a good reputation. He doesn't withhold food and abuse his passengers the way some famine ship captains do."

"I need to find Mary before I leave."

We finish the wine, and then she stands up.

"I'll be back soon," she says.

She returns two hours later. I meet her at the boat, and we walk back to the tent.

She opens a satchel, hands me several buttons, some thread, a needle, a pair of wool trousers, and eight pounds sterling. "This is all the money I could find. It should be enough for two steerage tickets to America."

"Thank you." I shove the money into my pocket.

"I brought something else that will help you escape."

She pulls some scissors and a straight razor out of her satchel. "You mentioned that you wore a monk's cloak while you searched for Mary. The wanted posters say you have long, curly black hair. You'll be harder to recognize if I cut your hair and shave your face."

"That's a great idea, Elizabeth. I see that you're as smart as you are beautiful."

She chuckles. "You think so, huh?"

I sit down cross-legged on the grass, facing away from her, and she cuts my hair short with her scissors. She then mixes some soap and water in a cup, lathers my face, and starts to shave my sparse whiskers with the razor.

"This is fun," she says.

"Can you shave my head too, so I'll look like a monk? There's a monk's cloak at Creevelea Abbey I can use to complete my disguise."

"Sure. I'll do my best."

She lathers my head with soap after she finishes my face. "I watched you play music in the meadow a few weeks ago," she says, as she carefully scrapes the hair off my head. "You looked very handsome... sitting on that Viking rock."

"That's nice of you to say."

"You play very well. I think I heard Beethoven, Mozart, and Shubert. Is that right?"

"Yes, indeed. I had an excellent violin teacher—a French monk named Brother Bernard. He returned to France a few weeks ago. He teaches at the music conservatory in Paris."

She finishes shaving the left side of my head and moves to my right.

"I watched you play your piano in the castle one night," I say. "I was standing in the forest watching you through the window. I played one of your melodies back to you, before I went to the Viking meadow."

"I heard that. You were gone when I went to the window."

"Your playing was marvelous."

"Thanks. I hope to study with Chopin when I return to London, but I'm not sure if that's going to be possible. Father wants me to find a husband during the Season next summer."

She gets up on her knees and starts to shave the top of my head.

"All done," she says a moment later.

She giggles as she stands up. "You look very different now, and I must say... you are *indeed,* a very cute monk."

I stand and face her. "Thank you, Elizabeth."

I take her right hand and press the back of it to my lips.

She smiles, folds her arms around me, and hugs me. We gaze into each other's eyes.

I want to kiss her, but I'm not sure if she wants me to.

I lean down, slightly, toward her lips.

She tips her head, the ends of our noses touch, and then our lips meet.

Her kiss sends a jolt through my loins. *I've never felt anything like that before*!

She looks into my eyes. She's trembling beneath my fingertips.

"Are you cold?" I say.

She shakes her head. "No. I've just never kissed anyone before."

"Neither have I."

I pull her close and we kiss again. I feel my heart drumming inside my chest.

She pulls back and smiles. "I need to get back. It's getting late."

She picks up a ringlet of my hair from the grass. "May I keep this... to remind me of you?"

"Of course."

She stores it in her satchel. She hugs me, and we kiss again, longer this time. She opens her mouth slightly, and the tip of her tongue finds mine, sending a quake through my body.

She laughs and pulls away.

I hold her hand as we walk to the rowboat. "May I have a lock of your angel hair?" I say.

She giggles and pulls out her scissors.

"I love your laugh," I say. "It makes me feel warm inside."

She snips off a two inch sliver of hair and hands it to me. "I hope you don't forget me."

My fingertips brush the side of her cheek. "How could I ever forget you? You're the angel of Innisfree... my guardian angel. You saved my life."

She smiles. "You're a pretty smooth talker for a monk, Brian Boru O'Rourke."

She steps into the rowboat, sits down, and grabs the oars.

"I'm curious," I say. "Why are you being so nice to me? I'm a Catholic, and you're a Protestant. I thought you wouldn't care about someone like me."

She rows left a few strokes to turn the bow of the boat toward Parke's Castle.

"This isn't about religion," she says. "I love you, Brian O'Rourke."

She giggles. "Don't you remember... when we played together as children? I told you I loved you then too. We promised each other we'd get married someday."

She smiles as she rows away.

I realize what she was talking about as she starts to disappear in the mist. *She must be Beth!* Her mother used to bring her to our house when we were children. She *did* tell me she loved me... and I told her I loved her too. Of course, we were just children then.

13. BRIAN O'ROURKE

Innisfree.

THE COMFORT OF the army tent helps me sleep well past dawn.

I eat several chunks of bread, the ham, and an apple, and then I take off my trousers and sit down beneath a tree to sew. I bind the wool trousers Elizabeth brought me outside of my own, and embed the jeweled cross between the layers below my left pocket. I reinforce the perimeter around the cross three times to make it secure.

Fashioning a sheath for the dagger is more complicated. If I need it, I'll need it fast, and it needs to slide out smoothly without cutting me. I stitch a scabbard on my right thigh below my right pocket between the trousers, and open the pocket so I can retrieve the weapon quickly.

A miasmatic mix of fog and peat fire smoke creeps over the island as night arrives. The ash-gray clouds are hiding the moon.

I hear Elizabeth before I see her. I can tell that she's strong as I listen to her breathing, rowing forward, and back, forward, and back, propelling the rowboat through the water.

"I'm here, Elizabeth," I say, when she's close.

"Thanks for telling me. It's hard to see in this fog."

She changes direction, rows a few more strokes, and pushes to the shoreline. I pull the bow of the boat up into the grass, and she steps out.

"I followed Sergeant Milton to the hills in Doonkelly," she says. "That's where I lost him. I couldn't keep up with his horse."

"I'll start my search there tonight after I retrieve the monk's cloak from the abbey."

I stuff a loaf of bread and several apples she brought into my backpack, and sling it over my shoulder. "Thanks for saving my violin when you rescued me."

"Of course. I know it's important to you. That's how I found you. Your music lured me to the meadow. I hope we can play music together someday."

"I hope we can too."

I take her hand. "Do you think we'll ever see each other again after tonight?"

She nods. "I hope so. It's up to us to decide what we want from the future."

"Ah, yes... like that play by Shakespeare called *As You Like It*."

"Hmm. Maybe so. I'm not familiar with that one."

"I've been thinking about what you said last night, about knowing each other when we were children. Are you the little girl with the rich mother that used to visit us from Parke's Castle?"

"That's right." She smiles. "I'm not so little anymore, though."

"I can see that. You've grown into a very beautiful woman, Elizabeth Reilly."

We stare into each other's eyes.

I bend down slowly to her lips. Her kiss makes me instantly aroused.

I pull away after a moment. "We should go," I say. "I need to find Mary."

I pick up the tent. "I folded up the tent so you can return it to the barracks. I don't want you to get in trouble if someone suspects you of taking it."

"Thanks."

We walk to the rowboat, and she sits down. I stow the tent and my backpack in the boat, push it away from the shore, jump in, and start to row. The fog is thick, so I row slowly.

"How are you going to save Mary from Sergeant Milton?" she says. "My father said that Milton's been a soldier for over thirty years. He's been in lots of battles, and he's killed many people."

I stop rowing, pull the oars in, and slide my dagger from its sheath beneath my right hand pocket. "I'll use this," I say, as I hand it to her.

She examines the blade.

"I found it in a cave on Innisfree," I go on to say. "It has my O'Rourke family crest on the handle. One of my ancestors must have left it there."

She hands it back. "Be careful. I don't want to lose you."

I slide the dagger back into its sheath and start to row. "Is it all right if I take the rowboat to the trail near the Bonet River? It's quicker from there to the abbey."

"Sure." She smiles. "By the way, your monk haircut looks good."

"Thanks."

I row to the shore, step out of the boat, and sling my backpack over my shoulder. She steps out and we face each other.

"I'll come back for you someday if you'd like," I say, "after I make my fortune in America. People say that it's easy to get rich there, if you work hard."

She pulls my head down to her lips and kisses me passionately, pulling me into her body. She leans back after a moment, and looks into my eyes. "Are you serious?"

"Yes, I'm serious. I love you too, Elizabeth Reilly. I remember telling you that when we were children. I'll come find you so we can get married, once I get my life sorted out."

"I'd like that, Brian O'Rourke."

She removes a slip of paper from her satchel and hands it to me. "This is my aunt's address in London. I'll be there by the time you reach America. Will you write to me?"

"Indeed."

I unbutton the hidden compartment for the cross I made beneath my left hand pocket, and remove the hair she gave me last night, which I fashioned into a braid to keep it together. I fold the braid inside the slip of paper, shove it back into my pocket next to the cross, and button the compartment so it's secure.

"I have an idea," she says.

"What's that?"

"I'll look at the moon at five a.m. every morning, and you could do the same at midnight. There's a five-hour time difference between England and New York."

"Indeed. The moon can be our touchstone until we're together again."

We kiss, and now I don't want to leave. I want to stay with her, but I need to find Mary.

I stare into her eyes. "So, we're promised to each other?"

She nods with a grin. "Yes. I'll wait for you... no matter how long it takes."

"Goodbye, Elizabeth. I'll come to London someday to find you, and then we'll get married."

"I'll be waiting."

Another kiss, and then another, and then I turn and run toward the abbey.

The stone key opens the entrance to the crypt, and I step down the spiral staircase. I light a candle, walk past the skeletons, take the brown monk's robe off the hanger on the wall, and pull it over my head.

I stuff two dresses that are still hanging on skeletons into my backpack for Mary, climb back up the stairs, close and lock the entrance, and scatter some rocks to hide the keyhole. I then drop the key back into the well.

The rolling hills have many diverging trails as I head northwest toward the mountains. I explored some caves near Glencar Lough with my brothers once. It would make sense for Sergeant Milton to hide Mary somewhere like that. It's very secluded.

I see a horse with Crown insignia on the far side of the meadow as I approach the caves. I circle the perimeter cautiously. There are shadows from flames dancing on the walls inside one of the caves.

There's another cave nearby that looks like a passage tomb—a grave used by the ancients to bury the cremated remains of their clan, so their souls would pass back into the earth.

The horse whinnies and snorts.

I freeze.

After standing still for a moment, I remove my backpack, stow it near the horse, and pull my dagger from its sheath. I slither sideways to the entrance of the cave and peek inside.

Mary is sleeping, half-covered by a blanket. Her back is naked. She has a two-inch thick rope tied around her right ankle. The other end of the three-foot rope is attached to a round hook embedded in the rock wall.

Sergeant Milton is asleep next to her. His Dragoon handgun sits atop a pile of his clothes near the entrance to the cave—out of Mary's reach.

I shove my dagger into the pocket of my cloak, and step slowly toward the gun. Two more steps and I reach it.

I pull the handgun from its holster, and aim it with two hands. "Untie her!" I yell.

Milton stirs, and then he jerks upright.

Mary screams. She covers her breasts with her arm and scoots sideways to the wall.

Milton stands. He's naked too. He's a few inches taller than I am and heavyset—even bigger than Da.

"You must be Brian," he says. "That's a clever disguise. No wonder I couldn't find you."

He steps toward me.

I back up. "Stop—or I'll shoot!"

Milton laughs. "Go ahead."

He takes another step.

I pull the trigger. Nothing happens.

Shite! I forgot to cock the hammer.

Milton swats the gun out of my hand.

I yank the dagger from my cloak and lunge at him as he reaches for the gun. The blade pierces his back.

"Damn you!" he yells.

He picks up the gun and cocks the hammer with his right thumb.

I dive at his knees to tackle him.

A searing heat screams through my left shoulder when he shoots me as we tumble to the ground. He crushes me beneath him on the dirt.

I hold the hilt of my dagger with both my hands as I thrust the blade deep into his gut, twisting the tip up toward his heart. He screams as it slices through his intestines. Blood gushes over me as I ratchet the blade back and forth with all my strength.

His grip finally loosens, and then he goes still.

Mary's screams break through my consciousness as his blood spews out over me.

I push his heavy body aside and crawl across the dirt to her. "Are you all right?"

She continues to scream, cowering against the side of the cave.

I'm wearing a monk's cloak, covered with blood, and my hair is gone. Maybe she doesn't recognize me.

"It's me," I say. "Brian!"

Her screams taper to whimpers.

I crawl to Milton, wrench the dagger out of his gut, and wipe the blood off the blade on my cloak.

"I'll get rid of your shackle," I say.

I cut through the thick rope on Mary's ankle using the dagger like a saw.

I retrieve my backpack from outside, pull out a dress, and hand it to her. "Put this on. Hurry! We need to get out of here before someone comes."

She trembles, staring at me without moving. Her blood-swollen lips and the black and blue bruises on her face, chest, and shoulders make her almost unrecognizable.

I pull the monk's cloak and my shirt off over my head, and examine my gunshot wound. There's a gash on my shoulder from the bullet. It's not deep, but it's bleeding quite a bit—*and it hurts like hell!*

I reach into my backpack, pull out the other dress, and slice a two-foot strip of cloth from the bottom with my dagger. I wrap it around my shoulder over my wound. It's a struggle, trying to tie it by myself with one hand.

"Let me help you with that," Mary says.

She wraps the cloth around the two-inch gash and ties the ends, which stops the bleeding.

"We need to leave before the soldiers come," I say. "They'll kill me if they find me here."

I put my shirt back on, pull the bloody cloak over my head, and strap on my backpack. Every movement I make sends a fiery pain through my shoulder.

She stands up, pulls the dress I gave her over her head, pushes her arms through the sleeves, and tugs it down past her knees to cover her nakedness. I hold her up with my good arm, and we stagger past Milton's body and leave the cave.

I place her left foot into the horse's stirrup and lift, and she mounts the saddle military style. I jump up behind her, using the back of the saddle for leverage.

"We should go to Lough Gill to get cleaned up before we go to Sligo," I say, "and then we'll buy passage on a ship to America. I have money for two fares."

We ride two miles west and veer southward toward Lough Gill. We dismount at the western edge of the lake half an hour later.

I remove the monk's cloak and my shirt, and dive into the frigid water.

"Jesus, that's cold," I yell as I stand up.

Mary steps into the lake still wearing her dress, until the water reaches her neck. She dunks her head beneath the water and starts to rinse her hair.

I'm trembling as I wash the blood out of my shirt and cloak. The fact that I murdered someone troubles my soul, as I think about what just happened.

We emerge quickly from the water, shivering in the cold.

"Let me help you with your hair," I say.

She sits down in the grass without speaking. I sit behind her and start to unsnarl her hair with my comb.

"Is it a sin... what I did?" she asks plaintively after a moment. "If it wasn't my choice."

"I don't think so."

How about what I did? I ask myself. I'm a murderer now.

"I killed Sergeant Milton. Do you think that's a mortal sin?"

"No! He used me as his whore... and he stole my virginity. No man will want me now."

I clench my jaw. "How'd you get those bruises? They look painful."

"Milton kept beating me, trying to get me to tell him where you were. He didn't believe me when I said I didn't know. He also beat me when I resisted him... and other men."

"That's terrible."

I move around her, combing from the bottom up to remove her tangles.

"That's the best I can do for now," I say when I finish.

"Thank you."

She checks the bandage on my shoulder. "The bleeding has stopped," she says, "so I don't need to change it. I'll change it later today... perhaps when we're on the ship."

She helps me pull my wet shirt over my shoulders, and I pull the cloak over my head.

I grab her flute from my backpack. "Look what I found under the ashes."

She looks at it with an apathetic stare.

"I'll keep it for you." I shove it back into my backpack next to my violin.

"Thank you, Brian," she says, "for saving me... for saving my life."

"I'm sorry it took me so long to find you."

"Where were you?"

"I was hiding in a crypt beneath Creevelea Abbey. I went out looking for you every night. Ma was with me in the crypt... until she died of starvation in the meadow."

I open the horse's saddlebags, and fill a canteen I find with water from the lake. I shove it into my backpack, along with some hardtack biscuits, dried beef, and a pewter cup.

Mary pulls a wool blanket out of the other saddlebag and wraps it around her waist.

"Let's go to St. Patrick's Well," I say. "I want to see it one more time before we leave."

We jump up on the saddle, cross a bridge, and ride a short distance to the well.

"I need to ask God for forgiveness," I say as we dismount. "This seems like a good place. Da said our ancestors have been coming here since St. Patrick blessed the well."

I drop to my knees and dip the fingertips of my right hand into the water. I make the sign of the cross and say a silent prayer. *Please God, forgive me for my mortal sin.*

Mary stands next to me, watching me without kneeling.

The dawn twilight appears on the eastern horizon.

I hand Mary an apple from my backpack and take one for myself, and we sit down to eat.

"This is good," she says as she chews. "The only food Sergeant Milton brought me was hard rolls."

"Solicitor Reilly's daughter, Elizabeth, gave these to me. She rowed me across the lake to Innisfree so I could hide, and brought me food at night. She also followed Sergeant Milton so I could find you, and she gave me money to buy tickets for our voyage to America."

"That was kind of her."

"We shouldn't ride the horse into Sligo. People will know we stole it when they see the Crown insignia. We'll leave it here. I'm sure the soldiers patrolling the roads will find it eventually."

She nods.

"I have something to show you," I say, when we finish the apples.

I unlatch the buttons inside my left pocket, and pull out the jewel-encrusted cross. "I found this in a cave on Innisfree. It was with a skeleton, next to the dagger I used to kill Sergeant Milton."

She examines the cross closely. "It's beautiful."

She hands it back to me.

"Perhaps this will keep us safe during our voyage," I say as I look at it.

Mary smirks. "I doubt it. I prayed to Jesus for weeks while Sergeant Milton and his men kept raping me, but no one ever came."

I shake my head. "Maybe that's how I was guided to you."

She clenches her jaw angrily, but she doesn't say anything.

I slide the cross into the niche below my left pocket, and latch the buttons to hold it in place.

"We can't tell anyone about the cross," I say. "It could be worth a lot of money."

"Don't worry. I won't tell anyone."

I pull the dagger from beneath my right pocket and hand it to her. "Look at this."

She examines the handle. "It's marked with our family's coat of arms."

"Indeed. I think the skeleton I found in the cave must have been one of our ancestors."

"There's still some blood on it."

She shoves the dagger into the holy water, washes it, and hands it back to me.

"That was very brave of you," she says, "the way you fought with Sergeant Milton."

"It happened so fast, I didn't have time to think. My rage took over when I remembered what he did to our family. I'll go to confession when we get to America. I don't want to go to hell with murder on my soul."

She grabs my wrist. "That wasn't murder. Sergeant Milton deserved to die."

"Perhaps you're right."

I slide the dagger through my pocket and secure it in its sheath.

The sun peeks over the mountains, heralding the start of a new day.

"Let's go," I say. "I want to board the ship before someone

recognizes us."

Mary helps me secure the bulky backpack across my shoulders, and we walk west toward Sligo. We pass a family trudging slowly down the road—bird-thin skeletons wearing ragged clothes. They beg us for food, but we don't respond.

We pass the lifeless body of a young man lying in a ditch a quarter of a mile later.

"I know the terror that starvation can paint in the mind now," I say as we walk. "I almost turned myself in to Sergeant Milton just for the promise of a bite of bread."

We stop a few minutes later at the roofless ruins of Sligo Abbey.

"I need a break," I say. "Every step I take sends a shooting pain through my shoulder."

She nods as I sit down.

"I studied the history of this abbey with Brother Bernard," I say.

"What did he tell you?"

"It was destroyed in 1642 by Sir Frederick Hamilton, when he slaughtered three hundred men, women, and children in retaliation for cattle raids by our O'Rourke clan. Hamilton received five thousand five hundred acres in and around Manorhamilton, the town that now bears his name, during the Protestant plantations—land that used to be ours."

Mary walks to a nearby tree, pulls off a wanted poster, and returns. "It says Sergeant Milton is promising a five-pound reward to anyone that discloses your whereabouts."

"I know. There are posters like that everywhere along the roads."

She folds her arms across her chest. "I see what you mean about having a price on your head. The monk's cloak is a good disguise, especially with your shaved head. You look very different. I'm your liability now. Milton's soldiers know he imprisoned me."

She looks at the ground. "He brought other soldiers with him." Tears fill her eyes. "Milton sold me to them... as a whore."

My head jerks sideways. "I can't imagine the terror you've endured."

She starts to cry, covering her face with her hands.

I stand up and hug her. "It'll be all right," I say. "We'll start a new life in America. No one will ever know."

Her sobs fade to silence after a moment.

"We should get down to the harbor," I say when she releases me. "I want to board as soon as we can. It's dangerous for us out in the open."

We start walking west toward the harbor.

"I feel defiled," Mary mumbles somberly. "No man will ever want me now."

I'm not sure what to say. I want to comfort her, but I can't lie. We both know that what she says may be true.

"You can never tell anyone what happened to me," she insists. "Never!"

Our gazes connect as we walk across a footbridge. "I won't tell anyone."

Most of the pedestrians on the streets are heading the same direction we are. We come up behind a crowd of people veering left to avoid a family—two parents with six children. The family is naked, crawling on their hands and knees on the rocky street. Their bony hips and ribcages are clearly visible beneath their translucent skin.

"Shouldn't we give them something to eat?" Mary whispers after we pass them.

I shake my head. "No. I hate to be selfish, but we'll need what we have for ourselves. Brother Bernard said that famine ship passengers often starve to death when a ship captain doesn't give them the food rations they've been promised."

"I hope the captain of our ship is a fair man."

"I do too."

We turn a corner, and the ships tied up next to the wharves come into view. I count one hundred and forty people queued up on the quay as we approach the barque *Dromahair*. The vessel is impressive, with three tall masts holding twelve sails, and a long bowsprit extending forward from the prow. The conical masts, four feet thick at the base, soar like church spires into the sky above the yardarms.

Two sailors balanced high on the riggings are unfurling and inspecting the sails. Six sailors on the wharf are hauling barrels up the gangplank to the main deck.

I pull the money Elizabeth gave me out of my pocket when we reach the ticket booth. "We'd like two tickets on the *Dromahair* to New York," I say.

The agent stares at me. "Are you traveling together, Brother?"

84

"Yes. This is my sister."

"You're lucky," he says. "There are only two spots left in steerage."

I pay the agent three pounds eight shillings for each ticket. That leaves us with one pound four shillings from the eight pounds Elizabeth gave me. I stow our money in my left pocket next to the concealed cross, and button the compartment securely.

Six soldiers with rifles on their shoulders march past us on the quay. I turn away so they don't see my face.

The agent points at a well-dressed man talking to the passengers in line. "The doctor will examine you before you board. I'll give you a refund if he rejects you."

There are two tall stacks of sheepskins on the wharf. The sailors are carrying them to the main deck and down into the cargo hold now that they've finished loading the barrels.

"Are those sheepskins for us to sleep on?" I say.

The agent laughs. "No. That cargo is going to America. They're taking it down to the orlop deck below the steerage hold—in the bowels of the ship. The cargo provides ballast to keep the ship steady, just like the passengers in the steerage hold do."

He gives us our tickets, and we walk to the end of the steerage passenger line. Most of the people in front of us are thin, shoeless, and dressed in rags. Some of the men have leather boots, long black coats, and floppy top hats.

There's a much shorter line close to the boarding ramp for the cabin passengers: six well-groomed men dressed in suits, and four women wearing colorful floor-length dresses with matching shawls.

A man in front of us points at them. "Those are the jumpers."

"Jumpers?" I say.

"Aye. They used to be Catholics. They jumped to the Protestant Church to save their hides."

"Why are *they* taking a famine ship to America?" Mary says.

The man's lips curve derisively. "The poverty caused by the potato blight and the mass evictions has destroyed the Protestant merchant class too. I know lots of shopkeepers, teachers, carpenters, and masons that are leaving to seek a new life in America. I used to work with several Protestant carpenters in Galway. There's no work for any of us here now."

"What's your name?" I say, offering my hand. "I'm Brian, and this is my sister, Mary."

"Glad to make your acquaintance. My name is Aiden Lynch."

He points at a wooden box next to his boot. "I'm taking my tools to New York. I'll send money home to my wife so she can bring our four kids over, after I find work."

His gaze looks west to the ocean. "Assuming they're still alive by then."

The cabin passengers show their tickets to the captain, walk up the gangplank, and disappear down the stairs to the cabin deck.

A red-haired sailor with a peg leg jumps up on a crate next to the loading ramp. "Each adult passenger gets eight cubic feet for luggage," he shouts, "two feet by two feet by two feet." He makes the shape of a box with his hands. "You'll need to leave the rest here."

His comments elicit loud groans and lots of commotion. Many steerage passengers have carts overflowing with their belongings. Some even have donkeys pulling their carts.

A man with a family pushing a cart full of furniture says, "We brought our possessions fifty miles. We can't leave them here."

"You won't be allowed to board if you don't heed my instructions," the sailor yells. "Show your tickets to the captain as you board."

There's chaos in the line as families argue about what to take, and what to leave behind. Several rough-looking men are swarming around us. They immediately take possession of the carts as they're abandoned. Within minutes, several carts pulled by donkeys and pushcarts filled with furniture, suitcases, clothing, cutlery, and books, disappear into the streets of Sligo.

The doctor approaches us. He's dressed in a sturdy wool overcoat with silver buttons.

"Are you well?" he says to me.

"Yes," I reply.

"Stick out your tongue."

I obey.

He looks at my tongue and moves to Mary, asking her the same question. She responds affirmatively, and sticks out her tongue.

"You can both board the ship," he says.

He doesn't ask Mary about the dark bruises on her face and arms.

"That wasn't much of an inspection," I say to Mary.

She nods. "I imagine it's pretty easy for someone with an illness to board the ship."

I survey the harbor as we approach the loading ramp. Several sailors in a merchant ship next to us are dumping the contents of a wagon filled with grain into the hold. Four Royal Irish Constabulary and eight soldiers of the Crown are guarding the ship while the sailors work.

Another merchant vessel loaded with livestock has just pulled up its anchor. The strident protests of bleating sheep and mooing cattle below deck are audible throughout the harbor as the ship moves away from the wharf.

The six Crown soldiers patrolling our quay march by. I hide my face again as they pass.

We show Captain Pyne our tickets.

"I don't think I've ever had a monk on my ship before," Captain Pyne says.

I nod without speaking.

"What are your names, ages, and occupations?"

"Brian O'Rourke. I'm sixteen. Mary, my sister, is seventeen."

The captain writes our names and ages in his ship manifest. The agent that sold us our tickets is standing next to the captain, copying his manifest.

The captain studies me. "You're Paddy O'Rourke's boy, aren't you?"

I look around for soldiers. My gaze returns to him. I nod affirmatively.

"There's a reward out for you," the agent says.

I stare at the captain—prepared to run if I have to.

Captain Pyne looks at Mary. "You look like you've had a rough time of it. I heard a British soldier kidnapped you. I'll list you as a spinster, since you aren't married."

He writes this in his manifest, as does the ticket agent.

"You better get below deck before the soldiers see you," Captain Pyne says.

"Thank you, sir."

We scurry up the gangplank to the main deck and climb down a steep stairway into the steerage hold. The pungent aroma of feces, urine, body odor, and mildewed food accosts us as we stop to let our eyes adjust to the darkness.

Several rambunctious children are running around in circles. Two babies at opposite ends of the hold are bellowing loudly, trying to outdo each other.

We locate our sleeping cubicle at the far end of the steerage hold, where we find out that we'll be sharing the eight-foot-by-eight-foot compartment with John Keenan, his wife Maria, and their two children. There's barely enough space to stow my backpack against the creaking hull.

I remove my monk's cloak and lay it on the uneven wooden planks where we'll sleep. Mary and I then sit down on the cloak.

"The captain told me our voyage will take between three and six weeks," John Keenan says. "I imagine we'll get to know each other *quite well* by the time we get there."

I speculate that John and his wife Maria are thirty years old. Their daughter, Celine, looks like she's ten, and their son, Matthew, looks like he's eight.

"This isn't so bad," Maria says with a smirk. "I wouldn't be comfortable sleeping on a mattress in a private cabin berth anyway. We'd miss the show."

The hold echoes loudly with the nervous chatter of strangers thrown together by dire circumstance. The passengers span a wide age range, from newborns to the elderly.

There are thirty-two sleeping compartments—sixteen on each side. The compartments are stacked on top of each other—one near the floor, and the other halfway to the ceiling. We occupy the compartment near the floor.

Our tickets say that each adult gets eighteen inches of sleeping space, and three feet of headroom. Children get half that amount since their tickets are half price. Some of us will have to sleep sideways in our cubicle for there to be enough room.

The teenage grandsons of an extended family in the cubicle next to us carry their frail eighty-year-old grandfather down the stairs to their bunk. He's unable to sit up or walk on his own, which could make his days miserable in our tight quarters.

The grating screech of an iron chain silences everyone except the babies. We hear Captain Pyne shouting commands on the main deck above us as the sailors haul in the anchor.

The ship begins an undulating roll a moment later, forward and back, forward and back. The hull creaks and groans beneath the forces exerted by the masts, sails, and riggings.

The captain follows his peg-legged first mate down the stairs into the steerage hold.

"My name is Jack," says the redheaded, red-bearded sailor.

His thick Scottish brogue makes him difficult to understand. He has a black scarf tied around his forehead over his red hair, which sticks out like a bushy hairbrush above his ears.

The children run and hide behind their parents.

"You'll be allowed on deck for an hour each day when the weather is good," he hollers. "You can use the grill to boil hot water for tea or oatmeal for your burgoo, but you have to finish in an hour. You're to remain here in the steerage hold the rest of the time."

"That's not enough time for all of us to cook," a rough-shaven Irishman yells.

His blond hair and muscular build betray his Viking ancestry. He has a wife and ten children in the cubicles behind and above him.

"You'll have to work that out among yourselves," Jack says.

Many people grumble, but there's nothing we can do. It's Captain Pyne's ship and his rules, and a perfect setup for skirmishes between mothers trying to feed their families.

Jack raises his hands and yells, "Settle down."

The agitated banter subsides.

"Don't get in our way when you're on deck," he says with a raised voice, glaring at the children. "Keep your youngsters in line, or we'll send them back below."

The smaller children cower behind their parents.

"Your food ration is one pound of hardtack biscuit or cereal per day," Jack says. "Children receive a half ration. There are no fires of any sort allowed downstairs, including candles. Fire on a ship is never good. Do you have any questions?"

A hollow-cheeked teenage boy raises his hand.

"Yes," Jack says.

"Can we stay up on the main deck if we help the sailors?" the boy asks.

Captain Pyne frowns. "This is no place for amateurs."

The captain turns and climbs back up the stairs to the main deck.

Jack points at a bucket-sized ceramic toilet urn tied to a partition in the center of the hold. "No one asked me the most important question." He chuckles. "Where's the privy? Well, there it is. Someone will need to bring it up and dump it over the side each day. You'll need to decide among yourselves who does it. Make sure you keep it tied to the bulkhead when you return. It makes an awful mess when it spills over."

Everyone stares at the foot-high ceramic chamber pot in the middle of the hold. Having privacy when nature calls is obviously a luxury we didn't pay for.

"You can come up on deck now if you'd like," Jack says. "This will probably be the last time most of you will ever see Ireland again."

All of the passengers except for the eighty-year-old man climb the stairs. The dark green hills of Rosses Point are visible as the *Dromahair* moves west from Sligo.

"It really is beautiful," I say to Mary.

"I'm glad we're leaving," she replies derisively. "I hate it here after what happened to me. I'm never coming back."

Her chin churns with anger as her hair flows behind her ears in the breeze.

It'll take some time for her to recover from what Sergeant Milton did. That's understandable. I'm *glad* I murdered him.

My gaze returns to the hills. Dabs of red and yellow are visible in some of the trees—the first signs of autumn, my favorite season.

The gyrating, up-and-down roll of the ship makes me queasy. The wind picks up, filling the sails as we move farther away from the shore, and the coastline quickly recedes behind us.

Many passengers are wiping tears off their cheeks as they say their silent goodbyes.

"Time to get below deck," Jack barks.

We descend the stairs into the shadows, which instantly turn black when Jack closes the hatch. Two small porthole windows, one on each side of the hold, provide a faint gray light.

We cram into our sleeping berths and lie sideways, scrunched together.

Several arguments break out among the passengers—some within the same family. Accusations fly between two men confronting each other about taking more than their fair share of space. A fistfight erupts on the other side of the hold.

Four men jump up and hold the fighters back from each other.

"I have a feeling this is going to be a long voyage," I say to John Keenan.

"Yes, indeed." An impish smile bends his lips. "I wish they had let us bet on the match before they began. We may as well make some money if people are going to fight."

I pull out my dagger, slice an apple into four pieces, and hand the quadrants to John and his family. Their only possessions are the clothes on their backs, a toolbox, and a blanket.

They thank me as they savor the fruit. Mary and I share a second apple.

We're luckier than most, having brought something to eat with us. Many of the emaciated passengers will have to rely on the meager food and water rations passed out by the first mate once a day—a pound of grain, and six pints of water for drinking, cooking, and cleaning.

Several young women are whining to their parents about the chamber pot. They need to go to the bathroom, but don't want to do it in public. Their protests end without a resolution.

"I'm not feeling well," Mary says.

I cover her with the wool blanket. "You'll feel better once you get some sleep."

Some of the passengers—either through laziness or inclination, since they've never known anything different—lean out of their bunks and vomit on the floor, including the family above us. Others urinate on the floor without using the chamber pot.

An elderly man in the cubicle across from us jumps down from his top bunk, drops his trousers to his ankles, squats down, and defecates.

"Is that what you meant by missing the show?" John Keenan says to his wife.

"Exactly," she replies with a smirk.

Mary bolts upright. "I'm getting sick."

She jumps off the wooden planks, runs to the toilet urn, and pulls off the cover. Everyone watches as she empties her guts.

She returns and lies down next to me on the wooden planks.

I offer her water from the canteen, but she refuses.

Her illness sets off a chain reaction, with one passenger after another becoming seasick, including me. I empty my guts twice in the toilet urn, which is overflowing by the time nightfall arrives.

The meager gray light from the portholes disappears after the sun sets, leaving us immersed in total darkness.

14. ELIZABETH REILLY

Parke's Castle.

MAYBERRY ENTERS the dining room while we're having lunch.

"Excuse me, Mr. Reilly," he says. "One of the soldiers wants to speak with you. He says it's urgent."

"Please bring him in," Father says.

Mayberry leaves the room and returns with the soldier a moment later.

"How may I help you, Corporal Wilcox?" Father says.

"My uncle... my uncle... Sergeant Milton, is missing," Wilcox says. "One of our patrols... our patrols... found his horse wandering... on the road... last night. We need... we need to send... send out a search party... to find him."

"Oh, dear," Miss Hughes says. "I hope he's not hurt."

Father frowns. "Do you have any idea where he may have gone?"

"He likes to ride... ride his horse... into the hills... into the hills north of here... in the evenings," Wilcox stammers.

"Ask the sergeant to come see me when you find him," Father replies.

I'm very curious about what happened. I hope Brian is all right.

Mayberry enters the parlor later that afternoon. I'm sitting on the sofa next to Father reading a book. Miss Hughes is sitting in the rocking chair embroidering a napkin.

"Corporal Wilcox has returned, sir," Mayberry says. "He wants you to come out to the barn."

"May we go with you?" Miss Hughes says.

Father nods affirmatively, so we follow him outside. Several soldiers are standing around a wagon. Sergeant Milton's blood-soaked body is lying in the back.

Miss Hughes gasps and covers her mouth with her hand. "Oh, no!"

"He's... he's been murdered," Corporal Wilcox says. "He was

killed... killed by that O'Rourke boy... that O'Rourke boy... we've been looking for—Brian... Brian O'Rourke."

"Why do you think it was him?" Father says.

The soldiers glance at each other.

"He wanted... he wanted... revenge," Wilcox says.

Father turns to me. "I think you should go inside."

"Yes, Father."

I conceal my trepidation as I return to the house. Brian must have found Mary. I hope they got away to America yesterday.

Miss Hughes is sitting with Father at the dining room table when I come down for breakfast the next morning. I sit down, pour myself some black tea, and garnish it with some cream.

"I think I'm ready to return to London," I say. "It's time to resume my studies."

"I agree," Father says. "You should leave here soon, before the weather worsens."

"I'll go to Sligo today to purchase our tickets. Perhaps a couple of soldiers can ride beside the carriage to keep me safe." I face Miss Hughes. "That way you won't need to go with me."

Miss Hughes nods. "That sounds fine, dear."

I look through the carriage window at Innisfree on the other side of the lake as I ride west toward Sligo an hour later. Remembering my kisses with Brian makes me smile.

We arrive at the harbor a few minutes later. I step down from the carriage.

"You should stay here," I say to the two soldiers who accompanied me. "I don't want anyone to steal the carriage. I'll be back in a couple of minutes."

"Yes, ma'am," one of them replies.

I ignore several beggars that confront me on the quay as I walk to the ticket booth.

"May I see the passenger list for the *Dromahair*?" I ask the ticket agent. "I believe it departed two days ago. I want to see if my friends were on board."

"Certainly, young lady," he says.

He opens his passenger notebook, finds the manifest for the *Dromahair*, and rotates the notebook a hundred and eighty degrees so I can see. "Were they in first class... or steerage?"

"Steerage, I think."

My eyes scan the page. I find Brian and Mary's names at the bottom. *Excellent*!

"Thank you, sir," I say. "It looks like my friends are on their way to America."

I purchase two first-class cabin fares for a ship that departs from Sligo to Cobh tomorrow. We'll buy another pair of tickets in Cobh for the voyage to London.

I gaze west at the ocean. *I hope you arrive safely in America, my love. I'll wait for you—no matter how long it takes, and then we'll spend the rest of our lives together.*

London, England. One week later.

IT FEELS GOOD to be back in Aunt Bess's parlor. I missed our Royal Crescent townhouse on Holland Park Avenue in Kensington, especially the modern indoor plumbing.

Aunt Bess is reading and Miss Hughes is doing needlepoint while I practice my piano. The oil lamps provide plenty of light, allowing me to practice after dark.

I love Chopin's music. His Étude op. 10, no. 3 in E Major makes my heart soar every time I play it.

"I've heard that Frédéric Chopin is looking for students," Aunt Bess says, when I finish the piece. "My friend, Jane Stirling, is his assistant. He's with her in Scotland now, but they should be returning to London soon."

I turn sideways to face her. "Do you think I'm good enough to take a lesson with him?"

"Of course you are, my dear. Your playing is lovely. Besides, I hear he needs the money. He charges a guinea for a one-hour lesson."

"That's expensive. Can we afford it?"

"It *is* a lot of money, but how often do you get to study with a genius?"

Aunt Bess is so good to me. She always makes me feel precious. Maybe that's because she never had any children of her own, or married again after her husband died.

"Thank you, Aunt Bess. I'd love to have a lesson with him."

"Did your father talk with you about coming out next spring?"

I sit down beside her on the sofa. "Yes, he did."

"Good. I submitted your application while you were away. The Lord Chamberlain assured me that you'd be getting a royal summons. You're very lucky to have Viscount Clements and your uncle John as sponsors. Their service as military officers guaranteed your admittance. Only daughters of the clergy, military officers, physicians, and barristers can be presented to the Queen in her drawing room at St. James's Palace."

"I'm really excited to be going."

She smiles. "It will be a grand affair. Prince Albert, the Queen's handsome consort, will be there too. We should start working on our evening gowns soon."

"That does indeed sound grand, Aunt Bess."

"You'll receive invitations to parties, balls, and afternoon teas after you're presented. These social events will give you an opportunity to meet many fine young gentlemen. Did your father speak with you about that?"

"Yes, he did. I told him I want to be a concert pianist, but he didn't listen. Most men are just looking for wives to manage their households and produce children when they get married. I'll never realize my dreams if I do that."

She squeezes my hand. "We'll just need to find you a husband that supports your dreams then. The season lasts until the middle of August, so you'll have plenty of time to meet someone that's a good match."

My gaze settles on the logs smoldering in the fireplace. I can't tell Aunt Bess I've promised myself to Brian. Father would certainly never approve, and neither would she.

I'll have to be careful—keep men at arm's length—while I wait for Brian to contact me. I'll tell them I'm going to be a concert pianist. That should deflect the affections of self-centered young men that are just looking for a woman to produce their progeny.

"Did you attend any more abolitionist meetings while I was gone?"

I say.

"No. The British and Foreign Anti-Slavery Society is meeting again in a couple of weeks. Would you like to go?"

"Yes, indeed."

"Good. The meeting's at Finsbury Chapel. Reverend Fletcher invited a speaker who's raising funds to support the Underground Railroad in America."

I nod. "I'll never forget that meeting where Frederick Douglass spoke to us."

"That was special, wasn't it?"

Aunt Bess picks up a pamphlet from the coffee table. "Reverend Fletcher has a statement Frederick Douglass made during that speech in his brochures," she says. She starts to read. "Douglass said that 'Slavery is one of those monsters of darkness to whom the light of truth is death. Expose slavery and it dies. Light is to slavery what the heat of the sun is to the root of a tree; it must die under it.'"

"I remember that. He was quite an eloquent speaker. Where is Frederick Douglass now?"

"He returned to America last year after we bought his freedom."

"What's the Underground Railroad?"

Aunt Bess's gaze returns to the pamphlet. "The Underground Railroad is a network of secret routes and safe houses used by fugitive slaves while they're escaping captivity from the South in the United States. The speakers are raising money for two abolitionists—Thomas Garrett and William Still—who were recently convicted of openly harboring slaves. The men have provided safe houses for hundreds of escaping slaves. Both men were given huge fines after their convictions, fines that will render them bankrupt unless they receive donations—fifty-four hundred dollars in Garrett's case."

"That sounds like a good cause," I say. "Can we really afford to donate? Father says our financial situation will change after Viscount Clements terminates his employment next spring."

Aunt Bess smiles. "Your father told me that in a letter. Don't worry. We'll just give them a small gift. Hopefully you'll be married soon, so you won't have to worry about money."

"Will we have to move if Father can't find work?"

Aunt Bess shakes her head. "No. I don't have a mortgage. Your father has been very generous to me over the years. I purchased this townhouse with the money he sent me."

"Should I seek new employment after the season ends next summer?" Miss Hughes says.

"That would probably be prudent," Aunt Bess replies.

"Why do I have to get married?" I say. "I can support myself teaching piano lessons."

"Managing money and fighting wars are affairs best handled by men," Miss Hughes says. "I don't think a women's brain is designed to handle financial matters. God built our bodies to have babies. You need someone to support you while you're raising children."

I don't agree with her, but I don't feel like arguing. We've had this discussion before.

"I forgot to mention," Aunt Bess says, "a young man named Stephen Cunningham came by looking for you last week, Elizabeth. He left his card. He said you agreed to have tea with him when you met at Lough Rynn. He seems like a nice young man."

"Is that what he said? I think he's a bit of a rogue, don't you, Miss Hughes?"

Miss Hughes spears me with a needle-eyed stare. "Mr. Cunningham will be offended if you don't keep your promise."

She turns to Aunt Bess. "Mr. Cunningham's father is very wealthy. He'll be leasing tens of thousands of acres from Viscount Clements for livestock production after Clements removes the papists."

"I don't want to have tea with Cunningham," I say, raising my voice. "He broke into my room and molested me at Lough Rynn."

"Now, now, dear," Miss Hughes says. "I'm sure it was just a misunderstanding."

"No it wasn't. I don't like him."

"It may not go well for your father if you humiliate Stephen Cunningham," Aunt Bess says. "He may take his livestock business elsewhere. What would Clements think of your father then?"

"So much for the idea that women shouldn't get involved in business," I say sarcastically.

Aunt Bess smiles. "You don't have to marry him. Just meet him for tea. Do it for your father. That would be the polite thing to do. Besides, Miss Hughes will be with you."

It's obvious my feelings don't matter.

"I'm tired," I say as I rise from the sofa. "I'm going to bed." I leave the parlor and hurry up to my second-floor bedroom.

It's still early, but I want to go to bed now anyhow. I need to rise before dawn to catch a glimpse of the moon at 5:00 a.m. Maybe Brian will be looking at the moon from the *Dromahair* tonight. I doubt that they've arrived in America yet.

I fondle the heart-shaped silver locket around my neck where I keep Brian's hair. *I miss you, my love.*

I close my eyes. *Please God—let him be safe.*

15. BRIAN O'ROURKE

Somewhere in the middle of the Atlantic Ocean.

I FIND MYSELF longing for the frigid serenity of the Creevelea crypt after a week in the steerage hold. It's not just the cramped sleeping quarters or the uneven wooden planks that make sleep almost impossible; it's the ceaseless weeping of scared children, crying babies, and grieving mothers that keeps us awake at night. The late-night banter of passionate couples copulating in the dark also contributes to our insomnia.

Life on a famine ship has been a shock: peculiar and surreal— beyond the realm of anything I could have imagined. Thrown together by circumstance, our lives woven together in casket-like cubicles, we struggle to survive the best we can. Many people had never been farther than twenty miles from their homes before they arrived in Sligo, let alone lived on an ocean.

The constant heave and row of the ship, diving deep to the fore and shuddering aft in a gyrating, agitated roll, is relentless and dizzying, exerting forces that dwarf any natural phenomena I've experienced. Most of us just vomit on the floor now when we get seasick, since it's impossible to reach the chamber pot in time when the waves are rough.

The nausea that claims us, coupled with the predilections of the peasants who prefer to urinate and defecate wherever they feel inclined, has left the floor coated with a slushy, putrid, layer of brown, fetid waste. The disgusting stench of feces, urine, vomit, flatulence, bad breath from rotting teeth, and body odor emanates from every crack and pore of the steerage hold now.

Mary and several other young women are refusing to use the public toilet urn. They witnessed the lascivious stares and pernicious taunts of men who laughed at women courageous enough to defecate in the center of the room.

The young women devised another solution. Sneaking away surreptitiously in pairs, they squeeze into the narrow orlop deck below steerage—the lowest level of the ship that holds cargo and supplies—and answer the call of nature in the dark. They go in pairs so that one of them can ward off the water rats with a stick while the other one does their business.

Neither Jack nor the captain has come down to the steerage hold since the first day, nor have any of the other sailors. They must know the squalor they'd find if they did.

Jack opens the hatch and shouts down to us: "You have one hour on the main deck, so use your time wisely. Make sure you bring the toilet urn up with you."

It takes ten minutes for everyone to climb up the stairs to the main deck. The family of the eighty-year-old always leaves him below. His translucent skin and trembling hands indicate he isn't doing well.

"Don't drop the toilet urn over the side when you empty it," Jack reminds the man carrying the urn today. "You won't have anything to shite into if you do."

The main deck feels like heaven after the filth of the steerage hold. A crisp autumn breeze fills the sails today. There's a band of dark gray clouds to the east of us. Captain Pyne is pointing at an iceberg far to the north—the second one we've seen during our voyage.

The first mate gives each of us a hard biscuit and pours a pint of water into whatever container we present to him—our rations for the day. The water tastes awful, like vinegar, probably because it's stored in used wine casks, and the biscuits are as hard as stone. It's important to let the biscuits soak in tea or water before we bite into them. A child broke her tooth biting into a biscuit she didn't soften.

Mary and I try to sit near the quarterdeck every day—the compartment near the helm reserved for the captain. That way we can smell the aromas of something good cooking in the captain's galley, usually some kind of meat and fresh-baked bread.

"I'm glad we brought some food with us," I say to Mary as we share an apple. "But this is the last of it. We'll be on ship rations for the rest of the trip."

"Indeed," she replies, "unless I can entice one of the jumpers to throw me an apple."

The male cabin passengers near the quarterdeck always stare at Mary. They laugh and make comments we can't hear—probably things that wouldn't be acceptable in polite company.

Jack jumps up on a barrel. "Captain Pyne is giving you a special treat today since we're making good progress. I'll be handing out another ration of oatmeal and water."

We applaud as we line up on the deck. Jack accepts our thanks with a smile when we reach him. This is the first time he's given us extra rations, so everyone is elated.

Most of the passengers mix their oatmeal with water and eat it raw. A few of the families combine their rations in a large pot and cook their cereal on the brick-lined stove.

Mary pours our oatmeal rations into a pot Mrs. Keenan is preparing, and we eat together.

Jack points out three sharks following the ship. Several teenage boys lean over the railing, trying to catch a better glimpse.

"You watch out there, lads," Jack says in a serious voice. "Those sharks will snap you in half with their razor-sharp teeth if they see you. I saw it happen once. The only thing left were the man's two legs, standing upright—right where you are."

The boys jump back from the hull like crickets.

All the sailors laugh.

Our hour is up, and Jack orders us back below. I always cover my nose as I slosh through the muck to our cubicle.

I've been playing my violin the past two evenings now that my shoulder has healed a bit. Mary joins me on her tin whistle flute during the Irish songs.

The passengers have been pleased for the most part—except for the Flannigan brothers. They've told me more than once to stop torturing them with my "highbrow music," when I play Mozart or Beethoven. The other passengers shouted them down last night, so I kept playing. The music helps to calm the children, which allows everyone to sleep better.

Mary and I pull out our instruments as darkness takes hold. We begin tonight with a song called "The Last Rose of Summer." Maria Keenan joins us, singing with her lovely soprano voice.

I feel the passengers' rapt attention even in the dark. They applaud when we finish.

Moonlight is coming through one of the porthole windows tonight. It paints strange shadows on the liquid muck sloshing back and forth on the floor.

I remember Elizabeth's kiss as I steal a glance at the moon.

We play two Irish folk songs: "Molly Malone," and "The Wild Rover." Maria and John Keenan lead the singing, which is loud and rambunctious, since the audience knows the words. People would be dancing if the floor were clean, but nonetheless everyone seems pleased.

It's time for the children to settle down, so I play a song Brother Bernard taught me called "O Holy Night," written by a friend of his named Adolphe Adam. The pastoral phrasing of the ballad is slow and melancholy.

Frankie Flannigan jumps down from his top bunk, sloshes through the sewage across the floor, and stops in front of me. "Stop playing that shite!" he yells.

I stop abruptly.

"I told you not to play that shite last night," he says.

His words are slurred. He's been drinking again.

Several people brought rum and poteen with them when they boarded the ship, including eighteen-year-old Frankie Flannigan and his sixteen-year-old brother, Jimmie. Their drunkenness has been a source of arguments between them and other passengers every evening. Tonight looks to be no different.

Jimmie Flannigan jumps down from his bunk and joins Frankie.

I lay my violin on the wool blanket next to Mary.

Frankie grabs Mary's hand. "Come here, darlin'," he says. "Don't you think it's time to sleep with a real man?"

It's impossible to ignore the people fornicating in the dark every night. Frankie and Jimmie have been harassing all the young women, looking for partners so they can join in.

Frankie tries to yank Mary out of our cubicle.

She slaps him hard, across the face.

He raises his fist to punch her. I jump in front, and his fist grazes my cheek.

I tackle him, and we're both on the floor grappling in the sewage. I plant a solid punch on his nose before several men grab our arms and pull us away from each other.

"I'm going to kill you," Frankie yells, as blood trickles down his chin.

Frankie, a farmer by trade, is thirty pounds heavier and four inches shorter than I am. I think I can beat him in a boxing match. I have good skills. Da used to let me box with my brothers and the Ribbonmen when they trained.

"Let's settle this up on deck tomorrow," I say, wiping the sludge off my trousers. "I'll bet you one pound sterling that I'll whip your ass. I also want you to apologize to my sister."

That will leave us four shillings if I lose, I figure, or two pounds four shillings if I win—a much better nest egg to have when we land in New York.

"I'll take that bet," he says. He smears the blood off his face with his wrist.

The men release him, and he returns to his bunk with Jimmie.

John Keenan jumps to his feet. "I'll match odds that Brian will win," he shouts, displaying a half crown in his raised hand.

Someone on the other side of the steerage hold takes his bet.

"Are you sure you can win?" Mary asks me.

"I hope so," I say.

"Thanks for sticking up for me. I hope you beat his arse to a pulp."

I smile. "The pleasure will be intoxicating if I do."

My proposal to settle our conflict with a boxing match excites the passengers. Da always said that gambling was next to drinking on the list of addictions that plague an Irishman's heart.

I figure the boxing match with Frankie Flannigan will help me tune my fighting skills before we land in New York. Several passengers have said that the Five Points neighborhood where we'll settle—since it has the cheapest rents—is teeming with gangs, vice, and criminals.

The fight will also help me settle a score. Frankie and his brother have been hassling Mary since we boarded. I'm looking forward to laying into him.

Wagering among the passengers continues for the next half hour.

"I have an idea," I say to John Keenan.

"What's that?"

"Let's ask Captain Pyne if he'll let the cabin passengers get in on the action. You could ask the jumpers to create a purse for the winning pugilist. I'll split the proceeds with you if I win. Mary and I need the money. We have no idea where we're going to live when we land in New

York."

"I'll bring it up with Captain Pyne tomorrow."

I fondle the cross in between the layers of my trousers. *Please Jesus—help me win,* I say silently. *I know this might not be a proper thing to ask, but I figure you can decide what's best.*

Captain Pyne agrees to let us fight on the main deck when we go up for our meal the next afternoon. The cabin passengers are pleased to oblige when Keenan asks them to get in on the fight action. They place bets among themselves, and establish a two-pound purse for the winner.

"I don't feel like eating," I say to Mary, as I hand her my canteen and biscuit ration.

She shoves my biscuit into her pocket. "I'll save it for you."

Jack ties a rope between the port and starboard sides of the hull next to the foredeck, where the cabin passengers are standing. The hull provides two sides for our trapezoidal boxing ring. A longer rope farther aft separates the steerage passengers from the ring. Sailors hanging high up on the riggings will have the best view.

Jack walks around on his peg leg inside the ten-foot-by-fourteen-foot area, while Frankie and I stare at each other from opposite corners.

"Frankie and Brian will fight until one of them gives up," Jack yells, loud enough so that everyone can hear. "There are no breaks." He looks at us. "Is that acceptable to you?"

I nod my agreement, and so does Frankie.

We circle around each other with raised fists. We've both taken our shirts off even though the wind is cold. I have a four-inch reach advantage, but he's more muscular.

Men and women are shouting, egging us on. Many of the women want me to win. They despise the Flannigan's for harassing them.

Frankie throws a right hook.

I lean back and it flies past me, twirling him around.

I jab a left hook into his ribs and a right uppercut to his chin.

He backs away and laughs, but I know I surprised him.

He comes at me flailing both of his fists.

Da always said, "Let the big fellows wear themselves out, and then go in for the kill." I cover my face and chest with my arms to defend his barrage, until I can scoot away.

He did some damage. I feel blood streaming down my face above my right eye.

I can tell that he's already tired when I see his fists dropping. I circle him, bobbing and punching, bobbing and punching, attacking every opening. I duck beneath his right hook and connect with a hard left to his chin.

He slams backward into the hull. His face flushes red with anger. He lunges at me swinging his fists like a raging animal.

I jump sideways and he lands in the rope.

"Stand and fight," he yells.

I continue circling, bobbing forward and back.

He has a straight stance. He comes at me with his right again—a swing and a miss.

I hook the left side of his jaw. This dazes him and he staggers backward.

I follow up with several pounding blows to his stomach and an uppercut to his chin.

He falls back against the ropes, leaning into the crowd. They slingshot him back to me.

He swings with a ferocious right hook, but I jump away, and he spins around.

I can tell he hasn't boxed much. He always leads with his right, which is starting to drop as he tires.

I bob back and forth and throw a left jab at his nose.

His nostril instantly starts to bleed.

His punch to my stomach surprises me. I step back to the hull, shielding my face with my arms as he pummels me. I've handled this kind of punishment before from my brothers. I always wait until they get tired, and then I attack.

Frankie steps back, exhausted after his barrage. His fists are low, fatigued.

I connect right-left-right, right-left-right to his face.

He's wobbly, staggering on his feet.

His next punch goes wide, and my right hook connects hard with his jaw. He crashes backward to the hull.

I pound his gut and chest with several blows and move up to his face, hammering him relentlessly with everything I have. Blood is streaming from both of his nostrils when I step back.

The crowd is screaming, urging us on.

His left whiffs past me without connecting.

My left catches his right eye and I go to work there, battering his eyebrow mercilessly as he's pinned against the hull. I step backward to the center of the ring to catch my breath.

His right eye is closed—puffy and bleeding. His nose is broken, pointing sideways.

It's time to go to work.

I strike him several times in the stomach and move to his face—twenty blows before I stop.

He grabs me around the waist and drives me backward into the hull. I feel a sharp pain in my kidneys.

I kick him in the face with my knee so he'll let me go.

He steps backward, wobbly, bending low as he sneers at me.

The crowd is shouting at the top of their lungs now, even the women—*especially* the women—urging me to finish him.

Frankie's right hook goes wild when I step aside, and then I attack, battering his face until his left eye is puffy, almost closed. His fists are up, but they're barely moving.

I circle around him. My right hook knocks him back to the hull.

He careens sideways and grabs the rope on the cabin passenger side of the ring.

The men in suits laugh as they push him back to me.

I pound his stomach and chest, and then my rage erupts—the rage I've been holding inside for weeks. I punish him for the brutal murders of Da and my brothers, and for Ma, and for Clements and his eviction brigades, and for my anger toward Ireland—the country that betrayed me, that betrayed our people, leaving us to rot and die in the ruthless hands of the landlords.

I'm screaming while I attack his bloody nose and eyes, his mouth and his ears, his stomach, kidneys, and chest. He falls sideways onto the deck and I jump on him continuing to punch him.

Keenan and one of the sailors grab my arms and pull me off.

Frankie is motionless.

"DO YOU GIVE UP?" I yell. "DO YOU GIVE UP?"

I see Jimmie Flannigan duck under the ropes. He jumps on my back before I can turn.

I flip him off my shoulders, and he crashes into the hull.

My dagger slides out of my pocket and then I jump on him. I jab the tip into the base of his throat.

The spectators hush.

"Give me the money you owe me!" I press the tip until blood dribbles down his chest.

He coughs, reaches into his pocket, pulls out a British pound, and hands it to me. I take it and stand up.

The crowd exchanges the money they've won or lost on their bets.

Jack dumps a bucket of seawater on Frankie to revive him.

"Where's Mary's apology," I yell as he sits up.

The crowd hushes again, waiting to see what will happen.

"I'm sorry," he mumbles in her direction.

I slide my dagger back into its sheath beneath my right pocket.

One of the cabin passengers hands me two pounds; the purse I've won. I give half of it to John Keenan.

"Time to get below deck," Captain Pyne says. "Make sure you tie down your belongings. It looks like a storm is brewing."

I see a huge bank of dark cumulous clouds behind the ship as we line up for the stairs. The strong scent of ozone warns us that the rain is coming.

I look back at Frankie at the end of the line. An older woman is fussing over him washing the blood off his face with a wet washcloth. His eyes are swollen shut and his nose is crooked, obviously broken. I suddenly feel bad for venting all my suppressed rage on him.

My face, chest, and shoulders bristle with pain when I lie down on the wooden planks. Mary cleans the cut over my eye with water from our canteen, and I fall asleep soon afterward.

The ship jerks aft and drops with a shuddering growl in the middle of the night, waking everyone up. An ebony darkness fills the hold. There's no light coming through the portholes. Many of the children start crying.

Jack opens the hatch. "Looks like we have a squall," he shouts down to us. "Tie down your belongings. I won't be opening this again until it's over." He slams it closed.

The growl of the squall grows gradually louder over the next hour, until it's loud enough to drown out the children's cries. The winds are heaving our ship sideways in a dizzying dance with the waves. I vomit on the floor next to our sleeping berth—a minor addition to the poisonous slop already there

The gale force winds are roaring by the time daylight arrives. The ship shudders as if it's going to split apart with each bone-jarring plunge, diving forty-five degrees in a stomach-churning lurch, followed by a ninety-degree rise.

Loose possessions in the hold are flying from one side to the other with each pounding wave—cutlery, clothing, boxes, books, chests, luggage, and the occasional screaming child. I'm holding eight-year-old Matthew Keenan in my arms, bracing my legs against the railings to keep him from flying across the room. John Keenan is doing the same with ten-year-old Celine.

"I'm scared," Matthew cries.

"Just pray to Jesus," I say. I move his hand so he can feel the cross on my leg. "He's with us here. He'll protect us from the storm."

Please God, I pray silently. *Please let us live, or end this quickly to stop the torture.*

The toilet urn flips over, adding more excrement, urine, and vomit to the sodden floor. Seawater seeping in from the entry hatch adds more liquid to the sewage stew. Pretty much everyone is vomiting onto the floor now.

The glassy-eyed eighty-year-old man dies amid the chaos.

His family wraps his body in a blanket, and they lay him on the floor. Each battering wave launches him from one side of the hull to the other, pummeling him against the wooden parapets below our bunks. He eventually flops out of the blanket. His pulverized muscles and brittle bones leave him unrecognizable as a human a few hours later. The horrifying spectacle triggers hysteria in some of the children.

The storm continues throughout the night. No one gets food or water while the tempest rages. It's too dangerous to move, so people heed the call of nature where they lie.

The dizzying pitch and yaw of the ship begins to subside as a trace of gray appears in the round porthole windows. A firm breeze still grips us when daylight comes.

Jack opens the hatch a few hours later. "Come on up," he says, "but be careful. Hold on to the railings. The waves are still pretty rough."

He hands out twice-baked biscuits and water—our first meal in two days.

The family of the eighty-year-old wraps his macerated body in a blanket and brings it upstairs.

Everyone stands with bowed heads—including the cabin passengers—as Captain Pyne reads Psalm 23 from the Bible. "The Lord is my Shepherd; I shall not want. He maketh me to lie down in green pastures. Yea, though I walk through the valley of the shadow of death, I will fear no evil, for Thou art with me. Surely, goodness and mercy shall follow me all the days of my life, and I will dwell in the house of the Lord forever. Amen."

Everyone responds with, "Amen."

The sailors dump the corpse over the railing, entrusting the man's body to the sea.

Captain Pyne turns to face us. "I know your ordeal was difficult," he says, "especially in the steerage hold. That was quite a hurricane. Fortunately, the wind was at our backs, so we made good progress after we raised our sails. The storm knocked four or five days off our voyage."

One of the steerage passengers, a twenty-year-old man traveling alone, collapses on the deck, shivering uncontrollably. A red rash covers his face and hands. His trousers are soiled. It's obvious he has severe diarrhea. He starts to cough, a continuous, dry, painful, hacking cough.

The captain feels the man's forehead. "You're hot," he says. "Do you have a headache?"

The man barely nods. He's holding his stomach, twitching and shaking.

Captain Pyne turns to us. "I think he has typhus. We'll need to segregate him from the passengers and crew so no one else catches it."

People near him back away.

The captain looks at his ship manifest. "I'm sorry, Mr. Cullen, but I've seen this before. I don't think you have long now. Would you prefer to stay up here with us?"

He nods.

"It's time to go back below deck," the captain says. "You folks in the same sleeping bunk as Mr. Cullen are at risk of catching his illness. You need to bring up his belongings and throw everything into the ocean. You also need to throw away your mattresses and blankets if you have them. They may be infected. Then you'll need to strip off your clothes up here on the main deck and scrub yourselves thoroughly, and do the same with your clothes. I'll give you soap after you throw his belongings and your mattresses overboard."

Cullen's cubicle mates follow the captain's orders. The rest of us go below and try to locate our belongings. I'm lucky. My backpack didn't break away from the side of the hull where I secured it. My violin is safe. Keenan's toolbox also survived.

Modesty has long since departed by this point in our voyage. The people who slept near Cullen strip down naked, even the young women, and bring all their clothing up to the main deck. I'm sure they must be washing themselves and their laundry in front of the crew.

They tell us the captain let them hang their cloths on the rope reserved for the cabin passengers when they come back down. He also gave them blankets to cover themselves while their clothes dry.

Jack opens the hatch early the next morning. "Mr. Cullen died a few minutes ago," he says. "We committed his body to the sea after a prayer by Captain Pyne."

He closes the hatch.

Everyone is quiet, absorbed in thought, even the children.

"I don't feel well," Mary says.

Mrs. Keenan wets a washrag with water from my canteen and holds it on Mary's forehead. "This should make you feel better," she says.

I hug Mary, trying to comfort her, and then she falls asleep in my arms.

16. BRIAN O'ROURKE

New York Harbor. November 1, 1848.

JACK OPENS THE steerage hatch just after dawn. "You all better get up here," he shouts. "We've just sighted land."

Everyone jumps out of their cubicles and stands in the muck chatting excitedly, until we can stagger up the stairway to the main deck. There's a faint outline of land on both sides of the foredeck ahead of us. The sailors are working the jib and square-rigged sails, tacking starboard as Captain Pyne steers the rudder with his wheel.

"That's Staten Island to the left," Captain Pyne bellows from behind the helm. "Long Island is to the right. We need to stop at the quarantine station near Staten Island before we proceed to New York."

Jack jumps up on the cabin roof. "Steerage passengers need to remove all of your bedding from the sleeping berths," he shouts. "Bring your mattresses, hay, blankets, pillows, and anything else you used for bedding up to the main deck and throw it overboard. That will make the inspection by the medical officer go much smoother."

One of the passengers says, "I paid good money for my mattress. I want to keep it."

"The quicker we clear quarantine, the quicker we'll tie up at South Street," Jack says. "You don't want to hold everybody up, do you?"

I return to the steerage hold to retrieve the monk's cloak and blanket Mary and I used in our cubicle. Many of the passengers are grumbling as they haul their filthy mattresses up the stairs to throw them overboard. I have no such problem getting rid of our smelly bedding.

Jack fills ten buckets with seawater and sets them on the deck. "You can rinse your clothes in these buckets," he says. "That way you'll be clean when you arrive in America."

Many people, including Mary and me, take off our clothes and dunk them in the seawater. We then wring them out with our hands and put them back on.

"Where will you be staying?" John Keenan says to me.

I shake my head. "I don't know. I've heard that Five Points is a good place to find lodging. I'm not sure why they call it Five Points, though."

"My older sister lived there when she first came to America. She told me it's an intersection where five streets come together. Be careful. Five Points is the most crime-ridden slum in the world, but at least the rent is cheap. She stayed in a place called Bottle Alley with some other Sligo immigrants. She said it's important to stay with your own people."

"Thanks for the advice. We'll look for it when we get there."

"We'll be meeting my sister on the wharf," John says. "She and her husband live in a place called Greenwich Village now. We'll be staying with them until I find work."

Many people have talked about the rough gangs in New York during the voyage. My hand slides through my pocket to the comforting handle of my dagger. I'm ready to fight if I need to.

A small schooner appears on the water, tacking toward us.

Our sailors heave to, bring the *Dromahair* to a stop, and drop anchor.

The schooner stops fifty feet away. Several sailors in white uniforms lower the schooner's sails and drop a large rowboat into the water. Two seamen paddle the rowboat to the *Dromahair* while another sailor stands in the middle, inspecting us. Three sailors remain with the schooner.

"Boat heaving to, off the port bow," Jack bellows.

The medical officer, who'd been standing in the rowboat, jumps onto a ladder on the outside of our hull and climbs up to the main deck.

Captain Pyne comes down from the quarterdeck to greet him. He tells the medical officer about the two deaths during the voyage.

The officer walks around the deck with the captain inspecting the sailors, cabin passengers, and us. He then follows Captain Pyne down the stairs into the steerage hold.

"That man speaks with a peculiar accent," Mary says.

"Indeed, he does," I reply. "He probably thinks we do too."

The medical officer emerges thirty seconds later. His dry shoes reveal that he didn't step into the sludge submersing the floor. He says goodbye to the captain and returns to his rowboat, and his sailors ferry him back to the schooner.

Captain Pyne tells our sailors to weigh anchor, and soon we're heading north.

The panoramic view of New York City is breathtaking as we approach the southern tip of Manhattan. Everyone is chattering excitedly as we pass through the narrows. A beautiful park populated with large trees filled with the colors of autumn comes into view.

Captain Pyne points at an oval-shaped brick building protruding into the water. "That's Battery Park," he says.

I retrieve my backpack from the steerage hold, and secure the straps across my shoulders. Mary and I then line up behind John Keenan and his family on the main deck.

"I hope we can find a place to stay tonight," I say to John.

"I'm sure you will. My sister told me in one of her letters that there are more than enough cheap lodgings in Five Points to absorb the three hundred refugees that arrive each day."

Ships of all shapes and sizes populate the wharves on the east side of Manhattan. A few have masts taller than the *Dromahair*'s.

Our crew drops our sails, and we slow to a crawl. Jack throws two large hawser ropes to some sailors standing on the pier. The sailors use the ropes to guide the *Dromahair* into a berth between two immense three-mast barques. They secure our ropes to moorings on the wharf, and extend a gangplank to our hull.

Several surly-looking men swing on riggings from the adjacent ships and drop like pirates onto our deck. They target the families with children first, offering to help them move their belongings to "comfortable lodgings." The men's Irish accents and smooth-talking sycophancy convince some of the beleaguered passengers to trust them.

Captain Pyne warned us before we docked about these ruthless hooligans—runners working for taverns and boardinghouses who take people's luggage and hold it for ransom, until the passenger pays an exorbitant cartage fee. Even so, many passengers inclined to trust a Cork or Kerry man with a familiar accent follow the runners down the gangplank. This is especially true of families with children.

A tall man with a Dublin brogue lets the Keenans pass since they have no luggage. The Dubliner steps in front of me and jabs his finger into my chest. "The law requires me to carry your backpack down the gangplank," he says.

"I don't need your help," I say.

Two of his friends appear beside him, blocking our way.

"Let us by!" I yell.

My right hand fondles the hilt of my dagger in my pocket. I won't use it unless I have to.

Their menacing stares melt beneath my glowering reprisal. They move aside and surround the family behind us.

Another Irishmen accosts us when we cross the gangplank to the crowded wharf. "Welcome to America," he says. "Let me help you with that backpack. We have comfortable lodgings where you can rest your weary heads after such a long journey."

We push past him without responding, and turn left on South Street. A fiddler playing Irish music entices us to turn right on Maiden Lane. We pass several saloons, a gambling hall, and three hotels. We almost trip over a pig that has its snout stuck in a pile of vegetable scraps.

"I'm surprised it's so filthy here," Mary says.

"Maybe that's just this area."

We circumnavigate a pile of horse manure and turn right on Water Street. Pigs roaming the streets aren't an anomaly we discover—they're everywhere, digging through garbage.

We wait at a corner for a wagon pulled by two horses to pass. I feel a tug on my pocket when someone clutches my leg.

I grab the pickpocket's wrist—it's a young girl, probably ten years old. She's filthy, with matted hair, wearing a threadbare dress with no shoes.

"What are you doing?" I say.

"Leave me alone, mister," she screams, trying to pull away.

She kicks my shin. "Help, help," she yells, clawing at me with her free hand.

I let her go, and she instantly vanishes in the crowd. There's a stream of snot on my trousers where she grabbed me.

"Looks like Captain Pyne was right," Mary says. "This place is filled with criminals... and some of them are pretty young."

We cross the street and drift past several packed saloons, a lottery ticket office, and a theatre. Most of the saloons have piano players inside. One of the saloons has several topless women leaning out of its second-floor windows.

"You can bring your girlfriend with you if you'd like," one of women yells down to me. "She's cute, and we have ways to pleasure both of you."

The women laugh.

Mary pushes me down the wooden boardwalk when I stop to look at them.

People hurry past us like water flowing in a stream: Irishmen wearing oversized black coats and crooked top hats; policemen with billy clubs on their belts; women pushing carts selling vegetables; young boys selling newspapers, advertising the headlines with large front and back placards hanging from their necks.

We stop when we see a black man approaching us, something we never saw in Ireland. He nods as he passes us, and we continue down the boardwalk.

Many women in fancy silk dresses are walking alone. They smell of heavy perfume.

"Those must be the whores," Mary says. "Maria said that women that walk alone are prostitutes."

A man in front of us stops to talk to a woman in a fancy dress, and they disappear down a dark alley. I see people having sex standing against a wall as we pass by.

We turn down Mulberry Street, and stop when we reach a triangular plaza with a withered sign that says *Paradise Square*. The ramshackle wooden shacks on this street look as if they're ready to fall down.

Mary holds my arm as we push through the crowds. The squalid streets and shadowy alleyways are swarming with people. We step over several passed-out drunks slumped sideways against a building. Beggars accost us every few yards. They move on when we ignore them.

Another pickpocket—an old man this time—reaches into my left pocket as he bumps me.

He won't get anything. I've stored our money in a buttoned cubbyhole beneath my pocket.

I grab his wrist and stare angrily into his eyes.

"Let the devil take you," he shouts in a thick Connemara brogue.

I release him, and he slinks away in a dark alley.

The crowds are so thick we can barely move. We have to walk

aggressively to avoid letting people shove us into the gutters, which are littered with garbage and horse manure.

Several horse-drawn carriages on the street bounce clippity-clopping over piles of rotting food, animal hides, intestines, and fish guts. A woman almost baptizes us with human waste when she empties a chamber pot from an upper-floor window.

I hear several flavors of English around us—the American accent being the most foreign to my ears. There's also German, French, Italian, and Yiddish. We pass by some Asian men with long black hair that are smoking skinny ceramic pipes, speaking a language I've never heard.

"I wonder if that was opium they were smoking," I say.

"It could be," Mary says. "Maria said a lot of Chinese sell opium in New York."

I ask several boarding house proprietors along Mulberry Street to show us their rooms. We realize quickly that we need to be cautious after we view the accommodations. Mary vomits when we inspect an outhouse with shite overflowing the hole in the seat.

"Most of the landlords are crafty liars," I say, after we inspect our third tenement. "They describe their rooms with unwarranted praise that couldn't be further from the truth."

"Aye," Mary says. "The wooden staircase at that last place was so steep and rickety; I thought it was going to crumble beneath us as we climbed to the fifth floor. The passed-out drunks and shameless couple fornicating in the room we'd have to share were disgusting."

"These places aren't much better than the steerage hold of the *Dromahair*."

"Aye, but at least we don't have the sickening motion of the waves."

"It's getting dark. We need to find somewhere to stay soon."

I stop an Irish woman carrying a small child. "Where can we find Bottle Alley?" I say.

"That's at 49 Baxter Street... where the Sligo immigrants live," she replies. She looks at my backpack. "You don't want to go there, though. You'd have to share a room with fifteen murderers and thieves. They'll slit your throat or steal your backpack while you're asleep."

She scoots by us and hurries away.

"We need to sleep somewhere safe," I say. "Perhaps we'll have better luck farther away."

We turn right on Canal Street, pass several small men smoking long pipes, and take another right onto Mott Street. A sturdy building has a *Room for Rent* sign in the window.

I stare at the front, trying to find the address. "Is that a sixty-two?" I say, pointing at the gold numbers above the door.

"I think so," Mary says.

There's light behind the red curtains. Someone inside is playing a piano.

I listen for a moment. "I think that's Beethoven," I say.

"Let's go in." Mary knocks on the door.

A young woman answers, lets us in, and sits back down on one of the sofas.

The parlor is elegant; its walls, decorated with burgundy-red wallpaper, surround a hardwood floor populated with oriental rugs, three sofas, and five armchairs.

A young man with short, curly black hair is playing a Beethoven piece on an upright piano. He stops and looks at us when we enter.

Three young women in silk dresses are lounging on the sofas. Their stylishly coifed hair compliments the jewelry around their necks. There's an open bottle of wine on a small table in front of them.

An older woman in her thirties approaches us from the kitchen. She glances at Mary's bare feet and says, "Just off the boat, huh?"

"That's right," I say. "Do you have a room for rent?"

The women on the sofas laugh.

The proprietor smiles at them. She turns back to us and crosses her arms over her chest. She circles Mary first, scrutinizing her filthy bare feet and threadbare dress up to her matted hair. She then circles me the same way.

"I don't normally rent to refugees," she says. "How did you find me? Most Irishmen just off the boat don't make it past the saloons on South Street."

"We've been walking around for hours," Mary says.

Mary takes a step into the room. "This is quite nice." She assesses the three women on the sofas. "Your clothing is beautiful."

The women smile. One of them says, "Thank you."

"I usually just rent to ladies of pleasure," the proprietor says with a twisted smile. "Women who want to join my business. Do you have jobs lined up?"

"No, not yet," I say. "We'll be finding jobs tomorrow."

"We can both read and write," Mary says, "and we know arithmetic, algebra, and French. What kind of business do you have here?"

The proprietor chuckles, as do the women on the sofa.

"We're seamstresses," she says. "That's why we have such nice clothes."

This elicits a hearty laugh from the women as well as the pianist.

Mary and I look at each other with puzzled expressions. We're not sure why they're laughing.

"How much do you charge?" I say.

The dark-haired beauty that answered the door says, "For what?" with a French accent.

Everyone laughs again except us.

"Was that Beethoven you were playing?" I ask the pianist.

He flashes a warm smile. "Yes. It's his piano Sonata number 8 in C Minor—second movement."

"I play the violin," I say.

The proprietor frowns. "You're not going to bring in other family members to share your room, are you?"

"Our parents and brothers are dead," Mary says somberly. "They were murdered... by British soldiers."

A tear trickles down Mary's cheek, and she quickly wipes it away.

"Sounds like you've had a rough time," the proprietor says. She studies us for thirty seconds with her arms across her chest. "I have a premonition about the two of you, and I could use some help. Would you like to earn your rent? I'll give you free room and board and pay you a few dollars a week if you're willing to do some work around here."

Mary and I look at each other, wide-eyed, surprised by our good fortune.

We smile and nod at the proprietor.

"That sounds wonderful," Mary says. "But may we look at our room first?"

"Of course."

The proprietor rubs my head. "What happened to your hair?"

"It's a long story," I say.

The woman extends her hand to Mary. "My name is Rebecca Weyman."

"How do you do?" Mary says. "I'm Mary O'Rourke, and this is my brother, Brian."

I shake hands with Miss Weyman.

"May we see the room and the outhouse before we decide?" I say.

The women in the parlor laugh.

One of them, a thin girl with long blond hair says, "They're learning quickly. Just off the boat and they're already checking the outhouse. That's the most important indicator of how well a place is run."

Miss Weyman grins. "That's true." She looks at Mary. "I can put you to work making good money right away if you like the company of men."

"I'm not interested in that," Mary replies emphatically.

"Suit yourself."

Miss Weyman points at my shoes. "You'll need to leave your boots down here before we go upstairs. I don't want to be rude, but they smell quite awful."

"I understand." I remove them and place them next to the front door.

Miss Weyman turns and says, "Follow me."

The pianist starts to play as we walk up the stairway to the third floor.

Miss Weyman opens a door, and we enter a room with two small beds set up cattycorner to each other next to the walls. The mattresses have sheets, a pillow, and a blanket. There's a table with a washbasin and a small desk next to one wall, a wardrobe for clothes next to another, and a chamber pot in the corner.

"This looks grand," Mary says.

Miss Weyman nods. "I'm glad you approve."

We follow her downstairs, exit through a rear door in the kitchen, and walk to the outhouse at the back of the property.

"It's very clean," I say when we look inside.

Mary smiles and nods at me. "We'll take it," she says to Miss Weyman. "Your room and outhouse are much nicer than the others we've seen today."

"That's why I need some help keeping the place clean. I run a high-class operation here. My customers expect the best." She flashes a sly smile. "They should, based on what I charge them. They certainly don't come down here to Five Points for the scenery."

Mary and I exchange wary glances.

"Is this a brothel?" Mary says.

"Yes, but just the rooms on the bottom two floors. Our patrons won't bother you."

Mary looks at me quizzically as we follow Miss Weyman back to the house. I pick up my boots, and we follow Miss Weyman up the stairs to our room.

"Can we play music here?" I say as we enter.

"What do you play?" Miss Weyman says.

"Violin… and Mary plays flute. We hope to make money playing for tips in the evenings after our jobs during the day."

Miss Weyman studies me. "Are you any good?"

"Let me play something for you."

I wiggle my arms out of the straps of my backpack, retrieve my violin, and tune it. The pianist is playing a different Beethoven Sonata in the parlor. I join in, matching the melody note for note—even though I just heard the piece.

Miss Weyman stares at me with her mouth open.

"That was wonderful," she says, when I finish.

The piano player stands at the bottom of the stairs and looks up at us. "Hey, that was really good. We should play together sometime."

"I'd like that," I yell down to him.

"How do you play Beethoven without reading music?" Miss Weyman says.

"I don't know. I've always been able to hear something once and play it back. My teacher in Ireland said I have perfect pitch. Mary plays flute too, and she has a lovely voice."

"Excellent. I'm looking forward to hearing both of you. Perhaps I'll hire you to play music with Adam when I entertain. Looks like you need some rest tonight, though. I'm sure it was a hard voyage."

"That would be grand," I say.

We hear a man squeal in a room on the floor below us.

Mary and I stare at Miss Weyman, wondering if someone is getting hurt.

"There's something you need to know," Miss Weyman says. "I have six courtesans, so I'm sure you'll hear the sounds of passion at times. Don't worry about it if you do."

"What do you mean?" Mary says.

"Our specialties are French Love, whips, ropes, and braces." A mocking smile bends her lips. "Some men enjoy pain."

Mary and I look at each other with puzzled frowns.

I have no idea what she's talking about—but I don't want to ask.

Miss Weyman lights two candles on our writing desk and hands me a key. "This will get you into the front door. Always make sure you lock it when you go out. There are hordes of thieves in the neighborhood. We pay a New York policeman on the corner to keep watch for us, but he's either drunk or asleep half the time."

She turns at the doorway. "Come see me in the morning, and I'll show you your duties. We'll need to get you cleaned up, Brian, if you want to find a job, and I imagine you'll both need to learn some table manners."

"Thank you, ma'am," I say.

"And Mary—I'll pay you an additional two dollars a week if you can do some bookkeeping for me, in addition to your housecleaning and cooking. Can you do that?"

"Bookkeeping?"

"Yes, writing down my expenses and the revenues I take in from my girls. You said you know math."

"Sure, I can do that."

"Good. My courtesans pay me twenty dollars a week for room and board, and a dollar for each client they entertain. Their clients pay for the booze they consume. I need you to keep track of that. I'll be managing another brothel for a friend of mine soon, so I'll need you both to keep an eye on things here when I'm not around. Do you think you can handle that?"

Mary and I nod.

Miss Weyman studies me for a second. "I know the perfect place for you to play your violin," she says. "I have many connections in town."

There's a knock on the front door. The French girl lets two men into the parlor.

"I'll see you in the morning," Miss Weyman says. She turns and walks back down the stairs.

I lock our bedroom door and open the window. The air is cool and crisp.

Mary stands next to me while we stare down at the street. People are milling about, talking, and shouting. Two drunks leaning against the wall of a seven-story building across the street are fighting over a bottle, snatching it away from each other every time one of them takes a drink.

A woman in a fifth-floor apartment above them opens a window and empties a chamber pot. Some of the effluence lands on the drunken men.

They raise their fists and curse at the woman. She ignores them and shuts her window.

Mary turns to look at our room. "This is a palace compared to what we had in Ireland."

"I can't believe our good fortune," I say. "It's nicer than the rooms we saw on Mulberry, and we're getting paid."

I lie down on one of the beds. "This mattress is wonderful."

We venture back down the stairs to the outhouse in the backyard. Mary vomits after she drinks some water from the well at the corner. I drink some too. It doesn't taste good and it smells bad, so I don't drink very much.

We return to our room and look out the window again.

"This is fantastic," I say, as I look up at the stars.

"Yes it is."

Mary sits on the mattress and tests it with her hand. "I've never slept on a soft bed before."

I stare at the waxing crescent moon above the horizon. *You got us here, Elizabeth. I hope you are well, my love.*

We fall asleep a moment later still wearing our clothes—too exhausted to undress.

17. BRIAN O'ROURKE

New York City.

A LOUD KNOCK awakens us. I launch myself out of bed and open our door.

"Time to wake up," Miss Weyman says. "Daylight's burning. There's something I'd like to show you."

Mary and I follow her down the stairs and through the empty parlor to the kitchen. She opens a door and we enter a small room. There's a three-foot-tall circular wooden tub in the center, and ten tin buckets filled with water lined up against a wall. A washbasin on top of a cabinet sits below a mirror on another wall. Two buckets filled with water are heating up on top of a cast iron stove.

Miss Weyman points at the circular tub. "Have you seen one of these before?"

"No," we both reply.

"It's a bathtub, which is why we call this the *bathroom*. You need to take baths before you do anything today."

Miss Weyman smiles at me. "You need to be presentable if you're going to find a good job."

She pulls on thick leather gloves, lifts each bucket from the stove, and pours the hot water into the tub. She then adds two buckets of cold water and feels it with her hand. "There, that's a good temperature."

She turns to me. "Why don't you refill these buckets while I get your sister situated? There's a communal well on the corner of Canal Street. You'll need to fill these water buckets each morning at sunrise from now on." She grins. "No more sleeping late after today."

"Yes, ma'am," I say.

"You need to keep quiet while you're working. Most of the courtesans sleep until ten when they work late."

Mary and I nod.

"You may wonder why I call my girls *courtesans*."

Mary and I look at each other, and turn back to her. We're unsure what she means.

"Calling them courtesans sounds better than calling them whores in a high-class establishment like mine. I used to be a courtesan myself, before I became a madam. I always preferred that term. You'll meet the girls this afternoon, but I'll tell you a little about them now."

Mary and I nod.

"Celeste Dubois, the twenty-five-year-old French girl with long dark hair you saw last night, is originally from Paris. She came to America when she was eighteen with her husband, but he died of cholera soon after they arrived."

"Gracie Jefferson is a twenty-year-old mulatto from Georgia—an escaped slave. You need to keep quiet about that since she has a price on her head. I don't want a slave hunter to take her back to the plantation she escaped from outside Atlanta. Her owner was a mean brute."

"What's a mulatto?" Mary says.

"She's half-Negro and half-white. Her father is the plantation owner, although he doesn't acknowledge her as his child."

We both nod.

"Nora Mullins, an eighteen-year-old Irish girl from Galway, has long auburn hair and green eyes. She arrived on a famine ship from Ireland six months ago. Both of her parents and two of her brothers died of typhus during the crossing."

"Angela Myers—she's hard to miss with her buxom physique and large breasts—is a twenty-two-year-old German originally from Bavaria. She has long blond hair and brown eyes. She's been in the U.S. since she was fifteen."

"Alice Chambers, the thin, blond-haired twenty-one-year-old you saw last night, is originally from Boston." Miss Weyman chuckles. "She's from a well-to-do family, so she has no financial reason to be whore. She chose the profession because she likes sex."

"Teresa Orsini, whom you also saw in the parlor last night, is a twenty-year-old Italian from Naples. She came to the U.S. as an orphan when she was sixteen. Both of her parents died on the ship during their voyage across the Atlantic."

Miss Weyman points at a coal bucket next to the iron stove. "I need you to fill this bucket with coal in the basement and bring it up here to get the stove going every morning. You'll need to do the same thing with the potbellied stove in the parlor."

"Yes, ma'am," I say.

"After you get the fires lit, you need to boil two buckets of water, bring them into the kitchen, and dump them into the water dispenser. I did that this morning while you were asleep. I'm not sure why, but boiling the well water makes it taste better, and we get less illnesses. It's something my parents used to do in Hamburg, so I continued the practice here."

"It sounds like it's working," I say.

She turns to Mary. "Each woman pays for their room and board, which includes meals and housecleaning. I hope you know how to cook. If not, I'll have to teach you."

"I can make a few things," Mary says.

Mary's eyes go wide when Miss Weyman stirs a fragrant smelling liquid labeled *Bubble Bath* into the water.

I leave with two buckets and walk outside to Canal Street. There's a line of people waiting to fill their buckets at the well. I learn that most of my neighbors are Germans and Eastern European Jews when I introduce myself. Some aren't friendly, or at least it seems that way.

A young woman in line behind me says, "Don't worry about them." She chuckles. "Most Germans are reluctant to speak English because they don't want to make a mistake. Some of us are perfectionists that way. I studied English for a year before I'd speak to Americans."

"And now you speak very well," I say.

"Thanks. Where do you live?"

"My sister and I just moved into the house at 62 Mott Street."

The young woman's friendly demeanor drains away. She turns around and starts talking with the person behind her, ignoring me.

I fill the buckets and return to the boarding house.

Mary is in the tub with her head above the bubbles when I enter the bathroom. She smiles at me. "This is marvelous," she says.

Miss Weyman is sitting in a chair, washing Mary's hair with soap from a bottle called *Shampoo*.

"Look at the clothes and boots Miss Weyman is giving me," Mary says. "I've never worn shoes before."

She points at a floor-length periwinkle-blue dress hanging on a hook on the wall. There are some women's undergarment drawers, a corset, and a petticoat stacked on top of the dresser next to the washbasin, and a pair of new leather boots on the floor.

"Those look grand," I say.

"They're clothes I'm not using," Miss Weyman says. "Why don't you give us ladies a little privacy? Mary will come and get you when she's finished. Then it's your turn in the tub."

Miss Weyman points at a stack of clothes next to the water buckets. "Try those on up in your room. We can exchange anything that doesn't fit. I guessed your sizes when I bought them at the Marble Palace this morning. It's a wonderful department store owned by one of your Irish compatriots, a fellow named Alexander Stewart. You can pay me back after you find a job. I told Alexander that I'd be bringing you by for an interview later today."

"Thank you, Miss Weyman. That was very kind of you."

"I'm pretty sure Mr. Stewart will hire you. I'm one of his best customers after all. I take my girls to the Marble Palace to shop all the time." She puckers her lips and smiles. "Girls in our line of work gotta dress well."

Mary and I laugh.

I pick up the stack of clothes, which includes a pair of black trousers, two white linen shirts, four men's undergarment drawers, and several pairs of socks.

She points at some new leather boots on the floor. "Take those too. You'll need some nice clothes for your audition this evening. A friend of mine owns the Astor House Hotel on Broadway. His manager is always looking for good musicians to entertain their guests in the courtyard. Adam plays there too. He's the piano player you heard in the parlor last night. It's a high-class establishment, so the pay is very good. However, your manners and wardrobe must be impeccable to work there."

"Yes, ma'am."

I hurry up to our room and try on my new clothes and boots. Everything fits perfectly.

I'll discard the boots Brother Bernard gave me, I decide. They stink worse than awful after traipsing through the sewage in the steerage hold of the *Dromahair*.

Mary enters our room a few minutes later wearing her new

periwinkle dress. Her reddish-blond hair is shiny, brushed out past her shoulders, with small curls dangling gracefully around her face.

"You look lovely," I say as she sits on her bed.

"Thanks. Miss Weyman told me about my job while I took a bath. I'll put fresh water—water that's been boiled and has cooled—into the whores' washbasins each afternoon, cook three times a day, and keep the parlor, bathroom, outhouse, and kitchen clean. I also need to keep track of the client payments and house expenses in Miss Weyman's bookkeeping ledger."

"Sounds like you're going to be busy."

"Yes, indeed, but she's giving me four dollars a week! She left a razor for you in the bathroom. She suggested that you shave before your bath. You'll have to use the same bubble bath water I had in the tub, unless you want to drain it and get more."

"That's fine. I can't believe our good fortune here in America."

"I can't either."

Mary frowns, the look she gets when she has something more to say.

"What is it?" I ask.

"I got sick again during my bath. Don't worry. I didn't puke in the tub."

"Are you feeling better now?"

"A little. I still feel a bit nauseous, though."

"Well... try to get some rest. I'll be back in a few minutes, and then we can eat."

"Miss Weyman said to come to the kitchen to get some turkey and vegetable soup when we're done."

"What's a turkey?"

"I don't know. We'll have to ask her. I feel so ignorant."

"Me too."

"We never had a bathtub in Ireland either, except for the lake," she says with a smile.

It's good to see Mary getting back to being herself again.

I hustle down to the bathroom, shave in front of the mirror, take my clothes off, and sit down in the bathtub. It is *indeed* a wonderful invention.

I dress in my new clothes afterward and face the mirror. My dark, bristly hair is almost a half an inch long. It hasn't started to curl yet.

Miss Weyman knocks on the door.

"Yes," I say as I open it.

She smiles and nods. "You look dashing, Brian O'Rourke. It's going to be hard to keep my girls away from you."

"Thank you, Miss Weyman. I feel very fortunate to have your help."

"I'm sure you'll get a job at the Marble Palace dressed like that. We'll go this afternoon, before we go to the Astor House for your violin audition."

She bends down, sticks her hand into the water, grabs the rubber stopper, and yanks it out of the drain. "This is how you empty the tub."

The water rushes through a hose beneath the tub and drains through the wall.

"That pipe empties into the cistern beneath the outhouse," she says.

"What a great invention."

She chuckles. "It certainly is."

"Thank you, Miss Weyman, for everything. Why are you being so kind to us?"

"I have a feeling about the two of you, as I said last night, and I always trust my intuition."

I nod.

"Either you or Mary will need to clean the floor after the courtesans finish their baths each afternoon," she says. "My girls are known for their good hygiene, which is important for securing wealthier clientele. I'll show you how it's done."

I get down on my knees next to her, and we dry the floor with two small towels. We throw the towels into a laundry basket when we finish.

"I'd like you to keep watch with Mary in the evenings when I'm not around," she says, as we walk into the parlor. "We do get ruffians here from time to time—mostly men that drink too much alcohol. I need a brave man like you to protect my girls. Your sister tells me you're good with your fists... and a knife, when that's required. You'll be back by eight thirty if you get the job at the hotel with Adam. Are you comfortable keeping watch?"

I nod. "I'd be happy to help."

"I'd also like you to handle my graft payments each week. Can I trust you with that?"

"What are graft payments?"

"Payoffs I make to the police department and Tammany Hall—the Irish syndicate that controls New York. I give ten dollars to Sergeant Collins of the New York Police, and another ten to Peter Flynn, the ward boss. They come by every Monday night. They always try to coerce the courtesans into giving them free pleasures. Just be firm with them, and they'll go away."

"I will, Miss Weyman, and I'm pleased that you trust us. We won't let you down."

"One thing you'll learn soon enough is that the police are just as corrupt as the criminal gangs that run the neighborhoods here."

I'm not sure what to say, so I just nod. The Irish Constabulary is under the thumb of the British, so it's probably like that here too.

"Go fetch your sister, and I'll meet you in the kitchen to teach you some table manners. I imagine you haven't used forks or spoons before."

"That's true," I say, "only a knife."

Miss Weyman starts our table-manners lesson by showing us how to cut and clean our fingernails. She then teaches us how to use a napkin, how to eat with a spoon and fork instead of our hands, how to pass food bowls around a table, and how to chew with our mouths closed.

"It takes longer to eat this way than with our hands," I say.

"I assure you," Miss Weyman says, "this is required etiquette if you want to fit in."

Mary and I return to our room to retrieve the clothes we wore during our voyage. I stow our money, the cross, and my dagger under my mattress. Miss Weyman then shows us how to wash our laundry in the tub, and how to hang our clothes on a clothesline outside to dry.

I wait in our room while Miss Weyman shows Mary her housecleaning duties. This is a good time to write to Elizabeth, I decide.

There's a quill pen, an ink well, envelopes, and writing paper in the desk drawer. I hold Elizabeth's hair braid in my hand as I write the letter. I describe our harrowing voyage across the ocean, and the good fortune we've had since we arrived in New York. I don't reveal that we're living in a brothel. That would be too difficult to explain in a letter.

Miss Weyman gives me directions to the post office near City Hall. I pass a bank on Chambers Street when I walk to the post office to mail my letter. I enter the New York Bank for Savings as I return.

"You need to be eighteen years old to open an account," a bank teller says.

"Mary, my sister, just turned eighteen. Can she open an account?"

"Certainly. New York law allows women to have their own accounts now. Just come by with her when you're ready."

I return to the Mott house and finish my chores.

Miss Weyman accompanies me to the Marble Palace on Broadway and Chambers in the afternoon. She introduces me to Alexander Stewart, and sits down with me in front of his desk.

"Do you think you can learn to do bookkeeping?" Mr. Stewart says.

"I'm a quick learner," I say, "and I've studied all of Euclid's *Elements*."

"That's impressive. I'd like you to start on the sales floor, which pays three dollars a week. I'll move you to my bookkeeping office after you know all the store's products, with a raise to five dollars a week."

"That would be grand, Mr. Stewart. I have a question for you, though."

He nods. "What would you like to know?"

"I'm a Catholic, and I think you're a Protestant, from what Miss Weyman told me."

She nods. "I told Brian I've seen you at the new Grace Episcopal Church on north Broadway."

"That's true," Stewart says. "I'm a Protestant. So what's your question?"

"I guess I'm just surprised that you'd hire me since I'm Catholic."

He chuckles. "We're all just Americans now. The First Amendment to our Constitution guarantees freedom from religious persecution, freedom of speech, and freedom of the press. You gained those rights the moment you stepped off the ship."

I nod and smile. "Thank you, Mr. Stewart. I won't let you down."

Miss Weyman loans me money to buy a present for Mary, and then we go to the Astor House Hotel. Adam is there for my audition. The manager hires me after he sees how quickly I learn the songs Adam plays. We then return home.

I pull Mary's present out of my backpack while we're getting ready for bed. "I bought this for you," I say, handing her the knife. "It should fit nicely inside your boot."

She grasps the handle of the dagger and pulls the four-inch blade out of its scabbard. "This is marvelous." She slices it back and forth in the air. "It has a nice feel to it."

"It's very sharp, and it has good balance. Try throwing it at a tree tomorrow. I think you'll be pleased. I figured it would be good for you to have some protection."

She shoves the blade into the scabbard and stows it in her right boot next to her ankle. "It fits perfectly. Thanks!"

Mary and I rise at dawn the next morning. We finish our chores and walk toward the bank on Chambers Street after lunch. She stops when we reach the park outside of City Hall. Several vagrants are asleep on the grass.

She pulls the knife out of her boot. "I want to try it," she says.

She aims for a tree twenty feet away, and flings her knife hard. The dagger flies end over end and spears the center of the tree.

"Ah," she says as she walks to retrieve it. "I haven't lost my touch."

"Indeed!" I chuckle. "I'm glad I'm not that tree."

The manager of the New York Bank for Savings helps her open an account with both of our names. I then deposit the money I had left over from Elizabeth, and the money I earned during my fight on the *Dromahair*.

"We'll pay you interest on your savings," he says.

"America is full of surprises," I say. "I've never heard of such generosity."

The manager nods. "The more money we have on deposit, the more we can lend out to our customers. We earn profits when they repay the interest on their loans."

I pull the Innisfree cross out of my pocket. "I need somewhere safe to store this."

His eyebrows rise as he examines it. "This looks quite valuable. You can rent a safe deposit box if you'd like. However, I'd suggest that you show this to Mr. Tiffany when you have a chance. His store is south of us, on Broadway. Everyone calls him the 'King of Diamonds' now. He purchased a huge cache of gemstones from aristocrats that fled Louis Philippe's regime in France earlier this year. He should be able to tell you what the cross is worth."

"Thank you. I'll try to make his acquaintance. In the meantime, we'd like to rent a small safe deposit box."

November 14, 1848.

MISS WEYMAN IS hosting a party tonight for some of her "big spender" guests from Philadelphia. Mary is helping her prepare a cake in the kitchen, while Adam and I rehearse in the parlor.

I've been playing music with Adam at the Astor House Hotel three evenings a week, as well as here, when Miss Weyman invites us to entertain her guests. Adam plays very well, so we've been having a lot of fun together.

Mary's main job in the evening is to serve alcoholic beverages to the clients. She also handles the money, and documents the client's courtesan expenses and payments.

"That's a nice suit you have," Adam says, after we finish playing a song.

"Thanks. I bought it this week after Mr. Stewart promoted me to bookkeeper. There's something I'd like to play with you if you know it."

"What's that?"

"I don't know what it's called. I heard it in Ireland."

I place my violin beneath my chin and play the melody.

Adam nods. "I think I have that."

He dives into his music satchel, pulls out Schumann's "Träumerei," and starts to play.

"That's it," I say. I join him a third of the way through, doubling the melody.

Mary steps out of the kitchen with a wine bottle and places it on the coffee table. She's wearing a floor-length red dress that accentuates her lithe figure and curves.

She opens the bottle and pours wine into four wineglasses.

"Just one drink," she says as she hands Adam and me a glass. "Miss Weyman says that's all you can have while you're playing."

"That's right," Miss Weyman says from the kitchen. "You need to keep your wits about you. You'll learn a lot from our three customers tonight. They've rented all six girls for the evening."

"I'd like to make a toast," Mary says.

Miss Weyman steps into the room carrying a large double-layer lemon cake on a serving tray. She sets it down on an embroidered linen tablecloth on the dining room table.

"I think that's a good idea," she says.

Adam stands.

Miss Weyman picks up the remaining wineglass.

Mary raises her glass. "To you, Miss Weyman, for everything you've done to help us begin our new lives here in America."

"Why thank you, Mary," Miss Weyman says.

We each take a sip.

Miss Weyman has been a godsend. We have nice clothes and money now—not a lot, but enough to get by. She likes to shop, so she's popular with the merchants. It's been invaluable for us, getting to know New York with her guidance.

She's a good businesswoman. We're learning a lot from her and her courtesans—including sex talk our parents would never approve of; but they're not here, so I guess it doesn't matter.

Adam sits back down in front of the piano, and I stand next to him with my violin. Mary sits in a leather armchair and focuses her gaze on him. I can tell that she likes him.

"It's nice to have a party," Mary says to Miss Weyman.

"I like to combine business with pleasure whenever I can," Miss Weyman says. "As I said earlier, we have some big spenders coming tonight—shady stock market dealers. Although they're charming, they'll steal the shirt off your back if you let them. They're here from Philadelphia, probably with some phony stock market scheme they'll use on Wall Street."

Miss Weyman's six courtesans walk down the stairs. They're wearing colorful silk dresses with low-cut necklines, to show off their cleavage and jewelry. Their long hair is pinned in a bun at the back of their heads, with curls dangling along the sides of their faces. They always fix each other's hair in Celeste's room before they come down each evening.

They take seats in pairs on the three sofas.

Adam plays a few bars of Schumann's "Träumerei" and stops. "This is a beautiful piece. Where'd you hear it?"

"I was listening to Elizabeth Reilly play her piano." I close my eyes for a second and sigh, suddenly struck by my longing for her.

"Who's Elizabeth Reilly?" Adam says.

"She's the woman who saved my life. I was standing in the forest watching her through the window in Parke's Castle as she played. She was…" I search for the right word, *"angelic,* is the only way I can describe her."

The courtesans laugh.

"That's something I can never be accused of," Alice says.

We all laugh this time.

There's a knock on the front door. Miss Weyman answers it, and three men in their early thirties enter the parlor. They're wearing tailored suits, white shirts with black bow ties, and short black top hats—not the tall stovetop hats the Irish peasants prefer.

They greet the courtesans and sit down between the girls on the sofas.

"Would you like some wine?" Mary says.

"Certainly," says a tall man with a beard. "Bring us each a bottle, and bring some glasses for all of us."

Mary places wineglasses on the coffee tables in front of each sofa and fills them with wine. She opens a third bottle and leaves it on the table.

"You sure are a cute," the bearded man calls out to Mary. He chuckles. "Why don't you join Celeste and Alice tonight?"

He squeezes toward Celeste to make room for Mary on the sofa. "There's plenty of room here."

"I'm just a server," Mary says.

She's rejected many propositions since we moved in, so she's getting good at it.

"Would you like to pay for your evening separately, or together?" Mary says, making eye contact with each man. "It'll be thirty dollars for your two courtesans and five dollars for each bottle of wine, so that's one hundred and five altogether, or thirty-five apiece."

Miss Weyman gives Mary an approving smile. She's been teaching her how to manage all aspects of the business, including how to collect money from the men that visit the courtesans. She told Mary to collect the money from the men as soon as they incur an expense.

"It's easy for them to get argumentative if you wait," I heard her say, "especially after they've been pleasured, or when they're drinking alcohol."

"How about I give you a share of stock in our new California gold mine?" the bearded man says to Miss Weyman. "The par value is one hundred and fifty dollars per share, so you're getting a forty-five dollar bonus."

Miss Weyman chuckles. "Show me one of your stock certificates."

The bearded man pulls a folded sheet of paper out of his coat pocket and hands it to her.

Miss Weyman opens it and stares at the writing. "The engraving looks very good," she says. "Who did that for you?"

"I did," the short man with glasses says.

"May I show this to everyone?" Miss Weyman says.

The bearded man nods. "Sure."

Miss Weyman hands the certificate to Adam. He looks at it and passes it to me. I study it and pass it to Mary, and it slowly circles the room.

"How many certificates are you going to sell?" Miss Weyman says.

The men chuckle.

"As many as we can," says the bearded man.

"I need cash," Miss Weyman says.

The bearded man looks offended. "Are you sure? The shares are for a gold mine a few miles from Sutter's Mill in California. That's where gold was discovered northeast of Sacramento."

"Is this leasehold land?" Miss Weyman says.

"That's right."

"I only take cash."

The bearded man smirks. He stands up and pulls three ten-dollar liberty eagle gold coins, and five silver dollars out of his pockets. The other two men do the same, and hand their payments to Mary.

She counts their money and says, "Thank you."

She then leaves the room and goes to the kitchen, where she'll deposit the money in a metal lockbox and document the transactions in Miss Weyman's accounting book. Miss Weyman only distributes the prostitutes' earnings to them when their clients aren't around.

Adam and I play softly so the men can converse with the girls.

"We need three more bottles," the tall man says, a few minutes later.

Mary retrieves the wine from the kitchen and each man pays her five dollars.

"Would you like some cake?" Miss Weyman says.

"What's the charge for that?" the bearded man says facetiously.

"Oh, there's no charge," Miss Weyman says. "We baked it for you."

He smiles. "In that case, we'd *love some*."

Mary cuts the cake, puts it on plates, and distributes it to everyone.

The men stand up when they're finished. They carry the wine bottles as they ascend the stairs with their courtesans hanging on each arm.

Adam and I finish the song we're playing.

"So, what did you think about their gold mine scheme?" Miss Weyman says.

"I don't know," I say. "Was it real?"

"I asked them to show us the stock certificate to teach you something. As you heard, they create their own certificates. The man with the glasses is an engraver. Essentially, they create as many stock certificates as people are willing to buy. All their customers own in the end is just a piece of paper, though. The men may or may not have leased the land where they say they're going to build a gold mine."

"Isn't that illegal?" Adam says.

"No. Perhaps it should be, but it isn't. That's why I wanted cash. They're using the California gold rush as a ploy to sell mining stock on Wall Street. I've witnessed their shady operations before. They'll disappear in a few days, and I won't see them again for another six months, when they show up with another get-rich-quick scheme."

"That doesn't seem right," Mary says.

"It isn't, but in their minds, the fools that buy their stock certificates are greedy schmucks. They have no qualms whatsoever about taking advantage of them."

I rise early the next morning, light the coal in the potbellied stoves, and retrieve ten buckets of water from the well on Canal Street. I boil two buckets of water, and fill the dispenser in the kitchen.

Teresa Orsini, the twenty-year-old Italian courtesan, is heating water on the bathroom pot-bellied stove when I enter with the last two buckets.

"You're up early today, ma'am," I say.

"Yes, I am. I have some errands to run, so I want to get an early start."

She pulls on the leather gloves, picks up a bucket of hot water, and dumps it into the bathtub.

"Let me help you with that," I say.

She smiles. "Certainly." She pulls off the gloves and hands them to me.

I put them on, pick up the other bucket, and pour it in. I then pour two buckets of cold water into the mix.

She feels the water with her hand. "Thank you," she says. "The temperature is perfect."

I pull the gloves off and lay them next to the wood stove.

"I'll see you later," I say as I turn to leave.

"Wait."

I turn to face her.

She smiles as she drops her bathrobe to the floor.

Her nakedness shocks me. She's beautiful... like a model in a painting.

"Can you help me?" she says, as she steps into the tub and sits down.

Her beauty triggers an uncontrollable reaction in my loins. I squirm and look away to hide my embarrassment.

She pours bubble bath into the water, mixes it with her hand, and pulls a round sponge out of her toiletry bag. "Can you wash my back with this?" She hands me the sponge.

I avert my gaze from her breasts as I kneel down behind her. She's quite shapely.

Teresa pulls her long dark hair in front of her left shoulder so I have access to her back. I wet the sponge in the warm water and rub it gently across her skin. Strong, uncomfortable surges pulse through my loins, the way they did when Elizabeth kissed me.

"That feels nice," she says.

She turns her head to watch me. "You can look if you want. There's no reason to be shy. You're gentle, even with your strong hands. I like that."

Her warm Italian accent makes me feel excited... and nervous.

"How long have you been doing this?" I say. "I mean... how long have you worked for Miss Weyman?"

She chuckles. "I became a whore last year. I worked as a seamstress for a couple of years after I arrived from Italy. Both of my parents died on the ship on our way to America."

"I'm sorry for your loss."

She nods. "I'm a whore because of the money. I earned fifty cents a day as a seamstress. I can make thirty dollars on a good night as a whore."

"That's quite a difference."

She leans forward, and I rub the wet sponge on her hourglass-shaped back down to her buttocks.

"How old are you, Brian?" she says.

"Sixteen. I'll be seventeen in April."

A surge pulses through me when she turns around and leans back against the edge of the tub. The tips of her breasts are pointing at the ceiling.

I pass the sponge to her as I avert my gaze to the floor. "I'm done."

I'd stand, but I'm too uncomfortable.

She hands the sponge back to me. "Now you can wash my front."

My body stiffens. I'm not sure what to do.

She chuckles. "I see you have a problem," she says, pointing at my private area. "I can pleasure you there if you'd like. I won't charge you anything."

My jaw drops. I'm aroused, uncomfortable—hard, ready to run, or stay... I'm not sure. "Um, I don't think I should do that."

"It's all right. Really. I like it. Then you can pleasure me. I'll show you how to make a woman happy."

I stare into her eyes. "I'm promised to someone. It wouldn't be right."

"That's really sweet," she says, eyeing me inquisitively. "What's her name?"

"Elizabeth. I met her in Ireland before we came to America. We promised we'd wait for each other... no matter how long it takes."

There's a quick knock on the doorjamb and Mary enters.

Teresa chuckles. "Hi, Mary. Brian was just helping me with my bath."

I feel guilty, sheepish, as if I've done something wrong.

Mary stares at Teresa. "I can take it from here," she says, reaching for the sponge.

"Thanks," I say, looking at the floor.

Mary hands the sponge to Teresa. "I think you can wash yourself, can't you?"

I rise and stagger out of the bathroom.

"Thank you, Brian," Teresa calls after me.

I feel awkward as I walk up the stairs. What just happened? Did I do something wrong?

I won't help Teresa wash herself again. It's too uncomfortable. *Was she just teasing me?*

A vivid dream consumes me that night. I'm with Elizabeth, rowing her across the lake to Innisfree. Her figure merges into Teresa, naked, leaning backward against the tub.

I wake up when the warmth jolts through me, soiling my drawers. It shocks me.

I change quietly in the dark so I won't wake Mary. It was something I've never felt before, something I can't explain. I hope this doesn't mean that I'm sick or something.

18. ELIZABETH REILLY

London, England. November 18, 1848.

I ARRIVE AT 4 St. James Place near Green Park at 2:00 pm. Gerald, our coachman, helps me step down from the carriage, and then I knock on the front door.

Jane Stirling, Chopin's assistant, opens it, and says, "Come in, Elizabeth."

I follow her into the parlor.

Frédéric is lying prostrate on a sofa next to the piano. He stands up with effort. "Good afternoon, Miss Reilly. It's nice to meet you."

"It's good to see you again," I say, offering him my hand. "We met at one of your concerts this past July, before you went to Scotland."

He grasps my fingers and looks into my eyes. "I remember you now."

His touch is gentle. I wonder how he can play the piano so passionately with such delicate hands.

He sits down in an armchair next to the piano, and motions for me to sit on the bench.

I hand Miss Stirling a guinea for the lesson.

"Thank you," she says. She stows the money in her satchel, sits down on the sofa, and opens a book.

My stomach is a bundle of butterflies as I sit down on the piano bench.

"How was your trip to Ireland?" he says.

He does remember me!

"It was good, and at the same time—heart-wrenching. The famine caused by the potato blight is terrible. I saw death and starvation everywhere."

He nods. "I'm sorry to hear that. It seems that turmoil has affected almost every country in Europe this year. So what would you like to play for me today?"

"I've been working on one of your nocturnes—the one in E-flat Major."

"Ah, very good." He leans back, joins his fingertips together as if he's in prayer, and closes his eyes. "Go ahead and play."

I place the music I brought on the stand—even though I've memorized the piece. I inhale a slow breath to calm myself, and then I begin.

The melancholic splendor of the notes comforts me, and my anxiety quickly drains away. I'm floating on the melody, propelled by the perpetual broken chords, until I can barely breathe, and in four and a half minutes, I'm done. I hold the pedal down so the last chord resonates throughout the room.

"*Très bien, mademoiselle*," he says, studying me intently.

I think I see a tear in his eye, but I can't be sure. Yes. He wipes it away.

"That piece brings back good memories," he says. "I wrote it for Marie Pleyel, a concert pianist I was enamored with as a young man. We were quite close. It was... difficult. She was married to Camille, one of my closest friends."

Jane looks up from her book. She presses her lips together, and returns her gaze to *The Three Musketeers,* by Alexandre Dumas.

It's a good story. I studied the novel in French with Miss Hughes.

Chopin starts to cough; a slugging, aching, relentless assault from deep within his lungs that goes on for a minute. He clears his throat, puts a handkerchief to his mouth, and spits out phlegm.

I saw him do this several times during his concert in July. His skin is pale, and his frame is thinner now, though. Perhaps his malady is worsening.

Miss Stirling pours water from a decanter into a glass, and hands it to him.

He drinks, and says, "*Merci.*"

He stands up and starts to pace. "You are very talented, my dear," he says. "Watching you play reminds me of Marie. Perhaps you'll be like her one day. She's one of most important concert pianists in Europe now."

"I hear she's taken a teaching position in Brussels," Jane says, "away from her husband."

Chopin nods. "I'm not surprised."

He sits down next to me on the bench and opens the score to the middle of the piece. "Let me show you something," he says. "Music is all about dynamics and expression. The written notes are just a framework. It's up to the musician to bring them to life."

He plays for a moment as he looks at me. "Hear how I retard the tempo here to catch my breath before I resume the journey? Each note and phrase should always be in motion, never stagnant, like the palpitations of your heart when it soars on the wings of love."

I watch, awed by his expressiveness as he plays, his passion flowing, always moving, pushing forward vivaciously and holding back cantabile, ambivalent joy and sorrow, tender caprice and burning desire, coaxed in subtle nuances from his fingertips, releasing the depths of his yearning. He's a new soul, sitting up straight—invigorated—not the sickly waif of a man I saw folded into a chair a moment ago.

He smiles when he finishes. "Did you feel that?" he says, his face six inches from mine.

"Yes... I did."

I wipe a tear from my eye. This piece always affects me that way.

"I've written many nocturnes," he continues. "It's best to play them late in the evening as a palliative, to elicit pleasant dreams before bedtime. Nocturnes are a musical form popularized by one of your Irish compatriots, a brilliant composer named John Field. Here's one he wrote in the same key: E-flat Major. Perhaps you can hear the way he influenced me."

Chopin plays Field's nocturne from memory without a pause.

I'm captivated as I watch him. Every phrase he plays is in motion, rising and falling, haunting and serene.

He stares deep into my eyes when he finishes. "Now, wasn't that lovely?"

"Yes, it was. I'll work on some of Field's nocturnes before our next lesson."

"Good."

He rises from the piano bench and returns to his chair. He has another coughing fit, drinks some water, and blows his nose.

"I'd like to have you as my pupil," he says, "but I'll be returning to Paris next week."

"Oh. Well, perhaps I can study with you there next year—after the Season ends in August. I have some obligations here until then."

He nods. "Go to Pleyel's piano store in Paris. Camille will know where to find me."

He coughs for two minutes. I see blood mixed with phlegm when he spits into his handkerchief.

Jane puts her book down. "You should probably get some rest before your concert tonight, Frédéric." She looks at me. "I hope you enjoyed your lesson."

I stand and pick up my music. "I did."

I face Chopin. "Thank you, sir. I'm looking forward to hearing you play at the Guildhall fundraiser for Polish refugees tonight. My Aunt Bess is taking me."

He grasps my outstretched fingers for a second and lets them go. "I'll see you there."

Jane Stirling walks me out while he lies back down on the sofa.

"He's very ill," she says when we're outside. "I'm sorry I had to cut your lesson short, but he needs some rest before he plays tonight. In addition to the Polish royals, there are rumors that the deposed French king, Louis Philippe, will be there. The royal family is living in exile at Queen Victoria's house in Claremont now."

"I understand. I'd like to continue my lessons with him in Paris next fall."

"I hope you can. Paris is marvelous in September. I'm sure you'll enjoy it. I'm looking forward to seeing your Aunt Bess at the concert this evening."

"She's looking forward to seeing you too."

We shake hands, and she goes back inside and shuts the door.

Gerald has been waiting while I had my lesson. He helps me into the back of the carriage and I sit down.

Aunt Bess is spellbound when I describe what happened after I return home.

Chopin's playing is superb on the Broadwood grand piano at the Guildhall that night. However, the audience is disappointed when he only plays for an hour.

Aunt Bess thanks him personally for taking me on as his student after the concert.

"I think your niece is a fine pianist," he says to Aunt Bess. "Her beauty and talent remind me of Marie Pleyel."

I feel myself blush from his compliment.

His deteriorating health is the main topic of conversation the rest of the evening.

"Chopin doesn't look well," Aunt Bess says, as we ride home in the carriage.

"I agree. He had a couple of severe coughing fits during my lesson."

A waning quarter moon hovers above us as we approach her townhouse.

I wish I could tell you about my lesson with Chopin, I say silently to Brian, as I study the moon. *This has been one of the best days ever, my love—almost as good as the day we first kissed.*

London. December 2, 1848.

AUNT BESS and I brave a cold wind to attend the abolitionist society meeting at Finsbury Chapel. Reverend Fletcher says a brief prayer. He then introduces us to a speaker who's raising funds to support the Underground Railroad.

The speaker points at a large map of America tacked to the wall as he describes the routes used to smuggle slaves out of the Southern states. He passes around several illustrations depicting slaves being beaten and tortured. The pictures are graphic, and quite disturbing.

Something gnaws at me as the Delaware abolitionist chatters on about the terrible treatment of the slaves. My thoughts cogitate into an observation when Reverend Fletcher asks the audience if we have any questions.

Should I bring it up? It could be divisive, especially among the antipapists in the audience.

My trepidation smolders into a gentle burn, haunting me, tugging at me, as I remember what happened to Brian's family. It just isn't right. I have no choice but to ask, regardless of their antipathy. I raise my hand.

Reverend Fletcher acknowledges me with a nod and a smile.

I'm sitting next to Aunt Bess and Miss Hughes in the front row, so everyone sees me when I stand up.

"I don't want to seem impertinent," I say, "since I agree that raising funds to support the Underground Railroad is a good idea." I scan the audience in the pews behind me. "It's a just cause, and they need our help."

Everyone nods.

My gaze returns to Reverend Fletcher. "However, I find it ironic that we're helping the repressed people of another country, while we ignore the cataclysmic catastrophe endured by our British subjects in Ireland. How can we commit ourselves to eliminating injustice in the United States when we're blind to the suffering of our fellow countrymen?"

I expect an earthquake of protest to erupt behind me. I hear quiet murmuring instead, so I sit down.

"Your question is thought provoking," Reverend Fletcher says. "Perhaps we can discuss the plight of the papists in Ireland another time. I'd like to keep our discussion focused on the topic at hand this evening: gathering funds to support the tireless efforts of the freedom fighters operating the Underground Railroad in America."

Reverend Fletcher tells the audience to, "Dig deep into your hearts when you donate money to our guest."

Aunt Bess, Miss Hughes, and I line up with everyone. We drop two pounds sterling into the abolitionist's hat as we leave the church.

"That was brave of you to ask your question," Aunt Bess says, as we ride back to her townhouse. "I'm proud of you for speaking your mind."

"Thank you, Aunt Bess. I guess I'm feeling distraught after what I saw in Ireland."

Miss Hughes scowls. "Well, I don't think it was appropriate. The Irish Catholics brought their problems upon themselves by giving their loyalty to the pope instead of the Queen."

We ride in silence the rest of the way home. I don't feel like fighting with Miss Hughes, knowing her entrenched bigotry, and I'm guessing Aunt Bess doesn't either.

The map of America sparked my curiosity, especially about New York. I must learn all that I can, I decide.

The Angel Of Innisfree

I gaze at the waxing quarter moon outside the carriage window. *I will live with you there one day,* I say silently to Brian. *I know you're in New York now. The ship report in the newspaper said the* Dromahair *arrived safely. It's been almost two months since you left.*

My longing grows deeper with every passing minute. Please write to me soon.

19. AUNT BESS

London, England. Two days later.

ELIZABETH IS practicing piano in the parlor when Miss Hughes enters the kitchen. The scowl on her face indicates she's upset.

"Look what I found in the mailbox, Bess," she says.

She hands me an envelope addressed to Elizabeth. It's from Brian O'Rourke in New York.

"I'm glad you brought this to me," I say.

Miss Hughes sits down across from me at the kitchen table. "I told you about Sergeant Milton, the handsome English soldier who was murdered—how someone gutted him with a knife."

"I remember."

"Corporal Wilcox told me that he's sure Brian O'Rourke murdered his uncle."

"How did it happen?"

Miss Hughes frowns. "He said he didn't want to upset me by revealing the details. I don't know how Brian knows Elizabeth, or why he's trying to contact her, but I think it's dangerous for her to get involved with him."

"I agree. Maybe she doesn't realize that he's a murderer."

I stare at the envelope, trying to decide what to do. "Let's open it."

I slice the side with a knife and remove the letter. The first several paragraphs describe their difficult voyage on the famine ship, and their good fortune finding jobs and lodgings in New York. The last two paragraphs are so outrageous; I have to read them twice:

I know we only had a few short hours together, my love, so I hope you still believe me when I say that I'm eternally committed to you. I don't care how long it takes, or how far I have to travel, I'll come for you as soon as I can, and then we'll be together forever. I know this is true when I look at the moon to feel your presence every night.

It is preordained for us to be together. Da used to say that our O'Rourke clan and your O'Reilly clan intermarried for hundreds of years during our reigns in Ireland, before the English came. I feel blessed to have found you. Thank you for saving my life. Sweet dreams, my love.

I pass the letter to Miss Hughes.

Concern furrows her forehead as she reads. She lays it on the table when she finishes.

"It's a good thing you found the letter before Elizabeth did," I say. "She'll ruin her life if she gets involved with a murderer. The scandal would be ghastly. No one would want her."

"I'll send a letter to Corporal Wilcox at Parke's Castle," Miss Hughes says. "I'm sure he'll want Brian's New York address so he can track him down. He swore he'd seek revenge for his uncle's murder."

"Good idea. I'll keep Brian's letter in my lockbox so Elizabeth doesn't find it. We'll need to watch the mailbox carefully from now on, in case he sends her another one. It's obvious Elizabeth needs protection from herself. She's always had a wild streak."

Miss Hughes nods. "Indeed. She probably got that from her Irish mother."

20. BRIAN O'ROURKE

New York City. December 15, 1848.

I ADJUST MY tie while looking at the reflection in our bedroom mirror, and turn to Mary when I'm satisfied.

"Let's stop at the bank before we go to the Astor House," I say. "I met Charles Tiffany during a reception at the hotel last week. He said he'll give us an estimate for the cross if I bring it to him."

Mary smiles. "I have some money to deposit too. I feel rich now that we have sixty-three dollars in our savings account."

"Indeed. I'm making five dollars a week at the Marble Palace, two dollars a week from Miss Weyman, and two dollars a week at the Astor House. Adam and I also make at least a dollar apiece when we split our tips each night."

She pulls five silver dollar coins out of her satchel. "We'll have sixty-eight dollars in savings after today. Miss Weyman told me she's going to be managing a brothel owned by Mary Gallagher at 90 West Broadway, so she won't be at the Mott house in the evenings. She said she'll raise my pay to ten dollars a week once I take over for her."

"That's excellent. Why is she managing the brothel on Broadway?"

"It has fifteen prostitutes, so she'll make more money. She said the West Broadway property is also in a better location, so her courtesans can charge more. It's across the street from the new Girard House Hotel."

I chuckle. "It must be noisy in the evenings. It's bad enough here with six courtesans."

"It amazes me when I see how much money Miss Weyman makes from her alcohol sales. I saw her invoice for the wine. She pays fifty cents a bottle, and sells it for five dollars."

"That's an excellent profit margin. No wonder she's so wealthy."

"Indeed. I met Miss Gallagher yesterday. She said she's hiring Miss Weyman so she can travel in Europe without worrying about her property."

"She must be doing well to afford a trip like that. I wonder if she's related to the Gallagher family I met in Manorhamilton."

"I'll ask her if I see her again."

Mary's gaze turns serious. "Miss Weyman said she doesn't want any of her courtesans or their customers smoking opium in the house. She's going to kick them out if they do. She wants us to figure out who's doing it."

"Why is that?"

"We smelled it the other night while you were gone. It was probably one of the courtesan's clients."

"Why is it bad?"

"Miss Weyman said the drug is good for relieving pain, but it also makes people imagine things in their minds. People get addicted, and then they lose all their motivation to work."

"I've seen the Chinese on Canal Street smoking it in long bamboo pipes."

"Miss Weyman said those men import opium from China."

I pick up the hard-shell violin case I recently purchased, and swing the strap over my shoulder. We leave Miss Weyman's boarding house and walk south on Mott Street, turn west on Bayard, south on Centre, and proceed to the bank on Chambers. Mary makes her deposit, while I retrieve the cross from the safe deposit box.

We then go west on Chambers to Broadway, turn left, and walk a short distance to Tiffany's Stationary and Fine Goods store. One of Mr. Tiffany's employees ushers us into his office.

"Have a seat," Mr. Tiffany says, after I introduce him to Mary.

We sit down in front of his black walnut desk.

"This is the cross I told you about," I say, as I hand it to him. "Can you tell us what it might be worth?"

Charles pulls out a large magnifying glass. He examines the cross, scrutinizing each gemstone carefully. He pulls a jar of clear liquid from a shelf, wets a corner of a velvet cloth, and rubs the cross. The metal changes color to gold as he cleans it.

He places it on a black silk cloth when he's finished.

We admire it for a moment before he speaks.

"I'm sorry," he says, "but I may not be able to determine an accurate value."

"Why is that?" I say.

He picks it up, turns it over, picks up his magnifying glass, and shows us a symbol embedded in the metal at the bottom of the cross.

"The inscription is the symbol of King Philip the Second of Spain," he says. "The year inscribed below the bearded image of the king says 1575."

"What does that mean?" Mary says.

Charles strokes his beard and smiles. "I can give you an appraisal for the gems and gold if they're sold separately, but that's probably only a fraction of its value. Where did you get this?"

"It's from one of our relatives," I say. "He was one of the Spanish Armada soldiers who settled in Ireland after his ship crashed in 1588. I brought the cross with me from Ireland."

He nods. "That makes sense. The historical significance and beautiful design could make it worth several thousand dollars to a collector. The gemstones will probably only bring you about five hundred dollars if they're sold separately."

Mary and I turn and stare at each other with disbelief.

"Thank you, Mr. Tiffany," I say.

"Let me know if you'd like me to sell it for you. I'll take a twenty percent commission."

"How long will it take you to sell it to a collector?"

"That depends. You'll get more for it if you're patient. I'll show it to the wives of some of my wealthy clients to get them to bid on it." He chuckles. "They'll drive the price up trying to outdo each other when they start chattering about it."

Mary and I look at each other and nod our agreement.

"Excellent," I say.

Mr. Tiffany stands up and shakes our hands. "I'll stop by the Astor House to see you once the bids start coming in."

I swing my violin case over my shoulder, and we leave his store.

Mary and I hug each other when we reach the street.

"I can't believe it," she says. "We're rich."

"Not quite. I'll believe it when I see it."

We walk on the west side of Broadway to the Astor House Hotel, which takes up the entire block from Barclay to Vesey.

The mood is festive inside. There's a tall Christmas tree filled with ornaments in the lobby, and holiday decorations on the walls. A woman dressed like an elf is handing out cups of cinnamon-spiced apple cider near the massive fireplace.

"I'm glad I finally get to see where you've been working in the evenings," Mary says.

"I am too. You look lovely in your new dress tonight, by the way."

"Thanks. Angela gave it to me." She chuckles. "I had to take it in a bit at the front. She has more up on top than me, but we're the same height, so it fits well."

"I heard a rumor that Angela may be leaving Miss Weyman."

"She'd like to. Angela told me she's only working as a courtesan until she earns enough money to have a good dowry. She thinks she has enough now."

We stop when we reach the elf, and she hands us cups of warm apple cider.

I smile mischievously as I face Mary. "The manager said you can play a couple of songs with us tonight if you'd like. I put your tin whistle in my violin case."

"You did?" She punches me gently on the shoulder. "We'll have to see. You know I get nervous in front of an audience."

"You'll do fine. They're always appreciative, and I know how much you enjoy playing music with Adam. We'll also split our tips with you."

She grins. "I'm looking forward to seeing Adam again. He hasn't been around for a while."

"He's been busy. As you know, he's studying law at New York University. He told me this is a hectic time of the year for him at the school. He says that playing piano at the hotel three nights a week is his stress relief from all the reading and tests he has to take."

"It sounds like he's working hard. I'm sure he'll be very successful someday."

Mary surveys the well-dressed men and women standing around the Christmas tree. "How much does it cost to stay here?"

"Two dollars a day."

"That's a lot of money."

"Indeed."

We place our empty cups on a table near the elf, and continue our stroll around the lobby.

"It's like a museum in here," Mary says, as she admires the oil paintings on the walls. "These must have cost a fortune."

"I imagine so."

"I'm glad you invited me. It's nice to have a night off. I wish you were around more often, though. I don't like being there when you're gone. Some of the men get aggressive... propositioning me for sex, especially when they've had too much to drink. Miss Weyman's courtesans are pressuring me too, saying how easy it is to make money. They charge five dollars for a half hour, or fifteen for an evening. They charge even more if the men want to do strange stuff with whips or handcuffs."

"That *is* a lot of money, but I'm sure you'd never do that."

She scowls. "Never! The thought of a man touching me makes me want to vomit."

"We'll find a safer place to live after we sell the cross."

Mary nods. "I like Miss Weyman, and she pays really well; I just feel scared when you're not around. I lock myself in the kitchen sometimes so that men can't harass me."

She turns in a circle, looking around the lobby. "This place is like a miniature city."

"Lots of famous people have stayed here, including a couple of presidents. Charles Dickens—the English writer—stayed here when he visited New York."

We veer into a corridor lined with shops.

"The hotel has many innovations," I say, "the most notable being the gas lighting. This is the first hotel in New York with hot and cold running water. Reservoirs in the attic provide running water to seventeen bathing rooms and two showers. A steam engine pumps hot water to all the floors. It also has water closets with flushing toilets."

I stop in front of a water closet, open the door, and flush the toilet to demonstrate.

Mary's eyes go wide. "That's marvelous. I want one of those."

"Indeed. Maybe we can buy a house with running water and a toilet after we sell the cross."

We continue down the corridor to the dining rooms.

"A printing press in the basement produces new menus for the dining halls each day," I say. "The large dining room is exclusively for men. The smaller one allows women, but only if a man accompanies them. The hotel manager doesn't want courtesans trolling the dining room looking for customers."

We laugh as we pass a smoking room filled with men. Most of them turn to admire Mary as we walk by. We enter another hallway and walk past a barbershop, a hairdresser, a boot maker, an apothecary, and stop in front of the tailor's store.

"Let's go in here," I say.

I enter the tailor's shop and Mary follows.

A man with a mustache looks up from behind his lockstitch sewing machine. He stands and offers me his hand. "Hello, Brian."

"Hello, Mr. Rubin. I'd like to introduce you to my sister, Mary O'Rourke."

He grasps her fingers and bows. "How do you do, Mary? You look lovely, my dear."

She blushes. "Thank you, sir."

"This is Adam's father," I say.

"Is that so?"

"Adam is already here," Mr. Rubin says. "He's looking for you."

"We should go," I say. "I need to get ready to play."

I turn to Mr. Rubin. "Will we see you later?"

He sits back down. "I'll stop by if I finish my customer alterations."

We walk back through the lobby and enter a large rotunda. A large group of men is standing three deep in front of a huge hand-carved bar. Most of the businessmen are wearing tailored suits, white shirts with bow ties, long topcoats, and black hats. The rotunda has several small water fountains mixed in among the tables.

"Adam used to play here alone," I say, "until he and Miss Weyman talked the manager into hiring me."

"That was nice of them."

"Our job is to play background music for the business people. It's a good place to make contacts. Adam's father was John Jacob Astor's tailor. That's how Adam got his job playing piano here. This is also where I met Mr. Tiffany."

Mary grins. "I wonder what Miss Weyman's relationship with the hotel is."

"She knew Mr. Astor before his son took over. I'm not sure how."

We stop at the grand piano in the corner of the rotunda.

"We occasionally get some generous tips in our jar," I say. "We received five silver dollars from Cornelius Vanderbilt last week."

Mary sits down at a table next to the piano while I remove my violin from its case.

Adam appears as I finish tuning. He stops in front of Mary, bows, and extends his hand. "It's nice to see you again, my dear."

Mary smiles and takes his hand. "It's nice to see you too."

Adam, twenty-two years old, is five feet ten inches tall, with dark curly hair and brown eyes. He's charismatic and extroverted, with impeccable manners.

We both keep our faces clean-shaven, whereas most of the men here are sporting beards, or wide sideburns in the style popularized by Prince Albert in England.

Adam removes his jacket and sits down in front of the piano. We begin with a Cracovienne, which is a fast-paced traditional Polish dance. Adam likes to begin with this song because it reminds him of Poland. He lived there with his parents before they immigrated to New York when he was five.

I accompany him without reading music.

We then play "The Two Grenadiers," by Schumann.

A few people clap when we finish. We don't usually get much applause.

We play for an hour, and then Adam says, "We should take a break. There's someone here I'd like you to meet. I'll be right back."

I sit down at the table beside Mary. The courtyard is crowded now, standing room only.

Adam returns with a man who received a lot of attention when he entered the rotunda. Mary and I stand to greet him.

"This is Samuel Morse," Adam says to us.

He turns to Morse. "This is Mary O'Rourke and her brother Brian."

"How do you do?" Morse says, shaking our hands. "I like your music."

"Thank you, sir," I say.

"He's the inventor of the electrical telegraph... and Morse code," Adam says with a chuckle. "He's also teaching at NYU now. I'm taking a course with him."

Adam turns to Morse. "I think there are a lot of good business opportunities with your invention. I'd like to discuss these with you after I receive my law degree."

Morse smiles. "Let me know when you're available. I'm involved in lots of litigation, trying to lock down all the patents related to my invention. I'm looking for investors to help us build telegraph lines across the country. That's why I'm here tonight."

"Is it all right for me to attend your lectures?" I say. "I'm interested in your invention. We tried to use a visual telegraph using flag signals between hilltops in Ireland, but that didn't work out very well."

"My telegraph works in any kind of weather," Morse exclaims proudly. "You'll learn this if you attend my lectures. The Astor House is installing a telegraph line. The hotel will need a telegraph operator if you're looking for a job."

"Thanks for letting me know. I'll check in to it."

Morse turns toward the bar. "You'll have to excuse me, but I see that Judge Selden and Mr. Sibley have arrived from Rochester. They're organizing a new business venture called the New York State Printing Telegraph Company."

We shake hands with Mr. Morse, and he walks over to Selden and Sibley.

"That went well," Adam says with his eyebrows raised.

"Yes, it did," I say. "Why wouldn't it?"

"Mr. Morse is a staunch anti-Catholic, and he hates immigrants, so I wasn't sure how he'd react to you. He ran for mayor of New York as a member of the Nativist Party in 1836."

Adam grins. "Of course, he didn't get many votes. New York is full of immigrants after all."

Adam smiles at Mary. "He was probably nice to us because he was enchanted by you."

She returns his smile. "Is that so?"

We play for a half hour, and then Mary joins us, standing next to me facing the audience. Several people stop to listen as we begin a song called "Amazing Grace." The animated conversation in the rotunda drops several decibels when Mary starts to sing.

A raucous swell of applause erupts when we finish. Her lovely voice has captured everyone's attention.

Mary plays tin whistle on a few songs, and sings on a few others. Several men come forward to meet her at the end of each song. They leave large tips, and the jar fills quickly.

Our last song for the evening is a traditional Irish jig called "The Irish Washerwoman." We accelerate each time we repeat a verse. People clap along with us trying to keep up, until we reach a riotous climax at the end. The applause is boisterous when we finish.

Mr. Boyd, the hotel manager, smiles at us from across the room and gives us a thumbs-up to indicate he's pleased.

Adam walks us home after we finish. It's obvious that he's smitten with Mary.

"I'm glad I met your father," she says, when we arrive at the Mott house. "He seems very nice."

"I'll let him know you like him. You should join us again. We received lots of tips tonight."

Adam turns to me. "I'm not sure how to do this... being that we have different cultures—me being a Polish Jew and you being Catholics—but I'd like to become better acquainted with your sister. Would it be all right for me to call on her sometime?"

He turns to Mary. "I'm sorry. I mean, if it's all right with you. I don't want to be presumptuous."

This is the first time I've ever seen Adam act flustered.

"I'd like that," Mary says. She smiles and squeezes his wrist.

I chuckle. "I guess I'll have to be your chaperone then."

We laugh.

Adam says goodbye, and Mary and I enter the parlor. There are four men sitting with the courtesans on the sofas.

"How did it go?" Miss Weyman says from the kitchen.

"It was great," Mary says.

We bid them good night, and walk up the stairs to our room.

"There's something we need to talk about," Mary says, as we lie down in our beds after we put on our nightclothes.

"What's that?"

She pulls her blanket up to her chin.

There's a candle burning in a glass-fluted candleholder on the corner table between our beds. It's throwing odd shadows on the walls.

"Miss Weyman... took me to a doctor today," she says hesitantly.

I jerk upright. "Are you sick?"

I see tears on her cheeks in the candlelight.

She turns to face me. "No. I'm pregnant."

Oh shite! I'm at a loss for words... so I stare at her.

I sit on her bed and rub her back while she cries into her pillow.

"Miss Weyman says she knows someone that does abortions," she says. "She said that's an option I should consider, especially since I'm not sure who the father is."

"That would be a sin," I say.

Mary turns away to the wall, crying louder.

She's still sobbing when I fall asleep hugging her.

21. ELIZABETH REILLY

London, England. April 10, 1849.

I AWAKEN JUST before 5:00 a.m. and look out my window at the moon. *Why won't you write to me, Brian? It's been six months. I trusted you.*

My hand finds the heart-shaped silver locket over my chest. I open it and remove the lock of his hair I picked up on Innisfree. My gaze returns to the moon.

Did something happen? I say, as I massage the strands between my fingertips. *Have you forgotten about me?*

I twist the hair back into the locket and snap it shut. The feel of the cold metal is comforting when it drops between my breasts. *I like having you there, next to my heart.*

I turn away from the window, light the oil lamp, and face the mirror. The silver locket gleams in the reflection. *I'll wear you under my dress,* I say to myself, *so you'll be with me when I meet the Queen today.*

I look through the window at the moon. *Ha! Just what you want, huh?* I chuckle at my mischievous irreverence.

Aunt Bess and Miss Hughes are preparing breakfast when I enter the kitchen.

"The seamstress will be here to make last-minute alterations to our gowns in a few minutes," Aunt Bess says.

"I don't think I'll need any," I say. "However, the long silk train that streams out from behind may need an alteration. I think it's too long."

"We'll have her measure it to see."

We spend the rest of the morning with the seamstress.

"I'm going to take a nap," I say after she leaves. "I want to look rested when I meet Queen Victoria. Don't wake me for lunch. I'm too excited to eat anyway."

Aunt Bess enters my bedroom and wakes me at 1:00 p.m. She's

wearing a cerise-colored evening gown adorned with handwoven white flowers.

She helps me put on my crinoline petticoat and lavender-colored gown, and then we look at our reflections in the mirror. My gown doesn't have shoulders, whereas hers covers her arms up to her neck.

"Don't forget to stand up straight," Aunt Bess says. "Keep your shoulders back with your chest out. It's important to exude confidence."

"I'll remember. How could I forget? The memory of the butter knife you tied to the back of my chair when I was a child so I'd have good posture is indelibly imprinted on my brain."

She chuckles. "Good. Mr. Cunningham came by while you were taking your nap."

"What did *he* want?"

Her gaze moves to the locket I'm fondling between my breasts, so I let it go.

"He wants to share a carriage ride in the park with you after you come out this evening."

"I'm not interested in him."

I adjust the train attached to the back of my gown and look sideways in the mirror.

"You look lovely," she says.

"You do too, Aunt Bess."

She pulls my silk train all the way out behind me and smooths it with her hand. "Are you excited to meet Her Majesty?"

A smile fills my face. "I am! I could hardly sleep thinking about it."

"You'll get many invitations to social events after you're presented. You can't blame Mr. Cunningham for wanting to be at the front of the queue."

I frown. "But I don't like him."

"I'm sure he's learned his lesson after his indiscretion at Lough Rynn. He told me that he thinks you're beautiful. Perhaps you should give him another chance. He *is* a good catch after all. You'll be financially secure for the rest of your life if you marry him."

I'm holding the locket again. I let it fall into my cleavage and turn away from the mirror.

"Who is it?" she says.

I stare at her. "What do you mean?"

"Who is it… that holds your heart in his hand? I've seen how you favor that locket since you came back from Ireland. Did you meet someone there?"

She won't approve, but I want to tell her anyway. It's time. I don't like keeping secrets from her. She's been like a mother to me since I was seven. Maybe she won't pressure me to find a husband if she knows about Brian.

"Where's Miss Hughes?" I say.

"She's watering the flowers in the garden."

I close the bedroom door and turn to her. "I'll tell you, but you'll have to promise to keep it to yourself. You can't tell Miss Hughes. People's lives are at stake."

She nods. "I will."

"I hope you don't judge me, but I guess that's up to you."

"That's enough teasing. Who is it?"

"It's Brian. Brian O'Rourke."

Worry lines crowd her forehead as her hands go to her hips. "Isn't he the boy who Miss Hughes talks about—the one that killed the British soldier in Ireland?"

"I'm sure it was self-defense, Aunt Bess. Sergeant Milton was an evil man."

"Our soldiers in Ireland don't think so. Sergeant Milton's friends gave Corporal Wilcox two hundred pounds so he could travel to America to avenge Milton's murder. Wilcox came here to talk with Miss Hughes before he left last week."

I gulp air. "America? You mean he's going there to hunt for Brian?"

"That's right. Corporal Wilcox just finished his military obligation to the Crown, so now he's going to America to avenge his uncle's death."

My heart sinks. I try to keep my fear from showing, but I can't.

How can I tell Brian he's in danger?

"What's wrong?" she says.

"I'm worried. I haven't heard from Brian since the day before he left on the famine ship."

Tears fill my eyes before I can stifle them. "I've been waiting for him to write to me."

Aunt Bess hugs me. I let go and cry into her shoulder.

"I saved... his life." My words come in mumbles. "I love... him."

I pull away and stare at Aunt Bess. "We're promised to each other."

She gasps. Her admonishing gaze burns into me. "You can't be. Your father hasn't given you his permission, and I doubt that he ever will. That's just silly. You can't marry a man you barely know—a criminal, with a price on his head. How did you meet him?"

I tell her about hearing Brian's violin, how I watched him play for starving families as they waited to die in the Viking meadow. "I took him to Innisfree in a rowboat when he was dying of hunger, and nursed him back to health."

"You'll get over him when other men start pursuing you. I'm sure we'll find you a brilliant match—a proper Englishman, who will support your dreams of becoming a concert pianist."

It's a lost cause, I realize. I'll just have to pretend while I play her game—until I can leave.

"Will you let me go to Paris to study with Chopin in September," I say, "if I'm not engaged by then?"

"That will be up to your father. You can ask him when he moves back here at the end of May. I know he'll be disappointed if you don't entertain prospective suitors, though. Your introductions to aristocratic courtiers and their parents will also open doors for him. He told me in his last letter that he'll be seeking a position as a barrister. That requires good connections."

Aunt Bess pins three white ostrich feathers to my hair. The center plume in the headdress is slightly higher than the feathers on each side. This is the required headdress for all debutantes presented to the Queen.

She steps back and looks at me. "I think you look gorgeous. Do you remember how to carry the train so you don't trip in the throne room?"

I pull on my white gloves, gather up my train, and drape it over my left wrist.

"Very good," she says.

Miss Hughes knocks on the door and enters the room. "The carriage is here."

The ceremony begins in two and a half hours, but we need to go now to be on time. We waddle down the stairs in our huge gowns to the front foyer, and exit to the porch. Two footmen dressed in livery are standing at attention next to the carriage as we approach.

"I hired another footman to accompany Gerald," Aunt Bess says. "They look nice, don't you think?"

"They do indeed," I say.

"They're wearing the heraldic badges for Viscount Clements on their livery," she continues. "Clements was an aide-de-camp for the Lord Lieutenant of Ireland as well as a member of Parliament, before he took over the management of his father's property empire."

They help Aunt Bess mount the step, and I follow her into the carriage and sit down. Our expansive gowns take up all the space available.

We arrive an hour later, and queue up behind a long line of coaches. There will be two hundred debutantes presented to the Queen today, so the line is quite long.

Thick crowds of commoners line both sides of the street. They're part of the pageantry. They *ooh* and *ahh* as we pass, pointing at our fancy carriages, gowns, and jewelry. Some of them wave at us trying to get our attention.

Aunt Bess says I should ignore them since we're aristocrats, so I do. I guess this is what it's like to be a snob.

It takes an hour in the queue for our carriage to reach the entrance to the castle. Aunt Bess exits first beneath the colonnade. I gather up my train, and Gerald helps me step down.

Everyone turns to assess us as we enter the St. James's Gallery. I wasn't nervous until now.

We proceed forward in a seemingly endless procession, until we reach a large stateroom. The elegantly wallpapered, high-ceilinged walls display majestic oil painting portraits of previous generations of the royal family. The jeweled necklaces and diamond tiaras adorning the older women's heads make the room sparkle beneath the crystal chandeliers. The male escorts are wearing red livery with shiny metals hanging on ribbons. It's chaotic with everyone herded together, especially when the men entangle their swords with the debutantes' long silk trains.

"I smell a lot of different perfumes here," I say to Aunt Bess.

She smiles. "There are indeed. Even the men are wearing cologne to mask their body odor."

Aunt Bess introduces me to several people she knows, but I quickly forget their names. I'm concentrating on staying still so the ostrich feathers in my hair don't go awry.

The banter rumbles to a hush when the orchestra starts to play "God Save the Queen."

We stand in silence and bow, as the royal procession moves down the red carpet to the Queen's Drawing Room.

Soldiers in red uniforms flank both sides of the entrance when we approach an hour later. I see several members of the royal family surrounding the Queen and her consort in the inner chamber. An attendant spreads my train out behind me, and I hand my card to the Lord Chamberlain.

He announces my name: "Miss Elizabeth Reilly."

I walk through the great room with my head held high, trying to appear serene—although I'm trembling inside. It's not good form to look nervous or dismissive. Tripping or stumbling would be a ghastly disgrace. People would talk about it forever.

Her Majesty the Queen is standing in front of her throne next to the Prince Consort. Aunt Bess stands behind me and to the left with her head bowed.

I curtsy until my knee is almost touching the floor. I rise and kiss the back of Queen Victoria's extended hand, curtsy to Prince Albert and the other royals next to him, and give a final curtsy to the Queen.

She smiles at me, which makes me explode with joy inside—but I only acknowledge her with a gentle smile.

I reach for my train, drape it over my left arm with the assistance of the lords-in-waiting, and step backward, making sure I don't turn away from the Queen until I reach the threshold of the door. I curtsy again, and then I'm on my way through a corridor with Aunt Bess.

Then we wait. It takes another half hour for the Queen to meet the rest of the debutantes, and then the orchestra plays the national anthem. We squeeze backward and bow our heads as Her Majesty and Prince Albert parade past us, and then the formal part of the ceremony is over.

The line is slow as we migrate to the Supper Room. We pass through the entrance a few minutes later, and then we're standing in line at a long buffet table packed with an impressive panoply of hot and cold cuisine. The rest of the room contains rows of tables covered with white linen tablecloths for the nearly six hundred guests.

Servants bedecked in royal livery place portions on our plates when we ask for a sample. I was too nervous to eat earlier, so I'm famished now. A footman follows behind me holding my plate as I select ham, carrots, potatoes, cod, baked beans, and orange slices from America. The footman then carries my plate to a table with a card displaying my name. Another footman pulls out my chair, I sit down, and the footman with my plate places it carefully in front of me. Aunt Bess sits down beside me.

The place setting is perfect. The water goblet is above the knife to the right of my plate. A smaller goblet for wine is to the right of the water goblet, and an even smaller goblet for sherry is next to that.

The main topic of conversation is the upcoming teas and charity balls at the houses of the aristocracy. Verbal invitations come my way from parents at the table with eligible sons. They promise Aunt Bess they'll send me formal invitations by post.

I survey the animated throng effused with gaiety and laughter after we've had dessert, and an odd thought occurs to me. No one has spoken about the terror transpiring on their Irish plantations, for surely there are landed gentry here among us. The decadent opulence of this cherished aristocratic ritual suddenly upsets me. No one has mentioned the hundreds of British subjects, mostly Catholics, who will die of starvation in Ireland today.

Is this what I want from life? I ask myself. Do I really need to find a wealthy man to take care of me so I can live an aristocratic dream?

Aunt Bess is unsympathetic when I mention my confused feelings during our ride home.

"Who among the starving in Ireland would not change places with you in an instant if they could?" she says. "It's God's providence. Wealth accrues to those most capable of managing it. This is your station in life, my dear, so you may as well get used to it and enjoy yourself."

22. BRIAN O'ROURKE

New York City. May 7, 1849.

THERE'S A KNOCK on my door—Mary's knock by the sound of it. She and Adam live in the three-story row house next to me. We moved out of Miss Weyman's brothel into our newly constructed homes on Patchin Place in Greenwich Village last month.

I rise from my sofa and open the door. "Come on in."

Mary enters my parlor and twirls around in a circle. "How do you like my new dress?" she says. "I know I don't look like a ballerina with all this weight I'm carrying, so be honest with me."

I chuckle. "You look lovely."

I sit back down on my sofa—the only furniture I have so far, except for a bed, a writing desk, and a kitchen table with four chairs. Mary sits down next to me.

"I'm attending Friday night Sabbath services with Adam's family at their synagogue tonight," she says. "We're having dinner at his parent's house afterward. I'm sure you'd be welcome if you want to join us."

"No, thanks. I need to do some reading for my finance class. We're studying the tactics Cornelius Vanderbilt used to create his ferry service monopoly. It's very interesting."

"Look at this," I say. I slide my dagger out of the sheath inside my coat. "Adam's father fashioned a scabbard for my dagger when he tailored my suit. It came in handy last night. Someone from the Forty Thieves gang jumped me as I was walking back from NYU. He backed off after I sliced an *X* in his shirt with my blade."

She pulls her dagger out of her boot. "I still keep mine with me, just in case."

"Indeed. Greenwich Village is supposed to be safer than Five Points, but it's good to have protection anyway."

We shove our knives back into their scabbards.

"Miss Weyman came to see me while I was working in the

telegraph office at the Astor House today," I say. "She said someone came to her Mott house brothel looking for us yesterday—someone from England. She thinks he's a soldier from his countenance, the way he strutted around with his chest out when he walked. He offered her money for information about us, which made her suspicious. Miss Weyman didn't tell him anything, though."

"Hmm. What else did she say about him?"

"The stranger paid for sex with Celeste. She told Miss Weyman afterward that the soldier interrogated her, offering her five dollars for our address. Celeste didn't tell him anything either. The Englishman wouldn't give her his name."

"Who do you think it is?"

"I don't know. I'll write another letter to Elizabeth tonight and ask her if she knows about an Englishmen that might be looking for us. I need to send her my new address anyway. We should keep our eyes open in the meantime."

"Haven't you written to her six times? Sorry to say this, brother, but I think she would have responded to you by now if she was interested."

"Indeed." I stare at the floor. "I can't believe she hasn't written back to me. We promised ourselves to each other."

Mary nods. "The Swedish nurse you met in Dr. Ryan's office, Cornelia Ericson, is interested in you. She told me she thinks you're cute. Maybe it's time for you to find someone new."

I remove my tie and unbutton my shirt. "When is your baby due?"

"Dr. Ryan said it should arrive sometime in June."

"That's good. Are you nervous about changing religions?"

"Aye, a little. Adam's mother isn't pleased that he married a gentile, especially a *pregnant* gentile, so our relationship is getting off to a rocky start. She wasn't pacified when he told her I'm converting to Judaism. I think part of it has to do with us living at the brothel. She thinks I'm a prostitute. She didn't come when I bathed in the *mikvah* at the Shaarey Zedek synagogue yesterday. That's a purification ritual required before someone can become a Jew. I hope she accepts me after the rabbi admits me into his congregation."

"How was it—bathing with all those women?"

"It was... very spiritual... and purifying. They were very kind to me."

"Aren't you going to miss being a Catholic? I think St. Joseph's is a good church. I'd be happy to take you there sometime if you'd like. Adam may like it too."

She shakes her head. "I prayed to Jesus after Sergeant Milton kidnapped me, but no one ever came. Besides, look what happened to the Catholics in Ireland. Remember how Father Murphy used to tell us to accept our poverty and focus on the afterlife. He implied that it was God's providence for us to struggle. I don't believe that anymore."

I nod, mostly because I'm not sure what to say. Her points are valid, and there's enough strife in the world caused by religion as it is, so I change the subject.

"We need to talk about our bank account," I say. "I think we should have separate accounts now that you and Adam are married. I have other reasons as well."

"What are you thinking?"

"Well, we received eight thousand dollars after Tiffany's commission for our cross, and we spent four thousand for these townhouses, so we have four thousand left. With the six hundred dollars we've saved, we'll each have twenty-three hundred if we split the account."

"I think Adam's father was right about these houses," she says. "They were a bargain, especially with the discount we received for purchasing two at the same time."

"I agree. Mr. Rubin knows a lot about real estate. It's nice to have our houses paid for. The main reason I want to separate our accounts now, though, is so I can do some stock speculating. I don't want to put your savings at risk."

"What are you going to invest in?"

"I see many opportunities at the hotel when I send and receive telegraph messages for businessmen. Primarily, I want to invest in telegraph companies. I think they're going to make a lot of money someday. Telegrams are expensive after all. Most of the money is profit once the telegraph lines are in place. I think the value of telegraph stocks will rise even more as they expand across the country, and most of them pay at least twelve percent in dividends every year."

Mary strokes her chin as she stares at me. "Adam said the same thing about the telegraph. He accepted a job as an attorney with the New

York State Printing Telegraph Company yesterday."

"I'm glad to hear that. I think he'll have a good future there."

"Why don't we leave six hundred in our account so we'll have funds for an emergency? That way you'll have four thousand to invest. Perhaps we can buy some more real estate too. Adam's father thinks real estate is a much safer investment than stocks."

I smile and nod. "Maybe we'll be like the Lord of Leitrim someday—charging people rent... and kicking them out when they don't pay."

She chuckles. "Wouldn't that be grand?"

"Mr. Rubin is probably right. Stocks *are* risky, and there's a lot of fraud in the market. I've seen speculators at the hotel manipulating railroad stocks by issuing fake shares. I'll always make sure it's a viable business before I invest in anything."

She squeezes my hand. "I trust you, brother."

"Guess who I saw at St. Joseph's Church last Sunday?"

She shakes her head. "I can't imagine."

"Teresa Orsini—the Italian courtesan we lived with at Miss Weyman's house. She took a job as a madam at a brothel on Mercer Street. She's buying the property with monthly payments over five years."

"She's only twenty-one. That's young for that kind of job."

"It is, but she said she got tired of being a courtesan, and she makes a lot more money as a madam. She wants to visit us after you have your baby."

"That's kind of her." Mary frowns. "Maybe I can treat her better now that she's no longer a courtesan. I didn't like the way she was always flirting with you at Miss Weyman's."

I chuckle. "She *was* quite a flirt, but we never did anything."

Mary stands up. "I need to get back. Adam will be home soon."

She shuffles to the door.

"Tell Adam I'll be coming over tomorrow afternoon," I say. "I want to find out what he'll be doing in the job he just accepted."

"Aren't you happy working as a telegraph operator at the hotel?"

"I am, but I don't want to do that the rest of my life. I see opportunities everywhere now that I understand what businessmen do."

She nods. "Why don't you come over for lunch tomorrow?"

"I will."

She closes the door as she leaves.

I read my finance book using an oil lamp until midnight. Then I begin my letter:

Dear Elizabeth—My Angel of Innisfree,

Are you looking at the moon tonight? Can you feel me reflecting my love to you? Do you remember how we promised we'd share this together?

As I mentioned in my last letter, I'm attending business classes at New York University now, and I still have my job as a telegraph operator at the Astor House Hotel. I enjoyed working as a bookkeeper at the Marble Palace, but I'm more interested in the telegraph industry.

You may recall me talking about how we tried to set up a visual telegraph in Ireland. Well, the telegraphs here run on electricity, so it operates at night, and in any kind of weather.

Adam and I still play music a few evenings a week at the Astor House Hotel. By the way, Adam and Mary got married last month. She's pregnant and expecting her baby in June. We bought new homes next to each other in Greenwich Village.

I would love to hear about your life in London. Please write, even if it's to say you're no longer interested in me. I pray with all my heart that you still want me, though.

With love and affection – Brian

"This may be the last letter I send to you, Elizabeth," I say aloud, as I stare at the moon through the window, "if you don't write to me."

I envision her rowing the canoe across Lough Gill as I fall asleep.

Adam invites me in when I knock on his door the next day. I sit down next to him on their sofa. Mary says "hello" from the kitchen, and I reciprocate.

"She's preparing chicken and vegetable soup for lunch," Adam says.

"Excellent. Tell me about your new job."

"The business has a great future. I'll be dealing with a variety of legal issues as we expand our lines across state borders. There's no case law, so we'll be making it up as we go."

"That sounds exciting."

"I can get you a job there too, if you'd like. You've met the owners, Hiram Sibley and Judge Selden. They like to listen to our music at the Astor House."

"Indeed. I remember them well. They're the ones that met with Samuel Morse."

"That's right. Mr. Sibley told me they have major expansion plans. They need men to construct telegraph lines and offices, and someone to train operators."

"I could do that."

"You'd be traveling a lot, so you'd get to explore other parts of the country too."

"I'd like that. I'll talk to them when I finish my classes at the end of the summer."

Adam nods. "I'll arrange an interview for you when you're ready. I think the company will be very profitable someday. We have contracts with the railroads to construct our telegraph lines along railroad tracks in exchange for free use of the telegraph. It's a win-win situation for both of us. The telegraph will help the railroad keep track of their trains, which will allow them to schedule more trains on the same tracks without having accidents."

June 28th, 1849.

MARY AND ADAM'S baby boy, whom they named David after Adam's father, was born eight days ago. Strong and healthy, he weighed almost nine pounds.

Today is his bris. I'm holding him, waiting in the parlor for the ceremony to begin. Adam and Mary gave me the honor of being David's godfather. His godmother is Rachel, Adam's older sister.

Adam and Mary purchased a new table with six chairs and two new sofas so they'd have seats for their guests. We also brought in the table and chairs from my townhouse next door.

Close to fifty people are waiting for the ceremony to begin. Most of the guests are friends of the Rubins'—immigrants that came to America with them from Eastern Europe.

Miss Weyman and her courtesans from Mott Street are here too. So are the Keenans, our sleeping compartment brethren in the *Dromahair*. Their two children, Celine, who's now eleven, and Matthew, who's nine, have been frequent visitors to our homes since we moved to Greenwich Village. They live two blocks away on Waverly Place.

Miss Weyman and Maria Keenan assisted Mary during her delivery.

I've been teaching Matthew how to play the violin. He's a good student, so he's learning quickly. We're like brothers these days, even though I'm eight years older than he is.

A few of the Jewish women gave the courtesans icy stares when they arrived, but everyone seems friendly now that the wine is flowing.

Adam hushes the crowd in the kitchen, a signal that he's ready to begin.

I lay David on a silk pillow, and carry him carefully into the kitchen. Rachel is at my side. She picks up the baby and hands him to her father. Mr. Rubin smiles as he takes his grandson. Then his expression turns serious.

The mohel that will perform the circumcision, a bald-headed man with a long salt-and-pepper beard, starts cantillating a Hebrew prayer called the *Baruch Haba*. His singing voice is beautiful as he intones the sacred words. Adam told me earlier that the words mean, "Blessed is the one who has arrived."

The mohel then chants some other Hebrew prayers.

Adam asks him to perform the bris for David, and hands him the *izmail*—a knife with sharp edges on both sides of the blade.

The mohel places a couple of drops of red wine in the baby's mouth, presses a thin piece of wood against the penis to shield it, and carefully slices off the foreskin.

I see Mathew Keenan cringe when the mohel cut David's penis.

The cut draws a few drops of blood and a brief cry from David. The mohel dabs a cotton swab on the wound to dry the blood.

Adam recites a prayer in Hebrew. He taught Mary and me the response, so we join the Jewish guests when they say, "Just as this child has entered into the covenant, so may he enter into Torah, the marriage canopy, and into good deeds."

The mohel recites another prayer in Hebrew, and announces David's name. He picks up a cup of red wine, places another drop in the baby's mouth, and hands the glass to Mary. She drinks a sip and hands it to Adam. He finishes the glass, and the main part of the ceremony is over.

Rachel picks up the baby, hugs him, and hands him to Mary.

I join Adam and the other men in the backyard. Adam dug a hole there earlier today. He places the foreskin cut from the baby into the hole and buries it. We then adjourn to the kitchen.

The food smells wonderful. I begin with Jewish onion bread, challah bread, some delectable babka cake, bagels, and lox. They're all delicious, especially the lox. I recall Ma baking salmon for a special occasion in Ireland once. I'd forgotten how good it tastes.

Matzah balls in chicken soup are an excellent invention. I follow that with some fried potato pancakes called *latkes*, smothered with a spoonful of applesauce—yummy. I can't eat another thing after I eat a few bites from a baked vegetable and fruit casserole dish called *kugel*.

Mary is radiant as she floats around the room, carrying the baby among the guests.

"Your Jewish community seems to have accepted Mary with open arms," I say to Adam.

"They have," he replies. "She's even getting along well with Sarah, my mother. They cooked together all morning, preparing for the ceremony."

Dr. Kingberg, one of Adam's law professors at NYU, approaches me while I'm talking with Miss Weyman. "How does it feel to be an uncle?" he says.

"It feels marvelous, especially after all this wonderful food. I hope they have some more boys soon."

He chuckles. "I hear you're taking finance classes at the university."

"I am. I enjoy them very much. I've learned how to read income and financial statements, and how to float stock and bond offerings to raise capital."

"Very good. It's important to know the difference between a real company and a shell created by charlatans. Seventy percent of the companies I review are frauds. Charlatans thrive on the greed of naive gamblers wanting to get rich overnight."

"That explains why most of my stock investments have turned

sour," Miss Weyman says. "I wish there was a way to identify good companies without getting flogged."

"That won't happen until there are better security laws," Kingberg says. "Anyone can fabricate a beguiling story to issue stocks and bonds now, even when their company is worthless."

"That's true," I say. "I've seen quite a few crooks doing that at the Astor House Hotel. They stay there as a ploy... to make their naive customers think they're rich while they're fleecing them."

August 25, 1849.

ADAM AND I arrive in Rochester on the afternoon train after our journey from New York City. He'll attend my interview with his bosses today. They wouldn't normally meet with someone applying for a construction job, but Adam convinced them I'd be a good management candidate, even though I'm only seventeen.

Hiram Sibley and Judge Samuel L. Selden, the founders of the New York State Printing Telegraph Company, remember me from the Astor House when I introduce myself.

Judge Selden smiles as he shakes my hand. "You're the boy who plays Beethoven and Mozart from memory. I've always enjoyed your music."

"Thank you, sir," I say.

The four of us sit down around Judge Selden's massive desk.

"Adam tells me you'd like to have a career in the telegraph industry," Sibley says.

"Yes, I would. I've been working as a telegraph operator at the hotel. I was a bookkeeper at the Marble Palace before that. I'm also taking finance classes at NYU."

"Excellent," Sibley says. "You'll start off working on a construction crew. We'll make you a manager once you learn how to hire crews, train operators, and handle the books. We need good people willing to travel and learn the business."

"That sounds exciting, sir. When can I start?"

"Next Monday. We'll put you on the crew we're sending to Ohio."

"May I take half of my pay in stock certificates? I've heard that's a good way to accumulate wealth as the business expands."

The owners look at each other and smile.

"I think that would be fine," Judge Selden says. "We like your attitude, that you're willing to take a long view of our business. There are more than fifty telegraph companies in the U.S. right now. Some use Morse's patents. Most of our lines use Bain's patents. It's a real problem sending messages over long distances because of the re-keying required between the different systems."

"I've seen that too, sir, at the hotel. We have to use telegraph systems from three different companies with three different code sets. It's a mess. It would be more efficient to have a standard code scheme."

"We agree," Sibley says. "Our vision is to have one telegraph system that operates across the United States. The industry needs consolidation to enforce a standard. Which code system do you prefer? We use Bain's telegraph on some lines, and Morse's hand telegraph on others."

"I'm not sure," I say. "Bain's punched paper tape system is very fast, and you don't have to be there to catch the message when it's sent, but the Morse code technology is cheaper to operate."

"Morse is litigating," Adam says, "trying to get Bain's patents overturned. He's filed injunctions trying to preclude us from using Bain's system in the United States."

"Looks like the future of the telegraph industry might be decided in the courts," Judge Selden says. "Morse is tenacious. He'll stop at nothing to get his way."

"May I continue to live in New York City?" I say. "Or do I need to move to Rochester?"

"You can stay in New York just as Adam does," Sibley says. "We handle a lot of our business there. Besides, you'll be travelling with your installation crews most of the time anyway. We can always send you a telegram if we need to contact you."

"I guess that's another advantage of the telegraph," I say. "People can work remotely from each other and still get things done."

A surprise awaits us when Adam and I return to New York the following afternoon. I find the front door to my home kicked in, dangling from its hinges.

"What the hell?" I say.

"Can you come here?" Mary says, from behind her screen door.

A medium-sized man who looks to be about thirty points a pistol at us when we enter.

"What do you want?" Adam says.

The man smirks. "My name... my name... is Henry Wilcox. Mary, your whore... your whore wife, tells me... I might be... I might be... the father of her child. That's why... that's why... she's still alive."

My heart starts hammering in my chest.

The man points his pistol at me. "I'm here... I'm here... to avenge... Sergeant Milton's death. He... he was... he was my uncle."

"I killed him in self-defense when I rescued Mary," I say.

"I told him that," Mary says, "but he doesn't believe me."

David, who was asleep in Mary's lap, wakes up and starts to cry.

She stands up. "I need to change his diaper."

She walks out of the parlor to the bedroom without waiting for Wilcox to respond.

Wilcox stares at me from behind his Colt Dragoon revolver. He hasn't cocked the hammer with his thumb—the same mistake I made with his uncle. Maybe Mary saw that too.

"Where's... where's... your money?" he says.

"It's at the bank," I say. "Why?"

"You won't need it... after I kill you, so you... you should... you should give it to me."

There's something odd about this man. I get the sense that he's a little slow by his demeanor, and the way he speaks.

I can see Mary through the doorway behind Wilcox. She's changing David's diaper.

"You're making a mistake," I say. "You'll get caught and spend the rest of your life in prison... unless you kill all of us."

His shoulders droop as he scowls at the floor. "No... no I won't... you'll... you'll be dead."

I nod. "What are you going to do with the baby?"

His eyebrows rise. He looks into the bedroom and returns his gaze to me.

"I'll... I'll... I'll take him back... take him back to England."

Mary lays David in his crib. She signals to me with a finger on her lips to keep quiet as she creeps toward Wilcox.

I need to keep Wilcox distracted, keep him talking.

"I'll give you some money to leave us alone," I say. "How does a thousand dollars sound?"

His eyes widen. "Where... where's your bank?"

"A few blocks from here."

Mary raises the dagger clenched in her fist. She scowls as she rams the blade into Wilcox's neck.

"AHHH!" he screams.

He drops his pistol as he falls forward to the floor. His arms splay out, gyrating wildly as if he's having an epileptic seizure.

I yank my dagger from its sheath and hammer it into his back between his shoulder blades.

Blood sprays over me as he bellows a deep-throated whine. His body convulses and flops around for several seconds, and then he goes still. The blood streaming out of his back ebbs to a stop. A circular red pool spreads out beneath him on the wooden floor.

I yank my dagger out of his back, and pry Mary's blade from the vertebrae in his neck.

"Thanks for saving our lives," I say to her.

She stares at Adam. She's shaking. "He's one of the men who raped me," she says.

Adam goes to her and hugs her without saying anything.

David starts to cry. Mary returns to the bedroom and picks him up.

I close the front door and turn to Adam. "We need to get rid of the body."

Adam is trembling as he assesses Wilcox with a wide-eyed, horrified stare.

"I'm going to rent a horse and wagon from the livery stable on Greenwich Avenue," I say. "I'll be back in a few minutes. Could you wrap his body in a blanket while I'm gone?"

He nods.

Mary and Adam help me move Wilcox's body into the back of the wagon at midnight. We throw yard tools on top of him to hide his corpse.

"How do you feel?" I say to Mary.

"I feel good... like I finally got some justice. I'd kill the lot of them if I could."

Adam and I pull our hats down low over our faces as we approach Bandit's Roost at 59 Mulberry Street. The alley is empty tonight.

We dump the body on the ground and remove the blanket so it will look like the crime happened here. We then jump back into the wagon and return to Greenwich Village.

"I emptied his pockets," I say as we ride away, "so the police will assume he was murdered during a robbery by one of the gangs. It happens all the time there at Bandit's Roost."

"I'm glad Mary is good with knives," Adam says. "I'm not sure what we would have done if she hadn't stabbed him. That took a lot of courage. Your sister has many mysteries about her."

"Indeed. She had plenty of reasons to be angry with Wilcox."

Adam nods. "She told me about her ordeal in the cave back in Ireland. I can understand why she wanted to kill him."

"I just hope someone else doesn't come looking for us. I don't want to be haunted by the past for the rest of our lives."

23. ELIZABETH REILLY

London, England. September 2, 1849.

I'M PRACTICING a Mozart piano concerto and Aunt Bess is sitting on the sofa reading when Father enters the parlor. He's grinning when he comes and stands next to me, so I stop playing.

"Sorry to interrupt," he says, "but I have some exciting news. I just met Stephen Cunningham and his father at their club. Stephen asked me if he could marry you. I gave him my permission, so he'll be coming by tonight to propose to you."

I feel my jaw drop. I'm too stunned to say anything.

"I'll be one of Mr. Cunningham's barristers here in London if you accept," he says. "When shall we schedule the wedding?"

I rise from the piano bench and sit down next to Aunt Bess.

"That's wonderful news," Bess says, squeezing my hand. "I imagine you'll be living in London as well as Dublin part of the time. I hear they have a summerhouse on the Mediterranean coast in Cannes too. That should be fun, especially for your children."

"I don't want to marry him," I say.

Father sits down across from us in an armchair. The lines on his forehead furrow with concern. "But I've already given him my permission. It'll be embarrassing if you don't accept. Why don't you like him?"

"I rode in his carriage several times at the park this summer with Miss Hughes as our chaperone. Stephen and I don't have anything in common, so it didn't take long for us to run out of things to talk about. I'm sure he won't tolerate my dreams of becoming a concert pianist. He doesn't attend concerts, plays, or art exhibits. He's more comfortable in gambling dens or bawdyhouse saloons—where he has quite a reputation with the whores, by the way. Most importantly, we disagree on the issue of slavery. I'm an abolitionist, whereas he believes that slavery is the natural order of things."

"Miss Hughes said he was charming," Aunt Bess says.

She *would* say that. I'm glad Miss Hughes accepted a governess position with a family in Chelsea after the Season ended. She was really getting on my nerves.

I shake my head. "Stephen can play the part when he needs to."

Father frowns. "So that's it then? You're going to walk away from having financial security for yourself and your future children. A proposal like this doesn't come along every day."

I stare deep into Father's eyes. "I want to go to Paris to study piano with Chopin."

Father and Bess look at each other, as if they're sharing some kind of agreement. He rises from his armchair, and starts pacing around the room.

"I'm not going to support you if you leave," he says.

"I agree with your father," Aunt Bess says.

I stand up. "So, that's how it is, then? You'll just discard me if I don't follow your orders."

I hurry across the room and stop at the bottom of the stairway. "I'll pack my clothes and leave tomorrow. I've saved enough money to get to Paris by myself."

They don't say anything, so I hurry up the stairs to my bedroom and close the door. I pack my clothes in a suitcase, and fall asleep crying into my pillow.

Aunt Bess taps on my door a few hours later. "Dinner is ready," she says.

"I'm not hungry."

She leaves without trying to convince me to come down. She knows I'm stubborn when I've made up my mind.

I awaken before daybreak and do what I always do in the morning: look out the window, searching for the moon. It's full now, fading into the western sky as dawn arrives.

"Wish me luck, Brian O'Rourke," I whisper.

Father rides with me in the carriage to the railway station after breakfast. We don't talk much along the way. He seems worried.

I buy my ticket, and we walk to the boarding ramp. The train is ready to depart.

"Be careful," he says. He hands me fifty pounds sterling. "This should help you get started."

"Thank you, Father. That's very generous. I'll write to you when I'm settled."

"Indeed. There's a hotel in Dover you can rest at while you wait for the paddle steamer to Calais. You'll need to stay at a hotel in Calais tonight, and board a train in Lille to Paris tomorrow morning. Where will you live?"

"Somewhere near the *Conservatoire de Paris*. I hope they admit me. The competition is tough."

"I'm sure you'll do fine."

I hug him. "I'm sorry I disappointed you, Father."

He holds me close. "I just want you to be happy," he says.

He pulls back, holding my shoulders at arm's length. "I don't want you to marry someone you don't like. Besides, it's your life. You should live it the way you want."

"Thank you, Father. Tell Aunt Bess that I appreciate everything she did for me."

"I will."

I walk toward the train, stop after a few steps, and run back to hug him. He has tears in his eyes when I pull away.

I walk to the train, open the door for my compartment, stow my luggage on a shelf, and take my seat. The whistle blows, heralding an imminent departure. I wave at Father through the window as the train pulls away.

An odd question strikes me as the station disappears. Will I ever see him again... and what about Brian?

Paris. October 1, 1849.

Dear Father,

I played Chopin's Fantasie-Impromptu without any mistakes during my audition at the Conservatoire de Paris. The faculty granted me permission to enroll afterward. I'm sure that being Chopin's student also helped me secure my admittance to the school.

My life here is exhilarating. Camille Pleyel, Chopin's friend, gave me a practice room to teach piano students at his store. I don't have much money, but I love what I'm doing, so I don't care.

I've had a couple of lessons with Chopin. Unfortunately, he's been too sick to perform or teach recently. My piano instructor at the Conservatoire, Louise Farrenc, is wonderful, though. She's a virtuoso pianist in her own right, and we get along very well.

The creative arts scene in Paris is invigorating. I feel as if I'm living in a dream. The painter, Eugene Delacroix, one of Chopin's close friends—let me watch him paint the ceiling of the Galerie d'Apollon in the Louvre last week.

I went to a salon at Jane Stirling's house last night. Frédéric started improvising an idea he's been working on, and then he and Delacroix got into a discussion about the use of images, structure, and color in art and music. It was fascinating to listen to them.

I must go now. I have a lot of practicing to do before my jury performance next week. I'm memorizing all twenty-four preludes and fugues from the first book of Bach's Well-Tempered Clavier.

With love and affection – Elizabeth

October 30, 1849.

Dear Father,

I have tragic news. Chopin died thirteen days ago, on October 17. The doctor said it was tuberculosis. I've been quite distraught.

Musicians at the Church of the Madeleine performed Mozart's Requiem Mass during his funeral today. It was remarkable. The choir and soloists were grand. Thousands of people packed into the church. Strangely enough, Chopin's longtime lover, George Sand—a woman who took a man's name so she'd be taken seriously as a writer—didn't attend.

The physician removed Chopin's heart before the funeral. His sister is taking it back to Warsaw pickled in an urn. I find that quite bizarre, but apparently, it was Frédéric's wish.

I must stop now. My emotions are overloaded and sleep is beckoning.

Please give my love to Aunt Bess.

With love and affection – Elizabeth

I seal the envelope and fall asleep.

It's noon when I awaken. I feel lonely with Chopin gone, even with his fastidiousness and foul moods. He was the reason I came to Paris.

I debate with myself about returning to London, but then autumn creeps by, and soon winter is upon us. The gaslights paint eerie storefront reflections on the wet streets when I walk around at night now, and frigid winds grip the city when it snows.

I practice piano five hours a day, burrow into my studies during the long winter, and emerge stronger in the spring. My audience is growing every month when I give recitals at the acoustically marvelous Conservatoire performance hall.

Where are you my love? I say to the moon each morning, as I hustle through the deserted streets of Paris to the school. *I feel your presence reflecting in the moonlight, so I know you're alive. Why won't you write to me?*

Something awakens inside me when I see a brown-robed monk walking in the hallway at the Conservatoire. Could the monk be Brian's former violin instructor?

The monk's office door is open when I knock on the doorframe.

"Come in," he says. He studies me with wide, curious eyes as I approach him.

"Excuse me, but are you Brother Bernard?"

"That's me." He smiles. "How may I help you?"

"Did you teach Brian O'Rourke in Ireland?"

He leans forward and smiles. "He's the best violin student I ever had. Do you know him?"

"Yes." I tell him about Brian then, how I rescued him, and helped him escape to New York.

"I'm not sure he's still alive, though," I say. "He promised he would write to me, but I haven't heard from him. Is it possible to find out if he's still in New York, perhaps through one of the Catholic churches there?"

Brother Bernard folds his hands together. "I'll write to each of the churches to see if he's a member of their congregation. It may take a while to get a response, though."

"That would be grand. I'm anxious to know if he's safe."

He stands up and shakes my hand. "I'll let you know what I find out."

I don't hear from Brother Bernard until the middle of July. I'm in a piano practice room at the Conservatoire when he knocks on my door.

"Hello, Brother Bernard," I say as I face him.

"Hello, Elizabeth. I finally heard back from the churches in New York. Someone named Brian O'Rourke attends St. Joseph's Church in Greenwich Village."

"That's wonderful news. Do you have Brian's address?"

"No. I'm sorry. The priest didn't send it, for privacy reasons."

"Thank you, Brother Bernard."

"You're welcome." He turns and strolls away.

I close the door and stare at the piano keys. I'm glad you're safe, Brian O'Rourke, I say to myself. So why won't you write to me?

24. BRIAN O'ROURKE

New York City. April 4, 1856.

ADAM KNOCKS ON the doorframe of my office door.

I point at the chair in front of my desk. "Come in and have a seat."

"That was quite a celebration last night," he says, as he sits down. "I still have a headache."

"Me too. I don't usually drink whiskey during the week. Now I remember why."

"It was an important occasion, though, so you had a good excuse."

"Indeed. Mary and I are very pleased to be naturalized citizens now."

He smiles. "It made me very proud, watching the two of you at the courthouse yesterday."

"Thanks. I'm glad you came."

"I just heard some important news. By a special act of the New York legislature, our company will now be called the *Western Union Telegraph Company*."

"Ah. That *is* good news. I guess Ezra Cornell got his way with the name."

I turn and look at a large map of the United States hanging on the wall behind my desk. I've drawn our telegraph line topology in green, and our competitors' lines in other colors.

"I imagine we'll be consolidating even more companies now that he's joined forces with us," I say.

Adam nods. "I'm sure we will."

"What's going to happen with my stock certificates?"

"We'll convert your New York and Mississippi Valley shares into Western Union shares. You've made some astute investments. Your telegraph shares are now worth twenty thousand dollars. Are you ready to sell them? You could buy hundreds of acres on the coast of Long Island with that much money."

"No. I'm going to hold on to them. I think we'll get tremendous cost synergies once we consolidate the industry, and we have many new markets to explore. Using the telegraph to relay news across the country is already transforming the newspaper business, and having timely prices for stocks and bonds has dramatically affected speculation in the financial markets. I've made sixteen thousand dollars speculating on grain and cotton the last few months."

"How'd you do that?"

"Our telegraph employees in Chicago, Ohio, and New Orleans send me price information before anyone else. I learned that from the businessmen I met when I was a telegraph operator at the Astor House. They used sources in the field to gather information before they placed their orders."

Adam nods. "I'd buy more telegraph company shares if I didn't have three children to feed, with another on the way. My shares are only worth about twelve thousand now."

"I think they're bound to go higher. The exclusive right-of-way contracts you're negotiating with the railroads give us an advantage no other company can compete with."

"That was a stroke of genius, wasn't it? And it's cheap to give the railroads free use of our telegraphs in exchange for their right-of-ways, which bring us to the business center of every city. It would cost a fortune to purchase right-of-ways along the roads."

"Don't forget that half of my speculation account belongs to Mary. She gave me that money to invest for her too. How are your negotiations going with the other telegraph companies?"

"Very well. The four largest U.S. companies have agreed. I'd like to get Montreal to join us so we can control prices in Canada too, but they haven't warmed up to the idea. Regardless, we'll drive minor operators across the country out of business once our cartel is in place."

"I imagine we'll follow the Vanderbilt model, setting our rates low enough to drive our competitors out of business, and then raising them once we have a monopoly."

"Of course."

"We studied his strategies in my finance classes at NYU. He drove his steamship and ferryboat competitors out of business that way. He's doing the same thing now with ocean steamers, shipyards, and the railroads. He's a very smart man."

"Yes, he is, and he's ruthless when he targets an industry."

Adam shifts position in his chair. "Mary and I are going to buy a new townhouse across the street from Gramercy Park. We need more room for the kids. Do you want to move there too?"

"Mary told me you were looking around for a new home. I think I'll stay where I am for now. I like our little neighborhood on Patchin Place. It's close to the university, and I enjoy sitting in the park at Washington Square."

Adam stands. "I need to lock my office door before we leave. Do you want to join us for lunch on Sunday, after you go to church? Mary wants you to try her new potato latke recipe."

"I wouldn't miss it. There's something else I'd like to talk with you about."

Adam sits back down. "What's up?"

"Could you close the door?"

Adam leans back and pushes the door closed.

"Thanks," I say. "I wanted to let you know that I've decided to help the Underground Railroad."

His eyebrows rise. "Do you mean the people who smuggle slaves out of the South?"

"That's right. I got involved after one of our telegraph operators showed me an odd message sent from a plantation in Macon, Georgia, to a man named Rufus Jones in Wilmington, Delaware. The message directed Rufus to retain ebony in route to G. The telegram then gave a physical description of the slaves he was to capture, and their expected date and time of arrival. I determined that the letter *G* in the message stands for Thomas Garrett—the abolitionist. His home in Wilmington is rumored to be the last stop on the Underground Railroad."

"I see. So, what did you do?"

"I went to see Garrett. I asked him if any of the slaves he was helping to escape didn't show up. He was reluctant to speak with me at first. He opened up once I showed him the message. He told me that more than forty runaway slaves disappeared before they reached his house the past few weeks."

Adam strokes his chin with his hand. "They were probably captured and taken back to their owners. I imagine their beatings were quite severe after they returned."

"Indeed. Garrett told me that his abolitionist agents use the telegraph to coordinate their activities. I think some of our telegraph operators might be intercepting their messages and passing them on to slave hunters for the rewards. Rufus and other slave hunters like him then pick up their quarry when they arrive on the trains."

"That sounds very organized."

"It's an intelligence network, or rather... an espionage network. Garrett said that railroad personnel and night watchmen at the harbors as well as the police are on the slave hunters' payroll too."

Adam nods. "Very clever."

"It's actually pretty easy to intercept telegraph messages. All you have to do is splice a telegraph key into an existing line. Of course, you can also use the telegraph to send secret messages once you encode them with a cipher. I shared that idea with Garrett."

Adam folds his hands. "Does Mary know?"

"No. I wanted to let you know in case something happens. You *are* my attorney after all."

He laughs. "I'm a lot more than that, brother."

A veil of concern drops over his face. "Seriously though, the Fugitive Slave Act says that anyone helping slaves escape can be arrested."

"I know. That's why I told you."

He leans forward. "I agree with the abolitionists. Slavery is an evil scourge that's tearing the nation apart. The war in Kansas is likely to bleed into other states soon. I think we'll all have to take a stand before long, either *for* slavery, or against it."

"I think the disenfranchisement of the slaves is similar to what we faced as Catholics in Ireland. We became tenant farmers after the Crown confiscated our lands and gave them to Protestant soldiers and politicians loyal to their cause. The measly payments we received for our labor was then given right back to our English overlords as rent. We still had to grow our own food, and we couldn't vote because we didn't own property."

Adam nods. "There are some parallels. However, Irish Catholics *are* able to leave the country if they want, and they aren't sold as property, or beaten by their landlords."

I feel anger bubbling up from my gut. "I think our feudal subjugation in Ireland *was* a form of slavery. That's why I'm helping the abolitionists. The Negro struggle is like our struggle—what we faced in Ireland."

Adam nods. "I understand what you're saying. Jews have faced prejudice and oppression for thousands of years too. That's why my parents left Poland. So, how are you planning to help the abolitionists?"

"I've created an easy-to-use cipher to encode their messages. That way, the slave hunters can't monitor their activities. I showed it to Garrett, and he liked the idea. I told him I'd train his agents when I travel on business. Many of their hideouts are near railroad stations and harbors. Of course, I won't do any of this on company time."

"That's good. You don't want to get fired."

"There are other ways I can help them too. As you know, we carry our supplies by rail when we construct our telegraph lines along the tracks. I occasionally find Negroes hiding in our railcars. I've never turned them in, so I guess I'm already breaking the law."

"The Fugitive Slave Act is ridiculous. Many people ignore it. However, that doesn't mean the police won't arrest you."

"I'm willing to risk it. I wanted you to know, so you can bail me out if I get in trouble."

His eyes go wide. "Be careful. You don't want to cause a scandal."

I lean back in my chair. "One of the reasons I'm working in the telegraph industry is because I realize how important information is. Our Ribbonmen insurgents were powerless against the government authorities in Ireland because we were isolated, just as the Negroes are here. I imagine you've heard that the Sixty-Ninth New York State Militia is an Irish regiment."

"Yes, I have."

"One of its leaders, Michael Corcoran—who happens to be from Sligo, close to where I was born—is a Ribbonman too. I've had many discussions with him about using the telegraph as a tool of war. We could have chased the British out of Ireland if we'd had weapons, and if we'd been organized enough to coordinate our attacks."

Adam leans forward. "I didn't know you were involved with the New York militia."

"I'm sure you've witnessed the shenanigans of the secretive Know

Nothing Party, and their hatred for immigrants. We need to be ready to fight if they come into power."

Adam stands up. "You know I enjoy discussing politics, but I need to leave soon if I'm going to make it home in time for dinner. You can bring Teresa when you come over for lunch on Sunday if you'd like. I know Mary doesn't care for her, but I'm sure she'll treat her well if she comes."

"That's kind of you. I'll talk with Teresa about it tonight."

"What is it about Teresa that Mary doesn't like?"

"She doesn't trust her." I roll my eyes. "She thinks Teresa might still be a whore. Teresa assures me that she doesn't see other men now, and I believe her. She has no reason to. She makes plenty of money as a madam at the brothel she owns."

Adam chuckles. "She's very beautiful. Do you think you'll ever get married?"

Teresa brings up this question to me too, but I always change the subject.

"I don't know," I say. "Elizabeth still haunts my mind when I think about marriage."

I spend the following week managing one of our telegraph construction crews in Maryland. I stop at an address Garrett gave me near Baltimore, after my crew returns home on Saturday afternoon.

"Are you Alistair Green?" I say, when he answers his door.

"Yes." He stares at me warily. "Who wants to know?"

"I'm Brian O'Rourke. Thomas Garrett sent me."

His eyes widen as he smiles. "Come on in," he says with a distinct Scottish accent. "Have a seat on the sofa. I'll be back after I get my wife from the kitchen."

"I'm Martha," she says as she enters the room.

I introduce myself, and she sits down next to me.

Alistair sits down in an armchair across from us. "So, how can we help you?" he says.

I hand them each a sheet of paper. "I'm here to show you how to use a cipher to send telegraph messages. This will prevent slave hunters from spying on your activities."

"That would be good," Martha says. "A lot of slaves have been caught and sent back to their owners recently. Is that because they're intercepting our messages?"

"It could be," I say. "I have a formula to make your messages secure with just a few changes, as you can see on the paper I gave you. Here's an example. Suppose you want to send a message to Thomas Garrett saying that four adults and two children traveling by rail will arrive at four p.m. The main substitutions you make are for the method of travel, and the time of arrival. You call rail travel a *party*, you call boat travel a *wedding*, and you call coach travel a *wake*. The message would then be: G1, four adults and two children will come to the party at six p.m."

They stare at the message and look back to me.

"G1 is the code scheme," I say. "I call it G1, for Garrett 1. In this code scheme, you always add two hours to the actual time you expect them to arrive. This will confuse the slave hunters that are spying on your messages."

"I see," Martha says. "So, if we send a coach to Garrett carrying three men that are supposed to arrive at noon, our message would be: G1, three men will come to the wake at two p.m."

"That's right. I may send you other cipher schemes in the future, but this is a simple one that should work for now."

Alistair stands up. "I like it, especially since it's easy to use. Follow me. I'd like to show you something."

I follow him down a steep wooden stairwell into his dark basement. He lights a candle, which illuminates the faces of four frightened Negroes lying on cots.

"This is Mr. O'Rourke," Alistair says. "He's part of our network."

They stand up as we approach.

I say, "How do you do?" and shake their hands.

"These folks are going to Canada by way of Chicago," Alistair says.

He turns to me. "There's a man you should meet there named Allan Pinkerton. Allan's Scottish. We came over on the boat together from Glasgow in '42. He has his own detective agency now, and one of his homes is a stop on the Underground Railroad."

"Certainly," I say. "I'll look him up the next time I'm in Chicago."

I wish the slaves good luck, and follow Alistair back up the stairs.

"Would you like some tea?" Martha says when we enter the kitchen.

"I'd love some."

We converse about Scotland, Ireland, and America for the next two hours. I pull my money satchel out of my pocket when I'm ready to leave, and hand Alistair twenty silver dollars. "Here's a donation for the refugees downstairs, to get them started in their new lives."

Alistair nods. "Thank you. I'm sure they'll appreciate it."

"Someone special to me did the same thing before I left Ireland on a famine ship. It feels good to be able to return the favor."

25. ELIZABETH REILLY

Paris, France. May 15, 1857.

THE KNOCK ON my apartment door comes in the middle of the night, after I'm already in bed.

I open the door, and a young man hands me a telegram. I sign for it, and close the door.

The message is from Father: *Aunt Bess is very ill. Please come right away. Send me your arrival date and time. I'll meet you at the London Bridge railway station.*

I'm too worried to go back to sleep, so I pack my luggage.

I spend the rest of the morning informing my piano students that I'll be gone for an indeterminate amount of time. I then return to my apartment and tell my landlord that he can keep or sell my belongings, if I don't return by the end of the month.

With my luggage in hand, I go to the *Gare du Nord* train terminal, where I send a telegram to Father with my arrival details. I then send another telegram to my promoter, asking him to cancel my upcoming concert performances in Lyon and Geneva.

Father is waiting for me on the London Bridge terminal platform when I disembark from the train the following afternoon. His face looks drawn, as if he hasn't slept.

"I'm sorry to tell you this," he says, "but your aunt died of consumption last night. She tried to hold on until you got here, but she couldn't."

My tears pour out as we ride through the rainy streets in our carriage. We stop by the morgue to view her body before we continue home. The funeral four days later at the Episcopal church is a small family affair.

"Aunt Bess used to have many friends," Father says, as we ride back to her townhouse, "but her illness kept her at home the past several years, so she lost touch with most of them."

"I had no idea she was so ill," I say.

"She didn't want to worry you. She did want me to tell you that she's very proud of you. She always followed the concert listings in the newspaper to see where you were performing."

Father and I spend the next two days organizing her possessions. He'll be putting her townhouse up for sale soon. I'm packing the clothes in her closet when Father enters the bedroom.

"I think you should see these," he says. He hands me a fistful of letters. "Don't judge your aunt too harshly. I'm sure she thought she was looking out for your best interests."

The letters are from Brian. The envelope postmarks reveal that he sent several letters in 1848 and 1849, and a few after that.

I sit down on the bed. "I've been waiting for Brian to write to me for years," I say. My voice is cracking with anger. "And all this time she's been hiding his letters from me."

He nods. "Bess told me that she thought the O'Rourke boy was a murderer. I didn't realize she'd hidden his letters, though. Otherwise, I would have told her that Brian probably killed Sergeant Milton in self-defense when he rescued his sister. I overheard some of the soldiers talking about the cave where Milton held Mary captive. He was selling her as a prostitute."

My stomach churns with disgust. "That must have been awful for her."

"I'll leave you to read his letters now. I'll be in the kitchen when you finish."

All the envelopes are open. I pull out the first letter and read it twice. I then read each of the letters in sequence by date, following the evolution of his life in New York, Mary's marriage, her conversion to Judaism, his success in the telegraph business, and his last letter from a year ago, where he discusses the birth of Mary's fourth child. He says he won't write to me again if I don't respond.

Father is going through Aunt Bess's business papers at the kitchen table when I sit down across from him.

"I can't believe she would be so cruel," I say. "Brian and I promised we'd wait for each other, and all this time I thought he'd rejected me."

I break down and cry then, sobbing into my hands.

Father hands me a handkerchief. "There, there, now... it'll be all right."

"I've been turning into a spinster… while I've waited for Brian… all these years. I told Aunt Bess I made a promise. She tried to make me marry… Cunningham. She wouldn't listen…"

I blow my nose and wipe my eyes. "I want to go to New York to find him."

Father leans back in his chair. "You can't go to a place like that alone. It's too dangerous. I have some more bad news."

"What?"

"Aunt Bess showed me her will before she died. I'm the administrator for your inheritance."

He hands me the document. "She wants me to sell this townhouse. She believes I'll get at least five thousand pounds. This is to be used as a dowry for you with two caveats."

I scan the page. "What are the caveats?"

"You must marry a Protestant, and you can't marry Brian O'Rourke."

My mouth drops open. I'm shocked when I read these demands at the bottom of her will.

"I need some time alone," I say as I stand up.

I return to my room, burrow myself beneath the covers, and fall asleep crying.

A plan presents itself the next morning: I'll secure a husband in name only—without conjugal rights. I'll make that clear from the beginning—perhaps an older man from the United States looking for someone pretty to hang on his arm. I'll figure out how to get a divorce and marry Brian once I'm there.

Father is reading the newspaper when I enter the kitchen.

"We should move soon so you can put the house on the market," I say as I sit down.

"Certainly, my dear. I'll find us an apartment near Bond Street where I work."

I feel sorry for Father. He's working as a bookkeeper now. Viscount Clements's pernicious review of Father's legal abilities made it impossible for him to get a job as a solicitor after he returned to London.

We rent an apartment close to the clothing store where Father works the following week.

THE ANGEL OF INNISFREE

It's easy for me to arrange concert performances in London when I mention that I studied with Chopin. His music has grown even more popular since he died. Watching a former student perform his works seems to bring an aura of magic to the air. I get many inquiries about him when I meet my audience after I play.

My mid-August recital at St. Martin-in-the-Fields Church near Trafalgar Square goes very well, which means I didn't make any mistakes, and I played with emotion, feeling the music. Several attendees stand in line to greet me and get my autograph after I finish.

A man in his mid-fifties with salt-and-pepper hair, thick eyebrows, and bushy sideburns approaches me offering his hand. "That was very nice," he says.

I can tell he's from the Southern United States by his accent.

"What's your name?" I say, as I return his handshake.

"Jacob Butler. I really enjoyed your performance. We don't get music like that in Virginia."

"Virginia. That's near Washington, isn't it?"

"Yes, it is."

"I'd like to learn more about your state. Would you like to have tea with me after I finish greeting my fans?"

His forehead scrunches up quizzically as his eyebrows rise.

I must have surprised him. Maybe he's not used to a woman being so forward.

"Sure," he says.

He turns and introduces me to the middle-aged couple behind him. "This is my banker, Peter Stiles, and his wife, Joanna."

"How do you do?" I say. "Would you like to have tea with us? I asked Jacob if he'd tell me about Virginia."

"We'd be delighted to," Mrs. Stiles says.

They wait for me near the front door while I finish my greetings.

The rector brings me the payment for my performance—twenty pounds. "I'd love to have you play a recital here in the fall," he says. "Your playing was marvelous."

"Thank you. I'd be delighted to, if I'm still in London then. I'll let you know."

I approach the trio waiting by the door. "I'm ready."

We exit the church, flag down a carriage, and ride to Claridge's

Hotel in Mayfair, where Jacob Butler is lodging. The maître d' at the hotel restaurant seats us at a table beneath a fancy glass chandelier. There are four porcelain tea settings on the white linen tablecloth.

"I'd like whiskey," Jacob says when the waiter takes our order.

Mr. Stiles orders the same. Joanna and I order tea.

"Peter represents the Bank of England," Jacob says.

"So, tell me about Virginia," I say to Jacob.

"I own a six hundred acre farm southeast of Warrenton," he says, "which is about seventy miles west of Washington. It's hot and muggy this time of year, even warmer than London."

"What do you produce on your farm?"

"Dairy products—milk, butter, and cheese. I use most of my acreage to grow grass and corn to feed my three hundred head of cattle."

He turns to Mr. Stiles. "My land borders the Warrenton railroad spur of the Orange and Alexandria Railroad, which enables me to ship my products directly into Alexandria each day. There's a huge market for our dairy products in Washington, which is just a few miles north of Alexandria."

"That's quite a large operation," Mr. Stiles says. "I imagine it would be difficult to manage much more than you already have."

Jacob shakes his head. "I can handle it. I have plenty of help."

I feel Mr. Stiles studying me. Perhaps he's curious as to why I invited Mr. Butler—a much older man—for tea.

"So what's the holdup?" Jacob says to Peter.

"We already have a lot of capital at risk in the United States. I'm concerned about investing more. Land prices are dropping precipitously in the western United States because of the fighting between the pro-slavery factions and the abolitionists in Kansas. Your railroad stocks are also in trouble. Several have already declared bankruptcy. Our board of directors will consider these factors when we examine your loan request. However, several of them are in the South of France until the end of September."

Jacob frowns. "I can't wait that long. The land I want to purchase will be sold by then."

"I'm sorry to hear about your wife," Mrs. Stiles says, changing the subject. "How long were you married?"

"Thirty-five years," Jacob says. "Her heart just gave out one day.

My twenty-year-old son, Harland, is managing things while I'm away."

We chat about my life in Paris for half an hour, and then Mr. and Mrs. Stiles stand up.

"I apologize," Mr. Stiles says, "but we have another engagement."

Jacob and I shake their hands, and they walk out of the restaurant.

"I'd like to hear about the property you plan to purchase," I say.

The lines in Jacob's forehead bend with dismay. "I think business is better left to men."

I remain calm after his snub. It's not the first time I've heard men say this.

"I need to be on my way," I say as I stand up. "I enjoyed talking with you."

He walks me to the exit and takes my hand. "Would you like to have dinner with me here tomorrow evening?" he says.

"Certainly." I hesitate for a second. "I'd normally need a chaperone, since I'm not married, but you seem like a gentleman. Can I trust you not to think badly of me if I come alone?"

He smiles and nods. "I'd love to have your company."

I chuckle. "Some people might call me a spinster, since I'm twenty-five."

"I'd never call you that."

"I'll see you at seven p.m.," I say.

"Good. I'll be waiting for you here in the lobby."

We have a lovely dinner together the next evening. I'm ready to bring up my proposal as the waiter clears the dishes away, but I'm also reluctant. Jacob sucked down six whiskeys during the meal. I don't want to get involved with someone that has an alcohol problem.

"What religion do you follow?" I say.

"Methodist." He chuckles. "To be honest, I don't attend church very often. I'm too busy. That's one of the things about owning a dairy farm. We have to milk the cows every day, even on Sundays."

"How much do you need for your land purchase?"

His eyebrows bend into an incredulous stare.

"It's all right," I say. "I may have a way to help you."

"My neighbor is selling five hundred acres of forestland that borders my property. I need fifteen thousand dollars, or three thousand British pounds, at the current exchange rate. It'll be good farmland once I clear the trees. There's also a large spring-fed pond stocked with trout in the middle of the property."

He sucks down another shot of whiskey and scowls. "One of Mr. Stiles's clients sold my farm to me thirty years ago. I never missed a payment while I paid it off, so I would think they'd consider me a good risk. British banks already finance half the tobacco and cotton crops produced in the South. However, I've found that they're reluctant to finance dairy farms, probably because it's too expensive to ship the products to England. Dairy products spoil if you don't get them to market quickly. Tobacco, grain, and cotton are less risky, but I make more money from dairy and cattle. Mr. Stiles's biggest worry is a collapse in land prices."

"I see."

I'm not sure how to word my proposal, so I hesitate before I begin. I can tell Jacob's a proud man. I don't want to insult him with my offer. "I have an option you may want to consider."

He stares at me skeptically. "What do you have in mind?"

"I want to move to the United States, and I don't want to lose my dowry."

His eyebrows arch. "What does that have to do with me?"

"My father has a dowry of five thousand pounds for the husband that marries me."

I let this percolate in his mind for a moment before I continue. "You'll receive my dowry if we get married. You could use three thousand pounds to purchase your land, and then remit the rest back to me. However, I only want a platonic marriage. We'd have to sleep in separate rooms."

His eyes grow wide and then narrow into a stare. I can see that my proposition will take a while to seep into his brain.

"I know this is an odd proposal," I say. "The reason I want to move to the United States is because I promised myself to someone a long time ago. His name is Brian O'Rourke. He lives in New York. Of course, he may be married by now."

Jacob crinkles his forehead. "So, you'd give me three thousand pounds just to marry you?"

"Yes. That's right. You'd need to support my ambitions to pursue a career as a concert pianist, and buy me a nice piano with some of my dowry money. I practice several hours each day. I hope that wouldn't be an issue for you."

He nods. "No. I like your music."

"I'm sure I'll be able to find some concert venues in Washington, don't you think?"

"I imagine so."

I give him my best smile. "The advantage for you, in addition to the money, is that you'll have a pretty girl on your arm for a while, until I find Brian. Of course, you can have a woman on the side to get your needs met if you want, as long as you're discreet. We wouldn't want to be the target of gossip."

His eyes cloud over. He stares at the table with a muddled expression.

Maybe this is too much for him.

He stares at me with anger in his eyes. "What will happen if you find Brian?"

"I'm not sure," I say tentatively. "It will depend on his situation… he may not want me any longer, or he may be married by now. I don't know. We haven't spoken in nine years."

I stand up to take my leave. "Shall we have dinner here tomorrow night? You can give me your answer then, after you've had some time to think about it."

He stands and takes my hand. "You're very beautiful, Elizabeth." He's hesitant. "Your proposal surprised me. Yes. Let's have dinner here tomorrow night at the same time."

Jacob is waiting in the lobby when I arrive the next evening. The waiter ushers us to a table in the center of the restaurant. There's a huge bouquet of white lilies on the table.

He kneels down on one knee when I sit down. "Will you marry me?" he says.

This time *I'm* shocked.

"Umm, yes," I say, "once we write down our agreement."

He pulls out a ring with a large diamond and slips it on my finger.

The patrons in the restaurant stand and clap as he rises to kiss me.

I didn't expect to have to kiss him. I do it for show. *Just this one time.*

Father's elation about my engagement turns to shock when Jacob visits our apartment the next morning. I didn't warn Father that I planned to marry someone the same age as him.

I remain silent, watching with interest, as the two men discuss my dowry. We sold Aunt Bess's townhouse in July, so the dowry money is sitting in the Bank of England.

Father copies down the details required to transfer the funds in gold to one of Jacob's banks—Riggs and Company, located on Pennsylvania Avenue in Washington, D.C.

Father seems perturbed. He suggests a small wedding.

I readily agree, and so does Jacob. He wants to return to Virginia as soon as possible.

I wake up before dawn on the last Saturday in August—my wedding day. I feel numb, bereft, and joyless. It's not too late to back out, I tell myself.

I stare out the window at the quarter moon. *I hope you're still waiting for me, Brian. I don't know if this is the right thing to do, but it's the best plan I can come up with to get closer to you.*

I shove my nightgown into my packed suitcase. We'll board a steamship to America after the wedding. The ship is supposed to reach Norfolk, Virginia, in eleven days.

I pull out my packet of letters from Brian and read each one again. My gaze returns to the moon. *I may be making a huge mistake, but how else will I be able to reach you, and still have part of my dowry? I don't want to show up penniless and be your charity case. I have my pride.*

I pull out my stationary and compose a letter to Brian. I start by offering profuse apologies for the injustice Aunt Bess perpetrated. I then tell him about my farcical marriage with Jacob that will bring me to America. I don't have Jacob's address yet, so I tell Brian I'll contact him when I reach Virginia. I address the envelope to the location Brian used in his last letter.

My name will be Elizabeth Butler after my marriage, I realize. *Shite*! Elizabeth Butler! I always assumed my name would be *Elizabeth O'Rourke*.

I paste enough postage on the envelope to get it to America, and place it in the mailbox.

The rest of the day goes by in a blur. I feel disconnected, as if I'm watching my life from outside my body, as the Church of England vicar pronounces us man and wife. We arrive at the harbor in a carriage soon thereafter, and then Father is hugging me while he says goodbye.

"I'll come visit you soon," he says, "maybe next year, after you have your first baby."

I hang on to Father while my tears fall on his shoulder. It's too late to turn back now, I realize.

"I hope you do," I say, "even if I don't have a baby."

We walk across the gangplank to the steamship, and Jacob hands the first mate our tickets. Captain Reynolds escorts us to our quarters, while a porter follows us with our luggage.

"This is the wedding suite," the captain says, flashing a wry smile. "You'll be comfortable here."

I turn to Jacob. "Where's *my* room?"

He grins mischievously. "It's here, with me."

My fury ignites before I can control it. "I'm not sleeping with you!"

Jacob's face turns red with anger. "You're my wife now. You'll do as I say."

I turn to the captain. "Do you have another room? I'm not going unless you do."

Captain Reynolds looks at Jacob without answering me.

There's a long, uncomfortable silence.

"We better get her a room," Jacob says. "She's nervous, this being her first time and all."

The men laugh.

I'm outraged, but I control myself.

"There's a room next to mine," the captain says. "It'll cost you twenty-two pounds."

"That's fine." Jacob pulls out his money satchel and pays.

We follow the porter to my room. He places my suitcase on a stand, and Jacob gives him a tip.

"I'll see you at dinner," I say to Jacob. I close and lock my door.

Jacob is laughing about something with the captain as they walk away.

26. BRIAN O'ROURKE

New York City. September 10, 1857.

I MARCH UP the steps to the porch at number 3 Gramercy Park West, and knock on the door. There are four couples sitting on blankets in the park across the street.

It's hot this afternoon. I unbutton the top of my shirt and loosen my tie, as I study the intricately laced wrought iron facade above the veranda.

David, Mary's eight-year-old son, opens the door.

"It's Uncle Brian," he calls out behind him. He turns to me. "Come on in."

"How are you doing, David?" I say, extending my hand.

He smiles and returns my handshake. "Very well, Uncle Brian."

I follow him into the parlor. His two younger sisters, Sarah and Fiona, are playing with one-year-old Michael on the floor.

The girls rush to me, and I pick them up. They giggle excitedly as I twirl them around in a circle and dump them on the sofa.

David used to enjoy having me do this when he was younger. He's too mature for that now.

Mary enters as I pick up the baby. "Thanks for coming over," she says. "Let's go to the backyard so we can talk."

We walk through the kitchen to the back porch and sit down. I position Michael's legs over my thigh and hold him securely by the waist.

Mary pours tea from a decanter into a glass, hands it to me, and pours another glass for herself. "It's good to see you," she says. "Adam tells me you've been traveling a lot."

"I have. I spent the past month in Iowa, Kansas, and Nebraska. It's a different country out there—flat terrain, with luscious farmland as far as the eye can see. Da would have loved it."

She nods. "I want to talk with you about our investments. The newspaper says that stocks are crashing along with the price of land, and several railroads have shut down. Is our money safe?"

"Most of our speculation fund is in cash right now. I've been too busy to do much trading."

She sighs. "That's good. I've been worried. The *New-York Daily Times* said the collapse of the Ohio Life Insurance Company might cause other banks to fail. Some of my neighbors are worried that they won't get their money back. People are lining up at banks all over town to withdraw their savings. Should we do that too?"

"No. There's a panic now. I think it'll pass. I can transfer your half of our speculation account to you if you'd like. The value is close to sixty thousand dollars, half of which is yours."

She nods. "I have an investment idea I'd like to share with you."

"What do you have in mind?"

"Let's buy some land across the street from the lake in Central Park. Adam's father said there's a competition underway to hire an architect to design a new layout for the park. I'm sure the land around it will increase in value after the improvements are made."

"Sure. Why don't we use thirty thousand of our cash for that?"

"Excellent. Mr. Rubin is negotiating with the owners. He invited Adam and me to meet with them next week. You can come too if you'd like."

"I'll be traveling again." I chuckle. "I'm sure you'll negotiate a good deal for us."

"Of course. Thirty thousand will buy a lot of land. We'll have a good bargaining position."

"So, what else has been going on while I've been gone?"

"Miss Weyman came to see me and the kids last week. She's moving her brothel to a home she just bought on Broadway near the new hotels. She said she'll have enough money to retire and live comfortably for the rest of her life in about five years."

"I imagine so. She has a lot of money flowing through her hands. Whatever happened to the rest of the women who lived on Mott Street with us?"

"Nora, the girl from Galway, got married. So did Angela. That was a few years ago. A slave hunter captured Gracie Jefferson and took her back to Georgia. I'm not sure about the others. Of course, you already know about Teresa."

"Indeed. I'll be seeing her later tonight. Do you think you can find out where Gracie lives from Miss Weyman?"

"Why? Do you want to rescue her?"

Should I tell Mary what I've been doing? I don't want her to worry about me, but I also don't like keeping secrets from her.

"I want to help Gracie," I say. "It's awful to think of her being raped and beaten by that cruel master she used to talk about."

"That *is* awful."

"I guess Adam didn't tell you... about my involvement with the Underground Railroad."

Her eyebrows rise. "No, he didn't."

"I asked him not to tell you. I may be able to help Gracie if I find out where she lives."

Michael cries and starts squirming in my lap.

Mary takes him, pulls up her shirt, and places her breast in his mouth. "I'll ask Miss Weyman the next time I see her."

"Thanks. There's something I want to show you... to get your opinion."

I pull the envelope from Elizabeth out of my coat pocket and hand it to her.

Mary stares at the return address name. "Elizabeth Butler? Who's that?"

"Elizabeth Reilly, the girl who saved my life, when she took me to Innisfree."

"After all these years... she finally writes to you?"

"Yeah. I just received it."

Mary reads the letter while the baby suckles her breast. She snickers when she finishes.

"Well, I'll be," she says. "She *did* wait for you, but then she got married so she could come to America to find you? That doesn't make sense."

"That's what I thought."

"What are you going to do?"

I shake my head. "I'm certainly not going to chase a married woman."

She nods. "Indeed. That would only end in heartache. I know

several women at our synagogue who are interested in you. Of course, you'd have to convert to Judaism. I'm sure they'd never become Catholics."

"And I'll never convert to another religion, so I guess we'd be stuck."

We both chuckle.

"Maybe I should start thinking about finding a girl to settle down with, now that I know Elizabeth is married. I've been dating Teresa, but I'm not sure I'd ever marry her. I guess I've been hanging on all these years waiting for Elizabeth, and now this. It's very disappointing. What do you think she means, about getting married so she can be closer to me?"

"I don't know."

Mary's kids burst through the screen door and run into the backyard. The girls are chasing David, who has stolen one of their dolls. The girls run back to Mary and complain.

David throws me the doll over their heads.

I stand up, run into the yard, and throw the doll back to him. We then play keep-away from the girls. I let Sarah catch the doll after a moment, and return to my chair.

I chuckle. "It seems like just yesterday that Patrick and James were teasing *you* like that."

"Yeah. Too bad they never had a chance to meet their nieces and nephews."

"Yeah... too bad."

Memories of the past haunt my thoughts as we watch the children play.

"I'll be away for the next month and a half in Ohio and Illinois," I say.

"What are you doing there?"

"The same thing I've been doing—running telegraph lines along the railroad tracks between cities, building telegraph offices, and hiring and training telegraph operators and maintenance crews. I've met some interesting people during my travels. I met a fellow named Allan Pinkerton in Chicago earlier this year."

"What does he do?"

She takes the baby from her breast, places him on her shoulder, and pats him a few times.

"BURP!"

We both chuckle.

"That was a pretty loud burp for such a small baby," I say.

"He cries loud too."

"Pinkerton has his own detective agency. You can't tell anyone this, but he also helps the Underground Railroad. He smuggles runaway slaves across the border into Canada."

"That's nice of him. Speaking of interesting people, I want to introduce you to one of our neighbors—Cyrus Field, the president of the Atlantic Telegraph Company."

"I'd like that. Adam has mentioned him."

Mary stands up. "Uncle Brian and I will be back in a couple of minutes," she hollers down to the kids. "You behave yourselves while we're gone."

The kids nod, and return their attention to the sand pile where they're building a castle.

We walk through the house, out the front door, and down the stairs to the street. From there we walk to 123 East Twenty-First Street.

"I hope he's home," she says as she knocks.

A maid answers the door and ushers us through the foyer to a drawing room.

Cyrus enters a moment later. "Hello, Mary," he says, shaking her hand.

He tickles the baby. "And hello there, Michael."

The baby giggles and smiles.

"This is my brother, Brian," Mary says, "who I've been telling you about."

"Hello," Cyrus says as we shake hands. "I'm glad to finally meet you. Have a seat."

We sit down on a sofa across from him.

"I understand you work for Western Union with Adam," he says.

"I do. I've heard a lot about your plan to lay a telegraph line across the Atlantic Ocean between Newfoundland and Ireland. Connecting the continents will be a huge accomplishment."

He nods. "It will be. We ran into technical difficulties last month when the cable broke. I'm not giving up, though. We're going to try again next year."

"I wish you luck. I'm responsible for many of our telegraph expansion projects, so I know how difficult they can be. Deploying a line on the ocean floor for over twenty-two hundred miles seems like a daunting task."

"It is. However, we found a plateau two miles beneath the surface of the ocean that runs all the way from Newfoundland to Ireland. We call it the *telegraph plateau*. I believe God must have put it there because he intended for us to connect our continent with Europe. Otherwise, it would be nearly impossible to snake a cable through all the canyons seven miles below the surface."

"Adam told me that you worked for Stewart's Marble Palace dry goods store when you first came to New York."

"I did."

"I worked there too, after we emigrated from Ireland."

Mary smiles. "Brian learned how to pick out nice clothes when he worked there."

Cyrus chuckles. "I learned a lot about business from Mr. Stewart. He's a good man."

"He is indeed."

Mary stands. Michael has fallen asleep on her shoulder.

"We need to get back," she says. "Adam will be home soon, and I need to get dinner started."

"I'll be following the status of your project," I say. "Let us know if we can help. I'm sure Mr. Sibley will want to connect our telegraph to your Atlantic cable once it's in place."

"Yes. I've already spoken with him about that."

We shake hands, and his maid escorts us to the front door.

"I'll take my leave now too," I say to Mary, when we reach the sidewalk.

I hug her and return to Greenwich Village.

Teresa walks home with me after we attend church together the next morning. "I always enjoy coming to your cute little place," she says, when we enter my townhouse.

We unlace our boots and leave them by the front door.

"It would be a good place to start a family," she says. "There are only two things missing."

"What's that?"

"You need a larger bed... and you need a wife."

I laugh. "So, the bed's too small, huh?"

She nods. "I'm sure you'd be more comfortable in a larger bed with how tall you are."

Her gaze becomes serious. "What about marriage, or are you still waiting for that English girl—Elizabeth—that you talk about sometimes?"

"Not really," I say. "How about you? When are *you* going to get married?"

She chortles. "You may not believe this, but I used to get lots of proposals when I was working as a courtesan."

"I *bet* you did."

She pulls me into my bed and gets on top of me, straddling me with her legs. She then leans forward and kisses me tenderly.

Electricity shoots through my body.

"I guess I just haven't met the guy I want to spend the rest of my life with," she says.

I chuckle. "Is that so?"

She giggles as she pulls my shirt off over my head. "Going to church always gets me in the mood," she says. "Perhaps it's the bottled up passion I feel from the priests that rubs off on me."

We laugh.

She glides her finger down my forehead and over my nose to my lips. "You might just be the man I pick if you play your cards right."

"I'm pretty good at poker... so you better watch out."

She traces the scar on my shoulder with her fingertip. "Does this hurt?"

"Not anymore. I was lucky. The bullet exited without hitting the bone. A half-inch lower, and I probably wouldn't be able to play my violin."

27. ELIZABETH BUTLER

Richmond, Virginia. September 11, 1857.

OUR VOYAGE ACROSS the Atlantic was uneventful. I ate my meals with Jacob, and spent the evenings alone in my room. He continued to pressure me to "consummate our marriage," as he calls it, ignoring my protests whenever I reminded him of our agreement.

We disembarked from the Atlantic steamer at the harbor in Norfolk, Virginia, yesterday, stayed in separate hotel rooms last night, and boarded a steam-powered ferry this morning. It took a few hours for the ferry to wind its way up the James River to the port at Richmond.

"I need to conduct some business in Shockoe Bottom," Jacob says, as we come ashore. "We'll stay here tonight, and take the train home tomorrow."

"What are you going to do?" I say.

"I need to send a telegram to Harland telling him I've arrived with my new wife. I don't want him to be surprised when he sees you tomorrow."

He stops and stares at me. "Then I'm going to buy some slaves at an auction house. We may as well while we're here. This is the largest slave market in America, other than New Orleans. We'll need more slaves to clear the land I'm going to purchase with your dowry."

My naiveté has blinded me. I hadn't thought to ask Jacob if he owned slaves... and he hadn't mentioned it.

"How many slaves do you own?" I say.

"Sixty-eight that are able to work, which means they're five years old or older. A few four-year-olds will join their parents in the fields next year."

My God! Five years old? That's despicable!

I'll keep my opinions to myself for now. I want to see how the process works before I do anything.

Jacob hires a Negro porter to carry our luggage as we leave the harbor.

"May I join you at the slave auction?" I say.

Jacob's thick eyebrows rise. "Sure, if you don't get in the way."

He pays for two rooms at the St. Charles Hotel, and the porter carries our luggage into our rooms. The porter frowns when Jacob gives him a measly tip.

We freshen up, and then we walk to a nearby hardware store, where Jacob buys a wooden board with a handgrip attached to a triangular slab of leather.

"What's that?" I say.

"It's a flogger—to keep our slaves in line."

He also purchases five sets of leg irons, and a chain to connect them. "Can you hold my purchases until tomorrow morning?" Jacob asks the proprietor.

"Certainly," the man says. "There's a slave auction underway at Lumpkin's Jail on Fifteenth Street this afternoon."

Jacob nods. "Thanks. I'll see what they have."

We walk up Fifteenth Street until we see a sign that says *Lumpkin's Jail*. There's a red flag hanging in front of the building on a pole.

"The red flag means he's having an auction," Jacob says. "I like buying slaves here. He has a jail we can keep them in overnight. We'll then pick them up in the morning, before we go to the train station."

Ten men stare at me when we enter the building. Their attention quickly returns to the fast-talking auctioneer.

There's a family of Negroes standing on two-foot-high wooden boxes—a married couple and their four teenage children, two boys and two girls. All of them are nearly naked, wearing rags that look like diapers over their genitals. The women are topless.

The auctioneer is attempting to sell the entire family. The bidders have offered three hundred dollars apiece so far.

"I only need the men," Jacob says to the auctioneer.

"Is this the same for everyone?" the auctioneer says to the crowd. "No one needs an entire family?"

Everyone nods.

"I'll bid on the three women," one of the customers says.

"All right," the auctioneer says. "We'll try this again. Just the three men this time."

"You can't split up the family," I say to Jacob.

He scowls. "Don't tell me how to run my business!"

Chuckles erupt from the men around us.

The auctioneer starts the bidding at three hundred dollars apiece. The price rises quickly to five hundred. Jacob outlasts a rival, and settles on a price of five hundred and fifty for each slave.

The scene is disturbing. I recall Frederick Douglass talking about the degradation he felt when his owner sold him like an animal. I can see the same kind of pain on their faces.

I'm not sure what I can do to help, so I say nothing.

"I'll pick them up in the morning," Jacob says.

The father says something in an African language to the women as the jailers push him and his sons into a crowded jail cell. The mother responds with an anxious wail.

A farmer from North Carolina purchases the three females for four hundred dollars apiece. He says, "I'll pick them up tomorrow," and the jailers push the women into the same cell as the men.

"I need two more men," Jacob says to the auctioneer.

The jailers retrieve two teenage brothers from the back of the jail cell, and steer them up onto the boxes. Jacob has to bid six hundred apiece to buy them.

"They're stronger than the others," he says when he finishes, "so they're worth more."

We then return to our hotel.

A Negro porter follows us with our luggage to the Farmers Bank of Virginia early the next morning. I wait with the porter out front while Jacob goes inside. We then walk to the hardware store to pick up the flogger and chains Jacob purchased yesterday, and continue to Lumpkin's Jail.

Jacob pulls a large satchel out of his pocket and pays for the five slaves with twenty-dollar gold coins. He hands the jailers the leg irons, and they shackle the slaves above the ankles.

The farmer from North Carolina arrives as we're about to leave. The family, realizing they're about to be split apart, starts chattering in their African language. The women are crying.

Jacob pushes the first of his five slaves toward the door. The three men from the same family resist.

"Stand back," a jailer yells.

We move away.

The jailer thrashes each of the defiant men once with his bullwhip. The iron tip bites hard into their skin, raising bloody welts on their backs.

"Thanks," Jacob says.

Jacob points his flogger at the exit, and the slaves stagger out the door. They learn quickly that they have to walk in a coordinated shuffle so they don't trip on the chain. Jacob strikes the slaves with his flogger when they don't respond promptly to his instructions.

The porter follows our entourage to the train station.

Jacob purchases seven tickets for Gordonsville at the Virginia Central Railroad terminal. He then directs the slaves to their seats and pays the porter.

I sit down across from Jacob in my own seat. I feel embarrassed and angry with myself for my naiveté. How could I marry such a cruel man? I ask myself.

The air is dripping with humidity. We're sweating profusely, even with the windows open. The slaves, wearing nothing but loincloths, look more comfortable than we do.

The seventy-six-mile trip to Gordonsville takes three hours. Jacob directs the slaves into a field after we leave the train. He points at the slaves' genitals as he urinates, implying that they should do the same.

They follow his orders.

One of the teenagers pulls down his loincloth, squats, and defecates. He wipes himself with a handful of grass when he's finished.

Jacob points his flogger to direct them down the street to the Orange and Alexandria Railroad terminal. He buys tickets for Warrenton, and then we stand on the railway platform, waiting for the train.

There are two wooden buckets filled with water next to the ticket office: one labeled *WHITE,* and the other labeled *BLACK.* Jacob picks up the *BLACK* bucket and hands it to one of the slaves.

The slave takes a drink with a ladle tied to the handle of the bucket, and passes it to the next man, while Jacob and I drink from the *WHITE* bucket. The BLACK bucket is empty by the time they've all had their fill.

The train arrives, we board, and soon we're on our way. The sixty-mile journey to Jacob's farm takes two and a half hours.

A muscular, sixty-year-old Negro is waiting on a ramp next to a barn when the train stops.

"This is William, my driver," Jacob says.

"How do you do?" I say, extending my hand.

Confusion fills William's eyes. He looks at Jacob without shaking my hand, so I pull it back.

"What's a driver?" I say to Jacob.

"He manages the other slaves, to make sure they get their work done. William is married to Emma, the head maid."

Jacob hands William the keys for the shackles. "Take these men to the empty cabin."

"Yes, sir, Mr. Jacob," William says. He motions for the slaves to follow him, and they shuffle toward a row of sixteen log cabins.

A light-skinned twenty-five-year-old Negro with dark red hair picks up our luggage.

"This is Johnny Red," Jacob says.

"Howdy, ma'am," he says.

Johnny and I follow Jacob to a white, two-story mansion. It has a covered wraparound porch supported by Roman-style columns, with a swing hanging from chains at one end. The mansion sits at the north end of hundreds of acres of rolling fields filled with brown-and-white cattle.

"This is quite beautiful," I say, as I stop to survey the land.

"I'm glad you're pleased," Jacob says.

We enter the house, and Jacob introduces me to Harland, his twenty-year-old son. The boy stares at me without smiling as he shakes my hand.

Three female Negroes standing next to each other greet Jacob with curtsies.

"This is Elizabeth," he says to them, "my new wife."

They curtsy for me as well.

"Emma is the head maid," he says, pointing at the oldest woman.

She looks to be in her late fifties.

She steps forward and says, "Pleased to meet you, Miss Elizabeth."

I reach for her hand and say, "Pleased to meet you too."

"Follow me," Jacob says.

I follow him up a long circular staircase to a second-floor bedroom. The maids and Johnny Red are behind me.

"This will be your room until you're ready to join me in our marital bed," Jacob says.

He turns to the maids. "Please make up a bath for Elizabeth."

"Yes, sir," they say in unison.

They scurry down the hallway to a bathroom, grab several buckets, and walk down the stairs—I presume to fetch water from a well.

I unpack my suitcase and place my clothes in a drawer.

It's charming here. My room is nice, and my window faces hundreds of acres of rolling green hills.

"Your bath is ready, Miss Elizabeth," Emma says a moment later.

"Thank you, Emma."

I close and lock the bathroom door. The water in the three-foot-tall wooden bathtub is cold, but it feels good after basting in humidity all day.

I return to my bedroom after dinner, and fall asleep instantly.

The crack of a bullwhip followed by a scream awakens me at dawn. I jump out of bed and look out my window.

Jacob is flogging the father of the family he separated in Richmond yesterday. The man is naked, with his arms stretched out, tied to posts with ropes. Harland is standing next to Jacob.

Jacob's bullwhip has a metal tip at the end. Each savage blow provokes horrifying howls from the man as the whip cuts deep into his flesh.

I have to stop this!

I dress quickly, hustle down the stairs, and run out the front door.

The slave is slumped over now, hanging by his wrists. The lacerations covering his back and buttocks have turned his skin into a bleeding mash of dark red pulp. Blood is streaming down his legs to the dirt. The slaves in the fields are holding their farm tools, watching with horrified stares.

"Why are you doing this?" I yell.

Jacob pauses. "He ran away. Harland caught him and brought him back. He needs to learn the rules."

"Do you have to be so cruel?"

Jacob raises the bullwhip and slashes the man's back, ignoring me.

I run to the slave and yell, "Stop!"

The whip cracks hard across my cheek.

"Damn you!" I scream.

I fall to my knees. The gash on my left cheek stings terribly. Blood is flowing down my neck to my dress.

Harland grabs his father's arm. "That's enough, Dad!" he yells.

Jacob glares at me. He coils his whip, attaches it to his belt, and walks into the house.

"Are you all right?" Harland says as he lifts me to my feet.

I point at the beaten slave. "You better tend to him first."

Emma rushes out of the house with a wet washcloth and places it on my cheek. "Hold this there, Miss Elizabeth," she says. "It'll stop the bleeding."

I point at the slave, who has passed out. "Can you do something to help him?"

"Yes, Miss Elizabeth." She bounds up the steps to the house.

"Untie him," I say to Harland.

Harland loosens the slave's arm shackles, and the man slumps to the ground. Johnny Red and William run from the field and help Harland lay the man on his stomach.

Emma returns with a bucket of water, washcloths, and a sheet. She cleans the wounds with a washcloth while Johnny Red cuts the sheet into long strips of cloth. William lifts the man into a seated position and holds him while Johnny and Emma wrap the cloth bandages around his torso to cover his lesions. Their proficiency indicates that they've done this before.

The man is semiconscious when they finish. William and Johnny Red pick the man up beneath his armpits, and they shuffle to the cabins.

I'm still holding the washcloth to my cheek. The pain is really taking hold now. The slaves in the field follow me with curious stares, as I walk into the house.

Jacob is sitting on the sofa. I ignore him and run upstairs to the bathroom. Emma is behind me. Blood flows from my wound when I pull the washcloth away.

"It's a deep cut," I say to Emma.

"Yes, it is, Miss Elizabeth. You'll probably get a scar."

She pulls a pair of scissors from a drawer and cuts a long strip of cloth from a towel. She then wraps the bandage tight around my head across my nose, to cover the wound on my cheek.

"That should stop the bleeding, Miss Elizabeth," she says. "Keeping the bandage tight over the wound should make the scar smaller."

"Thank you, Emma."

I walk down the stairs to the parlor to confront Jacob. I'm furious. "How can you treat your slaves that way? The poor man probably won't be able to walk for a week."

"Sit down," Jacob yells. He rises from the sofa. "I'll be right back!"

I obey.

Jacob goes into his office next to the parlor and returns with three sheets of paper.

"You need to memorize these rules," he says, as he hands the papers to me, "and stay out of my way next time!"

He stomps out of the house slamming the screen door behind him.

Each page has the words *Virginia Revised Codes* at the top, above a list of rules:

1. If a master kills a slave when he is correcting them, the master shall be free of all punishment, as if such accident never happened.

2. If more than seven slaves are on a road without a white person—twenty lashes apiece.

3. For visiting a plantation without a written pass—ten lashes.

4. For unhitching a boat—thirty-nine lashes for the first offense, and one ear cut off his head for the second offense.

5. For keeping or carrying a club—thirty-nine lashes.

6. For having any article for sale without a ticket from his master—ten lashes.

7. For traveling on a road that is not the most usual road when going any place—forty lashes.

8. For traveling at night without a pass—forty lashes.

9. For being found in another person's Negro quarters—forty lashes.

10. For hunting with dogs in the woods—thirty lashes.

11. For riding a horse without the written permission of his master—twenty-five lashes.

12. For riding a horse without leave, a slave may be whipped, branded in the cheek with the letter *R*, or otherwise punished as decided by their master.

13. A slave visiting his brethren without permission shall be dragged to a post, the branding iron heated, and the name of his master or

the letter *R* branded into his cheek or on his forehead.

14. There is no penalty for killing a runaway slave refusing to surrender.

The papers go on to list an additional seventy-one crimes for which a master can punish a slave in the state of Virginia.

The maids are staring at me from the kitchen when I look up. They seem anxious.

I rise and look out the window at Jacob. He's continuing his temper tantrum, yelling at the slaves in the fields.

I'll make you pay for this, you bastard, I promise myself.

We eat in silence during dinner.

"When can we go to Washington to buy my piano?" I say, when we finish. "I need to practice several hours a day to keep my skills up."

"We can't go until next Monday. The Bank of England should have transferred the gold to the Riggs Bank in Washington by then."

I'm standing on the ramp ready to board the train when it stops next to the barn on Monday. Jacob's slaves, who've been milking cows since before dawn, load nearly one hundred, ten-gallon milk cans from the barn onto the train.

Jacob brings four slaves with us to haul the piano. One of them is Johnny Red.

The gash on my face has scabbed over, so I removed the bandage yesterday.

The train stops at several dairy farms along the way to pick up their produce, so it takes five hours to reach Alexandria.

"We'll have to take a different train to the long bridge that crosses the Potomac River to Washington," Jacob says.

The eight-mile journey on the next train is quick. We then board a coach, cross the long bridge into Washington, and proceed to the Riggs Bank on Pennsylvania Avenue, which is located across the street from the president's house.

I wait in the coach with the slaves while Jacob goes into the bank.

What should I do if they try to escape? I ask myself.

I'll just let them go.

Jacob returns a few minutes later. He grins as he sits down. "The gold arrived from London, just as your father promised," he says.

"I'm glad you're pleased."

We proceed east toward a music store near the Washington Mall. I count more than fifty men standing on high scaffolding as we pass the Capitol building.

"They're building a new iron dome for the Capitol," Jacob says.

"I'm sure it will look impressive when they finish," I say.

Jacob takes his slaves into the music store with us so he can keep an eye on them.

"I'd like to try some of your pianos," I say to the owner.

"Certainly," he says.

I sit down in front of a piano, and perform a Chopin nocturne.

"Where'd you learn to play so well?" the owner says, when I finish.

I tell him about my performances in Europe, and mention that I studied with Chopin. "I'm looking for some concert venues," I say, "if you know of any."

He nods. "I manage the concert schedule for the president and the legislature. We'd love to have you play a piano recital."

"That would be wonderful."

"Give me your address so we can correspond, and I'll send you some performance dates."

I turn to Jacob. "Can you write down our mailing address in Warrenton?"

"Sure," he says.

He jots it down on a sheet of paper, and hands it to the owner.

I memorized the address as he wrote. Now I'll have a return address when I write to Brian.

"What happened to your face?" the owner says.

I stare at Jacob. "I had an accident."

The owner nods. "Try this upright piano. We just received it from the Steinway factory in New York. The sound is marvelous."

I play the piano for several minutes. "It sounds great," I say. "How much does it cost?"

"Three hundred dollars."

Jacob pulls out his money satchel and pays for the piano with twenty-dollar gold coins.

The owner packs it in a wooden crate to make it easier to transport. "I'll contact you soon with some concert dates," he says, as we leave.

Jacob hires the owner of a horse-drawn wagon to carry the piano, and the slaves load it into the back of the wagon. The owner of the wagon follows us in our rented carriage as we ride through Washington and cross the long bridge to the train station terminal.

The slaves load the piano onto the train, and we proceed to Alexandria. From there, they move it off the train, load it onto another wagon we hire, and the driver hauls it behind our carriage through the streets to the Orange and Alexandria terminal. The slaves then load the piano onto the train that goes to Warrenton.

"The politicians don't allow the trains to connect in the same terminal, because they want to make it difficult for people to travel," Jacob says facetiously. "The riverboat captains, coach owners, and hotel owners have a lot of clout in the legislature. They're trying to protect their monopolies. The delay caused by having to walk across town to another terminal to change trains forces many people to stay in hotels overnight."

"That sounds like a ploy to make money," I say.

Jacob scowls. "That's exactly what it is. They use the excuse that trains shouldn't connect using the same tracks to avoid accidents."

It's past midnight when we arrive back at the farm in Warrenton. William holds a lantern for the slaves as they haul the piano across the field, up the steps, and into the parlor.

I change into my nightclothes in my bedroom, pull the curtains aside, and stare at the new moon. *Do you still think about me, my love? Can you feel me closer to you now?*

There's a knock on my door.

Jacob is standing in his nightshirt when I open it. "Are you pleased with the piano?" he says.

I smell whiskey on his breath. "I am."

He enters my room and closes the door.

"It's time to act like my wife now," he says.

He tries to steer me by my arm to the bed. I resist, free myself from his grip, and slap his face.

He slugs me in the chest, knocking me into the wall. My cheek starts to bleed again.

"I want the rest of my dowry," I yell.

"You're not getting another dime until you consummate our marriage!"

There's a knock on my door and Harland enters.

"What *do you* want?" Jacob yells.

"It's time for you to leave," Harland replies.

Jacob glares at Harland as he walks out of my room.

Harland walks over to me. "Are you all right?" he says.

"Thank you for helping me."

"I'm sorry this happened to you. Dad gets angry when he drinks. He used to beat Ma and me too, until I became strong enough to fight back."

Harland leaves my room. I walk to the bathroom, light an oil lamp, and cover my bleeding cheek with a strip of cloth. Will you still love me with my scar? I say silently to Brian, as I look at the mirror.

I return to my bedroom and lock the door.

A purple bruise between my breasts stares back at me from the mirror the next morning. The maids stare at me sympathetically during breakfast. I sense their fear. I imagine they've experienced Jacob's wrath too.

I mail another letter to Brian in the afternoon, telling him I hope to play some concerts in Washington soon. I don't tell him about Jacob's abuse. It's too embarrassing.

Please write to me, I say to myself, as I place the envelope in the mailbox. I'm here for you now.

28. BRIAN O'ROURKE

Bedford, Pennsylvania. August 16, 1858.

THE CONCIERGE AT the Bedford Springs Hotel ushers me into the dining room. "The president said he'd be here in a few minutes," he says.

"Thanks for showing me the way," I say, as I hand him a tip.

I shake hands with several executives from other telegraph companies I know, and sit down with them around a long table. There's a telegraph operator sitting in front of a keypad near the window, where a telegraph wire comes in from outside. He's capturing a message—the first transatlantic telegram sent from England to America.

We traveled to the Bedford Springs Hotel today because this is President Buchanan's summer residence. Mr. Field, Mary's neighbor, invited me here to witness this historic event. He isn't attending, though. He's with his team that laid the telegraph cable across the ocean floor.

"It's taken a long time to get to this point," one of the executives says.

"Yes it has," another executive replies. "The cable broke apart several times, before Mr. Field was finally able to connect the telegraph station on Valentia Island in Ireland with the Heart's Content station in Newfoundland."

We all nod. We've heard the story before. Newspapers on both sides of the Atlantic have provided extensive coverage of the calamities surrounding Mr. Field's attempts to connect America with Europe the past two years.

President Buchanan enters the room and we all stand. He stops near me, I introduce myself to him, and then he sits down at the head of the table near the telegraph operator. The audible dots and dashes continue to flow from the telegraph keypad.

"The message is still coming in," an executive says. "I'm not sure why the transmission speed is so slow. The telegraph operator in England sitting with Queen Victoria keeps repeating the same words. Perhaps he's experiencing trouble on the line."

Most of us in the telegraph industry know Morse code, so we're translating the message in our heads as we listen to the keypad. I've been listening for fifteen minutes, and I've only heard four words.

"The telegraph is very slow," the president says with irritation. "I can't see how this device is really useful. People tell me I should install a telegraph in the White House, but it seems like a waste of time when it's this slow."

"There must be problems on the line," the telegraph operator says. "It took several hours for the first part of the message to get here."

The president stands up. "Tell me when the entire message is here. I have other business to attend to."

We stand as he walks towards the door.

He stops and turns at the doorway. "I hope you have a chance to sample the healthy spring water at the hotel. It's supposed to cure all kinds of ailments."

"We will," one of the executives says. "We're all staying here tonight."

"Good. I'll talk with you later." The president walks out of the room.

"The signal strength of the transatlantic cable has been deteriorating during our tests the past ten days," the telegraph operator says. "This makes some words garbled, which requires them to be re-sent."

"That's unfortunate," I say. "Still, the idea that we can send messages at lightning speed between continents is quite an achievement."

Everyone nods.

We decide to stroll around the resort's lush gardens while we wait. I find out while we chat that most of the executives from the six major telegraph companies began their careers like me—keying messages as telegraph operators.

The operator receives the rest of the message from England late in the evening. We're having dinner with the president in a private dining room when we hear the news.

President Buchanan's curmudgeonly skepticism toward the telegraph seems to soften a bit after the operator reads the entire message from Queen Victoria.

The president hands the operator a note scribbled on a sheet of paper. "Transmit this to her." He clears his throat. "I'll check back with you in the morning to see if it's there yet."

"Will you be installing a telegraph in the White House, now that you've seen what it can do?" an executive asks the president.

"No. It's too slow, and it's still not clear to me how it's useful."

The president stands up, and we rise to show our respect.

"I bid you gentlemen good night," he says as he leaves the room.

I board a train in the morning and arrive in Washington that afternoon. A carriage transports me to the Willard Hotel on Fourteenth Street, and I check in to my room.

The *Washington Union* newspaper confirms what I read in the *New-York Daily Tribune* last week. A woman originally from Ireland named Elizabeth Butler will be giving a piano recital at the Smithsonian on Friday evening. The article says the young woman studied with Chopin in Paris before she moved to Virginia.

I'm ambivalent about attending, even after coming all the way here to see her. She's sent me four letters, but I haven't answered any of them.

She should know that it's inappropriate for a single man to have correspondence with a married woman, I remind myself. However, I'm still curious to see her.

It's been almost ten years since I left Ireland. Will she recognize me? Will she look the same? She'll probably be there with her husband. How will that feel?

I arrive at the Washington Mall early on Friday evening. I remain hidden on the other side of the promenade across from the Smithsonian Castle so I can observe the concert attendees.

A man in his mid-fifties escorts Elizabeth when she steps out of a carriage. She's beautiful in her long white dress—even from a hundred feet away. She disappears into a side door with her husband.

I've walked halfway back to my hotel when I stop. You may as well listen to her play, I tell myself. You're already here.

The concert has already begun when I return to the Smithsonian Castle, so I listen from the lobby. She's playing a piece by Chopin. The audience applauds enthusiastically when she finishes. I walk into the room behind the other late attendees, and sit down in the back row.

She begins a Beethoven piece, the *Appassionata*. She plays softly at first, teasing the melancholy melody from the piano. Her fingers then start flying across the piano keys releasing a flurry of notes, exposing Beethoven's passionate countermelody. Exhausted, she returns to the restful repose of the gentle first theme, and then the passionate refrain erupts again. The piece continues like this, juxtaposing delicate longing with turbulent exhortations of joy.

My heart pounds beneath my chest as I listen, watching her, needing her more with each passing note. I'm mesmerized, transported through space and time back to Innisfree, surrounded by the lake shrouded in fog. I close my eyes and imagine her rowing through the mist to me. She holds me, embracing me in her arms, and the piece ends.

The audience rises to their feet, giving her a standing ovation.

Should I stand up or stay seated? I'm taller than most people are. She may see me.

I stand up when the applause continues.

She's bowing to the audience. Her smile is enchanting.

I see a scar on her left cheek. That wasn't there before. I'm sure we've both earned scars, I contemplate,—physical as well as emotional—in the years that have vanished since we last saw each other.

Her face freezes when she straightens. Confusion flutters across her eyelids as she takes another bow. She looks straight at me when she rises.

The audience sits down, and so do I.

She seems hesitant as she fidgets on her piano bench. She folds her hands and turns to the audience. "I'm going to play a piece that isn't on the program," she says, "called 'Träumerei,' by Robert Schumann."

Hearing her voice is a joyful shock. How long have I waited to hear that sweet melody in my ears? *Ten years!*

Her playing brings tears to my eyes. I've performed the piece hundreds of times with Adam, always thinking of her. I can't stand it... but I force myself to stay in my seat.

The audience applauds when she finishes.

She stands and takes a bow. I'm not sure if she's seen me. She looks right at me again. Then she sits down.

"The next piece," she says, "is Chopin's Prelude, opus 28, number 4 in E Minor. This was the last piece I played for Frédéric when I was studying with him in Paris—a week before he died. He was lying in his bed, too weak to sit up. Many of his friends came by to play music for him that day. He asked me to play this three times, and then he fell asleep. That was the last time I saw him."

Hushed emotion grips the audience.

She begins slowly, quietly, the notes almost imperceptible. We have to strain to hear.

She builds up the volume gradually, increasing the tension, making the tranquil solitude she expressed at the beginning of the piece even more poignant. We're entranced, spellbound. I feel her passionate yearnings and desires, raw and exposed, hanging thick in the air.

She's had so many interesting experiences since I saw her, so many adventures, performing as a concert pianist across Europe. Do we have anything in common anymore?

I can't stand it. My longing for her overwhelms me.

I rise and leave, quietly, shutting the door carefully so it doesn't disturb the audience.

I board the train for New York the next morning.

"You did the right thing," Mary says, when I stop by her house that evening to tell her what happened. "You can't set your heart on a married woman. That would only bring you pain."

"I had to leave. She was with her husband. He's much older than her."

I pour myself into my work the next several months to drown my melancholy. I also spend more time with Teresa, seeing her three times a week.

Mr. Sibley gives me a new role as a business account manager, encouraging me to develop new ways to use the telegraph. My subsequent sales of "on premise" telegraphs to publishers, shipping companies, the New York Stock and Exchange Board, hotels, and manufacturers, multiplies the number of telegrams sent on our network— as well as our profits.

My new role keeps me in New York, which finally allows me to pursue my dream of playing violin with a symphony orchestra. I practice diligently before my audition with the Philharmonic Society of New York. Carl Bergmann, the conductor, assigns me to the first violin section after I play for him.

Playing in an orchestra is definitely a "rainbow for the ears," as Brother Bernard described it so many years ago. Our performances at

Niblo's Garden and the Academy of Music on East Fourteenth Street are well attended and appreciated.

New York City. February 27, 1860.

I'D NEVER HEARD of the politician from Illinois until Adam invited me to attend the lecture at the Cooper Institute. I'm glad I went. Abraham Lincoln's clever words and passionate oratory captivated everyone in the audience.

"I'll walk with you to your house before I return home," Adam says, as we leave the building. "I want to discuss Lincoln's speech."

"Yes, indeed," I say.

"The man spoke eloquently about the federal government's power to regulate the spread of slavery when new states join the Union. His convincing evidence, using the subsequent actions of the original authors of the Constitution as examples, forcefully refutes the claims of politicians such as Stephen Douglas. The Federal Congress never gave state governments the sovereign authority to decide the slavery question themselves. I love the way Lincoln supports his arguments with sound legal reasoning."

"He's certainly a charismatic orator," I say. "I haven't read the Constitution, but what he said certainly makes sense to me."

"I think he's the Republican Party's best chance to get a moderate elected next fall. His proclamation that we should 'have faith that right makes might,' encouraging us to do the right thing, will stick with me forever."

"Me too. However, I'm disappointed he didn't declare slavery to be the evil scourge that it is. It's hard to know where he stands on the issue."

Adam nods. "That wasn't clear to me, either. Perhaps he's focusing on the legal issues surrounding federalism versus states' rights, so the slave states don't portray him as an abolitionist. That's a smart political move."

We stop at Broadway and wait for the traffic to pass. The street is always busy now, even late at night, as New York City's boundaries rapidly expand to the north. We spot an opening, run across quickly, and continue west on Tenth Street.

"I spoke with Horace Greeley," I say, "the owner of the *New-York Tribune,* while we were waiting to meet Lincoln. He said he's going to publish the entire speech in his newspaper."

"That should give Lincoln some great exposure."

"Did you hear Lincoln talk about his tour of the new House of Industry orphanage in Five Points yesterday?"

"I did. It made quite an impression on him. His empathy for the poor and support for public institutions such as orphanages indicates he genuinely cares about people. Most of the politicians I've seen are just trying to line their pockets with gold."

I chuckle. "The politicians in America seem just as corrupt as the absentee landlords in the British Parliament that confiscated our land in Ireland."

We wait at the corner for several coaches pulled by horses to pass. We then run across Fifth Avenue as fast as we can to avoid being run over.

Adam chuckles when we reach the other side. "I guess some aspects of human nature never change. The corrupt Tammany Hall politicians that run New York—most of whom are Irish Catholics—learned their lessons well from their British overlords. Most of the jobs in the city administration as well as the police force are handed out by Tammany's Democratic political machine. Sounds similar to what the Protestants were doing in Ireland."

"You know, I hadn't thought of it that way until you pointed it out, probably because a lot of my Irish friends have benefitted from Tammany's benevolence. Of course, their assistance comes with a price. They're required to vote for Tammany's candidates in every election."

"I heard that the Dead Rabbits gang went to graveyards throughout the city, gathering names for the Democrat voting rolls before the last election. Tammany then sent their people back to the polls several times using the names of the deceased each time they voted."

"Yeah, I heard that too. I guess that's one way to win an election. Hey, before I forget—can you pass along a message to Mary for me?"

"Sure."

"Tell her that my Underground Railroad colleagues in Georgia found Gracie Jefferson. We transported Gracie and her family to Chicago last week."

"That's wonderful news. I'm sure Mary will be pleased."

Rochester, New York. June 17, 1860.

HIRAM SIBLEY, the president of Western Union, sent me a telegram yesterday saying he needed to see me. I arrived by train in Rochester this afternoon, and took a carriage to our headquarters building.

Mr. Sibley's secretary ushers me into his office and closes the door. I shake hands with Sibley, and we sit down.

"Did you hear that Congress passed the Pacific Telegraph Act yesterday?" Sibley says.

"Yes. I read that in the newspaper. That's good news."

"Yes, it is, especially since we won the contract. That's why I called you in here today."

I nod, waiting for him to explain.

"First of all," he says, "I'd like to thank you for all the new business you've generated in your role as an account manager. You've opened up several new markets for us. I wanted to thank you personally for your help before I give you your next assignment."

Hmm. I like what I'm doing. Why do I need a new assignment?

"Thanks," I say. "I enjoy coming up with new ways to use the telegraph."

"You'll need to put that job on hold, when I send you to California."

California? That's on the other side of the country. Why do I need to go there?

I *have* fantasized about exploring the west, though. The photographs of snow-covered mountains and desert landscapes I've seen look magical.

"When would you like me to go?"

"I need you there by December first. You'll be working with Jeptha Wade. He needs someone to handle contracts and manage construction teams as we build the transcontinental line from California to Salt Lake City. The first thing we need to do, though, is consolidate the various telegraph companies operating in California. We don't want to attach our transcontinental line to a bunch of companies using different technologies."

"That's a good idea. It was inefficient when we had multiple technologies before."

"You'll be working with Jeptha to merge companies such as the Pacific Atlantic Telegraph Company with the California State Telegraph Company. Bring your stock certificate printing kit. You'll need that when we create the Overland Telegraph Company."

"What should we define the capitalization to be?"

"Jeptha will negotiate that with the California companies. I'm guessing it will be somewhere north of a million dollars. We'll take shares too, of course, for organizing everything. My long-term goal is to fold the California companies into Western Union."

"Indeed. Once we control the lines, we can set our rates low enough to generate lots of business, while still being quite profitable."

"Exactly," Sibley says. "Where'd you learn to be such an astute businessman?"

"I watched the way Vanderbilt drove his competitors out of the market to create his shipping and railroad monopolies. The British Parliament did the same thing to us in Ireland. They controlled the land, the roads, the military, and the cost of labor—which was essentially nothing, after their tenant farmers paid their wages back to the landowners as rent. That allowed them to set prices wherever they wanted. Their ownership rights also allowed them to export products grown on Irish soil to England, even when millions of people were starving to death."

Sibley nods. "That was a terrible tragedy."

He turns and points at a map of the western United States on his wall. "Jeptha should have the companies consolidated by the end of the first quarter next year. You'll work with folks from the California Telegraph Company while he's doing that, negotiating contracts to purchase supplies, hiring workmen, and arranging transportation to the worksites."

He stands up. "Your team will build the line from here in Carson

City." He traces a route on the map with his finger. "To Salt Lake City."

He turns and smiles. "Although the government is funding most of the cost, we'll be joint owners with the California Telegraph Company when we finish."

"That's a shrewd way to increase the value of our stock."

"It certainly is." He points at Nebraska on the map. "We'll have another team building the line west from Omaha across the Rocky Mountains to Salt Lake City."

"How long does it take to get to California from here?"

He sits back down. "The quickest way is by steamer from New York to Panama. From there, you'll cross the isthmus to the Pacific by train, and take another steamship to San Francisco. The entire trip takes about twenty-five days. There's a stagecoach—the Butterfield line—that runs from St. Louis to San Francisco in twenty-five days, but then you'd have to add on the time it takes to get to St. Louis. You'll be much more comfortable traveling first class on a steamer than you'd be on a rickety stagecoach with outlaws and Indians to contend with."

"I think I'll take the steamer."

"Go to the Wells Fargo office on Montgomery Street when you get to San Francisco. They'll convert the deposit notes we receive from the government into the funds for your contract disbursements. Wells Fargo will be our bank out west."

We continue our discussions for the rest of the afternoon. I have dinner with Sibley that evening, and return to New York by train the next day.

As usual, I sit with Teresa at church on Sunday. I accompany her to her house afterward. I love her delicious Italian cuisine, and she loves to cook, so we've made this a ritual on Sunday afternoons. I tell her about my pending trip to California as we walk. "I won't be leaving on the steamer until early November, which will get me there by December first. I may be gone for a year—perhaps longer."

"I have a cousin who lives in San Francisco," she says. "She's written to me several times, trying to convince me to move there. She says the men treat courtesans like queens because there aren't enough women, and they have lots of money from the gold they find in the mines. Some men even use gold nuggets to pay for their pleasure."

I chuckle. "That's a use for gold nuggets I hadn't considered."

We enter her kitchen when we reach her house on Mercer Street—a brothel she now owns. We wash our hands, and then she puts me to work chopping garlic, mushrooms, tomatoes, and green peppers for the pasta sauce she's preparing.

"So, what are you going to do," she says, "now that you found out that Elizabeth is married?"

"I don't know. I had my heart set on her for so long; I'm not sure what I'll do."

She sidles up behind me and massages my back.

"How about taking a bath with me before we make the pasta?" she says. "We never did finish what I started in Miss Weyman's bathroom years ago."

"I still remember that. I was only sixteen. How old were you then?"

"Twenty." She grins. "Your sister wasn't pleased with me for trying to seduce you."

I set the knife on the counter and turn to face her. She pulls me close, rises on her tiptoes, and kisses me.

A jolt surges through my spine to my belly.

She takes my hand and guides me through her bedroom to her private bathroom. She giggles as she starts to undress me. "Don't worry. I'll be gentle with you."

29. ELIZABETH BUTLER

Warrenton, Virginia. July 3, 1860.

THE SWING ON the front porch gives me no respite from the oppressive heat. I was hoping the temperature would drop after sundown, but it hasn't so far.

Jacob walks out of the house and sits down on the railing next to the swing. He loads his tobacco pipe.

I ignore him, hoping he'll go away.

Maybe he wants to talk about the concert I played at the Warren Green Hotel in Warrenton this afternoon. Most of his friends' wives were there. Perhaps he heard how appreciative they were. I even acquired five new students from parents wanting piano lessons for their children. That means I'll have fourteen students every week now.

I enjoy teaching, and earning my own money makes me feel good, especially since Jacob never gives me any. At least he can't rob me of my musical talents the way he stole my dowry.

Teaching piano at my students' homes also gets me out of the house. That allows me to meet with Reverend Brooks, my contact in the Underground Railroad.

The full moon looks huge as it climbs above the trees on the eastern horizon.

Jacob takes a deep draw from his pipe and releases a cloud of smoke toward me. I hold my nose until the pungent odor floats away. He knows I hate the smell of tobacco. That's why he torments me with it. He wants a reaction—even if it's to start a fight.

I'm not going to play his game. It'll just end in tears.

"As you may recall," he says, "I invited the Warrenton Rifles to our Fourth of July celebration tomorrow. Their wives and kids will be here too. Johnny Red and William will butcher two cows tomorrow morning so we'll have enough meat for everyone."

"Why do you call your friends the Warrenton Rifles?"

"John Marr formed the Warrenton Rifles after John Brown's raid on Harpers Ferry last year. We're lucky to have him. He taught at the Virginia Military Institute before he came back to Warrenton to be a commissioner. Our militia protects the citizens of Fauquier County from abolitionist raids. We also track down escaped slaves."

"Why do we need protection? There haven't been any abolitionist raids *here*."

"We need to be ready to defend ourselves if they come."

Be careful, I tell myself. Who knows where Jacob's violent temper might lead if he finds out I'm helping slaves escape.

"How many men are in the Warrenton Rifles?" I say.

"About ninety to hundred—it depends on the day."

"So, how many people are coming tomorrow?"

Jacob takes a deep draw from his pipe and releases the smoke toward the moon. It hovers there like a cloud, barely moving in the humid air.

"There could be close to four hundred since they're bringing their families," he says. "Some of my men will bring tables and chairs in the morning."

"What do you and Harland do when you go out riding with the Warrenton Rifles?"

"We mostly patrol the roads, looking for people smuggling slaves. They call themselves the Underground Railroad. We know they use homes here in Fauquier County as hiding places."

"How do you know that?"

He chuckles. "We have spies in their organization. However, they're pretty good at keeping things compartmentalized, so it's difficult to get the whole story."

"What do you do when you find a slave trying to escape?"

Jacob inhales a lungful of smoke and releases it.

"Several of our men are bounty hunters. They take 'em back to their masters and collect a reward if the slave surrenders peacefully." He chuckles. "We shoot 'em if they try to run away."

I need to tell Reverend Brooks his organization has spies. Perhaps he already knows. Maybe that's why he insists that we all work alone.

"Is that why I hear gunshots at night?" I say.

"That could be."

"I saw a dead Negro lying next to the road when I went into Warrenton last week. Was he one of your targets?"

"Probably. We spotted six of 'em coming out of Mrs. Morrell's house on Ball's Mill Road last week. Harland and some of my men took five of 'em back to their master in Charlottesville. We tracked the other one up here. He wouldn't stop runnin', so we had to shoot him."

The chirps of the crickets grow louder as I swing, magnifying the silence between us.

"What happened to Mrs. Morrell?" I say.

"Some of our men went back to her house the next day and burned it down. We needed to send a strong warning to others that might want to steal our property."

"By property, you mean slaves, right?"

"That's right, woman," he replies angrily. "You should know that by now. You sure are ignorant for someone that's supposed to be smart."

There it is again. His anger... always boiling... just below the surface.

"I don't think we'll have enough tables and chairs to seat everyone," I say, "even if we take the chairs out of the slave quarters."

"People can sit on the grass. We'll use the tables for the food and drinks."

"Are you going to let your slaves eat too?"

His forehead crinkles with confusion, as if he hadn't considered it.

He didn't drink much whiskey tonight, so perhaps he'll be reasonable.

"It's their country too, isn't it," I say, "now that they're here?"

"They can eat the leftovers after everyone leaves," he concedes.

"That's considerate of you, Jacob. Thank you. I'm sure they'll appreciate it."

He nods and takes another draw from his pipe.

This is the most amicable interchange we've had in quite a while, so I'll keep going.

"I was talking with Millie Carpenter after church last week," I say. "She's teaching their slaves how to read and write and do arithmetic. She says that slaves with schooling fetch higher prices than slaves that are illiterate."

I'll let his thick brain digest this for a moment. I know he needs to be in control—that the decision will have to be his and not mine. My real motive is to help Jacob's slaves survive after they escape. Reverend Brooks says that slaves often get lost when they can't read, which makes them vulnerable to capture by slave hunters.

"You could do that too," I say, "if you want your slaves to be worth more when you sell them. I'll teach them if you'd like. We could set up some desks and blackboards in the barn you aren't using."

"My slaves are here to work," he replies.

"That's true, but there are times when they're idle, especially in the winter months after the harvest. I could teach the children now, and the adults can come when they aren't busy. There are other advantages to teaching them some useful skills."

He expels a lungful of smoke. "What's that?"

"They're less likely to run away if they think you care about them."

The moon rises higher in the sky as he contemplates my proposal.

He knocks the ashes out of his pipe and puts it in his pocket. "I'll tell Harland to buy some tables and chairs and blackboards in town. Will that make you happy?"

"It will. Thank you, Jacob."

I squeeze his wrist, and quickly recoil my hand. This is the first time I've initiated physical contact with him. I forgot how queasy he makes me feel.

I don't want to bring up my next issue, but I feel I need to press my case. "When are you going to give me the rest of my dowry?"

He glares at me. "Goddamn it, women, I already told you—it's *my money*! I have no obligation to give it to you, especially since you won't share my bed."

"But you promised you'd give me the money when we arrived."

"That was when I thought I'd have a real wife! Don't bring this up again."

He stomps across the deck and slams the screen door behind him as he enters the house.

My tears come quickly, the only company I have in my desperate isolation. I have no real friends here. Although the women I've met are kind and well mannered, most of them take slavery for granted. They talk about Negroes as if God put them on the earth to serve white men, as if they're no better than horses, or a team of oxen pulling a plow.

Jacob's stinginess—forcing me to beg for money to purchase even the simplest necessities—is infuriating. The only clothes I have are what I brought with me from England.

He's a wealthy man. Women in Warrenton that invite me to their homes for tea say that Jacob is one of the wealthiest men in Fauquier County, and they assure me that our county is the wealthiest in the entire South. They seem to know about these kinds of things, so I believe them.

The women are always curious about me. I know they wonder why I married Jacob. His deceased wife told them that Jacob was quite a tyrant during their thirty-five years together.

Of course, I tell them nothing about the dowry, or our reneged bargain—a bargain that has left me destitute and alone on an eleven-hundred-acre farm. I let my tears run down my cheeks as I stare at the moon.

Was that you, Brian O'Rourke, at the concert in Washington last year, or were my eyes deceiving me? I'm certain you would have spoken with me after the concert if you were there. I waited thirty minutes for you to come, until Jacob was about ready to hit me.

Why won't you answer my letters?

A cloud sneaks in front of the moon as a bull bellows to a cow in the fields.

I would take a train to New York in an instant if I had any money. I need to keep my concert and teaching earnings hidden from now on. Jacob's been using my money to buy groceries.

Don't you love me anymore, Brian? You said you'd wait for me—no matter how long it takes. So why haven't you tried to find me!?

I dry my cheeks, stand up, and saunter through the house and up the stairs to my bedroom. As always, I double lock my bedroom door before I retire. Jacob hasn't tried to break in since Harland installed a solid door and two locks to protect me from his father.

30. BRIAN O'ROURKE

New York City. November 3, 1860.

I KNOCK ON Mary's door, and she invites me in to her Gramercy Park home. I hug the three younger children, and shake David's hand. He's eleven years old now, so he prefers handshakes to hugs.

"I'm giving you these Hanukkah-Christmas gifts early," I say, as I pass out presents, "since I'll miss your holiday celebration this year."

Her kids tear off the wrapping paper as I sit down next to Mary on the sofa.

"Don't forget to say 'thank you' to your Uncle Brian," Mary says.

The children thank me, and start playing with their toys on the floor.

David sits down in an armchair next to us and opens the book I gave him: *Aesop's Fables.*

I hand her my house key. "I've cleaned it thoroughly," I say. "I'm not sure how long I'll be gone. It could be a year or longer, so it's probably better to rent it out month-to-month. I appreciate you doing this for me."

"Sure." Mary stows my key in her leather satchel.

"Could you also open my mail and handle any bills that come up? I'll reimburse you when I get back."

"Of course."

"Teresa Orsini will be coming with me to California."

Mary frowns. "Why? You're not going to marry her, are you?"

I expected a question like that. Mary tolerates Teresa, but she doesn't trust her.

"No. She'll be visiting her cousin in San Francisco. She wants to check out the city to see if she wants to live there permanently."

"Is she keeping her brothel here?"

"No. She sold it for eight thousand dollars."

"That's a lot of money. Real estate prices just keep rising, don't they? Adam's father said the land we purchased across the street from

Central Park has doubled in value since we bought it. Some investors want to buy it from us now."

"What do you think we should do?"

"Mr. Rubin thinks we should lease the land rather than sell it, and I agree. It's bound to grow even more valuable over time."

"That's fine with me. Besides, I may move up there someday. I enjoy playing baseball in the park, and there's always a game on the weekends."

I hand Mary a note with my San Francisco address. "You can write to me here at the Occidental Hotel on Montgomery Street. Remember though, that even with the Pony Express running from Missouri to Sacramento, it still takes three weeks for a letter to get there."

"I'll remember. Tell me about your voyage."

"The first leg will take us by steamer to Aspinwall, a city founded by Americans on the east coast of Panama. That will take between eight and ten days, depending on the weather. From there we'll board the Panama Railroad, and ride forty-eight miles across the isthmus to Balboa on the Pacific coast. The steamer from Balboa to San Francisco will take another twelve days."

"It sounds like you're going to have quite an adventure."

"Indeed."

I hug Mary and each of her children when I say my goodbyes, and then I take a carriage to the North American Steamship Company, where I purchase two first-class cabin tickets. Teresa and I will occupy cabins next to each other.

"I'll tell anyone that asks that I'm your assistant," Teresa says, as we ride to the harbor the next morning. "That way I won't get harassed for being a single woman. I still have nightmares about my voyage from Italy to America. The sleazy sailors demanded sex from me in exchange for food after my parents died."

"That must have been awful."

"It was."

We arrive at the harbor and give our tickets to the captain. He lets us board, and a porter escorts us to our rooms with our luggage.

"Our first-class accommodations are dramatically better than the steerage hold of the *Dromahair*," I say to Teresa during dinner.

"I imagine so. The food is excellent. Thanks for taking me with you."

"You're welcome, my dear. I'm glad you came."

We pass the Bahamas six days into our trip. The next day we see Cuba. We see Jamaica the day after that. The islands, surrounded by aqua-blue water, look beautiful from a distance.

We arrive in Panama two days later. I've never seen anything like the jungles here when we ride across the country in a train. Gigantic vine-covered trees and mosquito-infested marshes border the tracks all the way to the Pacific.

Our steamer from Balboa docks at the harbor in Acapulco, Mexico, to pick up more fuel during our fifth day on the Pacific. The city, built around a majestic, horseshoe-shaped bay, has thick forests that flow gracefully down to its sandy beaches.

Everyone stands at the railing when our steamer resumes its voyage. We're enthralled as we watch several young men diving into the ocean from hundred-foot cliffs north of the city.

We arrive in San Francisco on November 29, disembark, and take a coach to the Occidental Hotel. Teresa and I check in to the same room. We've been sleeping with each other every night anyhow, so it seems natural at this point.

"One of my colleagues, a man named Jeptha Wade, will be meeting me in the lobby on December first," I say to Teresa, "so we can explore the city tomorrow on our own."

"I'm exhausted," she says. "Let's just get some sleep tonight." She smiles as she reaches for my hand. "That is, after we break in the bed."

"Indeed."

She chuckles as she stares at the oval-shaped bathtub. "Give me half an hour and I'll be ready. In fact, why don't you join me? It's large enough for both of us."

"That sounds like a great idea."

We rise early the next morning, eat breakfast, and leave the hotel. Thick fog fills the streets. I feel as if I'm walking in a dream. The fog dissipates a few minutes later, and the bay appears beyond the harbor.

"This is really beautiful," Teresa says.

"It certainly is. I can see why people want to live here."

We go to bed right after dinner. We're exhausted after walking up and down the hilly streets exploring the city all day.

Jeptha Wade is waiting for us in the hotel lobby the next morning. "It's good to see you again, Brian," he says, shaking my hand.

"This is Teresa," I say. "She traveled from New York with me."

He grasps the fingers of her outstretched hand. "You are a beacon of loveliness, my dear."

She grins. "Thanks for the compliment."

The maître d' at the hotel restaurant ushers us to a table, and we sit down.

"I'm meeting my cousin later this morning," Teresa says. "She wants me to move in with her. I'll decide whether I want to stay here permanently by the time you're ready to leave in the spring."

"We'll probably be here until May," Jeptha says. "I figure it'll take us that long to consolidate the California telegraph companies and procure supplies. We have a lot of work to do, and the weather is fickle in the mountains east of here early in the spring."

"Teresa and I hiked up and down the streets of San Francisco yesterday," I say. "The wooden shanties and saloons crowding the boardwalks reminded us of Five Points in New York. One difference here, though, is that people have money. I can't believe the prices in the stores."

"The gold rush in the Sacramento Valley has driven everything up," he says. "I'll need you to manage our finances carefully to make sure we have enough funds to complete the project."

"I will, sir."

He nods. "Where'd you learn to speak like that? Were you in the military?"

"Sort of. I was in the Ribbonmen in Ireland before my sister and I immigrated to America." I chuckle. "We were a motley crew of clandestine guerrilla fighters brought together by mutual desperation. Courage was our only resource. We only had one handgun... with no bullets."

"I see. I imagine that's where you learned how to manage money so well. Hunger is the best teacher when it comes to learning how to stretch a dollar."

His wisdom makes me smile. "Indeed. Starvation is a cruel but effective taskmaster."

I watch Teresa as she makes small talk with Jeptha. As always, she looks beautiful.

What would Ma and Da think of her, I ask myself? They'd probably like her... except for her occupation.

Elizabeth's image drifts into my mind. I remember how beautiful she looked as she rowed me across the lake to Innisfree beneath the moonlight.

Jeptha turns to me. "Did you notice that huge semaphore that looks like a windmill on the hill yesterday?" he says.

"I did. It looks like pictures I've seen of the visual telegraph in France. What's it used for?"

"The locals call that *telegraph hill*. Financiers, merchants, and speculators use the visual telegraph to describe what kind of cargo is on its way to the harbor. Commodity prices drop precipitously throughout the city when new shipments arrive."

I chuckle. "That's what the speculators in New York and Chicago do. Acquiring information quicker than a competitor gives traders a huge advantage. I sold lots of telegraph services to stock and commodity speculators this past year."

"I hear they're some of our biggest customers now."

"Indeed. So is the Associated Press. They use our telegraph to send stories to newspapers all across the country."

We adjourn to the hotel lobby after breakfast.

"I'll accompany Teresa to her cousin's house," I say, "and then I'll meet you here at noon."

Jeptha nods. "I hope you brought your violin. There are a lot of places for you to play if you want to sit in with musicians sometime."

"I did bring it. I always look forward to playing when I can."

I walk Teresa to the boarding house, and she introduces me to her cousin, Adriana Orsini. Adriana then gives us a tour. There's an owner's residence, and several rented rooms where Adriana lives on the first floor, below a six-room brothel on the second floor.

"Are you going to be comfortable here?" I say to Teresa.

"I'll be fine," she says. "I need to assess the business environment to see if I want to buy a brothel. This seems like a good place to start."

"I'm going to be busy the rest of the week. Shall I come by to see you on Saturday evening?"

"That would be lovely. Thank you, Brian, for taking me to

California. Our time together has been marvelous."

"It has indeed."

We hug each other for a long moment and kiss before I depart.

Jeptha introduces me to James Gamble when I return. The three of us then sit down on two sofas in the hotel lobby.

"James deployed the first telegraph lines for the California State Telegraph Company," Jeptha says.

"That was in 1853," James says. "There weren't any hotels along our route in those days. We had to sleep on the dirt at night as we made our way south to San Jose." He chuckles. "The natives we hired to help us, who'd learned about Christianity from the Spanish, thought our telegraph poles were built like crosses to keep the devil away."

The three of us exchange stories about our adventures stringing telegraph wire in the untamed wilderness. We then outline a project plan for our upcoming expedition, and order dinner in the hotel's restaurant.

"You should grab your fiddle," Jeptha says, when we finish, "and I'll show you around town."

I retrieve my violin case from my room, swing the strap around my shoulder, and we walk outside. It's a cool, pleasant evening. Most of the saloons, gambling halls, brothels, and opium dens have their windows open. We walk north several blocks and turn right onto Pacific Street from Montgomery.

"There's lots of music here," I say, as we pass a block filled with saloons.

"We'll need to be careful on this street," James says. "There are pickpockets and thieves everywhere. I brought my friend just in case."

We stop beneath a gas lamp. He opens his overcoat and displays a pistol in a shoulder holster.

"I have a friend too," I say.

I pull my dagger from its sheath inside my coat.

"May I see that?" Jeptha says.

"Sure." I hand it to him.

"It looks like it could do some damage."

He hands it to James, who studies it and hands it back to me.

"I brought it with me from Ireland," I say, as I point at the handle. "The design is my O'Rourke family crest. It's a good weapon. I've defended myself with it a few times."

"Have you ever killed anyone?" James says.

"Only in self-defense."

I stow it back inside my coat, and we continue our stroll down the crowded boardwalk.

"The lower section of Pacific Street near the docks here is especially dangerous at night," James says. "A lot of Chinese sailors jump ship to work in the gold mines after they arrive. That leaves the captain without a crew for his return voyage. Many captains go to bars to lure drunks back to their ship when they're ready to leave. Some of them even put opium in the drunks' drinks, or force them back to their ship at gunpoint. When the drunks wake up, the ship is already on the water, so they either have to work, or walk the plank and die. They call these kidnappings 'getting shanghaied,' because many of these ships are going to Shanghai."

"Thanks for telling me," I say. "I'll be careful. This is a pretty wild place, isn't it?"

"Yes, it is."

Jeptha enters the Old Ship Saloon, and we follow him inside. A scantily dressed female entertainer is leading the audience singing a popular song. The piano player next to her is dressed in a suit with a bow tie.

"Did you see that singer?" I say, as we push our way through the crowd. "Wow."

"Yeah," James says. "Her dress doesn't leave much to the imagination."

"I wonder if they'd let me play my fiddle."

"I was hoping you'd say that," Jeptha says. "I told the owner about you. He said you could sit in with them if you'd like. I know how much you enjoy playing, so I thought I'd surprise you."

"Thanks. This should be fun. Let me know when you're ready to leave." I chuckle. "I don't want someone to shanghai me on the way back to our hotel tonight."

I thread my way to the piano while James and Jeptha step up to the bar. I remove my violin from its case and immediately start playing their current song. The singer and piano player nod their appreciation.

I see immigrants from every corner of the earth as I look around. The next song is an Irish jig, which entices several drunken Irishman to sing and dance sloppily with each other on the dance floor.

We play an assortment of popular songs for the next three hours. I'm exhausted by the time we return to our hotel.

I work closely with James and Jeptha over the next six months, developing plans and signing contracts with suppliers. We also meet with telegraph company executives throughout the state, as we consolidate their companies one by one into the California State Telegraph Company. We're ready to begin our Overland Telegraph project by the middle of April.

"One of my associates," Jeptha says, "a man named James Street, left for Salt Lake last week. He'll hire the Mormons to procure enough poles to string three hundred miles of wire across Utah. He'll then manage the team that will install telegraph line westward as we work our way east. James plans to meet with several Indian tribes along our route. He's bringing them clothing, medicine, and food to gain their goodwill. I hope that persuades them not to attack us."

Teresa and I have been spending most of our free time together. She invited me to her boarding house tonight for dinner. I'm leaving for Sacramento tomorrow with James Gamble to begin our project.

She's preparing ravioli in the communal kitchen when I arrive. We hug each other, and then I wash my hands and start chopping vegetables for a salad.

"Our telegraph project may take six months," I say as I work. "I'm going to miss you."

"I'll miss you too. What will you do after that?"

"I'm not sure. I'll probably head east from Salt Lake City back to New York."

"I can go with you if you'd like," she says. "I enjoyed our trips to San Diego and Los Angeles. The weather was very pleasant there— much warmer than New York in the winter."

"It was nice having you with me, but I think it's better if you stay here. The terrain and weather will be challenging, and you'd be the only woman. I'll be working from dawn to dusk, and sleeping in a tent every night. It's not going to be a vacation."

She starts chopping spinach to put in the ravioli.

"The owner of this boarding house has offered to sell it to me," she says. "There are six courtesans here, plus the rental rooms, so I'd have a pretty good income."

I don't respond, mostly because I'm contemplating the details of my upcoming trip.

She finishes shaping the ravioli and faces me. "What do you think I should do?"

"What do you want to do?"

Her eyebrows arch—the way they get when she's angry. She puts her hands on her hips. "Do we have a future together?"

We've never talked about the future much, mostly because I avoid the subject.

"I'm not sure if I should wait for you, or move on," she goes on to say. "I'm thirty-two years old, and I want to have children someday. The window for making babies in my womb won't stay open forever."

I continue to chop vegetables without responding. My mind strays to Elizabeth, as it always does when I think about marriage—even though she's unavailable.

I can't share this with Teresa. I don't want to hurt her.

Her hand slides down my back and settles on my butt. "You won't have to use sexual continence to restrain yourself if we get married. That would be nice, wouldn't it?"

"I'm not sure what I'll do after we finish the transcontinental telegraph. I know I want to return to New York, though. I miss Mary and Adam, and their kids."

Teresa grabs my wrist so I'll stop chopping. I put down the knife and face her.

She crosses her arms. "So, the idea of marrying me hasn't occurred to you, huh?"

I pull her curvaceous body into mine.

She pushes my chest with her hands and backs away. "Are you still hung up on Elizabeth? Is that it?"

I watch her with an aloof stare. I don't want to admit it, but she's right. Neither the passage of time nor an occasional glass of whiskey has helped me wash Elizabeth out of my mind.

I know my silence infuriates Teresa. She already thinks that I "run away from my emotions." She's said that several times when we've had heated conversations.

Her face darkens with anger. She takes my hand and places it on her breast. "Can you feel this?" she says derisively. "Do you know what this is?"

A jolt surges through me. "Really nice," I say, trying to humor her.

She smirks as she moves my hand down to her crotch. "And this? I'm a real flesh-and-blood woman, Brian, someone that's here for you, not some fantasy from your past. I love you."

She starts pacing around the kitchen.

"I love you too, Teresa," I say, "I just don't think I'm ready."

"We're good together," she says. "We both work hard, we're passionate in the bedroom, and we're both Catholics. Doesn't that mean anything to you?"

She stops and glares at me. "You don't love me. Otherwise, you'd marry me."

Why don't you want to marry her? I ask myself. We know each other well. We practically grew up together these past thirteen years... but I've always envisioned myself raising a family with Elizabeth—the impossible dream... *the fantasy*, as Teresa calls it.

I take her hand, look into her olive-green eyes, and approach her lips for a kiss.

She pulls away and crosses her arms.

"I sense your sister's animosity toward me," she says. She starts to pace again. "That's why I wanted to get away from New York with you. I didn't just come out here to have an adventure. I was hoping we'd start a new life together."

I nod, watching her carefully as she walks back and forth.

She stops. "So, you can't see yourself marrying a former whore," she says indignantly. "Is that it?"

Maybe she's right. I know she had to sell herself to survive after her parents died. I shouldn't judge her for that.

"No, that's not the reason," I say.

"Are you sure? You know I've always been faithful to you."

I feel a surge of anger in my gut. "Have you?"

She doesn't blink. "Yes. Of course I have."

I didn't want to get into this before, since I don't think it's true, or if it is, I wasn't sure I wanted to know, but now that she's brought it up, I want to know the truth.

"Remember that New York stock speculator that rented a room here last month while I was in Sacramento?" I say. "Jonathan Edwards. He was waiting to take a steamer to Panama."

She folds her arms across her chest as her eyes go wide. "No, I don't remember him."

"Well, he remembers you. He told James Gamble that he paid you fifty dollars to sleep with him."

She looks down at the floor, avoiding my eyes. The air is suddenly thick, as if an impenetrable wall has risen up between us, tarnished by the stain of her deceit.

She unties her apron and throws it on the countertop.

"I'd like you to leave," she says, pointing at the hallway. "I'm sure I can find a man who will appreciate me. I have a good dowry, and I get propositions all the time."

My anger starts to boil as I think about her deceit. *She's trying to change the subject!*

She marches to the hallway. "Get out," she yells, pointing at the front door. "Now!"

"Fine!" I stagger out of the kitchen and down the hall.

I hear her crying as I exit to the street. I start walking fast to calm myself. What just happened?

The quarter moon is taunting me as I walk, peering in and out from behind the clouds. Inevitably, the moon makes me think about Elizabeth. *Will you haunt me for the rest of my life?*

I walk north and climb the trail to the top of Telegraph Hill. Fog rolling in from the ocean is cloaking the streets below me in a gray luminescent cloud.

I turn in a circle to survey my surroundings. The black silhouettes of Goat Island to the east and Alcatraz to the north look foreboding. Masts from several tall schooners jut out above the fog at the Vallejo and Mission Street wharves. The spire from St. Francis Church on Vallejo Street looks lonely—the church where Teresa and I attended mass every Sunday.

I walk down the hill and continue south to Market Street. I keep a firm grip on the handle of my dagger as I walk. The hoodlums lurking around the wharves are preoccupied with drink tonight, so they don't confront me as I pass.

I find myself outside Teresa's boarding house a few minutes later.

I'm ambivalent, unsure what to do. Should I go inside and tell her I'm sorry?

The moon is barely visible, a translucent yellow orb glowing behind the fog.

She deserves a committed partner, doesn't she? Why can't I give her that? Am I just destined to be alone? I can't trust her anyway. I know that now. Mary was right.

Would marriage make any difference? Would she be trustworthy then?

My anger urges me back to my hotel. I finish packing, and fall into a restless sleep.

Three taps... enter my dream, as I'm flying above the fog, soaring like an eagle over the city.

Three taps again.

I jerk upright, light a candle, and open my door.

Teresa scoots into my room without saying anything, and I close the door behind her.

She stares into my eyes as she drops her black dress to the floor. She pushes me back to the bed, gets on top of me, and our wanton lust consumes us—fierce, angry, passionate intimacy—without words.

Satiated, she kisses me tenderly, slides onto the bed, and presses her back against my chest. I wrap my arm around her, and we watch the candle burn down, the flame flickering, as the last quarter inch melts away.

"I'm sorry," she says. Her voice is soft, almost inaudible. "I'm sorry I lied to you. How long have you known?"

"Gamble told me when I returned from Sacramento."

"Why didn't you bring this up before?"

"I didn't believe him. I trusted you... so I just assumed it couldn't be true."

We stare at the candle for several minutes. The melting wax finally snuffs out the flame, and the room goes dark.

"I was angry at you," she says. "I'm jealous about your feelings toward Elizabeth. I want you to feel that way about me. That wasn't a good way to act, though..."

"Do you still love her?" she says after a moment.

I hesitate. "I do. It's hard to explain. I know it sounds crazy, especially since she's married, but we promised ourselves to each other. Our clans—my O'Rourke clan and her O'Reilly clan—have intermarried for centuries back in Ireland."

Teresa turns and faces me in the dark. Her fingertip circles my chest.

"You should go to her if you love her," she says. Her hand glides slowly down my stomach to my crotch. "I'd hate to lose you, but I want you to be happy."

I feel her heart beating when she hugs me. "I can't guarantee I'll be here if you change your mind," she says, as she sobs into my neck. "I want children, and I don't want to wait any longer."

"I understand."

Her warm tears trickle down my shoulder.

"I'm going to miss you," I say.

"I'm going to miss you too."

She's gone when the sun creeps through my curtains in the morning.

James Gamble is drinking coffee when I meet him in the hotel restaurant for breakfast. We eat a quick meal, check out of the hotel, and take a carriage to a warehouse near the Pacific Street wharf.

We hire two men with a coach there, and they help us move several oversized wooden boxes from the warehouse to the wharf. The boxes contain glass telegraph insulators we received by steamer from New York.

James and I pay the freight costs, and then we purchase cabin passage to Sacramento for fifty cents each. The men we hired load the boxes onto the steamer, and we depart at 4:00 p.m.

Thoughts of Teresa flood my mind as I watch San Francisco recede behind us. I'm angrier about her cheating and dishonesty today, now that I know the truth. It's my own fault. I should have confronted her before last night. Perhaps I wanted to keep my illusions about her alive.

The steamer passes Oakland and enters the mouth of the Sacramento River a few minutes later. James and I don't speak much as we watch the shoreline. I assume the complexity of our arduous project is consuming his mind, as it does mine. Several white pelicans start swimming beside us as we meander through the valley.

I have a restless night trying to sleep in the cabin. We arrive in Sacramento and dock at the base of L Street early the next morning.

We're quite busy the next few weeks, purchasing 26 wagons, 228 oxen, 10 mules, and riding horses for 50 men. One of the men James hires—Silver Hawk—is a Paiute Indian. He also hires three Chinese brothers—Hung, Jian, and Yong Lee.

"Silver Hawk is great with horses," James says, "and the Chinese are excellent telegraph line installers. They sidle up the poles without much difficulty. I've hired them for other projects. Of course, everyone is pleased to make good wages; especially the disgruntled miners who went broke when their mining claims didn't pan out."

May 27, 1861.

I MARVEL AT the diversity of our crew, as our expedition gets under way. In addition to Silver Hawk and several other Indians, and the Chinese brothers, we have several Mexicans, a dozen cowboys—including a Negro freeman originally from Texas—and an assortment of Germans, Irishmen, Scots, Frenchmen, Poles, and Scandinavians.

Progress is slow as our long caravan winds its way through the foothills toward the Sierra Nevada Mountains. The oxen are hard to manage on the narrow, pockmarked roads.

"The Placerville and Humboldt Telegraph Company completed a telegraph line across the mountains to Virginia City last year," James says. "As you know, they've been folded into the California State Telegraph Company now. Unfortunately, the line they constructed isn't reliable, so it's being re-strung."

"Why is that?" I say.

He chuckles. "They hung the telegraph wire on tree limbs instead of poles, so the lines broke and fell to the ground every time there was a heavy snow or a windstorm. Stagecoach drivers also used our wires to repair their wheels."

"That happened out east too," I say, "until we hung the wires high enough to make them difficult to reach."

"My team in Carson City should have the telegraph line deployed as far as Fort Churchill by the time we get there. We'll hire more frontier men and scouts as we head east across the deserts of the Nevada Territory. They know the rivers, canyons, and valleys, which will be important when we need to hunt and fish to augment our food supplies. We'll also need them to help us find trees to cut down for telegraph poles."

An assortment of mishaps plagues our expedition over the next several days. The oxen teams—pulling covered wagons filled with telegraph wire, insulators, tools, lumber, saws, ladders, tents, and provisions—often flounder on the muddy roads. We have to stop to repair several broken wheels, which slows everyone down.

A fierce windstorm one night keeps our tents rattling, making sleep impossible. Everyone is grumpy the next day when the weather is hot, which melts the snow, causing the mountain streams to overflow and wash out sections of the road.

A late spring snowstorm the following day hides the road beneath two feet of snow.

"We need to locate and mark the road so the oxen don't head over a cliff," James says.

Two trappers we hired in Sacramento, Norwegian brothers named Hans and Lars Olsen, pull some thin eight-foot-long flattened sticks with one end turned up from their wagon. They attach the sticks to their boots and secure them with ropes.

"We'll mark the trail," Hans says. "Do you want to go with us?" he asks James and me.

"I'd like to try," I say.

Lars hands me a pair of wooden sticks and helps me secure them to my boots. He then gives me two thin wooden poles. "Use these to keep your balance," he says.

I fall sideways into the snow several times, as I follow behind them. The men in our expedition laugh hysterically every time I fall, until I pass beyond their view.

Hans and Lars stop when we reach the bottom of a shallow ravine.

"Don't worry," Lars says. "You'll get the hang of it soon."

They pull thin strips of sheepskin out of their backpacks, wrap them around the bottom of each of our skis, and secure them with ropes over our boots.

"This will allow us to walk up the hill without falling backward," Lars says.

We trudge up several hills, using our poles for balance.

"I like this," I say, as I keep up with them. "Perhaps I'm better at going uphill."

I'm panting heavily when we reach the summit. The air is much thinner up here. The snow-covered mountains surrounding us look magnificent. There's a huge lake below us in the Tahoe basin.

"This is amazing," I say.

Lars and Hans smile and nod.

"These mountains remind me of Bergen, Norway, where we grew up," Lars says.

The trip back to our convoy is much quicker using the tracks we left in the snow. I'm good at keeping my balance by the time we arrive.

We reach the summit with our expedition the following afternoon.

"This is called the Central Overland Route," James says, as we begin our descent toward Carson City. "It was mapped out by Howard Egan, one of your Irish compatriots. He found this route while searching for a quicker way to drive cattle from Utah to California. This trail is two hundred and eighty miles shorter than the previous route up north along the Humboldt River."

Most of the snow melts during the next several days, making the muddy trails almost impassable, especially for the last wagons in the expedition. We finally arrive in Carson City a week later.

Our journey has given me lots of time to think about Teresa. Maybe she *is* the right person for me... I contemplate. We have a lot in common, and we do love each other. Can I really trust her to be honest with me, though, I keep asking myself?

I send a telegram to her after I check in to our hotel. I tell her that I miss her, and encourage her to write to me using the Salt Lake City telegraph office as my address.

We set our first pole at Fort Churchill, Nevada, on June 24. Working sunup to sundown, setting each pole twenty-five feet apart, we're able to deploy close to eight miles of telegraph line each day.

Our workday begins when we break camp at dawn every morning. After a quick breakfast, we hook the oxen to the wagons and march forward, finding, felling and stripping trees, digging holes, installing poles, crossties, insulators, and wire, until we set up camp again at dusk each evening. We're always exhausted by the time we've fed the horses, the oxen, and our men.

Several Pony Express riders gallop swiftly past us on their horses each day while we work. We're planting our poles along the same route they use to carry mail from St. Joseph, Missouri, to Sacramento. They bring us progress reports each day from Edward Creighton, the construction manager building the telegraph line westward from Omaha. We have a bet going with Creighton to see who finishes their line to Salt Lake City first. Our journey across the mountains took a month instead of the two weeks we'd planned, so we're already way behind schedule.

We're ravenous for news about the war. Lincoln's election last November triggered a rebellion across the South, prompting eleven states to secede from the Union by the end of June.

The war has made our expedition more dangerous, now that the U.S. Army has moved the troops that guarded the Pony Express trail back to the East Coast. Many of our men wear holsters with handguns. The rest of us carry rifles in our saddles to ward off attacks by Indians or criminals.

My thoughts dwell on Elizabeth each evening as I sit around the campfire staring at the moon. News about the war skirmishes in Virginia prods me to worry about her.

It doesn't matter if she's married, I decide. I'll make sure she's all right when I head back to the East Coast. This will give me a good excuse to see her again.

A newspaper left by a Pony Express rider in early July carries a story about New York Mayor Fernando Wood. He's calling for the city to secede from the Union, as he did in January. His suggestion is disturbing—but not surprising.

"The Tammany Hall Democratic machine that ensured Wood's election has always been corrupt," I tell the men, as we talk about politics that night around the campfire. "Thugs under his direction disrupted several abolitionist meetings I attended before I left New York."

"New York's wealthy gentry, especially those in the shipping industry, have always been pro-slavery," James Gamble says. "They make most of their profits shipping goods from our southern ports to

Europe."

"The owners of the garment industry in New York are also pro-slavery," I say. "Not only do they make enormous profits by paying measly wages to the women they employ, they rely on cheap cloth from the South. Many of New York's wealthy elite also finance ship captains that steal slaves. An investment of forty dollars buys a Negro in Africa. The captain then sells the slave for between four and twelve hundred dollars in Charleston, New Orleans, or Richmond. That's a huge return for a three-month investment."

I send a letter addressed to Mary with a Pony Express rider going east the next morning. I ask her to forward my mail to the telegraph office our men are building on Main Street in Salt Lake City. James told me we'd probably be there by the end of October.

31. ELIZABETH BUTLER

Warrenton, Virginia. July 8, 1861.

A BUGLER AWAKENS me when he plays reveille just before dawn. I sit up in my bed and look out my window. The morning twilight is creeping over the horizon.

Twenty tents filled with Confederate soldiers from the Seventeenth Virginia Infantry are astir in our fields. Smoke from their campfires last night is hovering over our cattle beyond their tents.

Jacob and Harland are sitting at the table dressed in their gray Confederate uniforms when I enter the dining room for breakfast. I sit down next to Jacob across from Harland.

Emma says, "Good morning," and pours black tea into a cup for me.

"Good morning," I reply. I add milk and stir the brew to my liking.

"General Longstreet is holding drills this afternoon," Jacob says, "so we'll be breaking camp this morning. I'm not sure how long we'll be gone."

Jacob, at fifty-nine, is older than most of the soldiers. However, his experience during the Mexican-American War in 1848 gave him skills the Confederacy sorely needs. His courage during the Warrenton Rifle skirmishes at the battle of Fairfax Court House and his substantial financial contributions have recently earned him a promotion to captain.

"I'm surprised Virginia seceded from the Union," I say. "Several people I know said they wouldn't have voted for secession, but they were afraid of retribution, so they didn't vote."

Harland frowns. "Farmers have wanted to secede from the Union for years," he says. "However, I agree that the vote didn't seem fair. I heard the reason the May referendum supported secession was because Governor Letcher's henchmen lost the ballot boxes from the northern and eastern counties. Now we have a mess on our hands. The northern counties of Virginia voted to secede from the Confederacy and return to the United States at their convention in Wheeling two weeks ago. That's going to split Virginia in two."

"I can't understand why they'd do that," Jacob says. "Why would they want to support a government that tramples their property rights by abolishing slavery? Half our wealth is based on the value of our slaves."

"I agree," Harland says, "but something was bound to happen when Governor Letcher insisted that everyone's vote be made public. I think his strategy backfired."

"The Yankees have no right to outlaw slavery," Jacob says. "It's insulting, the way they treat us. They say a higher power, what they call a message from God, prevents them from returning our runaway slaves, even though that's the law. They can't steal our property and treat us like sinners just because we own slaves."

"Their stance against popular sovereignty is ridiculous too," Harland says. "They should let each new state that joins the Union decide for themselves if they want slavery."

Jacob shakes his head. "I don't agree. Slavery should be legal in every state. The way things are now, the Yankees make it illegal for us to take our slaves to another state if we decide to move. They have no respect for our property rights."

I don't want to argue, but I can't help offering my opinion.

"Lincoln made a proposal to Congress to compensate slaveholders who release their slaves," I say. "That would have given slave owners a cushion while their states transitioned to a market-based labor economy. That seemed like a generous offer to me, especially since it would have averted a war. Why wasn't that considered?"

"The federal government has no right to tell us what to do," Jacob says.

Jacob hands me his flogger. "It'll be up to you to keep the slaves in line while we're gone. Don't be afraid to use this. They'll sense your weakness and take advantage of you if you don't punish them *immediately* for every infraction."

I lay the flogger next to me on the table. I'll never use it. *In fact, I have other plans for your slaves once you're gone—you bastard.* I smile inwardly about my devious plan.

"We're taking the cattle with us," Jacob says. "We need the meat to feed our troops."

"Are you leaving any for us?" I say. "Your slaves, especially the children, need milk."

He looks at me with a blank stare.

"You need to treat your slaves better if you don't want them to run away," I say.

He sneers. "I'll leave two cows here."

"I also need money to purchase supplies. Our pantry is almost empty."

He places a Virginia-issued ten-dollar Confederate note on the table. "This will have to last you through the rest of summer."

"What happened to my dowry money? I hope you're keeping it stored as gold in the Riggs Bank in Washington. Confederate money will be worthless if the Confederacy loses the war."

He chortles. "We won't lose. Besides, I used the rest of your dowry gold to buy Confederate war bonds. Those bonds will fund the purchase of uniforms and supplies for our troops. I also mortgaged my farm with Mr. Stiles's bank. He told me that England might join the Confederate cause if Lincoln doesn't rescind the blockade of our ports soon. The British textile industry depends on our cotton, so it's only a matter of time before they join us."

I'm startled—and furious. "That's a very risky investment you made with my money. What interest rate are you paying Rothschild's Bank of England for your mortgage?"

Jacob grits his teeth angrily. "That's none of your business."

"The farm will be Harland's one day," I say. "You're putting his legacy at risk by your actions."

Jacob jumps up from the table, knocking his chair back. "That's enough, woman!"

Harland looks at me with a blank stare. He obviously doesn't realize the risk his father is taking with his future.

I keep my composure while Jacob glares at me. My hand reaches for the handle of his flogger. I'll defend myself if I need to.

You'll regret using my money to support the Confederacy, I say silently to myself, when I help your slaves escape on the Underground Railroad.

A train stops next to the cattle barn a few minutes later. Jacob and his troops drive our cattle up the ramp and load them into the railcars. They then load their horses, tents, and supplies, and the train departs.

I don't see Jacob and Harland again until the afternoon of July 19.

"There's a major skirmish coming," Jacob says, as he enters the house.

"How do you know?" I say.

Harland and Jacob exchange glances.

"We have spies in Washington," Jacob says. "One of them, an Irish socialite who's involved with a Yankee senator, passed the information to us. She's part of our Confederate Secret Service."

He smiles. "We have many sympathizers in Congress, as well as the Union army."

"Really?"

"Of course. We can't stay long. We just came by to have a home-cooked meal before we rejoin our troops. How are things going?"

I smile to myself. I'm not going mention that I helped twenty of your slaves escape on the Underground Railroad.

"Everything is fine," I say.

I walk with Jacob and Harland to the porch after dinner.

"Where are you going next?" I say, as they mount their horses.

"East, to Manassas Junction," Jacob says. "The Yankees have a big surprise waiting for them." He flashes a sardonic smile as they turn and gallop away.

Echoes from distant cannons begin early the morning of July 21. I smell the caustic odor of gunpowder smoke from the battlefield twelve miles away when the breeze changes direction.

The air is sweltering hot and dripping with humidity by noon.

"The soldiers in their thick wool uniforms must be sweating terribly," I say to Emma.

"Yes, Miss Elizabeth. I imagine the soldiers are miserable on the battlefield."

Two white-canopied covered wagons appear on the road late in the afternoon. The drivers turn onto the trail that leads to our home and stop in front of our house. A man in his early forties wearing a suit with a bow tie jumps down from the first wagon.

"I'm Dr. Johnson," he says as he approaches me. "Captain Butler told us we could bring our wounded soldiers here."

"That's fine," I say. "I guess that means Jacob is still alive."

"He is."

I follow the doctor to the back of the wagon and look inside. Several men covered with blood are moaning. It's hard to make out how many.

I point at the barn we use as a classroom. "Take the wagons to that barn. We'll get it ready for you."

William runs up to me from the field. "Do you need some help, Miss Elizabeth?"

"Yes, William. We need to move everything out of our classroom to the hay barn to make room for the wounded soldiers."

"Yes, Miss Elizabeth."

I turn to Dr. Johnson as we enter the barn. "We use this as a classroom, so it's cleaner than the dairy barn where we milk our cows."

"That's fine," the doctor says. "I'll operate outside for now since the light is better. We'll move the patients into the barn to recover when we're done."

He turns to William. "Can you bring two of these tables outside? I'll need them when I operate."

"Yes, sir."

We move the chairs, blackboards, books, bookshelves, and supplies out of the barn. Dr. Johnson directs the soldiers driving the wagons to lay the wounded on the ground.

I count nineteen souls. Most are under twenty-five. Some are much younger. Two of the drivers and several of the wounded soldiers are wearing orange shirts.

Dr. Johnson covers the faces of two dead men with blankets.

"Can you bring me some buckets filled with water and some rags?" he says. "I need to clean the blood away to see their wounds."

"Certainly," I say.

I run back to the house, grab a handful of towels from the bathroom, fetch a bucket of water from the well, and return to the doctor. I dunk a washcloth into the bucket and start to clean the leg wound of the patient Dr. Johnson is examining on the table.

A driver wearing orange-and-blue striped pantaloons and an orange shirt picks up a washcloth and assists me. The soldier on the table is barely conscious. His right leg is a shattered mass of bloody pulp below the knee.

"Where are you from?" I say to the driver as we work. "I noticed your Irish accent."

"Our regiment is from New Orleans," he says. "I took a famine ship to America from Waterford in 1847. My name is Michael Nolan."

"It's nice to meet you, Michael. My name is Elizabeth Butler. My last name was Reilly before I got married. I was born in Ireland too, near Sligo."

"Half of our regiment is Irish," Michael says. "The rest are German, Dutch, and English, with a smattering of Creole and native-born Frenchman thrown in for good measure. Most of us worked on the docks in New Orleans before Major Roberdeau Wheat recruited us."

"Why are your uniforms orange?"

"Orange is the color we use to distinguish our battalion, the Louisiana Tigers. We haven't had a chance to get the official Confederate uniforms yet."

Another wagon arrives. Michael and the other drivers move the wounded to the dirt in front of the barn. They cover the faces of two more men with blankets.

Emma and William arrive with several buckets of water and more towels. They kneel down next to Michael and me and start bandaging the minor wounds of the injured.

"I need your help," Dr. Johnson shouts to us.

Michael and I rush to the patient lying on the table.

"Hold him down so he doesn't move," Dr. Johnson orders.

We grab the soldier's arms. Another soldier holds the patient's good leg.

The doctor inserts his finger into the wound.

Blood sprays over us as the soldier screams. It takes all my strength to keep him from jumping off the table.

"I'm probing for broken bones or bullets," the doctor says.

He removes his finger and looks down at the soldier. "I'm sorry, son, but we're going to have to amputate your leg. Your shin bone is shattered."

The doctor grabs a cotton handkerchief out of his medical bag, sprinkles it with liquid from a bottle labeled *Chloroform*, and places it over the soldier's mouth and nose. The patient starts to relax beneath our grip.

"Why are you cutting off his leg?" I say.

"It's the only way to prevent gangrene," Dr. Johnson says.

He pulls another instrument out of his bag. "This is called a *spiral tourniquet*." He wraps a thick rope from the device around the boy's thigh. "It'll stop the blood flow while I operate."

He turns a hand crank that tightens the rope, and the blood stops flowing from the wound.

"Keep the patient still while you hold him down," Dr. Johnson says, as he shoves a rubber clamp into the soldier's mouth. "Don't let him move, or I'll have to start over."

The doctor pulls a scalpel out of his bag. He cuts through the skin above the wound all the way around the leg, leaving a large, U-shaped flap on the thigh.

"We'll use that flap of skin to cover the wound when we're done," he says.

He slices through the muscles and ligaments until he reaches bone, and continues carving around the leg in a circle.

I bend over and puke into the dirt. I stand up quickly and return to hold the soldier down.

Dr. Johnson pulls a bone saw out of his satchel and shoves the jagged edge into the wound. "Here we go," he says.

The patient moans while the doctor saws through his leg.

"Give him more chloroform," the doctor yells to me. "Hold the cloth over his nose and drip a few drops into the rag."

Another soldier takes my place holding the soldier down. I move to the end of the table and follow the doctor's instructions.

"Don't give him too much," the doctor says as he continues to saw, "just a few drops to put him out again. Make sure you don't get any chloroform in his eyes."

The severed limb falls away and lands with a *thump* on the table. Dr. Johnson picks up the amputated leg. He pulls the muscles and ligaments away from the bone inside and shows us the wound.

"A fifty-eight caliber Minie ball makes a nasty wound," he says. "See how it shattered the bone?"

We nod.

The doctor tosses the leg into a bucket beneath the table.

He pulls an instrument with an ivory handle and a hook made of steel from his medical bag. "This is a tenaculum," he says. "We use it to hold blood vessels when we're operating. We need to sew his arteries shut so he doesn't bleed to death."

The doctor probes into the boy's thigh with the instrument, snags an artery, and pulls it out. "Hold this for me," he says.

I hold the instrument as he asked. It takes all my strength to keep the artery from snapping back into the soldier's leg, while the doctor ties off the bleeding artery using a sewing needle and silk thread.

"Good job," he says. He takes the instrument from me, eases the artery back into the soldier's leg, and detaches the hook.

He then pulls an iron file from his satchel. "This is to prevent the jagged edges of the bone from tearing through the skin."

He files the edges of the exposed bone, stretches the skin flap over the wound, sews it with silk thread, and cuts a small hole in the flap with his scalpel.

"The hole will allow puss to drain while it heals," he says.

He wraps the stump with gauze, ties it around the boy's thigh, and removes the tourniquet.

"Move him into the barn," the doctor says to the soldiers around him.

Four soldiers carry the patient away. I spread some hay on the dirt, and the soldiers lay him down.

Dr. Johnson is examining a man lying on the ground with a stomach wound when we return. He opens a bottle labeled *Opium*, raises the man's head, and holds the bottle to the man's lips.

"Drink this," he says.

The man drinks a mouthful, and the doctor lays his head back down.

"Take him into the barn," the doctor says to the soldiers around me.

The soldiers take the man away.

"A gut-shot like he has is always fatal," the doctor says to me. "We're just supposed to make those men comfortable while they bleed out."

I look at the soldiers lying around us. Most of them are moaning. Some are screaming.

"There are a lot of serious injuries here," I say. "Is it always like this after a battle?"

"I don't know," he says. "This is my first time in combat. I worked as a barber in Atlanta until I volunteered to become a surgeon a month ago."

He looks at me with a faraway stare. "The battle was awful. Both sides stood in lines, slaughtering each other with rifles and cannons."

The doctor tells his soldiers to lift another wounded boy onto the table.

"I'd hide behind a tree while I fired my rifle if I was a combatant," he goes on to say, "but that's considered cowardly to the officers."

"That's right," Michael Nolan says. "I want to face my enemy like a man when I die."

Dr. Johnson stares at Michael. "Facing each other standing shoulder to shoulder in lines seems stupid with the kind of weapons we have these days. The bore of a Springfield or Enfield rifle quadruples the accuracy and distance of a bullet compared to a smoothbore. Those bullets can travel up to a thousand yards now."

Michael nods. "I just do what the officers tell me to do."

"Smoothbore rifles were notoriously inaccurate and lacked distance in Napoleon's day," Johnson continues, "yet we're still fighting as if we're at the Battle of Waterloo."

He frowns facetiously. "But I'm not a general, so what do I know?"

"Can you dig a hole to bury the limbs we remove?" the doctor says to William.

"I'll do that right away, sir."

William picks up the bucket with the discarded limb, and walks behind the barn.

The doctor examines the patient on the table. I grab a washcloth, dunk it in the water bucket, and wipe blood and soot off the soldier's face. The soldier, who can't be more than sixteen years old, has a bone jutting out of his wrist above his right hand. One of his feet is a bleeding mash of tissue and cartilage.

"It looks like this one will need an arm *and* a foot removed," Dr. Johnson says.

"No," the boy screams.

I try to comfort the boy by putting a wet washcloth on his forehead.

The boy stares into my eyes. "Don't let them take my hand," he pleads. "I need it to work on the farm."

"It'll be all right," I say, as I wipe his tears away. I'm not sure what else I can tell him.

Dr. Johnson administers chloroform, and the boy slowly fades into semi-consciousness.

William returns with the bucket and sets it next to the table. "I dug a hole behind the barn for the body parts," he says.

"Thank you," the doctor replies. "Can you take over for Elizabeth?"

"Yes, sir." William takes my place.

"I'll call you over here if he needs more chloroform," Dr. Johnson says to me. "Can you get the next patients ready? Give the soldiers who have gut-shots a mouthful of opium, and then ask the drivers to take them into the barn."

"I will," I say.

I kneel down and wash a soldier's leg wound while Emma applies bandages to the lacerations on his face.

The front of my dress is stiff with ochre-brown blood by the time we finish our last surgery. Dr. Johnson is sharpening his bone saw with a file when another wagon filled with injured soldiers arrives just before midnight.

"The barn is already at capacity," I say to Dr. Johnson. "We'll have to take them into the house from now on."

"Light some oil lamps," he barks. "I can't operate in the dark."

"We'll set up an operating table for you in the parlor," I say.

William and Michael bring a table and the rest of the supplies in while I light the oil lamps.

The doctor amputates limbs throughout the night. He's performed forty-one amputations by the time he finishes. Dawn is breaking over the horizon when the drivers carry the last soldier upstairs and lay him on my bedroom floor. My bed already has two soldiers in it.

The chloroform the amputees received during their surgery only deadens their pain for a while. Their agony returns like a ferocious fire when they awaken. The screams emanating from the house and the barn are horrendous now.

I follow Dr. Johnson as he gives opium or laudanum drops to all the patients.

"We're getting low on pain medicine," he says, "so we'll have to ration it from now on."

"I need to take a break," I say to him. "I'll be back in a few minutes."

I cross the fields quickly, enter the woods, and walk down a trail that leads to a large pond. I sit down on a wooden bench and contemplate the placid water. I'd cry if I could, but my emotions are numb. I fall asleep then, but just for a few minutes.

"I don't think I'll ever forget these horrendous screams," I say to Dr. Johnson when I return. "I'm sure I'll have nightmares about it."

"You very well may," he says. "But this war is just getting started. Who knows what kind of horrors are waiting for us?"

The maids help me take care of the soldiers the rest of the day. Most of the soldiers can barely move, so we have to empty their bedpans and wash them after they defecate, hold cups of cool water to their lips, and feed them soup and baked bread by hand. None of the soldiers complains about having a Negro woman take care of them.

Six soldiers died last night and this morning, so we have ten bodies in the makeshift morgue by the afternoon. The morgue is a large tent the drivers set up next to the dairy barn.

Johnny Red approaches me with several male slaves carrying shovels. "Shall we dig graves for the deceased, Miss Elizabeth?" he says.

"That would be very kind of you, Johnny."

I survey the fields. "Let's bury the soldiers on the grassy knoll behind the barn."

He nods. "Yes, ma'am."

"Oh, Johnny," I say as he walks away.

He turns. "Yes, Miss Elizabeth."

"You better dig a couple of more graves. I'm sure we'll have others that won't make it."

"Yes, ma'am."

Several covered wagons arrive at sundown. The drivers move most of the wounded into the back of their wagons, and they head north to the hospital in Warrenton.

"Six of the patients' injuries are too serious for them to be moved right now," Dr. Johnson tells me. "We'll try to transport them tomorrow. Is it all right if I take a nap on your sofa?"

"Certainly," I say.

"Wake me up if a patient needs help. I'm going to stay here until we can move them. Michael Nolan said he'd bring us some more opium or laudanum from Warrenton."

"That's good. There's no more left."

PATRICK F. ROONEY

I realize I've barely slept for thirty-six hours as I stare at the rising moon. My clothes, plastered with dried blood, are stiff enough to stand up on their own now.

Jacob arrives in the middle of the night. He lights an oil lamp after he enters the parlor. I'm lying on the wooden floor half-asleep, my mind reeling with frightful images.

The shrieks of a soldier in the barn are nonstop. No one returned with opium, so his screams are his only refuge.

I sit up, feeling numb, detached, outside of my body.

"I saw Dr. Johnson in the barn," Jacob says. "He told me your assistance was indispensable. I see our home and barns have become a makeshift hospital."

"They have. I assisted him as much as I could, as did William and Emma and the rest of your slaves."

"Thank you. The Confederacy appreciates what you've done."

I nod. "Why is your face covered with soot?"

"That's from the cannon I was firing yesterday. My ears are still ringing from the explosions." He smiles. "But it was a great victory for the Confederacy."

"That's what I heard. All I saw were a lot of dead and mangled bodies, though."

He chuckles. "Yankee spectators rode out from Washington to have picnics while they watched the battle. The Union soldiers ran them over during their retreat. I saw a lot of overturned buggies and screaming women caught up in the milieu."

"Is Harland with you?"

"No. He's with Colonel Stuart tracking down Yankee stragglers and slaves trying to escape. He's making a good income as a slave hunter these days."

"How long do you think the war will last?"

He shrugs his shoulders. "I have no idea. I heard that the Yankees are drafting half a million soldiers. I'm sure we'll do the same, so the fighting is likely to continue for a while."

Dr. Johnson moves the remaining patients to Warrenton the next morning.

Jacob mounts his horse after the doctor leaves. "I'm heading back to the Shenandoah Valley. I'll see you in a couple of weeks."

I write another letter to Brian then, telling him about the battle at Bull Run, and how the Confederates used our barns and home as a hospital. I tell him that I'm scared, and implore him to write back to me.

I know you've received my letters, I say to myself, as I stare at the words. The mail carrier hasn't returned them, so I know they're reaching you. Why won't you write to me?

Could Brian be misinterpreting my situation, I wonder?

I don't want to be crude, but maybe you think I'm sleeping with Jacob, and looking for a relationship with you on the side. Could that be why you aren't writing back to me?

After much contemplation, I add a postscript: Just to be clear, I want you to know that I'm sleeping in a different room than my husband. I'm still a virgin, waiting for you, as I promised I'd do years ago.

I can't get much more explicit than that.

"The Union recently outlawed the exchange of mail between the North and South," I say to Emma, "so I'll have to get someone to smuggle my letter to a Union post office. I've arranged for Reverend Brooks to take Johnny Red and his family up north tonight. Would you mind asking Johnny if he could post this letter for me when he reaches Pennsylvania?"

"Certainly, Miss Elizabeth."

Emma takes my envelope to Johnny's cabin. She returns a few minutes later and says, "He agreed to post it for you. He also asked me to thank you again for arranging his escape."

Jacob goes directly to the slave cabins when he comes home a couple of weeks later. He then stomps up the porch stairs and enters the house.

"I see that I've lost half of my slaves," he yells. "When did they leave?"

"I'm not sure," I say.

"Those slaves are worth a lot of money. I'll tell the slave hunters to look for them."

"How can I pay them if they bring a slave back? I don't have any money."

He stomps away angrily without giving me an answer.

Jacob stays at the house every night—except when he goes out on patrol—until the end of August.

"I have to train another batch of recruits," he tells me one morning. "I'll be gone for several weeks."

There are no signs of the conflict the next few months. More of Jacob's slaves run away the last week of September. Ten adults are still here with their fourteen children. Emma is the only maid that stayed. William is here too.

"Where are we gonna go at our age?" Emma says, when I ask her if she wants to leave. "Running to catch trains and hiding in basements or forests would just be too much for me. Besides, I enjoy listening to your piano. When are you going to play again?"

I look over at my piano, and realize I haven't played in weeks. "I'll play today," I say.

I begin with Schumann's "Träumerei." My fingers find the piano keys and I close my eyes, imagining Brian playing his violin with me in my mind.

I continue to teach the children in the barn every day. Their parents attend too, since there's nothing to do around the farm with most of the cattle gone.

The children love my stories about faraway places like Ireland, England, Germany, and France. Their attention is riveted when I tell them about Frederick Douglass's anti-slavery speech in London.

Emma and William eat with me at the dining room table now, because I insist. Of course, Jacob would never allow this if he was home, but he's not, so I don't care.

32. BRIAN O'ROURKE

Salt Lake City, Utah Territory. October 24, 1861.

THE SUNSETS HAVE been spectacular each evening as we've marched across the arid plains of the Nevada and Utah Territories. The stars also seem brighter in the high-altitude sky.

I play music with Lars Olsen around the campfire on Saturday nights. Lars has an eight-string Hardanger fiddle he brought with him when he emigrated from Norway. John Espinosa, a twenty-year-old Californian from a wealthy farm family in Los Gatos, usually joins us on his Spanish guitar. He sings well too, and he has quite a repertoire of Spanish and Mexican songs. I double his melodies with my violin or add vocal harmonies when I'm comfortable. He's here more for the adventure than for the money. He'll be obligated to take up farming in the family wheat business when he goes back home.

We've overcome many challenges during our expedition. Our Paiute Indian scout, Silver Hawk, has been very helpful when we've run out of timber. He showed us hidden canyons sprinkled with enough trees to make poles for our telegraph lines. He also knew how to find safe drinking water—our most precious resource in the hundred-degree heat.

James Gamble returned to California a few weeks ago, taking the oxen, horses, wagons, and installation crews we no longer needed with him. He'll be in our San Francisco telegraph office when we send our first message across the line later today.

We met our team extending the telegraph line west from Salt Lake City a few days ago. James Street and I then rode east to Salt Lake, testing the line periodically and fixing problems along the way. We arrived in Salt Lake City this morning.

Edward Creighton—the team leader for the Nebraska telegraph team—walks in to the telegraph office on Main Street while we're hooking up the wires to the outside line.

"What took you so long?" he says. "My crew has been here since

October 18."

"We had a few problems along the way," I say. "I guess we lost our bet."

He nods. "The acting governor of the Utah Territory, Frank Fuller, received a message from President Lincoln on Sunday. Lincoln congratulated us for completing the line from Omaha to Salt Lake. I'm sure the president will be pleased to receive a message from San Francisco today. He's taken an active interest in our project."

"That's good to hear. President Buchanan wasn't really interested in the telegraph when I met him a few years ago."

A crowd of curious onlookers is gathering in the street in front of our office. Everyone is excited as we prepare to send our first message to San Francisco.

James Street sends a test message to General Carpentier, the president of our Overland Telegraph Company in San Francisco: *Line just completed. Can you come to office?*

The next message we send to Carpentier is from Brigham Young, the leader of the Mormon Church. He was the governor of the Utah Territory from 1850 to 1858.

Young congratulates Carpentier and our crew. He then suggests that we connect our lines to the Russian empire through northwest Canada so we can converse with Europe.

I laugh after he dictates his message. "That will have to wait for now, sir," I say. "We need to recover from our exhaustion before we begin another project of this magnitude."

"I understand," he says with a smile.

"We do want to thank you for all the help your church gave us. The telegraph poles you provided when we constructed our lines across the Utah Territory saved us weeks of work."

"I'm glad we could be of service."

Carpentier sends a message back to Brigham Young: *That which was so long a hope is now a reality. The transcontinental telegraph is complete. I congratulate you upon this auspicious event. May it prove a perpetual union and friendship between the people of Utah and California.*

Stephen J. Field, the chief justice of the state of California—acting on behalf of the governor—sends a message across our lines to President

Lincoln a few minutes later. In addition to congratulating Lincoln, he promises that California will remain loyal to the Union.

We nod and smile as James Street recites the judge's message. I think everyone realizes the inherent power of lightning-speed communication as we listen. In addition to connecting the eastern and western halves of our country, the telegraph has just facilitated the communication of an important political message during our country's darkest hour.

I pick up a bundle of mail sent to me at the telegraph office after our celebration ends. James Street and I then walk to a hotel called the Salt Lake House on Main Street.

"I hear that Brigham Young has forty-nine wives," James says after we check in.

I stare at him incredulously. "Are you kidding?"

He laughs. "Nope. The Mormon religion allows polygamy. However, some of his wives are former widows, and a few are older than him, so it's not clear if he's intimate with all of them."

I chuckle. "I guess that's his business. I'm certainly not going to ask him."

I heat some water on the woodstove in the communal bathroom after I check in to the hotel, and take a warm bath—the first I've had in months. I then return to my room. Too tired to read and anxious to enjoy the comfort of a mattress, I'm asleep as soon as my head hits the pillow.

I open my mail the next morning. Mary's first four letters are mostly about the kids. She writes the following in her last one: "There's something important in Elizabeth's letter, which I'm including here with mine. Please write to her. She needs you."

Elizabeth's letter surprises me, especially the postscript paragraph. All these years she's been waiting for me, I realize, and I didn't respond.

I pull paper, ink, and a quill pen from my suitcase and write a letter to her then, describing my trip to California and our transcontinental telegraph project. I end my missive with a promise to come to Virginia to find her, adding that I'm not sure how quickly I can get there. The snows have started in the Rocky Mountains, so it may take a while.

I'll tell her about Teresa when I see her in person. It's too complicated to explain in a letter. I mail my letter at the post office, and then I walk down the street to the telegraph office.

The telegraph operator hands me two telegrams when I enter. "These came for you this morning," he says. "I was just about to send them to your hotel with a delivery boy."

The first telegram is from Anson Stager, a Western Union superintendent I've worked with in Ohio: *Congratulations. The transcontinental telegraph project is a major achievement. Sibley has approved my request to bring you to the War Department in Washington. Please send me your anticipated arrival date. I'll explain your assignment when you arrive.*

The mysterious dispatch immediately raises my curiosity.

The second telegram is from Teresa: *Dear Brian. I met someone that wants to marry me and I've purchased the boarding house. I wish you a happy life.*

So... that's it then. Our relationship ends with a telegram. This strikes me as strange for some reason.

I write a message on a pad telling Mary that I completed my project, adding that I'll be heading home after a detour to Washington. I hand it to the operator, and he taps out the Morse code, while I jot down a message for Stager.

"It should be delivered to her in a few minutes," the operator says.

"Thanks. Here's another one."

The operator sends my telegram to Stager, telling him that I'll arrive in three weeks. That will work out well. I'll find Elizabeth—once I figure out how to sneak behind enemy lines—and then I'll go to Washington on my way back to New York.

I then send a telegram to Teresa: *Congratulations. I hope all your wishes come true.*

I walk down the street to the *Central Overland California and Pikes Peak Express* stagecoach office, and purchase a ticket for Atchison, Kansas, where the rail lines begin.

"Your journey will take a detour to Denver City in the Colorado Territory before it heads east," the sales clerk says. "Many of our routes include Colorado these days. Thousands of men are moving there after the silver and gold discoveries in 1858."

I board the stagecoach early the next morning. The Concord-style coach, pulled by six horses, seems comfortable as we leave Salt Lake. The curved body, fastened on a steel-spring suspension harnessed with leather braces, gives the coach a perpetual undulating roll as we ride across the rugged roads.

The drivers on top of the coach are sitting on a green Wells Fargo treasure box. One of the drivers carries a shotgun. Two men with rifles inside the coach tell me they work for Wells Fargo. They aren't friendly, so I don't ask questions. I assume the green treasure box must hold something important for them to be here.

Our stagecoach continues its journey twenty-four hours a day. The drivers stop every fifteen miles or so to change horses, which gives me a chance to step outside and stretch my legs, and then we're quickly on our way. We eat meals and change drivers at every fourth stop, which has a home station with a dining hall and a kitchen.

I become better acquainted with the men riding with me by our third day together. It turns out that they were wary of me at first. My stories about the telegraph project convinced them that I'm not a bandit.

"The treasure box is carrying currency for the bank in Denver City," one of the men says. "We're here to assist the drivers in case they run into trouble."

A fierce mountain blizzard during our fifth day has me wondering if we'll survive. The winds are blowing the snow sideways to the point where we can barely see. We almost go over a cliff when the coach slides sideways on a hairpin switchback.

We jump out of the coach to help the drivers each time the horses falter in a snowdrift. The blinding whiteout snowstorm pummels us with ice crystals as we work. I feel incredibly lucky that we can return to the coach when we're done. The drivers have no such luxury.

We arrive at Fort Laramie after fighting the storm for several hours. The fort's high wooden walls give us shelter for two days while we wait for the blizzard to blow over. We then board the stagecoach and head south toward the recently established Colorado Territory the next morning.

"The stagecoach feels like a torture chamber at this point," I say to the men as we ride.

"Tell me about it," one of them says. "We make this journey once a month."

"I imagine you've had some exciting times."

"We have," he says. "We've survived Indian raids, blizzards, washed-out roads, and outlaws. Several masked bandits chased our stagecoach for three miles during our trip in May. Our coach turned over after they shot our driver. We held them off for two hours until one of our stagecoaches going the other direction rescued us."

"So, I guess it's not all just beautiful scenery and majestic sunsets," I say.

The men chuckle.

"Not quite," the other man says.

We stop at Laporte, Colorado, that evening—a town founded by French-Canadian fur trappers in the early 1800s. It's snowing heavily when we arrive, so we stay at the home station overnight.

We continue our journey before dawn the next morning, going south on the Cherokee Trail. We veer southwest and stop at Boulder City for lunch. The massive, snow-covered rock slabs butting against the mountains look spectacular beneath the sunny skies.

A convoy of rifle-carrying men on horses from Gold Hill west of Boulder deposits what I assume is a bag of gold in the green Wells Fargo chest, and then we head southeast toward Denver City. We stop at the Clark & Graber's Bank at the corner of McGaa and G Street, when we reach Denver in the evening.

The two men in the coach stand guard while the drivers carry the green treasure box into the bank. I stand with them on the boardwalk, waiting for the drivers to return. I notice that most of the men walking along the streets here have revolvers hanging from their gun belts.

"It looks like there's a lot of building going on," I say to the guards. "I saw several saloons and hotels under construction on Larimer Street."

"There sure is," one of the men replies. "The city is booming. Almost seven thousand people have moved here since gold was discovered in Cherry Creek in 1858."

Two women wearing fancy silk dresses stop and ask us if we'd like some company. The guards agree to meet them in a nearby saloon.

"Denver's brothels have the most beautiful women in the west," one of the guards says, as the women stroll away. "I'm sure the drivers will want to see their girls."

The drivers exit the bank without the treasure box.

"We're staying overnight," one of them says. He points at the *Central Overland California and Pikes Peak Express* sign a block away.

"Be there at seven a.m. tomorrow morning, Mr. O'Rourke, and we'll get you on your way. Have a good time."

The four men walk down McGaa Street and enter a saloon.

I decide to see what the bank looks like inside since I'm already here. A bank teller protected by a metal cage says, "May I help you," when I enter.

"Your sign out front says that you mint gold coins," I say.

"That's right. You can bring in gold dust or nuggets and we'll give you the equivalent in coins. You can also purchase coins if you'd like."

"I'd like to see what you have."

He pulls out a wooden box and opens it. The shiny gold coins have an etching of Pikes Peak above the word *Denver* on one side, and the dollar denomination on the other.

I purchase several five-dollar gold coins, and pack them in a hidden pocket in my jacket. I'll give these to Mary's kids after I return to New York.

I then leave the bank and explore the city. It feels good to walk around after riding in the stagecoach for so long. It's a bright and sunny afternoon. This is surprising after the strength of yesterday's snowstorm, which left the mountains west of Denver covered with snow.

I'm surprised to see Confederate flags flying above some of the buildings. However, most of the flags are for the Union.

I check in to the Sutherland House on Blake Street as nightfall approaches. There's a dance hall on the second floor. I dance a few songs with a woman who's probably a courtesan, and return to my room alone to enjoy the comfort of a mattress before tomorrow's journey.

The drivers are loading the stagecoach when I arrive early the next morning. We make good progress with the nice weather, reaching Julesburg in the northeast corner of the Colorado Territory the following day. We arrive in Atchison, Kansas, four days later.

I stay at a hotel overnight, and board a train the next morning. I have to change trains four times over the next two days to reach Charles Town, Virginia, which is now a Unionist stronghold. Citizens from this part of Virginia voted to secede from the South and rejoin the United States a few months ago.

I walk down the street and enter a mercantile store after I leave the train station.

"I hear that you recently voted to return to the Union," I say to the proprietor.

"Yes, we did," he says. "The farmers that run the Virginia legislature don't speak for us. People here in the mountains don't own slaves. The rich farmers just don't want to lose their free labor. We figured that wasn't a good enough reason to tear the Union apart."

"I agree."

I walk up and down the aisles of his store trying to devise a plan that will allow me to sneak across the border. Posing as a violin player might provide a useful disguise.

I return to the proprietor. "Is there a theatre in town with a traveling minstrel show?" I say.

"Not that I'm aware of."

I buy a map of Virginia and study the roads from Charles Town to Warrenton. I then glance through a book he has that describes the demographics of every county in Virginia. A story in the newspaper about soldiers dying from malaria after the battle at Bull Run gives me an idea.

I'll disguise myself as a medical supply merchant.

I return to his medical supply shelves. One shelf has stacks of five-ounce tins of quinine.

"You have a lot of quinine and other medical supplies here," I say to the proprietor.

"Yeah, and I've ordered more from Philadelphia. There's a malaria epidemic in the army camps in Virginia. Doctors call the disease *Mal aria* because they think it comes from bad air. Quinine is a wonder drug for malaria. It comes from the bark of cinchona trees in South America. No one knows why it works, but it does, which is all that matters, I guess."

"How do people get malaria from bad air?"

"That's a mystery. However, they know it strikes people who sleep near swamps. The terrible chills, high fever, and headaches will eventually lead to death if it's left untreated."

"I'll be back to purchase all of your quinine in a while," I say. "And then I'll sell it in Virginia. I've been looking for a way to make some money."

He nods. "I'll be here."

I walk to a livery stable down the street and purchase two horses, and a small covered wagon.

"I'll be using this to sell medical supplies down South," I say to the blacksmith that owns the stable. "Can you replace the gray tarp covering the wagon with a white one, and paint the words *Medical Supplies* in capital letters on each side?"

"Certainly," he says.

I help him change the tarp and paint the wording after I pay him.

"You better have one of these too," he says. He attaches a long pole with a white flag to my seat. "You don't want to get shot."

"Thanks."

I drive the horses and wagon to the mercantile store, where I procure three hundred tins of quinine, forty boxes of wraparound cloth bandages, fourteen amputation kits, and twenty bottles of chloroform.

"Are you taking these to the Rebel or Union troops?" the proprietor says.

"I'll sell to both sides," I say.

I head south from Charles Town through Berryville to Salem, where I spend the night in the back of my wagon.

Three men on horses block my path as I head south from Salem the next morning. They aren't wearing uniforms. Their stern dispositions tell me that they're either bandits or soldiers.

The youngest man jumps down off his saddle. "We need to search your wagon," he says.

"That's fine with me," I say. "Do your troops need medical supplies?"

"Where's your travel pass?" one of them says.

"I didn't know I needed one. I've come here from Charles Town. I'm going to Warrenton and then east to Manassas Junction to bring medical supplies to the troops. Can you take me to your leader?"

"I'm the leader," one of them says. "My name is John Mosby."

"How do you do?" I say, as I reach for his hand.

He returns my handshake.

"Would you like to purchase some quinine for your troops that have malaria?" I say.

Mosby ponders this for a moment. "We'll accompany you to Warrenton. Several of our soldiers are sick with malaria symptoms."

PATRICK F. ROONEY

The man searching the back of my wagon pulls out my violin case and says, "What's this?"

"It's my fiddle," I say. "Shall I play something for you?"

He hands me the case. I remove my violin, tune it, and then I play "I Wish I Was in Dixie."

The men smile. One of them sings along. I finish with a flourish, and we all laugh together.

They surround me in front and back as we ride south to Warrenton. We reach a field filled with tents an hour later.

Mosby dismounts. "Stay here," he says. "I'll be right back."

He returns with a doctor.

"We just ran out of quinine," the doctor says. "You arrived just in time."

"I'm glad I can help."

He hands me Confederate dollars, and I give him forty tins of quinine.

I smile at Mosby as I jump up on my wagon seat. "I heard you had a magnificent victory at Bull Run. You chased those Yankees all the way back to Washington."

He grins. "We sure did."

"I imagine you must have other troops that need medical supplies. I'm thinking of heading east to Manassas Junction from here."

"I'm sure they need supplies there too."

Mosby scribbles something on a piece of paper and hands it to me. "Here's a travel pass."

"Thanks."

I steer my horses toward the center of town, and veer south after I pass the Warren Green Hotel. I expel a huge sigh of relief when I'm alone on the road.

A mailbox with the name *Butler* painted on the side appears on my left a few minutes later. I stop and survey the property. The fields are empty except for two cows. There are two barns and sixteen log cabins. I don't see any slaves working. This is surprising. I read about Fauquier County when I was in Charles Town. The statistics say that 55 percent of the population is slaves.

I steer my horses onto their private road, stop in front of the house, and jump down from the wagon. A heavyset Negro woman stares at me

from behind a screen door.

She walks out to the edge of the deck and says, "May I help you?"

"Hello, ma'am," I say. "I'm here to see Elizabeth."

"I'll get her for you."

The Negro woman walks down the stairs, crosses the yard to a small barn, and opens the door. "I think there's someone here to see you, Miss Elizabeth," she says.

Elizabeth appears in the doorway.

A passionate surge jolts my body when I see her. I grab the horse's harness to steady myself.

She's staring at me as she walks, and then she's running, and so am I.

"Oh, Brian," she says, hugging me hard.

A muscular Negro man appears at the barn door. He looks to be about sixty years old. I feel him studying me as Elizabeth sobs into my shoulder.

She pulls back and we look into each other's eyes. "I'm sorry about what my aunt did to us in England," she says. "I had no idea she was hiding your letters from me."

I brush the tears from her cheeks with my thumbs. "I understand. It wasn't your fault."

"Let's walk," I say.

"It's getting cold. I'll be right back."

She vaults up the stairs two at a time, disappears inside the mansion, and returns a moment later wearing her overcoat.

"Do you want to see my schoolhouse?" she says.

"Sure."

I walk with her to the barn and we look inside. A dozen children and ten adult Negroes are sitting at tables facing three blackboards.

"Can you lead the group reading the story, William?" she says.

"Yes, ma'am," the muscular Negro replies.

Elizabeth closes the barn door.

We walk back to the house and climb the porch steps to the deck.

"This is Brian," Elizabeth says, to the woman behind the screen, "the man I told you about from Ireland." She turns to me. "And this is Emma."

I open the screen door and extend my hand. "How do you do,

Emma?"

She shakes my hand. "Very well, Mr. Brian. I imagine you have a lot to talk about."

"We do," Elizabeth says. "We're going for a walk."

"Yes, ma'am."

Elizabeth takes my hand as we walk into the yellow fields.

"Thanks for writing back to me," she says. "I was surprised to see your letter was from Salt Lake City."

"I wasn't sure if it would get through. I've heard that mail going between the Confederacy and the Union is being opened and read by people looking for spies."

Elizabeth talks nonstop for several minutes about the bargain she made with Jacob Butler.

"It sounds like you've had a difficult time with him," I say.

"I have."

"Where is he now?"

"I don't know. I haven't seen him for weeks. He came home after the Battle of Ball's Bluff, but then he left the next day. He said it was another Confederate victory."

"I'm sorry I didn't talk with you after your concert in Washington. I was distraught after I saw you with your husband."

"He's my husband in name only, as I said in my letter. I should have been clearer about my relationship when I wrote to you. I just didn't want to be vulgar."

I chuckle. "I understand. Your husband seems a bit old to be a soldier."

"He served in the Mexican-American War, so he's helping to train recruits, although he also participates in battles. It's strange, actually. He's the happiest I've ever seen him now that he's a soldier. He was always in a foul mood before the war. He isn't happy about our escaped slaves, though. Most of them have run away on the Underground Railroad. Only one of the maids stayed—Emma, whom you just met."

"What do you think about the Underground Railroad?" I say.

"I agree with what they're doing. It's a noble cause."

I stop to survey the grassy hills. "This is beautiful. How much acreage do you have?"

"Jacob owns eleven hundred acres. He bought five hundred acres with the dowry money he received from my father. Actually, Rothschild's Bank of England owns the farm now. Jacob mortgaged it to get funds for the Confederacy. He'll be destitute if the South loses the war."

We resume our walk.

"He must feel confident," I say.

"He does, especially after the Confederate victories at Bull Run and Ball's Bluff. It seems that the Union is losing. It'll be awful if the Confederacy wins—for the slaves, that is."

We enter a trail leading into the woods.

"This is the land Jacob bought with my dowry," she says. "He hasn't had a chance to clear the forest here yet."

We cross a wooden bridge that traverses a small stream and continue on the trail. Red oak leaves propelled by a light autumn breeze drift to the ground around us as we walk.

"So, what do you want to do now that we've found each other?" I say.

"I don't know. What do you think I should do?"

"I can take you with me to Washington and put you up in a hotel. One of my Western Union colleagues asked me to meet him there."

Her hand comes to her chin as she contemplates my proposal. "What will happen to Emma and the rest of Jacob's slaves if I leave? Many of them have children."

"I could make arrangements to relocate them to Canada on the Underground Railroad."

She stops and faces me. "You're working with the Underground Railroad?"

"I am indeed. I developed the secret messages we use when we move runaway slaves."

She grins and squeezes my hand. "That's quite a coincidence. I've worked with the Underground Railroad too. We've been working together even though we didn't know it."

I chuckle. "I guess that's what happens to kindred spirits."

"How many people have you helped to escape?"

"I've taken close to two hundred up to Chicago, and at least four hundred to New York. Please keep this to yourself. What we're doing is illegal. I'm sure some slave owners would shoot me if they found out."

PATRICK F. ROONEY

"Don't worry. I won't tell anyone."

She turns back to the trail, and I hold her hand while we walk.

"I learned about the Underground Railroad when I attended abolitionist meetings in London," she says. "I work with Reverend Brooks now, a Methodist minister in Warrenton. He's helped me smuggle several slaves up to Pennsylvania. Of course, I need to be careful not to expose myself. Jacob might kill me if he finds out."

"I exchanged several ciphered telegrams with Reverend Brooks last year, when he needed to move some slaves out of Virginia."

She stops and faces me. "What a small world it is."

We stare into each other's eyes for a moment, and then our lips meet. My body starts to tremble inside as we kiss. I always felt a thrill with Teresa... but this is stronger.

She smiles as she looks up at me. "I've been dreaming about your kisses for a long time."

"I have too."

We continue on the trail until we reach a large pond surrounded by trees. She sits down on a wooden bench facing the pond, and I sit down next to her.

"This is my favorite place," she says. "The serenity here reminds me of our time together on Innisfree. I've sat here many evenings thinking about you while I've stared at the moon."

"I've often wondered if you kept your promise about using the moon as a touchstone, like we agreed to do when we were in Ireland. I've sent silent messages to you hundreds of nights."

I tell her about killing Sergeant Milton when I found him with Mary in the cave, our escape on the famine ship, our arrival in Five Points, finding shelter in a brothel, about Mary and Adam and their kids, about Corporal Wilcox hunting us down in New York, and finally—I tell her about Teresa.

She listens attentively until I finish.

"Do you love her?" she says.

"I did, but not the way I love you. It's over now. She sent me a telegram when I was in Salt Lake City, saying she's getting married. I wouldn't have gotten together with her if I'd known you were still waiting for me. She always knew I had strong feelings for you. She told me before I left San Francisco that I should figure things out with you."

284

"I *thought* that was you at the recital. I was upset when you didn't talk to me afterward."

"I'm sorry."

"I'm glad Corporal Wilcox didn't kill you. Several of Sergeant Milton's soldiers put up the money to fund his trip."

"He came to Mary's house with a gun, threatening to kill us, so we had no choice but to take him out."

I pull my dagger out of the sheath sown into my jacket. "Do you remember this knife I found on Innisfree?"

She nods.

"I take it everywhere I go." I slide it back into my coat. "So, do you want to come with me?"

I show her the travel pass I received from Mosby. "I'm representing myself as a medical supply merchant. This will allow us to travel behind Confederate lines, until we get close to Washington."

"Emma told me she doesn't want to travel on the Underground Railroad. She feels it would be too difficult at her age. I think the same would be true for the children."

She takes my hand. "I know we've been waiting to be together for years, but I need to ensure everyone here is safe before I leave."

"I understand. There's another possibility."

"What's that?"

"It's controversial, but slaves that reach the Union battle lines are being classified as contraband of war. This prevents the Union from having to send them back to their owners."

She smiles. "That would be much easier on the children."

I look into her eyes, and we kiss. The smell of her skin and hair ignites my passions.

She giggles and pulls back. "We should slow down. This isn't the right time, or place. I've dreamed of the day that we'll be intimate together. I want it to be special."

She pulls out a silver locket dangling on a thin chain from beneath the collar of her dress. She opens it, and removes a braid of black hair.

"Do you recognize this?" she says.

It takes me a moment to remember. "Is that from my haircut on Innisfree?"

"Yes." She smiles. "I've been keeping it in the locket between my breasts."

Incredible! She kept it all these years.

"I stored the lock of hair you gave me inside my copy of Shakespeare's *As You Like It*," I say. "My books are currently in storage in New York."

She closes her locket and slides it back under her collar.

We walk back on the trail holding hands, until we emerge from the woods. She tells me about a female Confederate spy while we walk—an Irish woman—operating in Washington.

"Jacob said the woman is having an affair with a Northern senator," she says. "The senator disclosed the Union's battle plans for Bull Run to her, and she passed the information on to the Confederacy."

"Is that so?" Her story brings me back to reality.

I jump up to the driver's seat of my wagon when we reach her house. "I'll be back to see you as soon as I can," I say.

She folds her arms. "Be careful when you come. Jacob is a violent man, and he knows that I love you. He'll probably kill you if he finds you here."

I shake the reins, and my horses lurch forward, pulling me away. Elizabeth is standing next to Emma on the porch when I wave goodbye from the road.

I ride southeast to Warrenton Junction, pass Catlett's Station, and veer northeast toward Manassas. I pull off the road into a field as night approaches, and sleep in the back of my wagon.

Manassas Junction is bustling with activity when I arrive the next morning. I count almost two hundred Confederate troops building warehouses, barracks, and a rail line to Centreville.

"Where can I find your hospital?" I say to a soldier, after he checks my travel pass.

"Go north a couple of miles to the tents," he says.

A column of Confederate troops appears in front of me as I'm heading north. I veer my wagon to the side of the road to let them pass, and then I continue toward Centreville.

I see several putrefied corpses in the fields as I approach Bull Run. The blue uniforms on the decomposing bodies reveal that they're Union soldiers. The stench of death makes me wretch as I pass them.

There are hundreds of Confederate soldiers building log cabin barracks when I reach Centreville. Some of the cabins have human crossbones nailed over their entrance doorways.

"Why do you have those bones?" I ask a soldier.

He smiles. "Those are from Union soldiers we skinned."

I pull on my horse's reins and dismount next to an enormous hospital tent. The doctors are pleased when I show them my supplies. They purchase most of my merchandise with Confederate dollars, and then I continue east on the Warrenton Turnpike toward Washington.

I pass thousands of soldiers building defensive bulwarks interspersed with artillery. Some of the cannons are actually logs painted to look like two-hundred-pound Parrott rifles or Rodman guns. *Very clever!* One regiment is playing baseball—my favorite game. I'm tempted to stop and ask them if I can play.

There will be plenty of time for games when the war is over, I tell myself.

Confederate troops occupy defensive fortifications most of the way to the Fairfax Court House. From there I pass into a no-man's-land.

A band of Union cavalry soldiers stops me as I approach Vienna, Virginia. They block the road with horses as they level their rifles at me.

"Put your hands up," one of them says.

I comply with his order. "I'm on my way to see Anson Stager in the War Department telegraph office," I say. I nod at a nearby telegraph booth. "Send a telegram to him if you'd like. Tell him Brian O'Rourke is on his way."

Two soldiers jump into the back of my wagon. They inspect my suitcase and violin, while another soldier talks to the operator in the telegraph booth.

"Let him go," the telegraph operator calls out a moment later. "The War Department confirmed his story."

I continue through the rolling hills of Virginia to the Long Bridge, and cross the Potomac River into Washington. I leave my horses and wagon at a livery stable on Pennsylvania Avenue, and check in to the Willard Hotel.

Exhausted after my journey, I retreat to my room and fall into bed without eating. An image of Elizabeth rowing me in her boat to Innisfree comforts me as I fade into sleep.

33. BRIAN O'ROURKE

Washington.

I APPROACH THE War Department building early the next morning. Two soldiers with rifles on their shoulders are standing guard.

"What business do you have here?" one of them says, pointing his rifle at me.

"I'm here to see Anson Stager. I'm with Western Union."

The soldier escorts me to a large room on the second floor. He stops and salutes when we enter. I see three telegraph operators sitting at desks against one wall.

"This man says he has business with Mr. Stager," the soldier says.

President Lincoln, Mr. Stager, and two men I haven't met stand up.

The president returns the soldier's salute and says, "At ease."

"Hello, Brian," Stager says, as he shakes my hand.

He turns to the president. "This is the man I told you about, Mr. President. Brian O'Rourke. He developed the encryption scheme for messages used by the Underground Railroad."

Lincoln shakes my hand. "I'm pleased you could join us."

"It's nice to see you again, Mr. President."

The president is tall—six feet four, an inch taller than I am—so we almost see eye to eye. He has a chinstrap beard he didn't have when I saw him speak at the Cooper Union building in New York. He also looks much older and wearier now, with dark circles under his eyes.

Perhaps it's the weight of the war bearing down on him, I speculate.

"This is Andrew Carnegie," Stager says, introducing me to the third man. "Andrew helped us take control of the railroad and telegraph lines around Washington."

I shake Carnegie's hand. "I recognize you," I say. "Did you ever visit the Astor House Hotel in New York? I believe I saw you there when I was playing violin in the rotunda."

"Ah, yes." He smiles. "I often stay at the Astor House when I'm in

New York City."

"And this is Edward Stanford," Stager says, "president of the American Telegraph Company."

I shake Stanford's hand, and we all sit down around a giant oblong table. There's a detailed map of the eastern United States spread out in front of us.

"I'm glad you arrived safely from Salt Lake," Lincoln says. "Anson tells me you were in the expedition that built the transcontinental telegraph from Carson City to Salt Lake."

"I was, sir. It was a difficult project. Everyone worked very hard."

"I'm sure they did. Were you in Salt Lake when the California Supreme Court justice sent the telegram promising that they'd stand with me to keep the Union together?"

"Indeed. I feel lucky to have witnessed that, sir. I also attended your Cooper Union speech in New York. It was very inspiring. I joined your Republican Party after that."

"Thank you. I enjoyed my visit to New York, especially the orphanage in Five Points."

"We have a special assignment for you, Brian," Stager says. "We'd like you to stay in Washington to support the war effort. You'll be working here at the War Department as part of the recently formed Military Telegraph Corps. Although the Corps is a civilian organization, you'll receive direction from the secretary of war."

Oh, no! This isn't what I planned.

"I was hoping to return to New York, sir," I say. "I've been traveling for more than a year."

"I won't force you to stay if you insist," Stager says. "However, we'll pay your living expenses and continue your salary at the same level if you do. We need your expertise developing message ciphers. Your extensive knowledge of our telegraph infrastructure will be useful too, and you know many of our operators since you trained them. In addition to working with the president and the secretary of war, you'll be out in the field with the Telegraph Construction Corps running lines to the battlefield."

This will change everything!

I've been looking forward to returning to New York. I miss my home on Patchin Place, and Mary, Adam, and the kids, and I want to play violin again with the symphony.

On the other hand, Elizabeth is here... and I want to be near her. She won't move to New York while she's married. I wouldn't want her to anyway. That would be scandalous.

Can she get a divorce? Is it legal in Virginia? I obviously need to sort things out with her.

Maybe it's God's plan for me to stay here. I say a silent prayer asking for guidance.

"Your country needs you," President Lincoln says. "None of us is anxious to fight a war, but sometimes sacrifice is necessary to ensure our freedom. We need to keep the Union together. Otherwise, every state would secede when they disagree with a ruling from Congress, and the country would dissolve into chaos."

Everyone is staring at me, waiting for my answer.

"You'll be working with Allan Pinkerton's Secret Intelligence Service on occasion," Stager says. "He'll be here in a few minutes to discuss some of their missions."

I nod at Stager and the president. "I'd be glad to help, Mr. President."

"We're pleased to have you on board," Lincoln says.

"Thank you, sir."

Allan Pinkerton enters the room with a woman, and everyone stands.

I shake Allan's hand. "It's good to see you again."

"How was your trip through the Rockies?"

"The snowcapped mountains and autumn colors in the trees were beautiful. Something about the high altitude makes the sky produce spectacular sunsets. A blizzard caught us on our way to Fort Laramie, though. I wasn't sure if we'd make it out alive for a while."

Pinkerton turns to the slender, brown-haired woman standing next to him. "This is Kate Warne, my assistant."

I shake her hand. "How do you do?"

She smiles. "Very well, thank you."

Everyone sits down around the table.

"General McClellan asked Allan to lead our secret intelligence service," the president says. "He thwarted an assassination plot in Baltimore while I was on my way here for the inauguration."

"That's right, Mr. President," Pinkerton says. "Kate is the real heroine, though. She infiltrated the assassination ring by pretending she was a Southern belle."

"How'd you do that?" I say.

She smiles demurely and opens her fan. "You know there's nothin' betta' then collard greens, chitlins, and fried chicken on a hot summa day," she says, in a sweet Southern accent.

We all laugh.

Allan looks at her affectionately. "She has a knack for fitting in, which makes her an excellent spy. Unfortunately, there are many secessionist spies in Maryland and Washington. We've been quite busy flushing them out."

Lincoln points at the map. "I need the ability to exchange encrypted messages with my troop commanders in the field. What do we need to do to make that a reality, Mr. Stager?"

Stager points at some red markers around Washington on the map. "Our first priority is to ensure these lines aren't compromised. The Confederates have cut the telegraph wires around Fairfax and Alexandria several times. Union cavalry patrols will need to be vigilant to ensure that doesn't happen again. We also need to train operators to handle encrypted messages."

Stager turns to me. "I'd like you to train our Military Telegraph Corps operators to use ciphers, Brian."

"I'd be honored to help, sir."

I turn to Pinkerton. "I have some information that may be useful in your search for spies."

"What's that?"

"A friend of mine in Virginia told me that a socialite in Washington disclosed the Union's Bull Run battle plans to the Confederacy. That allowed Confederate troops in the Shenandoah Valley to board trains and come to Manassas to join the battle. Apparently, the woman is romantically involved with a Northern senator."

Lincoln stares at Pinkerton and says, "That confirms what we've heard from other sources."

"My friend told me the female spy has an Irish surname."

"That's probably Rose O'Neil Greenhow," Pinkerton says. "We have her under house arrest. We intercepted a telegram sent to her by a

Confederate soldier after the battle at Bull Run. The telegram said the Confederate president appreciated the information she provided."

"That's an example of one of our missions," Stager says. "Intercepting and decoding Confederate telegrams. They're using ciphers too."

I nod.

"Having telegraph lines wired to the battlefield will give us a strategic advantage as the battle evolves," Lincoln says. "We'll also use the telegraph to coordinate logistics. We need easy-to-use ciphers our operators can apply and decode quickly. Can you help us with that?"

"Yes indeed, Mr. President," I say. "I'll certainly do my best."

Lincoln looks at Carnegie. "As you know, Andrew, many railroad lines run from city to city, but they don't have a common terminal. Some of the trains also use different widths between their rail lines. This is inefficient. We can't unload our troops and carry our supplies across town to another railroad terminal every time we reach a city."

"I agree, Mr. President," Carnegie says. "We need standard railroad gauges and lines that run through cities. I can build those if you give me the authority to override the local politicians. Many towns build their rail lines to be inefficient now. That enables the local townspeople to make money from the inconvenience and delays they impose on travelers."

"The same thing used to be true in the telegraph industry," Stager says. "We had to consolidate many companies before we could use Morse code as the standard for messages."

"I've asked Congress to allow the federal government to take control of the railroads and telegraph network until the war is over," Lincoln says.

He looks at Stager, Stanford, and Carnegie. "Of course, we'll pay you for your services during the war, and return control to you when it's over. We're not nationalizing your industries; we're just taking control to ensure military traffic has the highest priority. The decision from Congress should be coming soon."

The president leans forward, staring at Carnegie. "I'd like you to draw up plans to standardize the railroad gauge and extend the rail lines through cities to ensure we can move our troops and supplies efficiently. You did an excellent job securing the rail and telegraph lines around Washington. I trust that you'll take on this new assignment with equivalent vigor and speed."

"Yes, Mr. President," Carnegie says. "Will you give my railroad and steel companies the contracts to build this infrastructure?"

"Certainly," Lincoln says. "There's no time to waste. I'll press Congress to allocate the funds you'll need."

Lincoln turns to Stager and Edward Stanford. "The same will be true for the telegraph infrastructure we build to support the war effort."

Carnegie stands up. "I'll bid you good day now, Mr. President. I need to meet with my colleagues to get things moving." He shakes Lincoln's hand and leaves the room.

We spend the rest of the morning developing plans for our fledgling Military Telegraph Corps. Stager has already recruited thirty telegraph operators from Western Union, the American Telegraph Company, and the Southwest Telegraph Company to join us. Many of these operators will accompany generals in the field.

Pinkerton and Kate Warne help us develop the initial message ciphers. They'll use these to communicate with the president when they conduct clandestine missions.

"I'll assist you with your spy missions when I can," I say to Pinkerton.

"Good," he replies. "It'll be nice to have your help."

I figure this will give me an opportunity to check on Elizabeth when I'm in Virginia.

We adjourn at noon, and the president leaves to attend to other business. I accompany Stager, Kate, and Pinkerton outside to inspect a field telegraph wagon Stager's Telegraph Corps engineers are building.

"We'll be sending telegraph wagons like this into the field with each general," Stager says. "We'll run telegraph lines to them so they can communicate with us here at the War Department. As you can see, the large galvanic batteries take up most of the space in the back of the wagon."

"We're likely to have some casualties with our operators in the field," I say.

"That's true," Stager says. "Unfortunately, fatalities are an inevitable consequence of war."

I return to the Willard Hotel after dinner. Knowing that I'll be in Washington awhile, I check out of the hotel the next morning, and rent a room in a boarding house on K Street across from Franklin Square.

I then send a telegram to Mary: *Delayed in Washington with a new assignment. Not sure when I'll be home. Please continue to rent out my house until you hear otherwise.*

I don't tell her what I'll be doing. Pinkerton cautioned me that our work is top secret.

Most of our War Department messages the next few weeks deal with logistics—moving soldiers and supplies on trains, ships, and barges. We also decipher several messages captured by a Pinkerton agent who spliced into a Confederate telegraph line outside Fredericksburg, Virginia. We determine that most of the Rebel messages are also for supply logistics. These are still valuable, though, since logistic messages often accompany troop movements.

I'm sitting at my desk in the War Department when a soldier enters on the morning of December 13. "The president would like you to meet him at the White House," he says to me.

I follow the soldier to the south lawn behind the president's house. President Lincoln is conversing with a large group of soldiers when I approach.

Lincoln turns to me. "I'd like to introduce you to Brigadier General Thomas Meagher," he says. "He'll be leading the Irish Brigade from New York."

He turns to the general. "This is Brian O'Rourke, the man I told you about."

"How do you do?" I say, as I shake the general's hand. "I'm pleased to finally meet you. I heard about the Young Ireland Rebellion you led in 1848. I was sixteen years old at the time."

He nods. "The British almost hanged me for that. They commuted my sentence to life in prison, and sent me to Australia. I escaped from there to San Francisco."

General Meagher turns to Lincoln. "I understand we might give Britain a taste of the sword if they attack our ships. I'll lead the charge against England if you'd like. I'd love to exact revenge for the million souls they starved to death in Ireland."

President Lincoln frowns. "Let's not get ahead of ourselves. We need to fight one war at a time. We have intense diplomatic efforts underway with Britain over the Trent Affair. Your mission is to win the war here. I heard your men fought valiantly at Bull Run."

"Yes, sir, we did," Meagher says.

Meagher turns and smiles at me. "I believe I may have met your father. He was tall and strong, just like you. Big Paddy O'Rourke was his name."

"That was my father. The British killed him and both of my brothers when we wouldn't leave our land."

"I read about the terrible treatment of the Catholics in Ireland," Lincoln says. "It was a tragic affair. That reminds me, General Meagher. I will not tolerate religious prejudice in the ranks. I assume you're comfortable with Irishman of all faiths in your regiment, including Protestants, Jews, or atheists."

General Meagher straightens his back and salutes. "Absolutely, Mr. President. I've experienced religious persecution. I won't inflict that upon my soldiers."

"Good," Lincoln says. "I'd like to meet some of your men now."

Meagher stays with me when the president moves into a crowd of soldiers waiting to greet him.

"You returned from France with the new Irish flag," I say to Meagher.

He smiles. "Yes, I did. The French treated me very well, especially their beautiful women."

We chuckle.

"I'm working in the War Department's Military Telegraph Corps," I say.

"Excellent." He pauses. "What will you do if we go to war with the British? Would you join me to expel them from Ireland?"

You can't return to Ireland, I remind myself. *You may still have a price on your head!*

"I'm a U.S. citizen now, General Meagher," I say. "Ireland holds too many painful memories for me to ever live there again."

"The British Parliament is threatening to jump into the war with the Confederates to protect their investments in the South. Everyone in Europe is lining up behind the scenes—the French, the English, even Russia, who has come out in support of the Union. The Russian czar informed Lincoln that France and England are forming an alliance to side with the Confederates."

I nod. "I've heard that many abolitionists that are Protestants in Britain favor the Union. It's interesting when you think about it. The Protestants are more anxious to get rid of slavery than the Catholics. I heard the pope is siding with the Confederates."

"That *is* interesting," Meagher says, "and disappointing."

Meagher turns his gaze to Lincoln. "I'm going to catch up with the president. Perhaps we can have a drink together sometime. Your father and mother treated me very well when I visited them at Lough Gill. It was beautiful there as I recall. I understand why they refused to leave. He told me the Kingdom of Breifne was ruled by your O'Rourke clan for several centuries before the British came."

"That's true."

We shake hands, and he walks across the lawn and stands next to the president. Several soldiers I know come and greet me then—men I met when I attended Corcoran's Sixty-Ninth New York State Militia meetings. I'm surprised to see Matthew Keenan. The stripes on his uniform say he's a sergeant.

"It's good to see you, Sergeant Keenan," I say as I hug him. "I didn't know you joined the army."

He grins. "I signed up when Meagher said he needed soldiers for his Irish Brigade. I remember you talking with my father on the famine ship about how important it is to be able to defend ourselves."

"Indeed. That was a long time ago. How old are you now?"

"Twenty-one."

"I hope you get through this in one piece. I heard the battle at Bull Run was awful."

Matthew pulls out a metal cross hanging on a small chain around his neck. "Remember how Jesus protected us during that terrible storm on the *Dromahair*?"

"I do indeed. I held you in my arms the entire night. I thought we were going to die."

He laughs. "I did too, but the Jesus cross in your trousers protected us. This cross protected me during our battle at Bull Run."

I nod. *I wonder if wearing a cross on a battlefield really works.*

He slides the cross back beneath the collar of his shirt.

"Do you still play the violin?" I say.

"I do. I often play fiddle for our company when we're bivouacked in the field. It's a nice way to pass the time. Thanks for the free lessons you gave me all those years when I was a kid."

"You're welcome. I enjoyed teaching you. You're very talented. Perhaps we can play in the New York Symphony together when this is over."

"That would be fantastic."

He tells me about his life in the army, and I tell him about the transcontinental telegraph project I just completed. I shake hands with him when we say goodbye, and then I return to the War Department with Secretary Edwin Stanton.

"What do you think about our new Irish general?" Stanton says.

"I'm not sure. What do you think?"

"It's a popular political move that will help our recruiting efforts. General Meagher has enlisted thousands of Irishman in New York and Boston. However, he doesn't have the training our generals receive at West Point, so I'm not sure how well he'll do. Insisting that his men use the obsolete 1842 smoothbore musket instead of a Springfield or Enfield rifle has me worried."

"Why does he want to use the musket?"

"He feels it will do more damage to the enemy. The musket shoots a buck-and-ball shot that's deadly at close range. However, the long-range rifles the Confederates use may prevent the Irish Brigade from getting close enough to use their muskets."

A foreboding worry gnaws at me the rest of the day. Will the hundreds of soldiers on the White House lawn make it through the war? I say a prayer, asking Jesus to keep Matthew safe.

Lincoln doesn't use our War Department telegraph the next two weeks. Stager tells me that diplomatic letters crisscrossing the Atlantic trying to resolve the Trent Affair are consuming most of the president's energy.

I return to Virginia to see Elizabeth after Christmas. The travel pass from Mosby still allows me to sneak behind Confederate lines when I bring my medical supply wagon.

I'm not sure if her husband will be home, so I stop at Reverend Brooks's house in Warrenton, and ask him if he will contact Elizabeth for me. He accompanies me in my wagon to her farm. It rains for a few minutes, but stops just before we get there. I wait on the road while the reverend knocks on her front door.

He returns with her a moment later.

"Jacob isn't here," Elizabeth says.

"You can take my wagon back to Warrenton," I say to the reverend. "I'll walk back to your house to pick it up after my visit with Elizabeth."

The reverend tips his hat and snaps the reins, and my horses pull the wagon away.

"Let's walk in the woods," Elizabeth says.

We walk across the yellow grass and enter the trail that meanders through the forest to the pond. The sun paints the ground with spider web patches of shade from the barren tree limbs while we walk.

She stops and hugs me without saying anything. She then raises her lips and we kiss.

"Umm," I moan. "I've been dreaming about your kisses since my last visit."

She giggles and turns back to the trail.

"I love the way the forest smells after it rains," she says. "It reminds me of Ireland."

"It does indeed. It's very beautiful here."

We sit down on the wooden bench facing the pond.

"I'm glad you came to see me," she says. "I've been longing for you."

"I can't wait until we can be together... forever."

She studies my eyes, first one, and then the other. "Do you think that will happen?"

"I do."

"That would make me very happy."

I remove an envelope from my pocket and hand it to her. "There's a note with the address of my boarding house inside, as well as some money, and a pass to get you through the Union lines. I've made an advance payment for you at the Willard Hotel in Washington. You can ask for me at the War Department—which is next to the White House— if I'm not home when you arrive."

She stows the envelope in her pocket purse. "I'll be safe here for now, but thank you anyway."

We kiss several times—long, slow kisses that make the birds watching us chirp louder. We then walk back through the forest toward her house.

"I'll come again as soon as I can get away," I say. "I'll be traveling for a while, so I'm not sure when I'll be back. I'm managing telegraph projects for the War Department."

"What do you do for them?"

I need to be cautious. She doesn't have a need to know.

"I train operators and coordinate crews stringing telegraph wire—that sort of thing."

"Please be careful," she says. "I didn't get married to a stranger and come all the way here from England to have you taken away by a bullet."

"I will."

I walk her to her door, and then I return to Warrenton to retrieve my wagon from the reverend.

Paris, France. May 10, 1862.

THE FRAGRANT scent of chestnut and cherry-tree blossoms and flowerbeds lined with tulips fill my nostrils as I enter the Pont Neuf Bridge that crosses the River Seine. I recognize the brown-robed monk immediately as I approach him. He has less hair than fourteen years ago, but other than that, he looks the same.

"It's good to see you again, Brother Bernard," I say, extending my hand.

He smiles and embraces me, finishing with a kiss on each of my cheeks. "I've thought of you often over the years," he says. "Let's walk. Paris is enchanting in the spring."

"Indeed. I love the way the city uses trees and flowers to beautify its wide boulevards."

We walk north to the end of the bridge, and continue west on a footpath that borders the wide, fast-moving river.

"I was surprised to get your note," he says.

"I'm glad you could meet me on such short notice. I'm here on a diplomatic mission for President Lincoln."

He raises his eyebrows and studies me as we walk. "Is that so?

You've sure come a long way from your humble beginnings in Ireland."

"The education you gave me certainly helped. I'd like to thank you again for that."

"You're welcome, my son. I wasn't sure how well you'd be able to navigate the storms of life when I left. You weren't dealt a very good hand."

I nod. "I'm glad you suggested that I immigrate to America. My life totally changed after that. You told me once that you were an agent for the French government. Is that still true?"

He looks around furtively and returns his gaze to me. "What's on your mind?"

"I'm hoping that we can establish a backdoor communication channel between our intelligence services. I've brought some message ciphers we can use."

I hand him a piece of paper with the cipher instructions.

He shoves it into a pocket in his cloak. I feel him studying me again as we walk.

"We're pleased that your government hasn't recognized the Confederacy," I say, "at least not officially. Recognizing the Rebels could lead to war between our countries. We hope to avoid another war if we can. That's why I'm here."

"We haven't recognized the Confederacy, but many of Napoleon the Third's capitalist benefactors would like us to. They've loaned the Confederates fifteen million dollars, and they want a return on their investment."

"We're aware of that. I want to reiterate the position our ambassador, William Dayton, relayed to your emperor recently. We won't tolerate other countries meddling in our affairs. Your country's invasion of Mexico may already lead to further difficulties between us. We wouldn't have allowed a foreign power to establish a foothold in North America if we weren't already at war. This will change if your government provides official support for the Rebels."

He nods. "Many of us were pleased to see your country taking steps to abolish slavery. However, some of Napoleon's advisors don't care about that. They're more interested in exploiting the situation. They believe the Confederates are strong enough to prevent your Union forces from attacking our troops."

We cross the street and enter the *Jardin des Tuileries*, a huge park north of the river. Brother Bernard steers me toward a flower-lined walkway that leads to a giant Egyptian obelisk.

"The Catholic Church supports France's plan to establish a monarchy loyal to the Vatican in Mexico," he goes on to say. "The Vatican believes that recognizing the Confederacy with their backing will dissuade Catholics in the Union army from fighting the Rebels."

"Assuming we wouldn't attack your troops would be a grave mistake. Lincoln is the most determined man I've ever met, and our army and navy are strong, as you can see from our recent victorious campaigns down the Mississippi River to New Orleans."

We stop to assess the seventy-five foot tall, yellow granite obelisk in the center of the gardens. It's surrounded by picturesque flowerbeds and water fountains.

"This is quite beautiful," I say.

He smiles. "I'm glad you like it. I have something else I'd like to show you."

We start walking north.

"Our foreign minister, Édouard Thouvenel, has dissuaded Napoleon from aligning with the Confederates so far," he says. "I'll pass along your concerns to him, which should reinforce his position with the emperor."

We stop next to a post office mailbox on the east side of the square in *Place Vendôme*. He pulls a piece of chalk out of his cloak, and makes a slash mark on the side of the mailbox.

"Your agent should make a mark like this when he needs to pass me a message from you," he says. "I'll do the same when I have a message for you. There's a secret drop box we can use inside this bookstore."

We enter the bookstore, and stop in front of a shelf filled with religious books. He pulls an oversized Bible off the shelf.

"There's a nook in the wall behind this book," he says. He places his hand through the opening to show me. "I'll place my messages in here, encoded with one of the ciphers you gave me."

"Good. I'll show my colleague the mailbox and drop site before I leave tomorrow."

He re-shelves the Bible. "Tell him to erase the chalk mark on the mailbox outside after he picks up a message. I'll do the same after I retrieve a message from him."

We exit the bookstore and walk down the street to 12 Place Vendôme. He stops and points at an upper-floor window. "Your friend, Elizabeth, played the piano for Chopin in that room when he was on his deathbed."

"Thank you for showing me this place. I'll tell her I was here the next time I see her."

He chuckles. "She's quite a good pianist... and very attractive."

I grin. "She certainly is. I hope to marry her someday."

He smiles and pats me on the back. "I'm happy for you, Brian. She seems like a lovely girl."

We spend the afternoon sharing an excellent bottle of Bordeaux at a nearby restaurant. It takes a second bottle to catch up on the last fourteen years of our lives.

I show my American colleague the bookstore drop site and mailbox the next morning. I then board a train for Brest on the west coast of France, and take a steamer back to the United States.

34. ELIZABETH BUTLER

Warrenton, Virginia. June 2, 1862.

I KNOW SOMETHING'S wrong when Jacob arrives driving a wagon pulled by two horses. I see a wooden coffin in the back as he continues on to the grassy knoll where we buried the soldiers last summer.

He's sobbing next to the wagon when I approach. I understand why when I look inside the coffin. Harland is there, dressed in his Confederate cavalry uniform. A thick bandage soiled with dried blood covers his gut.

"What happened?" I say.

"We were protecting Richmond from attack," Jacob says, in a solemn voice. "Harland was riding with J. E. B. Stuart's cavalry brigade. We repulsed the Yankees several times before they retreated at Seven Pines. Stuart said Harland fought bravely after his horse went down. He brought me his body yesterday evening after the battle ended."

Jacob spears me with an angry stare. "A soldier from New York's Irish Brigade gouged him with a bayonet."

"That must have been awful."

"Stuart said it took two miserable hours for Harland to die. They couldn't do anything for him except wrap his wound. Can you tell the slaves to dig a grave?"

"Certainly."

I return a moment later with William. He's carrying a shovel.

"I'm very sorry for your loss, Mr. Jacob," William says, as he starts to dig.

"Where are the other slaves?" Jacob says.

"William and Emma are the only ones left," I say. "The rest ran away when General Geary's Union soldiers occupied Warrenton."

Jacob walks to the barn. He returns with a shovel and starts to dig next to William.

Emma comes out of the house and stands next to me.

"Shall I fetch the preacher from Warrenton?" I say.

"No," Jacob says. "Prayers won't do him any good now."

The men finish digging an hour later. Emma and I help them carry the casket from the wagon and set it down next to the hole.

Jacob slumps to his knees and starts to weep.

I kneel next to him and rub his back. "This is so sad," I say, releasing tears of my own. "He had his whole life ahead of him."

Emma is weeping too. "I cared for him... from the time he was a baby," she murmurs. "He was always so full of energy... and very respectful to me."

"I'm gonna make those Yankees pay for this," Jacob stammers.

William retrieves a hammer, nails, and two ropes from the barn. He carries the casket cover from the back of the wagon to the gravesite. Jacob positions the cover on top of the casket and nails it shut.

We stand at the four corners of the coffin, wrap the ropes underneath it at each end, and lower it carefully into the hole. The men then shovel the dirt back into the grave. They're just about finished when I return from the barn with a white cross. I painted the name *Harland Butler* in black letters on one side.

Jacob pounds the cross into the ground with the hammer. He then jumps up into the driver's seat and pulls away without saying anything.

I don't see Jacob again until the middle of August, when the rumble of fifteen hundred horses accompanies his arrival with General J. E. B. Stuart's cavalry troops. They veer into our fields from the road. It's been raining most of the day, so the fields quickly turn into mud when the horses' hooves churn through the grass. I watch from the porch as the soldiers dismount and relieve themselves.

Jacob brings General Stuart and four of his fellow officers inside and introduces me. The men are gracious and charming, leaning forward and bowing when they take my hand.

I've already heard about one of the men—Lieutenant John Mosby— from Brian. He's the one that gave Brian his travel pass, I realize, but I certainly can't say anything about that here.

"We just came by for a few minutes," Jacob says as they sit down. "I wanted you to meet these officers in case they come looking for a place to hide some night."

"We travel incognito when we can," Mosby says, "so we may not be in uniform. Most of our partisan soldiers still live with their families."

"What is it that would bring you here?" I say.

"We sneak out at night in small groups and travel behind enemy lines, where we cut the Union's telegraph wires and dislodge railroad ties to make their trains wreck. It's nice to have farms such as yours to hide out in when we're on the run."

"I'm glad we met before you show up at my door. I wouldn't want to shoot you."

The men chuckle.

General Stuart looks across the room at my piano. "My wife tells me that you're quite an accomplished pianist. It would be nice to hear you play sometime."

"I'd love to," I say.

Emma arrives with a pitcher of tea. She fills glasses and hands one to each of them. Jacob doesn't introduce her.

"This is Emma," I say.

The soldiers look at Jacob and then back at me without responding.

Emma scoots away to the kitchen.

The men guzzle down their tea and stand up.

"It was nice meeting you," Stuart says as they exit.

I walk behind them to the porch and watch as the officers jump up on their saddles.

"Where are you off to next?" I ask Jacob.

"We're going to Catlett's Station south of here." He smiles. "The Yankees have a supply depot there. We're going to destroy the railroad bridge, cut the telegraph wires, and tear up the train tracks."

"Won't the Confederate troops need those rail lines too?"

"We'll rebuild them after we chase the Yankees out of Virginia. They're using trains and telegraph messages to manage their troop movements, so the more we disrupt their supply lines, the better we'll do in the next battle."

"When did you join the cavalry? I thought you liked to fire cannons."

"I took Harland's place after he died."

The soldiers in the field follow the officers out to the road. The ground rumbles as the horses gallop away in the mud. The rain has started again.

I hear distant gunfire an hour later. It continues for half an hour.

It's almost dark when the Confederate troops pass by on the road heading north toward Warrenton. They're escorting a large contingent of bluecoat Union prisoners marching on foot with their hands tied.

Jacob rides up to the house and dismounts.

"How did it go?" I say.

"Great. We captured three hundred prisoners and twenty-five thousand Union dollars at the Catlett rail station. More importantly, we found General Pope's dispatch book, which contains the Union's war plans. It was raining too hard to set the railroad bridge on fire. We'll come back to do that later."

Jacob leaves during the day and returns at night the following week, so I figure his troops must be nearby. Something major must be coming with all the activity I see on the road.

I'm practicing my piano when I hear the knock. Emma opens the front door.

"May I speak with Elizabeth?" a woman says. She has a strong Southern accent.

She's wearing a blue dress with a matching hat. Her four-wheeled Concord buggy, drawn by two brown and white stallions, has a canopy top and two sets of leather seats.

Her driver remains in the buggy.

"I'm Elizabeth," I say.

She looks past me into the parlor. "My name is Kate. Would you mind if we talk a bit? I've heard that my brother may have been buried here."

"Not at all." I push the screen door open. "Come on in."

"I'd prefer to chat outside," she says. "We'd like to stretch our legs with a walk if you don't mind."

I exit to the porch and extend my hand.

"How do you do?" she says. She walks down the steps to the buggy. "This is Allan."

I shake her driver's hand, and the three of us start walking toward the grassy knoll where we buried the soldiers.

"Brian sent us," Kate says, when we're away from the house. Her Southern accent has disappeared.

"Oh. It's a good thing you suggested that we take a walk. My husband is inside."

She nods. "Brian wants you to come to Washington with us. He feels you'll be safer there."

"Why now?"

"Union soldiers are looting and pillaging homes suspected of helping the Confederate cause. It's not safe for you here."

"I'm not going to let anyone take my land—Union or Confederate."

My candor surprises me. Although I've never said it aloud, I realize now that I love this land, regardless of my relationship with Jacob. Besides, I have no place else to go—other than the hotel room Brian paid for in Washington. I don't want to be his charity case... unless that's my last resort.

We reach the grassy knoll dotted with white crosses.

Kate hands me a folded slip of paper. "Secretary of War Edwin Stanton signed this for you. It will allow you to travel behind Union lines. I think Brian already told you that he left a deposit with the manager of the Willard Hotel to cover your room expenses."

"Where is he now?"

"He's on an assignment," Allan says. "He would have come himself if he could."

We turn and walk back toward the house. Kate studies me sideways as we walk. "You're a lucky woman. Brian told me that you're his girl... even though you're married."

I nod. "I'm glad to hear that. My marriage situation is complicated."

"I imagine so."

Jacob comes to the porch when we reach the buggy. He's wearing his uniform.

"Who might this be?" he says.

"We're from Roanoke," Kate says. Her sweet-as-molasses Southern accent has returned. "I heard my brother might have been buried here. He died during the battle of Manassas Junction."

Jacob nods. "You can visit his gravesite whenever you'd like."

Allan helps Kate into the buggy seat and sits down beside her.

"It was nice meeting you, Elizabeth," she says.

Allan tips his hat, and then they're on their way.

"It was nice meeting you too," I call after them.

We watch until they disappear on the road. I follow Jacob back inside and return to my piano to continue practicing.

Jacob rises before dawn on August 28. I dress quickly and run to the porch as he mounts his saddle.

"Wish us luck," he says. "You should set up some tables outside the barn like you did before. We're bound to have some casualties today."

I hear cannon blasts east of us a few hours later. Wagons filled with casualties start to arrive at noon. A man named Dr. Jeffers accompanies the injured soldiers this time.

Emma and William keep the water buckets coming while the doctor performs his amputations. I assist, administering chloroform and opium to the amputees. I'm getting good at this by now.

The next two days go by in a blur. Cannons echoing in the distance accompany the casualties arriving from the battlefield at Bull Run—the second major battle north of Manassas Junction.

"It's a sordid mess, this business of war," I say to Emma, as we clean the amputees' chamber pots.

She nods. "It seems like such a waste... all these young men dying."

Dr. Jeffers and his aids cart the last of his patients to Warrenton the next morning. There are eighteen new coffins planted in our cemetery by the time he leaves.

I'm surprised to see Lieutenant John Mosby driving a wagon onto our private road that afternoon. Several cavalry soldiers on horses accompany him as he steers the wagon to the grassy knoll. His men lift a casket out of the back, and place it on the ground as I walk up to them.

Mosby extends his hand to me. "I'm sorry about your husband," he says. "We had to close the casket. The cannonball that hit him left his face unrecognizable."

The men retrieve shovels from the barn and dig a grave for Jacob's casket. William helps them. I'm numb as I watch. For some reason I can't cry. Emma comes from the house and stands next to me. She doesn't cry either. Our grief from burying so many young men has left us emotionally depleted.

"What happened?" I ask Mosby.

He looks at me with a frozen stare. "We were hiding in the trees ready to attack the Union's left flank, when some of our own soldiers mistook us for the enemy. We lost four men before they stopped firing their cannons at us."

How ironic and sad, that Jacob's own troops killed him.

A soldier opens a Bible and reads a prayer, and they lower Jacob's coffin into the ground. I watch without emotion as they fill the hole with dirt.

I return from the barn with *Jacob Butler* painted on a white cross. Mosby pounds the cross into the dirt. He then goes to the wagon and brings me Jacob's Confederate-issued Enfield rifle and some ammunition.

"Perhaps this will give you some security," he says.

I nod. "Thanks. Jacob showed me how to load ammunition and fire his rifle last year."

His men mount their horses. Mosby jumps up into his wagon, tips his hat, and they ride away.

Emma and William return to their chores, and then I'm alone, staring at the fresh mound of dirt.

"You were a hard man, Jacob Butler," I say aloud.

I try to think of something more to say, but my attention keeps drifting. I turn in a circle, looking at the rolling hills. The farm is mine now... with all its debts and encumbrances—or maybe it belongs to Rothschild's Bank of England. I should find out.

I return to the house and dig through the paperwork in Jacob's office. I break open a locked drawer with a screwdriver, and find the mortgage from the Bank of England inside. Jacob received six thousand pounds sterling in gold in return for pledging our eleven-hundred-acre farm as collateral. The mortgage interest rate is 10 percent per annum. The entire mortgage plus all accumulated interest—payable in gold—is due within six months of the end of hostilities between the Union and Confederacy, or within thirty days if Jacob dies.

I'll never be able to raise that kind of money.

I find a stack of bonds Jacob purchased with the gold. The six thousand pounds sterling purchased thirty thousand dollars' worth of Confederate bonds.

"*Shite,*" I say aloud.

Inflation has run rampant since the start of the war, significantly reducing the value of the bonds. I do some quick calculations using the currency rates in the Richmond newspaper. The six thousand pound sterling loan plus seven hundred in accumulated interest will now cost fifty-two thousand Confederate dollars at the current exchange rate—more, the longer I hold the loan.

I realize now that the Bank of England is the de facto owner of the land, the house, the two barns, the grain silos, and the sixteen log cabins where the slaves used to live. I'd hate to lose the farm, but there's no way I'll be able to pay off the loan on my own, and Father doesn't have any money. Viscount Clements ruined Father's chances of finding a solicitor position thirteen years ago. I'll just stay here until the Bank of England finds out Jacob is dead and kicks me off the property.

I retrieve a hammer from the barn and break open a metal lock box I find on a shelf. There are two hundred Confederate dollars inside.

"It smells wonderful in here," I say to Emma as I enter the kitchen.

Emma is pulling an apple pie she just baked out of the oven compartment of our pot-bellied stove.

She grins. "Thank you, Miss Elizabeth. I know you love apple pie."

"I'll sign whatever papers you and William need to secure your freedom. You'll be freemen from now on."

I see tears in her eyes as she comes to hug me.

"Thank you, Miss Elizabeth," she says into my chest. "That's been my dream since I was a little girl."

She releases me. "I need to go tell William."

I place the two hundred Confederate dollars on the counter. "You and William are free to leave, or stay if you'd like. This is all the money we have to live on until the war is over."

"I'll ask William what he wants to do. This has been our home since Jacob bought us at the slave auction in Richmond thirty years ago, so I think he'll probably want to stay."

"You can move into the house if you'd like. You can take Jacob's room. It's the largest."

"Are you sure, Miss Elizabeth?"

"Of course. I'd love to have your company. I don't want to stay in this big old mansion by myself."

"I'll ask William, but I'm sure he'll want to."

She grins. "He loves to listen to your piano. I'll be back in a minute," she says, removing her apron.

I watch through the parlor window as she runs into the field to William. He's milking a cow—the only cow we have left. Jacob took the other cow to his soldiers last month.

I watch him smile and hug her after she tells him the news. They walk back to the house together. He's carrying the milk pail with him.

"We'd love to stay here with you," William says, as he reaches for my hand.

"I'm glad," I say. "I'll pay you once I'm able to earn some money again."

"Don't worry about that, Miss Elizabeth. We're not going anywhere."

"Let's have some pie to celebrate," Emma says.

William and I follow her into the kitchen. The pie is half-gone when we finish.

Emma helps me pack Jacob's clothes into boxes, and we move them out of the room. I then help William and Emma carry clothes from their cabin into the house.

September 14, 1862.

THE SMELL of smoke awakens me at dawn. I see twenty Union soldiers in our fields when I look out my bedroom window.

They're burning down the log cabins!

I dress quickly, run down the hall, and knock on William and Emma's door.

William opens it. "What is it, Miss Elizabeth?"

"Union troops are burning down the cabins! We need to stop them."

I go to the office, grab the Enfield rifle, bite open the cartridge, pour the black gunpowder in, and ram a .577 caliber Minie ball down the barrel the way Jacob showed me. I then stick a percussion cap on the percussion lock.

William and Emma join me as I run out of the house.

Eight of the log houses are burning. The soldiers are just about to light a pile of firewood propped against the dairy barn.

"Stop," I yell, pointing my rifle at them.

The soldiers turn and stare at me. Some of them have whiskey bottles. Others have cans of kerosene.

One of them throws a burning stick into the pile of firewood. The kerosene-propelled flames instantly shoot up the side of the barn. The searing heat pushes us back toward the house.

Several soldiers approach us with their rifles leveled, surrounding us on all sides.

"So, you're the lady of the house," one of the soldiers says. He sounds drunk. "We know you use this as a field hospital for the Rebels, so we're burning you out."

"You can't do that," I yell. "There's no one here but us."

"What about all those Rebel graves behind your barn?"

"Get off my property!"

One of the drunken soldiers grabs the barrel of my rifle. He snorts a devilish cackle as he sticks the end of the barrel into his chest. "Go ahead and shoot, little lady," he slurs.

The other soldiers laugh.

I'm tempted to pull the trigger, but I can't. I'm sure they'd shoot all three of us if I did.

The drunk twists the rifle out of my grip and hands it to a soldier standing next to him. "Now why don't you be a good little girl and take me to your bedroom."

He grabs me and tries to kiss me.

I twist out of his grip and slap him across the face. "Don't touch me!"

"Ah, good," he says. "You're a feisty little tiger. I like that."

The soldiers chortle.

"I'll get her warmed up," he says. "The rest of you can line up outside her bedroom until I'm done."

William blocks the drunken soldier when he tries to grab me again. "Leave her alone," he yells.

A soldier smacks William in the head with the butt of his rifle, and he crumples to the ground. Emma and I kneel down next to him. William is dazed as we help him sit up.

A soldier rides up on a horse. He has more stripes on his shoulders than the other men—a lieutenant.

"That's enough," he says to his troops. "Get back to work. McClellan wants us to head north to Maryland today. We need to finish up here before we leave."

The soldiers move away and return to the log cabins.

One soldier stays, pointing his rifle at us. "Don't move," he says.

The soldiers set fire to the remaining log cabins and the barn we used as a classroom.

"Take all the food and valuables out of the house," the lieutenant bellows to his soldiers.

The soldiers carry food from our pantry out of the house and load it into the back of a wagon behind two horses. Another soldier ties a rope around the neck of our remaining cow, and attaches the rope to the back of the wagon.

Several of our neighbors, drawn by the thick columns of black and gray smoke rising into the sky, stand in the road, gaping at the burning buildings.

"Burn the house down," the lieutenant orders.

"No!" I yell.

"We're burning down everything used to support the Confederate war effort," he says. "People in town told us your husband is a captain in the Rebel army."

"But he's dead now!"

"That doesn't matter."

"Please don't burn my piano."

The lieutenant smirks. "We have no use for a piano."

He turns to his men. "Burn it down," he orders.

I watch with disbelief as they stack furniture in the center of the parlor. They douse the pile with kerosene, and throw a burning stick through the doorway. The house erupts with a massive boom, shooting flames out the windows.

Tears stream down my cheeks. Emma is crying too, holding on to me.

The soldiers watch the fires burn until the walls of the house implode. The barns and slave cabins have turned into rubble now. They depart with the wagon and cow heading north toward Warrenton.

My neighbors try to console me by expressing their outrage toward the Yankees, but I'm in a trance, unable to speak. The fire consuming our house has diminished into smoking embers by late afternoon.

"We should go to the Methodist church in Warrenton," William says. "Reverend Brooks has a room for people escaping on the Underground Railroad. Maybe he'll let us stay there tonight."

I nod. My shock and anger have left me sullen and quiet.

We walk north to the minister's home in Warrenton. Reverend Brooks brings us down to his basement after I explain what happened. There are several cots with blankets in his windowless cellar.

"You can stay here as long as you need to," he says. "I haven't smuggled anyone for a while. The Union troops protect escaped slaves now."

The reverend's wife is making breakfast when we come upstairs the next morning. "Have a seat," the reverend says.

We sit down at his table, and the reverend pours hot tea into cups for us.

"I have a cousin in Georgetown we can stay with for a while," Emma says.

"I have a friend in Washington too," I say, "at the Willard Hotel."

I turn to the minister. "I hate to put people out, Reverend Brooks, but do you know of anyone that could take us to Washington today?"

He smiles. "I'll take you there after breakfast. I can stay at the Foundry Methodist church rectory tonight, and return home tomorrow."

Mrs. Brooks brings scrambled eggs, bacon, and freshly baked bread to the table. "You better eat a good breakfast," she says with a smile. "You have a long day ahead of you."

"I'm going to give Emma and William their freedom," I say. "Do you know what I should write for that?"

"I can help you," the Reverend says.

He brings me two sheets of paper, an inkwell, and a quill pen. "Write out their names and ages separately on each sheet of paper, and say that you're granting them their freedom. We can sign the papers as witnesses. We should register these with the Clerk of the Court here in Warrenton before we go to Washington." He faces William and Emma. "That way you won't need to worry about being abducted by slave hunters if you return to Virginia."

I look at Emma and William. "I'm sorry to say this, but I don't know your last names."

William nods. "Mister Jacob told me once that our last name is Butler, the same as his."

I write down the particulars granting each of them their freedom, and sign and date my name at the bottom of each page. Mr. and Mrs. Brooks then sign and date the papers as witnesses.

William and Emma smile when I hand them their freedom papers.

"Thank you, Miss Elizabeth," Emma says, with tears in her eyes.

We walk down the street to the County Courthouse and enter the Clerk's office.

"We're here to register some slaves that have been granted their freedom," Reverend Brooks says.

The clerk, a bald, middle-aged man in his fifties, smirks as he looks at Emma and William.

"Those are Jacob Butler's slaves," he says to me. "I saw them when I came to the Warrenton Rifles picnic you had at your farm two years ago."

"Jacob and Harland are dead now," I say. "Here are Emma and Williams' freedom papers."

I place the papers on his desk.

He reads the papers, and then looks up at me with a wary eye. "I can't register your niggers just based on your word. I need proof that Jacob and Harland are dead. Besides, you're a woman. You have no right to do this."

"Jacob and Harland are buried behind the barn the Yankee soldiers burned down yesterday," I say. "You can go to our cemetery if you want proof. We've buried close to forty Confederate soldiers there."

"Trust me," Reverend Brooks says. "Mrs. Butler owns the farm now."

The clerk pulls out his Free Negroes registry and writes down William and Emma's names and ages.

We then return to the Reverend's house, pick up the sandwiches his wife made for us, and leave in his carriage heading east towards Washington. It's dark when we arrive in Georgetown.

We leave William and Emma with their cousin, and then the Reverend takes me to the Willard Hotel. There's a prepaid room for me, just as Brian promised.

I take a bath and go to bed. I'll go to the War Department to find Brian tomorrow morning.

35. BRIAN O'ROURKE

Washington. September 16, 1862.

MY TELEGRAPH RECEIVER comes to life at dawn. I raise my head from my desk and start jotting down the code words as the audible dots and dashes hurry by.

President Lincoln stirs from his slumber in his cot next to me, sits up, and yawns. He slept here in the War Department again last night. He's been doing this a lot lately, so he can stay in close contact with his generals in the field.

Lincoln watches over my shoulder as I decipher the encoded message. It's long and rambling, which is typical for General McClellan.

"He says General Lee has a hundred and twenty-five thousand troops, Mr. President," I say as I write, "and he only has eighty-seven thousand. He wants you to transfer the troops protecting Washington to him before he attacks."

Lincoln smirks. "I don't believe his estimates, and we can't leave our capital unprotected."

Lincoln turns to Secretary of War Edwin Stanton, who is sitting up on his cot next to Lincoln. "McClellan has overestimated Confederate troop strength in every battle he's fought," Lincoln says. "His timidity has made him squander every opportunity we've had to defeat Lee's army, and now he's doing it again."

Stanton nods his agreement.

I continue to write as I decode the message. "McClellan says Confederate General Hill is retreating from South Mountain, heading northwest toward Sharpsburg. The rest of Lee's troops are digging in west of Antietam Creek."

Lincoln stares at a detailed map of Virginia and Maryland tacked to the wall. "Why isn't McClellan attacking Hill now," he says, "before the rest of Lee's reinforcements arrive from the Shenandoah Valley?"

Stanton points at Sharpsburg in western Maryland on the map.

"Pinkerton's men told us last night that General Lee only has thirty thousand troops, and McClellan has eighty-seven. We should attack now while we have the advantage."

Lincoln points at the Hagerstown Pike road south of Sharpsburg. "McClellan could use one of his divisions here to crush General Hill while he's on the run from Burnside. This would significantly weaken Lee's defenses behind Antietam Creek."

Lincoln faces Stanton. "This is a crucial battle for us. We need a victory before I announce the Emancipation Proclamation. Our diplomats in Europe say that England and France are close to joining the Confederates. However, the abolitionists in their governments will exert strong pressure to keep them out of the war if we launch a moral crusade to free the slaves."

"I agree," Stanton says. "We must make our proclamation after a victory on the battlefield. Otherwise, our announcement will be perceived as an act of desperation."

Lincoln turns to me. "Send McClellan the following message."

I poise my quill pen above a sheet of paper.

"Destroy General Hill while you have him on the run," Lincoln says.

"Yes, Mr. President," I say.

Lincoln's message, as usual, is crisp and to the point. I encode the message with a cipher, and send it to McClellan's telegraph operator in the field—Stuart Jenkins—a man I trained.

McClellan replies thirty minutes later with a long diatribe accusing Lincoln of not understanding conditions in the field. He says an attack on General Hill will expose his lines and lead to a Union defeat, especially since Lincoln is withholding the troops he needs in Washington.

I don't write down McClellan's last words, where he tells Lincoln to "stop trying to control me." McClellan's gross insubordination will only stir up more enmity between them. I'll tell Secretary Stanton about this later and let him decide if he wants to inform the president.

"This is very frustrating," Lincoln says. "He's obsessing about his lack of resources again to justify his procrastination. That doesn't give him the right to disobey my orders."

Stanton nods. "McClellan is counting on his Democratic friends in Congress to defend his actions if we dismiss him. I know we need to replace him, but that's risky before a major battle."

Lincoln faces me. "How long will it take you to reach McClellan's lines?"

I stand up, look at the map, and calculate the distance from Washington to Sharpsburg.

"It's approximately sixty-nine miles, sir. The Confederates took Harpers Ferry yesterday, so I'll only be able to travel as far as Knoxville, Maryland, by train. I should reach our troops tonight if I ride the last fifteen miles like a Pony Express rider."

"Good. I'd like you to give me another set of eyes and ears during the battle."

Lincoln faces a soldier who's standing guard by the door. "Are you familiar with that part of Maryland, Sergeant Doyle?"

"Yes, Mr. President," Doyle says. "I used to hunt in those mountains with my father."

"Good. I'd like you to accompany Brian to McClellan's headquarters."

"Yes, sir."

Lincoln walks to the desk of another telegraph operator. "Please send a message to the B&O Railroad officials along Brian's route, telling them to clear the tracks. Make sure they have an engine ready at the New Jersey Avenue Railroad Depot in thirty minutes, and fresh horses available at the station in Knoxville."

"Yes, sir." The operator encodes the message with a cipher and starts tapping it out.

Lincoln turns to me. "I want a report every hour from McClellan's headquarters as the battle progresses."

"I'll do that if I can, Mr. President, but McClellan may not let me communicate with you."

"Why is that?"

"He threatened to have me court martialed during the Peninsula Campaign."

"Why?"

"He didn't like it when I reminded him of your order to pursue the enemy when they retreated."

"He can't do that. The Telegraph Corps doesn't report to the army, even though he'd like it to."

"McClellan was also upset that I informed you about his secret meeting with Fernando Wood and the other pro-slavery Democrats, when they came to the Berkeley plantation in Virginia."

"The Democrats shouldn't be courting him to be their presidential candidate in the middle of a war."

"He's made no secret about his disagreements with our administration," Stanton says.

"I know McClellan censors information he sends me from the battlefield," Lincoln says. "That's why I need a separate source of intelligence. Are there other telegraph wagons with our troops?"

"General Meagher from the Irish Brigade has one," Stanton says. "Meagher is bivouacked east of Antietam Creek."

Lincoln scribbles out a message and hands it to me. "Give this to General Meagher. I want you to observe the battle and send me reports using his Telegraph Corps wagon. I'm sure Meagher will be in the thick of things. He never misses a chance to confront the enemy."

"Yes, sir."

Lincoln faces Doyle and me. "Good luck, gentlemen," he says, "and may God be with you."

Sergeant Timothy Doyle and I salute the president—even though I'm not a soldier—and we leave the room. We arrive at the New Jersey Avenue Railroad Depot ten minutes later. There's a train engine with no railcars waiting when we arrive.

We sit on a bench behind the train engineer as he speeds northwest out of the city. The Knoxville stationmaster has two saddled-up horses ready for us when we disembark.

A misty rain is falling as we mount our horses. We ride west through a pass in the Appalachian Mountains, and head northwest toward Sharpsburg, arriving at our Union encampment just before 10:00 p.m. It's raining harder now.

We locate General Meagher after fumbling around in the dark for an hour. General McClellan told his troops that they couldn't have fires tonight. The cloudy skies to our west are yellow with the glow of hundreds of Confederate campfires.

We enter General Meagher's tent. He greets me with a handshake, and I hand him Lincoln's message. He reads it beneath an oil lamp and stuffs it into his pocket.

"Our troops have been sitting on their butts all day instead of confronting the Rebels," he says. "I hope McClellan doesn't change his mind and make us wait again tomorrow."

Meagher pours a generous serving of Bushmills Irish whiskey into three tin cups, and hands them to Sergeant Doyle and me.

He raises his cup, and we do the same. "To Ireland... and the Union," he says. "*Sláinte.*"

"*Sláinte,*" we reply, and then we put our cups to our lips and drain them dry.

I swill mine around in my mouth to savor the strong flavor before I swallow. "Thanks," I say. "That was delicious."

Meagher nods. "Our brigade will be facing the center of the Confederate line tomorrow. You should get some sleep. It's going to be a long day."

One of Meagher's Negro corporals departs with Sergeant Doyle to help him find his unit. Meagher exits his tent and points at his telegraph wagon ten yards away. "They'll set you up with a place to sleep," he says.

"Thanks, and good luck tomorrow," I say as we shake hands.

I walk my horse to the wagon, tie it to the wheel, and awaken the telegraph crew. I know both men. I trained them in Washington before we sent them into the field with General Hooker's I Corps.

They set up a cot for me on the ground and hand me a blanket. I'm unable to sleep with all the adrenaline pumping through my veins, so I rise from my cot, and walk around the bivouac talking with the troops. Everyone speaks in whispers so we don't alarm the Confederate patrols on the other side of Antietam Creek.

Many of the soldiers are nervous. I know they're wondering if they'll live another day. The Irish Brigade has taken many casualties— 30 percent or more—in their last two battles.

I find Matthew Keenan playing poker in a tent with some soldiers in his platoon. We sip a shot of whiskey together while I play a couple of hands.

I wish him luck, and return to my cot. The rain finally stops just as I pull the wool blanket over my head.

I've barely slept when a cannon boom awakens me before dawn. It's a dreary overcast day with drizzling rain.

"General Hooker's corps is attacking Lee's left flank," the telegraph operator tells me.

I encode a message saying the battle has begun, and send it to the War Department. I sign my initials at the end—B. B. O., for Brian Boru O'Rourke—so Lincoln will know I arrived.

I ride my horse north to a bluff overlooking the battlefield. Confederate cannons west of Antietam Creek are exchanging volleys with Union artillery on our side of the river. General Hooker's troops from Wisconsin, New York, and Pennsylvania are marching southwest toward a church to engage the enemy.

The acrid stench of burning gunpowder chokes the air. Gray smoke clouds are obscuring the battlefield, so I ride closer for a better look.

The Union line advances past the church to the northern edge of a vast cornfield after an hour. The rain has dissipated now, and the sun is starting to peek through the clouds.

I see hundreds of Confederate soldiers hidden among the cornstalks jump up and fire their rifles. The surprise assault inflicts heavy Union casualties.

It's difficult to watch the savage butchery through my binoculars. The fighting is fierce, with the Union soldiers getting the worst of it. The Confederate troops continue to hide among the cornstalks while the Union troops stand in straight lines going through the same ritual: loading their rifles, aiming and shooting, moving a step forward, loading and shooting, until they lurch backward in agony when a Minie ball or artillery shell finds its target. A soldier behind them then takes his comrade's place in the line.

The Confederates offer valiant resistance in the cornfield, forcing the Union to retreat several times with brutal counterattacks. Control of the field changes hands at least fifteen times, exacting hundreds of fatalities on both sides. There are hardly any cornstalks left by the time the Union's superior numbers overwhelms the Rebels, forcing them into a final retreat.

I scurry away to the telegraph wagon and send a terse ciphered message to Washington: *Heavy fighting with many casualties. The Union right flank is taking ground.*

I see dozens of Union troops—deserters— running through the trees as I return to the battlefield.

General Meagher's troops are marching toward the center of the Confederate line now. A priest, Father William Corby, is riding back and forth on his horse in front of Meagher's men, blessing them with the sign of the cross. He's giving them absolution before they die—granting their souls advance forgiveness for the murders they're about to commit.

The priest rides behind the troops and joins me as the Irish Brigade moves forward. I see Sergeant Keenan with his platoon. He turns to me and salutes, and I return the gesture. He nods, and marches forward with his platoon.

Please God, protect him in the battle, I pray.

Several rows of men from General Meagher's Sixty-Third, Sixty-Ninth, and Eighty-Eighth New York regiments augmented with soldiers from the Twenty-Ninth Massachusetts, advance in lockstep toward the Confederates. The first Confederate volley knocks a third of Meagher's officers off their horses. The next volley takes several more.

"The officers on horseback are always the first to go," Father Corby yells out to me above the din.

The thunderous cannon booms are making it difficult to hear.

"They want to eliminate the command structure to cause confusion in the ranks," I yell back.

Bullets topple the rest of Meagher's officers from their horses a moment later, including Meagher. The combatants from both armies are standing in lines now, immersed in smoke, slaughtering each other with torrents of bullets. Neither army seems to be gaining an advantage.

I see a woman helping wounded soldiers in the cornfield through my binoculars.

"Do you see that woman?" I yell to Father Corby. "She's in danger."

"That's Clara Barton," he shouts. "She's a nurse. I saw her at the Battle of Second Manassas and at South Mountain a few days ago."

The Rebels retreat to a sunken road next to a fence after an hour of heavy fighting. The embankment provides good protection as they fire thousands of bullets at the approaching Union soldiers. I see several emerald-colored Irish Brigade pennant flags go down as I watch through my binoculars.

I report status to Washington, and return to a bluff overlooking the sunken road. The warriors are fighting bayonet-to-bayonet now. The battlefield in front of the sunken road is thick with bodies.

I ride south after I report status. General Burnside's Union troops are attacking Confederate General Lee's right flank. Hundreds of Confederate snipers hidden in the bluffs are picking off Burnside's men as they try to cross a bridge over Antietam Creek.

I return to the bluff near the sunken road. Dead bodies are two people deep on the ground in some places. The Irish Brigade finally breaks through the line, splitting the Confederate defenses. I report this to Lincoln.

Burnside's troops have conquered the bridge when I return to the south end of the battlefield. They're pushing the Confederates back to Sharpsburg. The Union has an overwhelming advantage when I estimate troop strength.

I ride back to the telegraph wagon and report status—lots of good news this time. Sergeant Doyle rides up to me as I finish sending my message.

"I have something important to tell you," he says.

"What's going on?"

"McClellan ordered our division to hold the line instead of pursuing the Confederates. No one knows his battle plan because he doesn't trust his generals, so we're not sure what to do. We could cut off Lee's retreat if we take control of the bridge that crosses the Potomac west of Sharpsburg, but McClellan has ordered us to stay where we are. I think the president should know this."

"I'll be sure to tell him."

"McClellan is squandering a great opportunity. He's holding two of his five corps in reserve instead of committing all his forces to the battle. General Porter's V Corps and General Franklin's VI Corps are ready to engage the enemy, but McClellan told us to stand down."

"Thanks for telling me."

Doyle spurs his horse and rides back toward his unit.

I prepare another message—longer this time—and send it to Washington.

Psalm 23 comes into my mind when I reach the sunken road to estimate fatalities: "Even though I walk through the valley in the shadow of death, I fear no evil, for I know you are with me."

But where? I ask, as I look up at the smoke-filled sky. *Where are you, God*?

The psalm seems empty beneath the deafening roar of the battle that's raging half a mile from me. The horrific slaughter has turned the sunken road into a river of black blood. Hundreds of mutilated corpses stare at nothing in a frozen repose, with hollow-mouthed screams chiseled on their faces. I see bodies with heads partially blown away, guts ripped open, testicles hanging from broken pelvises, dangling eyeballs, missing limbs.

Many Confederates don't have shoes. Two combatants gripped by death are clinging to rifles, thrusting bayonets into each other.

Irish Brigade bodies fill the middle section of the road. Their emerald-colored pennants, flapping so proudly this morning, now lie trampled in the mud.

I find a Virginia Emerald Guard's body entwined with a Union Irish Brigade soldier—Irish fighting Irish in America, men that may have been friends before they fled from Ireland on a famine ship.

I recognize men I met in the New York militia, men that helped me string telegraph lines to the general's tents, men that danced Irish jigs while I played my fiddle during the Peninsula Campaign.

A shriek from a maimed horse captures my attention. Its hind legs are shattered.

I need to put it out of its misery. I jump down from my saddle, pick up a discarded musket, load it with a Minie ball and gunpowder, and shoot the horse in the head. The front of the horse crumples into a heap—silent.

I step carefully along the road to avoid tripping over bodies.

Oh God! Matthew Keenan.

I kneel down beside him. His guts are splayed open, pulverized by a cannonball. He's been like a brother to me since our voyage on the *Dromahair*.

My tears flow before I can stop them. *Thank you, God—for nothing*!

I cry as I survey the sea of contorted bodies around me—thousands in all directions.

Why are we here? Is it worth all this... to keep the Union together?

Only a cruel God would allow this kind of slaughter. *Is this some kind of lesson you're teaching us*? I say silently, as I look up at the clouds.

I remove Matthew's Jesus cross from his neck. I'll give it to his parents. It's all they'll have of him after the cleanup crews bury the dead on the battlefield.

There's someone moving beneath the bodies next to Matthew.

I pull three entangled corpses aside, and find a young Confederate, probably seventeen years old. I think he's saying, "Help me," as I stare at the fear clouding his eyes. It's impossible to hear above the earsplitting noise from the cannons and rifles.

His left wrist is a bloody stump. He has a bayonet wound in his right thigh.

Kill him! He's the enemy.

My right hand finds the handle of my dagger... but then I let it go. I grab a rifle on the ground and stick the tip of the bayonet into his chest. One thrust and it's over.

Terror reaches through his eyes to me as I stare at him.

Should I kill you? You'll probably die anyway. I'm doing you a favor.

This is God's work, I decide—if there *is* a God.

I drop the rifle and yank my belt off my trousers.

"Stay with me," I yell, as I wrap my belt around his bicep. I hitch it tight to stem the blood flow.

I cut the leather strap off the rifle, and use it as a tourniquet around the top of his leg.

"What's your name?" I yell.

He's losing consciousness. He doesn't answer.

I pick him up, drape him over my shoulder, and plod over bodies toward where my horse has wandered off. Clara Barton pulls up, driving a flatbed wagon pulled by two horses.

"Do you want me to take him to the hospital?" Clara yells.

"Does it matter that he's a Confederate?" I yell back.

"No! The Union will exchange him for one of our prisoners if he survives!"

I lay him on the wagon's wooden planks, jump up to the back, and we pull him forward between two Union soldiers.

"I'll take them to the field hospital," she yells, as she leaps over the railing to the driver's seat.

I jump down from the back. "I'll look for more wounded soldiers while you're gone!"

I guide my horse to the sunken road and tie its reins to a smashed cannon wheel. I'm not sure where to start as I look at the tangled muddle of dead bodies.

I pull a soldier out of the road, lay him on his back, and check his pulse to see if he's alive. Nothing. The man beside him has a shattered skull, so I move to a body draped over a fence railing.

I find a soldier who's still breathing after I've examined a dozen corpses. I cut a leather gun strap off a rifle with my dagger, and tie it around his groin to stifle the blood flowing out of his shattered knee.

I've lined up five wounded soldiers by the time Clara Barton returns. She has two medical soldiers with her now. They jump down from their wagon and start tending to the wounded.

The Union is consolidating their position west of Antietam Creek when I return to the battle line on my horse. Artillery from both sides continues to pound away, filling the air with projectiles and acrid gray smoke.

A fresh battalion of Rebel troops arrives. They march quickly into position to bolster the Confederate right flank. A standoff ensues as both armies bombard each other with grapeshot, cannonballs, and bullets. The Confederates, overwhelmed by the Union's numerical advantage, move gradually backward toward Sharpsburg in a slow retreat.

I report status to Washington. I then ride north along the river, estimating casualties and troop strength.

I barely hear the swooshing whistle of the shrapnel shell before it explodes. Flaming shards of metal rain down on me.

My horse neighs a horrifying scream, bucks me off, and runs away.

The molten flames sear the skin on my head and shoulders as I writhe on the ground. My screams are lost in the din of the battle as I crawl through the mud to the creek. I smell my skin and hair burning as I lunge into the muddy water to douse my burning clothes.

Muffled cannon blasts echo behind a vicious ringing in my ears as I drag myself up the embankment. My overcoat and shirt have disintegrated. Pain ripping my flesh screams like a lightning bolt through my consciousness. Blood is flowing into my eyes.

I yank my dagger and its leather sheath from the tattered shards of my overcoat, and shove them into my trousers beneath my waist. I wipe blood from my eyes, struggle to my feet, and plod toward the telegraph wagon a half mile away. I trip over corpses several times before I reach the operators.

"Tell Lincoln that the Rebels are backed up to Sharpsburg," I yell as I fall to my knees, "but McClellan isn't cutting off their retreat across the Potomac. We can capture General Lee if we act soon!"

One of the operators hands me a towel as the other encrypts and sends my message. I see his lips move, but I can't hear anything but a loud buzz.

I wipe my face and head. The towel is red with blood.

I trudge back toward the battlefield, and then I'm wobbling and tumbling as if I'm falling into a deep abyss, and then everything goes black.

36. ELIZABETH BUTLER

Washington. September 23, 1862.

I ARRIVE AT the entrance to the War Department building just after dawn.

"Has Brian O'Rourke returned yet?" I say to the soldiers guarding the door.

"No, ma'am," one of them replies.

I'm worried. I've looked for Brian here every morning for the past week, but he hasn't shown up for work. He's not at his boarding house either. News of the slaughter on the battlefields at Antietam is everywhere, but I don't even know if he was there.

"I need to find out if he's wounded," I say. "Isn't there someone I can talk with?"

"Wait here," the soldier says. "I'll be right back."

He walks inside and disappears.

I'm shocked when he returns with President Lincoln. The president extends his hand to me. "How do you do?" he says.

"I'm pleased to meet you, Mr. President," I say, returning his handshake.

"This is my secretary of war, Edwin Stanton," he says, introducing me to the man beside him.

"My name is Elizabeth," I say as I shake his hand. "I'm a friend of Brian O'Rourke's. I can't find him anywhere. I've been checking at his boarding house, but he's not there either."

"We sent him on a mission a few days ago," the president says. He turns to Stanton. "Can you find out where Brian is for this young lady?"

Stanton nods. "I'll do my best, sir."

Lincoln faces me. "Brian told me you're a concert pianist. I promised him I'd invite you both to play a recital at the White House soon. My wife will make the arrangements when you're ready."

"Thank you, Mr. President. I'd love to perform for you, but I need to find Brian first."

"Where are you staying?"

"I'm at the Willard Hotel. I heard about the Emancipation Proclamation you announced yesterday. I think it's wonderful that you're releasing the slaves from captivity."

He nods and tips his hat. "I must take my leave now, Elizabeth. We'll dispatch a courier to the hotel as soon as we know something."

Stanton walks back into the building as Lincoln departs toward the White House.

Should I follow Lincoln and tell him what his troops did to my farm? No. This isn't a good time. Perhaps I'll confront him after he finds Brian.

There's a knock on my hotel room door late in the afternoon. I open the door, and the concierge hands me a folded sheet of paper. "A soldier asked me to deliver this to you," he says.

"Thank you."

I close the door and read the message: Brian O'Rourke is at the Armory Square military hospital at Independence Avenue and Seventh Street. – E. Stanton.

I rush out of the hotel and run several blocks south to the hospital. It's near the Smithsonian Castle where I played a concert a few years ago. I find out when I arrive that the hospital has more than a dozen long rectangular buildings.

The scene is chaotic inside the first building. There are close to fifty patients lying in beds along the walls. A deceased soldier with a sheet over his head lies on a stretcher near the entrance.

"Where can I find Brian O'Rourke?" I say to one of the nurses.

"No one has a complete list of patients," she says. "You'll have to look for him yourself."

I search the building next door without results.

There's a tall, shirtless man sitting up in bed leaning against a wall in the third building. I'm not sure if it's Brian. The man has a white bandage wrapped around his head, and smaller bandages on his shoulders and arms.

His dark eyes draw me close. "Is that you, Brian?" I say.

He reaches for my hand. "My angel of Innisfree. Are you here to rescue me again?"

I sit down next to him on the bed. I want to hug him, but I'm afraid of his injuries. "I'm glad you're safe," I say. "What happened?"

"A shell exploded above me. I lost a lot of blood, and then I passed out. The bandage around my ears is there to protect my ruptured eardrums."

"Are you able to hear me?"

"There's a loud buzzing in my left ear. The doctor said it should heal on its own in a couple of months, although I may have some hearing loss. They're taking the bandages off tomorrow. They said they'd let me leave if my wounds are healed enough."

"That would be wonderful. I can take care of you."

He doesn't smile. I see a haunted, faraway look in his eyes. This is new, something I've never seen before. Maybe that's what happens to soldiers after a battle.

"The room at the Willard is nice," I say. "Thank you for arranging that."

"You're welcome. How did you get away from your husband?"

I tell him about Jacob's death, and about the Union soldiers who burned everything to the ground.

"That's awful," he says. "They had no reason to do that."

"I found the Bank of England mortgage in Jacob's office. It said we have to repay the original loan balance plus all accumulated interest in gold within thirty days after Jacob dies, or I'll be in default. I'm sure the property isn't worth much now with everything burned down."

"That's too bad." He takes my hand. "You'll be safe here in Washington until the war is over."

"Do you think it will end soon?"

He shakes his head. "It's bound to continue for a while. The fighting was ferocious at Antietam, but many of Lee's troops got away at the end. There's a lot of hatred between the North and South after all the killing and destruction."

There's a Jesus cross on the table next to Brian. His dagger, in its leather sheath, is there too.

I pick up the cross. "When did you get this?"

"It belonged to a friend of mine—Matthew Keenan. I found him on the battlefield. It obviously didn't do him any good... but I think his parents might appreciate it."

"I'm sure they will."

I survey the injured soldiers lining both sides of the ward. Many have amputations. One man has no arms. Two young men in wheelchairs only have bandaged stumps for legs.

My gaze returns to Brian. "President Lincoln invited us to play a concert at the White House."

His eyebrows rise below his bandage. "You met him?"

"I did, when I went to the War Department looking for you."

"The president is a remarkable man. He works harder than anyone I've ever met. He even sleeps on a cot in the War Department so he can be there when we get a telegram from the field."

"It sounds like you're doing important work."

He stares into space with a faraway look. "Do you know what I'd really like?" he says.

"What's that?"

"See that piano over there against the wall?"

I turn and look. "I do."

"Can you play some music for us? I'm sure the other patients would appreciate it too. Ask one of the nurses if it's all right."

"Sure."

I walk to the piano and sit down after a nurse gives me permission to play. He'll like this, I tell myself. I play Schumann's "Träumerei" from memory.

The patients—those who haven't lost their hands or arms, that is— and their visitors, applaud when I finish. Many of the soldiers have a mother, sister, wife, or friend sitting next to them.

Brian smiles and nods in my direction.

I then play Chopin's Nocturne in E-flat Major, opus 9, no. 2.

Several people tell me that they hope I can play again as I walk back to Brian.

"That was great," Brian says. "Thank you."

I arrive at the hospital early the next morning. I'm carrying Brian's violin case.

"Your landlady let me take this from your room after I told her you were in the hospital," I say.

He removes his violin from the case and tunes the strings. "I'm elated to see my old friend."

He plays for a moment, frowns, and puts the violin back in its case. "I don't think I can play yet. I still have a terrible buzzing in my left ear."

The doctor arrives with a nurse a few minutes later. He introduces himself, sits down in a chair next to the bed, and watches as the nurse removes Brian's bandages.

I'm shocked when I see the scabs on Brian's scalp, forehead, arms, and chest. He must have close to thirty wounds. Most are the size of a grape. There's a two-inch burn scar above his left eyebrow.

"You'll have scars where we removed the shrapnel," the doctor tells Brian. "The largest will be above your left eye. Most of your hair should eventually grow back to hide the scars on your head."

"Now you'll be like me," I say, pointing at the scar on my cheek. "You'll have a beauty mark."

Brian chuckles. "Elizabeth earned her badge of courage protecting a slave from being beaten," he says. "I think it makes her look even more beautiful, don't you?"

The doctor nods. "That's a good reason to have a scar. However, it's really not that noticeable."

He sticks a probe into Brian's ears and looks at his eardrums. "How's the buzzing?"

"It's gone in my right ear, but not my left."

"Your eardrums look good. The nurse will bandage them again to help protect them. The rest of your injuries should heal on their own if you keep them clean. I can release you now if you'd like."

"Indeed. That would be grand."

The doctor signs a sheet of paper at the bottom, hands it to the nurse, and stands up. "You should return in three days to have your head bandage removed. Make sure you don't get water in your ears for at least three months. You need to give your eardrums time to heal."

"Yes, sir."

The doctor moves to the patient in the next bed.

I watch as the nurse wraps a bandage around Brian's head. "Will you play something for us on your violin after the doctor finishes?" she says to Brian.

Brian looks at me. I nod and smile.

"Certainly," he says.

He puts on a green shirt, blue army pants, and a black jacket provided by the hospital, and shoves his dagger beneath his belt. "My shirt and coat were destroyed," he says, "so this will have to do for now."

Brian introduces me to several soldiers he knows from the Irish Brigade while we wait for the doctor to finish his rounds. One of the soldiers says, "Brian saved my life. I was wedged beneath a bunch of dead bodies. He pulled me out and tied a tourniquet around my leg to stop the bleeding. I would have bled to death if he hadn't found me."

Brian stands next to me at the piano after the doctor leaves. Our first song is the Schumann piece. Everyone claps when we finish.

"How did that sound?" Brian says to me.

"Great."

"The notes sound odd with the buzzing in my eardrum."

"I couldn't tell the difference."

"It's nice to play music with you finally, after all these years."

"It certainly is."

We play several more pieces. I'm impressed as I watch him. He listens while I play a song he doesn't know, and then he joins me without needing music.

"Your concert was good for the patients," a nurse says when we finish. "I hope you can come back and play again."

"I will," I say. "I can also come back to help you if you need a volunteer."

"That would be greatly appreciated. Our staff is overwhelmed. We could really use more help."

The air is sunny and warm when we exit the hospital. It's a beautiful autumn day.

"Let's take a walk," I say.

"I'd love to."

We stroll around the city admiring the architecture, and the colorful leaves of autumn. Several people ask Brian about his bandage, and he explains what happened. We arrive at my hotel three hours later.

"I'd like to go back to work tomorrow," he says. "Do you want to walk with me to the War Department in the morning?"

"Sure. I'll go to the hospital and volunteer afterward."

We kiss in the hallway before I enter my room, and he returns to his boarding house.

Everyone is pleased to see Brian when we enter the War

Department building the next morning. He introduces me to several of his colleagues in the Telegraph Corps. I then say goodbye, and continue south to the Armory Square hospital.

Brian comes to my hotel and takes me out to dinner that night.

This becomes our daily ritual. The Telegraph Corps or secret service—I'm not sure which role Brian is playing on any given day—doesn't send him out of town since he's still recovering from his injuries, so I have him to myself in the evenings.

"I can't discuss what I'm doing," he always says when I ask. "It's secret."

Brian arrives at my hotel accompanied by another man in late November. "This is Adam, my brother-in-law," he says.

Adam extends his hand. "How do you do, Elizabeth?"

I return his handshake. "I'm pleased to meet you."

Adam grins. "So, this is the woman I've been hearing about for the past fourteen years."

Brian chuckles. "Yes, this is the angel of Innisfree." He turns to me. "Adam came down from New York to meet with Secretary Stanton. I hope you don't mind if we discuss a little business during dinner."

"I don't mind at all."

"Let's eat at the hotel restaurant tonight," Brian says. "It's cold outside. Besides, Adam is staying here too."

We walk into the restaurant and the maître d' seats us at a table.

"Our company, along with American Telegraph, will take ownership of most of the infrastructure the Telegraph Corps is putting in place after the war ends," Brian says. "Adam is here to discuss this with Secretary Stanton."

Adam nods. "Incorporating the military lines into our network will extend our reach into hundreds of towns we don't currently serve. It's a good deal. The government is going to give us the telegraph infrastructure at a nominal cost for supporting the Union war effort."

"How are Mary and the kids?" Brian says.

"The kids are growing fast, and Mary and my father have become real estate moguls. We've bought several more lots across the street from Central Park. The trails the city built there are beautiful. She's still renting out your house on Patchin Place, and depositing the money into your account each month."

THE ANGEL OF INNISFREE

"I'll give you the gold coins I bought for your kids at a mint in Denver before you leave tomorrow," Brian says. "I've kept them in a safety deposit box at Riggs Bank for over a year."

"That sounds like a wonderful gift," Adam says.

Brian pulls a small Jesus cross out of his pocket. "Could you give this to the Keenans? I took it from Matthew when I found his corpse on the battlefield at Antietam."

Adam nods. He puts the cross in his jacket pocket. "That's very sad. John and Maria have been inconsolable since they heard about his death. I'm sure they'll appreciate having this."

Brian's physical scars gradually heal over the ensuing weeks. Most of the hearing in his left ear has returned by Christmas. His emotional scars are much deeper, often rendering him distant and far away.

We attend an afternoon reception at the White House on New Year's Day. President Lincoln is celebrating the official start of the Emancipation Proclamation, as well as the admittance of West Virginia into the Union. I meet many congressmen, Supreme Court justices, and military officers and their wives during the celebration.

Brian and I walk back to the Willard Hotel when the reception is over.

"May I come in for a moment?" he says, when we reach my room.

This is strange. Brian has always been a gentleman until now, adhering to moral codes of decency.

"I guess so."

We enter my room, and I close the door and sit down on my bed.

Brian sits down across from me. He seems anxious.

He smiles after a moment, kneels down, and takes my hand. "Will you marry me, Elizabeth?"

My heart starts racing in my chest. "Yes!"

He slips a ring on my finger. We stand, and he takes me in his arms and kisses me passionately.

We lie down next to each other on the bed after a moment.

"I'd like to get married in New York if that's all right with you," he says. "That way Mary and her family can attend, along with some of our other friends."

"That's fine with me."

"How soon can you be ready?"

I smile. "I'm ready now."

He chuckles. "I'll send a telegram to Mary to tell her the good news, and then I'll get us tickets for the train tomorrow. I've arranged to take two weeks off."

I giggle. "I guess it's a good thing I said yes then."

"I'd like to take you to the Bedford Springs Hotel for our honeymoon, after we spend a week in New York. It's a beautiful resort in the Appalachian Mountains. I met President Buchanan there when he received the first transatlantic telegraph message from Queen Victoria."

"That sounds wonderful. It'll be nice to see Mary again."

"Indeed. I haven't seen her for two years."

"What kind of church shall we get married in—Catholic, or Protestant?"

He shrugs his shoulders. "Which do you prefer?"

"I'd prefer Protestant, unless you're determined to have me convert, which may take a while."

He nods and looks at the wall, staring into the distance. "It doesn't matter to me. I lost my taste for religion after witnessing the slaughter on the battlefield at Antietam."

Hmm. Perhaps that explains why he seems so far away at times.

"How so?" I say.

"I think religion is a hoax... or if it isn't a hoax... then the world is run by a really cruel God."

"What do you mean?"

"The papacy has helped oppressive rulers subjugate the poor for centuries. Even now, the church is conspiring with France to recognize the Confederacy. The pope doesn't care about the plight of the slaves, and since his decisions are considered infallible because he represents Christ on earth, his support of the Confederacy will obligate Catholics serving in the Union army to abandon their fight against the Rebels. There are many other examples of religious cruelty throughout the centuries. Oliver Cromwell's slaughter of Catholics in Ireland is one. The various Catholic Crusades to the Middle East are another. The worst thing is what I saw on the battlefield. A compassionate God would never allow the slaughter I witnessed at Antietam."

This is a change, I ponder—Brian's antagonism and vexation toward religion. I hope he doesn't stay this way. I certainly don't want to raise our children as atheists.

"Let's get married in a Protestant church then," I say. "I don't want to wait."

"That's fine with me."

He traces his finger along my cheek. His hand cups my breast when he kisses me. His touch ignites my senses. I can't stand it any longer.

My hand settles below his belt. "We've waited long enough, don't you think?"

He's excited as he struggles with my blouse, so I help him. He helps me pull off his shirt, and then he holds me in his arms.

I let him lead the way. He takes everything slow, making sure I'm comfortable, until I'm about to burst inside. It must be the intimacy knowledge he learned from Teresa, I assume.

His body is strong and muscular, and then we become one. It's easier than I expected. The brief pain fades away, subsumed by my liquescent desire. I can't believe what I've been missing all these years!

It's even better the next morning. I write Father a letter that afternoon, telling him about my pending nuptials. I say that I don't expect him to cross the ocean, due to his health issues.

We leave for New York the next morning.

A wealthy investor Adam knows arranges for our marriage to take place at the elegant, tall-spired Trinity Church on Wall Street. The wedding is attended by Mary, Adam, their four children, the Keenans, some of Brian's friends from Western Union, and several ladies Mary and Brian resided with during their early days in New York. Mary is my bridesmaid, and Adam is Brian's best man. Brian looks very handsome in his suit, even with the burn scar above his left temple.

We stay at the marvelous Astor House Hotel during the first week of our honeymoon. The hotel staff treats us like royalty since Brian used to work there. We then board a train to Bedford, and stay at the Pennsylvania resort for a week.

Brian rents a three-room house near Emma and William in Georgetown when we return. He goes to work at the War Department each day, while I volunteer at the hospital.

We have a wonderful time performing together at the White House the following Saturday afternoon. Mrs. Lincoln is a gracious host. She asks us if we'll play there again, and we readily agree.

37. BRIAN O'ROURKE

Washington. September 14, 1863.

I FOLLOW PRESIDENT Lincoln as we exit the War Department building together.

"May I speak with you for a couple of minutes?" he says.

"Certainly," I say.

We walk toward the White House, taking long, quick strides. I feel fortunate to be tall so I can keep up with him.

"I'd like you to accompany my wife and her entourage to New York tomorrow," he says. "She'll be representing me when the Russian fleet arrives at the harbor."

"I'd be happy to, Mr. President."

"Good. Please keep an eye on her to make sure she's safe. Some of Pinkerton's agents will be traveling with her too. I'd like you to stay in New York after Mary returns to Washington. I have a special assignment for you."

We reach the front of the White House.

"Let's walk a bit more if you don't mind," he says. "I could use the exercise."

We continue through the mansion, exit out the back, and walk toward the south lawn.

"I need to figure out what's *really* going on with the Russians," he says. "We told the press that Russia is sending their squadrons to New York and San Francisco so they can assist us if England and France jump into bed with the Confederates. However, I think they may have their own agenda."

"It could be helpful to have Russia on our side. Defeating England on our own may be difficult. They have the strongest navy on the planet."

Lincoln nods. "It's giving the country a much needed morale boost to hear that Russia wants to be our ally. The public's jubilation after our triumphs at Vicksburg and Gettysburg wore off quickly after the draft riots in New York in July."

"Pinkerton's agents are infiltrating the circle of Confederate sympathizers that started the riots. I hope we find the traitors before they can instigate any more insurrection."

"I do too. England will think carefully about joining forces with the Confederates if they know they'll have the Russian navy as an adversary. However, I need to find out if Russia has an ulterior motive. See what you can find out when you talk with their officers. I hear you're a quick study when it comes to languages. Learning some Russian could help you get closer to them."

"I will, Mr. President."

"I'd also like you to infiltrate Fernando Wood's inner circle if you can. Wood's seditionist rhetoric since Tammany Hall's Democratic machine elected him to Congress is undermining our efforts to keep the Union together. I'd like you to find out if he's involved in any treasonous activities we can use against him. For instance, Confederate raiders on the high seas are raising havoc with our merchant marine fleet—stealing cargoes and sinking our ships. See if Wood or any of his cronies are involved in these raids."

"I will, sir. Wood made his fortune in the shipping business, and I'm sure he and his associates are involved in the illegal slave trade. I'll see what I can find out."

"He's committing treason if he's financing the Confederate blockade runners. England says they're remaining neutral in the war. However, their shipyards are continuing to build ironclad steam-propelled warships for the Confederacy. I need to know if Wood is working with them."

"I understand, sir. I'll bring my violin with me. My cover as a musician will allow me to travel in aristocratic circles, as well as the Irish pubs where Wood's accomplices spend their evenings. I'll use my contacts at the brothels to see what they learn from the Russian sailors they entertain. Men often open up to women when they don't perceive them as a threat."

He chuckles. "I imagine so. The New York aristocracy is going to make a valiant effort to impress our new allies. They'll be holding several celebrations in their honor. You should pack accordingly, so you can attend the festivities."

"I will, Mr. President."

"There are a lot of moving parts in this diplomacy. France and England are supporting Poland's plan to break away from Russian domination. I think the real reason Russia is sending their fleet to us is to prevent England from bottling up their warships in Russia's ports if they go to war. I need to know if Russia is serious about their alliance with us, or if this is merely a convenient way to protect their fleet."

"I understand, sir."

"Their first ship should enter New York harbor on September 16, with five more cruisers arriving soon thereafter. Another Russian squadron will arrive in San Francisco the second week in October. As always, you can send telegrams to me at the War Department when you need to communicate."

"Yes, sir."

We arrive back at the White House after circling the south lawn, and the president escorts me to the front door.

"I won't keep you any longer," he says. "I imagine Elizabeth is anxious for you to get home. How's she doing?"

"Very well, Mr. President. Thank you for asking."

"Give her my regards."

The president shakes my hand. "Good luck."

"Thank you, sir. I'll contact you as soon as I find out anything."

I walk northwest on Pennsylvania Avenue to Georgetown, and enter our home on Olive Street. Elizabeth is cooking dinner in front of the stove. I slide up behind her and hug her around the waist. "How's my angel doing today?"

She turns, smiles, and stretches on her tiptoes to kiss me. "How's that for an answer?"

"Indeed!"

She turns her attention back to the mashed potatoes.

I wrap my arms around her enlarged belly. "How's the baby?"

"It's kicking and moving around a lot this evening." She chuckles. "Perhaps it smells the potatoes. I'm afraid we may be bringing a true Irishman into the world."

I laugh. "Is that roast beef I smell in the oven?"

"It is."

She scoops the mashed potatoes into a bowl and carries it to the table. "I went for a checkup today," she says. "The doctor said I'm still on track for the first of December."

I move plates and cutlery from the cabinet and start to set the table. "Excellent. I need to go to New York tomorrow. I'm not sure when I'll be back. It could be a couple of weeks."

"Is this a social visit, or something else?"

"Both. I'm traveling with Mrs. Lincoln to greet the captain of the Russian warship that's coming to the harbor. I'm staying there afterward on a special assignment."

"Is it something you can talk about?"

"Not really. I'll send you a telegram every couple of days, or more often when I can."

I wash the dishes after dinner while she relaxes on the sofa. Her back has been bothering her as the baby has put on more weight.

She accompanies me to the train station the next morning. We sit on a bench, waiting for Mrs. Lincoln and her entourage to arrive.

"As always, you can withdraw funds from our account at Riggs Bank while I'm gone," I say. "I was thinking that you may want to hire Emma to help you around the house. What do you think?"

She smiles. "That would be nice. Thank you. I'm going to miss you."

"I'll miss you too, love."

Mrs. Lincoln arrives with more than twenty people. I recognize most of the dignitaries. We stand to greet Pinkerton and his associate, Kate Warne.

Mrs. Lincoln walks over to us. "How are you doing, my dear?" she says to Elizabeth.

"I feel fine, Mrs. Lincoln," Elizabeth says.

"I do look forward to seeing the baby. We'll have to celebrate."

Elizabeth's face broadens with a smile. "That would be lovely."

Our train for New York departs a few minutes later.

Two of Pinkerton's secret service agents in our railcar acknowledge me with a nod. I smile at them, and return my focus to the Russian language textbook I checked out from the Library of Congress.

PATRICK F. ROONEY

New York City. November 6, 1863.

I ENCODE MY message with a cipher, walk down the street to our Western Union telegraph office, and type the Morse code myself.

Dear Mr. President. I performed with the orchestra during the extravagant Soirée Russe at the Academy of Music last night. The Russians seem truly impressed with our hospitality. I've learned enough Russian to converse with one of their sailors I've befriended, a fellow named Nikolai Rimsky-Korsakov, who composes music as a hobby. He's teaching me Russian in exchange for violin lessons.

Your previous supposition is correct. The Russians moved their fleets to protect them from seizure by the British in the event of war. It's unclear if they would fight on our behalf unless the British-French alliance threatened them directly. My guess, after talking with several of their officers, is that they'd assist us if you make a formal request.

I've found no direct evidence of Wood's involvement in treasonous activities. However, I discovered two Confederate clandestine agents in his cartel.

I turned their names over to Pinkerton. I suspect their arrests are imminent. See you next week. – B. B. O.

Washington. December 3, 1863.

ELIZABETH HAS been screaming and moaning off and on behind our bedroom door for the past three hours. Hearing a baby's cry is a welcome relief after pacing back and forth in the parlor throughout the delivery.

Mary, who came down from New York to assist Elizabeth during the birth, opens the door and smiles. "It looks like you're a father," she says.

I enter the bedroom and approach the bed.

Emma is combing Elizabeth's hair, which is slick with sweat.

342

"Congratulations, Mr. Brian," Emma says.

"Thanks, Emma. I'm glad you were here to help."

Elizabeth reveals the baby suckling her breast. She smiles. "It's a boy. He latched on right away."

I'm mesmerized as I stare at our child. "Are you all right?"

"I'm sore, but that's to be expected. Come closer."

I sit down next to her, reach out tentatively, and cradle his tiny hand in my fingers. I'm too awestruck to know what to say.

Mary and Emma are gathering up the bloodstained towels and sheets.

"We're going to wash these," Mary says, "and give you some privacy."

They leave the bedroom and close the door.

"What shall we name him?" she says. "And we need to make arrangements for his baptism soon."

"It's up to you as far as his name goes. I don't care about getting him baptized. As you know, I'm skeptical about that sort of thing... although I did pray while you were in labor. I guess praying helped me feel less anxious; hoping that you'd both be safe."

She purses her lips. "Let's name him Patrick, after your father."

"That's nice. I don't think we'll be able to call him Big Paddy for quite a while, though."

She chuckles. "Probably not."

She gazes at me with conviction in her eyes. "I think it's important to get him baptized. Let's do it at St. John's Trinity Church next to President's Square. I like Reverend Smith Pyne."

Her imploring stare persuades me not to argue about the matter. "I'll ask Reverend Pyne tomorrow. Perhaps he'll perform the baptism after his church services next Sunday."

The baby gurgles and cries. Elizabeth lifts him to her shoulder and taps him gently on the back.

"Burp!"

We laugh.

"Sounds like he has a healthy appetite," I say.

"Would you like to hold him?"

"Sure."

She hands me Patrick, and I cradle him in my arms. "Look at his tiny fingers. They're perfect."

"They are. It looks like he got your dark hair and my blue eyes."

She puts her hand on my leg. "I feel stronger than ever that there must be a God, after experiencing the miracle of a baby growing inside me."

I nod, as I sway gently back and forth with Patrick in my arms. "What do you view God to be, now that you've felt the spirit of a baby growing in your womb?"

"I'm not sure. I certainly don't see him as some angry man with a beard whose main goal is to keep track of our sins so he can confront us at the Pearly Gates. It's deeper than that, like the air we breathe... or the water we drink, or the forces that keep the stars and planets aligned. I feel it the most when I play music," she chuckles, "or when we're intimate."

"Perhaps that's the Holy Spirit."

"Yes, that's what I mean. There's something more going on here than just this physical existence, something that makes us one with the universe; like the love that binds our spirits together eternally, even after we're gone."

I hand Patrick back to her, and she places his mouth on her other breast.

I take her hand and kiss her cheek. "Thank you... for giving me such a beautiful son."

She grins. "We'll make another one as soon as I'm healed up a bit. He needs a brother or sister to play with, don't you think?"

"I do *indeed*!"

Washington. April 9, 1865.

TWO OF MY Telegraph Corps colleagues are standing with me at the Navy Yard waiting to greet the president. He's returning on a steamer called the *River Queen* after two weeks of meetings with General Grant in Petersburg, Virginia.

The president, having departed for Washington from City Point,

Virginia, last night, is unaware of Lee's surrender at Appomattox this afternoon.

I hand the president a telegram from General Grant when he steps onto the platform. His entourage watches him as he reads.

He turns to Mary Lincoln. "This is good news," he says. "Lee has surrendered."

Everyone congratulates the president with handshakes and hugs.

"Per our instructions from Secretary Stanton," I say, "we've sent telegrams to your generals informing them of Lee's surrender."

"Good. There's no reason for any more fighting. Too many men have already given their lives."

We follow Lincoln's entourage in a horse-drawn carriage back toward the White House. The news of Lee's surrender has traveled fast. Bonfires on the street corners cast a pumpkin-orange glow on the jubilant faces of the revelers as we pass them. I hear many people shouting "Hooray," and "It's over," as we move through the city.

I say goodbye to my colleagues when we reach the War Department. I then run nine blocks on Pennsylvania Avenue, cross the bridge over Rock Creek, and enter our home on Olive Street.

"The war is over," I shout to Elizabeth as I enter.

"That's wonderful news. I was wondering what all the commotion outside was about."

We hug each other and dance around the parlor in a circle together.

I pick up Patrick from the floor—who, at the age of sixteen months, isn't sure if he prefers walking or crawling—and we dance with him cradled in our arms. Elizabeth's belly is large with our second child, which is due at the end of June.

"Let's walk down to the White House," I say. "The president is bound to make a speech."

Elizabeth puts on her cloak as I swaddle Patrick in a blanket, and we exit to the street.

There's an enormous crowd gathered outside the White House when we arrive. Many are Negroes—some of the thousands of refugees drawn to Washington, seeking protection during the war.

Someone begins a chant asking for Lincoln, and soon the uproar is deafening. We move back toward Federal Square to protect Patrick's ears from the noise.

The president appears at the balcony and the crowd cheers. Lincoln waves, makes a brief statement, and then leaves a moment later.

"He's probably exhausted after his trip," I say. "He was sick most of the time he was in Petersburg."

"That's too bad. It seems like he's been ill quite a bit the last couple of years."

"He has, probably due to all the stress he's had to deal with."

We walk northwest on Pennsylvania Avenue back to our home in Georgetown.

Church bells throughout the city start ringing early the next morning. Children and parents are bellowing through horns or ringing bells as I make my way to the War Department. People are shouting, "The war has ended, Lee has surrendered," or "The Union is saved," as I pass them on Pennsylvania Avenue.

Flags are flying from the tops of every building. Many men are marching arm in arm, singing at the tops of their lungs. There's hardly a dry eye anywhere.

The celebration continues throughout the day. Two bands assemble outside the War Department early in the afternoon. The bands play in formation, trying to get the secretary of war to emerge from the building.

Our Telegraph Corps inside is quite busy dealing with logistical matters. Every Union general across the country wants guidance regarding disarmament, disposition of Confederate prisoners, supply replenishment, and orders for their troops.

Per the surrender agreement signed by Lee, based on the directions President Lincoln gave to Grant and Sherman during their conference at Petersburg, we tell the generals that the Confederate combatants may keep their side arms and swords, as well as their mules and horses. The president wants them to return home quickly before the planting season ends. They must deposit all their remaining weapons and artillery with a designated Union representative. We also tell them to share their rations with Confederate troops in need, as General Grant did at Appomattox.

The terms seem generous to some of the generals who want retribution. We send a second telegram repeating our instructions when they ask for clarifications.

The bands playing outside move to the White House after an hour. I follow them. It's a good excuse to take a break after our busy morning.

THE ANGEL OF INNISFREE

A cheer erupts when the president steps out onto his second-floor balcony. He makes a brief speech and several jokes, saying he'll be better prepared to speak to us tomorrow.

Laughter and cheers erupt when he asks the band to play "Dixie."

He waves at the crowd afterwards, and retires from the balcony.

Friday, April 14, 1865.

ANSON STAGER and I, after one of the busiest weeks in our lives, are having a celebration dinner at Gautier's restaurant on Twelfth Street and Pennsylvania Avenue. We've just shared a sumptuous French meal. Stager is smoking a cigar while I have tea.

"Western Union will list on the New York Stock Exchange this fall," Stager says. "That should stimulate even more passion for our stock."

"I'm surprised at how much money we made speculating in gold and silver during the war," I say. "I'm glad you convinced me to join the Telegraph Corps."

"I recall your reluctance. The war turned out to be very profitable for both of us."

He takes a drag from his cigar and expels it toward the ceiling. "Having our finger on the pulse of each battle gave us a huge advantage over the speculators getting secondhand information on Wall Street. However, even I'm surprised at how much our Western Union stock increased in value during the war."

"Adam told me my stock holdings are worth close to a quarter of a million dollars now."

He smiles. "And our industry is just in its infancy. There are many new ways to make money with our messages. We've been discussing a stock ticker symbol quote service with some brokers on Wall Street."

"That will be quite valuable. We also installed more than fifteen thousand miles of new telegraph line during the war."

"I'd like you to stay on at the War Department for a few months before you return to New York. There are a lot of reconstruction projects

347

to organize, and I need your help negotiating merger agreements with the other telegraph companies."

"I'll tell Elizabeth we'll be moving to New York in October. Is that reasonable?"

"Yes, it is."

"Good. That will give us a few months with the new baby before we have to move."

A man bursts through the front door of the restaurant. "Lincoln's been shot at Ford's Theatre!" he shouts.

Stager and I look at each other with bewilderment.

Everyone jumps up at the same time to leave. We place the money for our meal on the table, and join the crowd queuing up at the exit. It's raining when we reach the street.

"Why would someone shoot the president?" I say. "The war's already over."

"I don't know," Stager replies. "I'm going to the theatre to see what happened."

"I have to tell Elizabeth, and then I'll join you. She's expecting me home soon."

We part company, going in opposite directions.

Emma is sitting with Elizabeth in the parlor when I arrive.

"Someone just shot the president," I say.

"Oh no!" Elizabeth exclaims. "Is he all right?"

"I don't know. I'm going to Ford's Theatre to find out."

She starts to cry, and Emma does too.

"Does that mean... we'll be slaves... again?" Emma says between sobs.

I kneel down and hold her hand. "Don't worry. That'll never happen. You have your freedom now."

I stand up and hug Elizabeth. "I'll be back when I know more."

I arrive at Ford's Theatre on Tenth Street at midnight. A crowd of hundreds has gathered outside in the rain.

"The president has been moved to the Petersen House across the street," Stager says.

Secretary Stanton arrives and asks us to follow him into the house. We thread our way through the crowd to the entrance.

"These men are with me," Stanton says to the soldiers guarding the front door.

Mary Lincoln is crying hysterically in the front parlor.

We follow Stanton to a bedroom near the back of the house. Lincoln is there, unconscious, lying diagonally across a bed. There's blood around his head on the pillow.

Joseph Barnes, the surgeon general of the United States, faces us. "The bullet is lodged in his brain. His prognosis doesn't look good."

Tears fill my eyes as I stare at the president. I force my tears to stop by concentrating on the vertically striped green-and-white wallpaper on the walls. Stager and I follow Stanton out of the room to a parlor at the rear of the house.

"We need to inform the cabinet," Stanton says to several soldiers in the room, "and send a search party to look for the assassin. His name is John Wilkes Booth."

He assigns the soldiers tasks, and they hurry away.

The rest of the night is busy. I leave the Petersen House several times to send telegrams to out-of-town cabinet members and congressmen for Stanton.

I've just returned when Dr. Barnes tells us that Lincoln passed away at 7:22 a.m. I enter the bedroom and kneel down with the rest of the men around Lincoln's bed.

Lincoln's war-weary countenance finally seems at peace. He's only fifty-six years old... but he looks much older.

I say a silent prayer for Lincoln's soul.

"Now he belongs to the ages," Stanton says.

I feel as if I'm in the midst of a bad dream when I exit to the street. The grief-stricken crowd is openly weeping now that they've heard the news, especially the Negroes, who view Lincoln as their savior.

The White House opens its doors to mourners wanting to pay their last respects on Tuesday morning, the eighteenth. Elizabeth and I arrive early, pushing a child pushcart with Patrick inside. The line behind us stretches several blocks down Pennsylvania Avenue by the time we enter.

Lincoln is in an open casket in the East Room. The bereaved in front and behind us include all races and colors—old and young, rich and poor, Confederate soldiers in gray, Union in blue. Our grief is palpable, heart wrenching, with most men and women openly weeping as they pass his casket to say goodbye, including us.

We hear later that thirty thousand visitors passed through the East Room by the end of the day, with thousands more still in line. Officials decide to move the casket to the Capitol building after his funeral tomorrow, so that additional mourners can pay their last respects.

The funeral ceremony at the White House the next day is private.

We watch the slow procession of his casket up Pennsylvania Avenue to the Capitol afterwards, along with thousands of other mourners. Twelve soldiers hoist his casket up the broad steps into the rotunda.

The line of visitors wanting to say goodbye to Lincoln as he lies in state extends half a mile from the Capitol. The rain is pouring down in buckets, but that doesn't stop hundreds of soldiers with amputated limbs and bandaged heads hobbling on crutches from the nearby hospitals. Government workers, cabinet members, state delegations led by governors and senators, foreign dignitaries, and hundreds of out-of-town visitors stand in line for hours to say goodbye.

Soldiers take the president's casket to the New Jersey Avenue B&O railroad depot on Friday morning. From there it begins its fourteen-day journey to his final resting place in Springfield, Illinois.

The newspapers display pictures of Lincoln's casket lying in state in different cities every day for the next two weeks. They estimate that millions of people watched the president's funeral train pass through their towns as he made his last journey home.

October 3, 1865.

ADAM AND HIS son, David, who's now sixteen years old, are waiting for us at the Jersey City railroad terminal when we arrive on the train from Philadelphia. They help Elizabeth and I carry our luggage to the Jersey City ferry.

"I can't believe how much you've grown," I say to David.

He smiles and says, "Thanks, Uncle Brian."

"He's as tall as I am," Adam says, "and he's still growing. I imagine he'll be as tall as you by the time he's done."

"Indeed," I say. "What do you want to do when you graduate from high school?"

"I want to study civil engineering at West Point."

"That sounds like an excellent idea."

David's straight brown hair, the shape of his face, and his height make it obvious he isn't Adam's biological son—at least to me anyhow. I wonder if anyone has ever brought this up with him. I'm certainly not going to say anything.

Elizabeth and I hold our two babies as we cross the Hudson River to New York. From there we board a horse-drawn carriage, and I instruct the driver to take us to our home on Patchin Place.

Patrick, who's now almost two years old, is trying to squirm out of my grip as he leans out the open window. Deidre, our four-month-old, whom we named after Ma, is asleep in Elizabeth's arms. We arrive at Patchin Place, bring our luggage into the house, return to the carriage, and continue to Adam's townhouse at number 3 Gramercy Park West.

Mary and her other three children greet us with hugs when we enter. Patrick is pleased with the attention he gets from his older cousins when they take him into the backyard to play.

Adam and I place the food Mary prepared on the table—roasted chicken, mashed potatoes and gravy, steamed carrots, green beans, watermelon, and freshly baked bread. Mary sits down on the sofa with Elizabeth to dote over Deirdre. She hasn't seen the baby since she came to Washington to assist Elizabeth with the delivery.

"Mary's found something you'll like," Adam says, speaking quietly so the women don't hear.

"Is that so? When can I see it?"

"Soon. She found out about it from our neighbor, Cyrus Field."

We spend the rest of the afternoon with Mary's family, and return home exhausted after dark.

There are several mergers in the telegraph industry the next several months. American Telegraph makes the first move in January of 1866, when they purchase Southwestern Telegraph.

Western Union merges with the United States Telegraph Company in March, and then American Telegraph in June, giving us a de facto nationwide monopoly. The value of my Western Union stock is worth

three hundred thousand dollars when the dust settles.

July 1, 1866.

THE RECENT RAINS and the hundred-degree heat have made the humid New York City air oppressive and unforgiving.

"Let's have a picnic north of the city," I say to Elizabeth. "It's cooler there. We should pack food and blankets. I asked Adam if he'd join us yesterday, and he agreed. They'll be ready when we arrive."

"That sounds like fun. It'll be nice to get out of this heat for a while."

We load the kids and supplies in a carriage, and the driver takes us to Mary's house.

Adam and I load their picnic supplies and children into a second carriage, and we depart for the Hudson River railway depot on Thirty-Fourth Street and Ninth Avenues. We exit a half hour later from the northbound train at the Irvington rail stop.

"Irvington was named after Washington Irving," Mary says, "the author who wrote *The Legend of Sleepy Hollow*, which is close to here. Irving lived north of here in Sunnyside."

"I remember him," Elizabeth says. "I read his stories when I was growing up in London."

I rent a large covered coach—large enough for all of us—from a livery station, and we load the kids, women, and supplies into the seats in the back. Adam and I sit up front, driving the horses. We head east on Irvington's Main Street out of town, and meander along a winding dirt road through the forest.

"Where are we going?" Elizabeth says from behind me.

"You'll see soon enough," I say.

We continue to a fork in the road, veer left, and stop a moment later when the road ends. Adam and I jump down from the driver's seat and help everyone out. The children start playing keep-away with a ball in a grassy two-acre field surrounded by trees.

"So, what do you think?" I ask Elizabeth as we look around.

"There's a marvelous view of the Hudson River," she says as she looks to the west.

"Indeed." I point north. "That's Hook Mountain on the other side of the river."

"It's beautiful." She turns to me with a puzzled look on her face. "But this is a long way to come for a picnic. Why did we come here?"

Mary, Adam, and I grin at each other.

"This is your present," I say to Elizabeth, "the land where we'll build our new home."

Her eyes narrow. "What do you mean?"

"I bought this land—eighteen acres of it anyhow. I'm going to name our estate Innisfree, assuming you approve."

She turns her gaze to the river and smiles. "I think that's a marvelous idea."

"The pond to our left is fed by a freshwater stream," I say. "It even has fish."

I walk in a circle around the blankets and picnic supplies. "This is where I was thinking we could build our house. We get the best views here. We'll put an indoor bathroom in the children's hallway, and another one next to our bedroom. Of course, we'll need a large parlor for the grand piano I'm going to buy for you."

"Many wealthy businessmen are purchasing land to build estates here," Mary says. "We bought the fourteen acres to the south of you. You can reach us by going right at the fork in the road. There's also a trail beside the pond that leads to our land."

Elizabeth's mouth falls open. "Really? That's wonderful. Our children will be able to play together while they grow up."

Mary grins. "Cyrus Field, our neighbor who built the transatlantic telegraph, told me about this area. He's looking for land out here too."

Elizabeth turns to me. "How will you get to work?"

"Adam and I will take the train from Irvington. We'll stay at our homes in the city when we need to work late."

Elizabeth hugs me and raises her lips, and I oblige her with a kiss.

"This is the best present ever," she says. "I guess I should tell you my surprise too."

"What's that?"

"I'm pregnant again."

EPILOGUE: ELIZABETH O'ROURKE

Innisfree Estate. Irvington, New York. September 18, 1898.

THE HORSES TIED to the hitching posts next to our barn are stomping and snorting as the motor carriage rumbles up our long circular driveway. Everyone from the party streams out of the house to see what's causing all the commotion.

Mary's son, Colonel David Rubin, steers his open two-seat convertible to the porch and turns off the engine. He's wearing his dark blue army uniform. He jumps out of the driver's seat and opens the door on the other side for Karen, his wife.

David hugs me when he reaches the porch. "It's good to see you, Aunt Elizabeth," he says.

I kiss his cheek. "I'm glad you made it back safely from Cuba. The Spanish-American War sure didn't last very long."

David nods. "No, it didn't. I appreciate you throwing a party for me. I'm looking forward to hearing you and Uncle Brian play music again."

David shakes hands with his male relatives and hugs the women. I count thirty-two of us here with Mary and Adam's children, spouses, and grandchildren, along with our own.

"Where did you get this?" Brian asks David. "And how much did it cost?"

"It's from the Winton Motor Carriage Company in Cleveland, Ohio. It was a thousand dollars. It has an odorless hydrocarbon engine that can reach twenty miles an hour, and suspension wire wheels that minimize passenger jostling on a bumpy road. Would you like a ride?"

"I'd love one."

Brian sits down in the passenger seat. David starts the engine and steers the car with the lever down the driveway.

I return to the kitchen with Mary, and we arrange the food we've prepared for the party on the countertops. It's an informal smorgasbord, so people can eat whenever they'd like.

All of the men and boys and a few of the women ask David for a ride. They migrate back to the kitchen and fill their plates afterward.

There are fourteen grandkids running around playing hide-and-seek. We have a large house with six bedrooms, so there are plenty of places to hide.

Brian hugs me from behind. "Shall we begin the concert soon?" he says.

"Sure," I say.

I dry my hands and turn to him, and he kisses me. His kisses still make my heart flutter, just as they did back in Ireland when we were sixteen. Our passion has always been strong.

We walk hand in hand to the grand piano in the parlor. I turn on the lights. The Edison light bulbs will allow us to play late into the night if we want.

Brian starts to tune his violin, which lures everyone into the room. They sit on sofas and chairs around us. The younger children are fidgety, but they soon settle down.

"We're going to begin with the first song I heard Elizabeth play," Brian says. "I was standing in the forest watching her through her window in Parke's Castle. I'd never seen anyone so beautiful."

Everyone chuckles and claps.

I feel my face tingle. Brian still makes me blush when he talks like that. Of course, the wine I had earlier is playing its part too—a fruity, red Bordeaux from one of the wineries we visited when we were on a concert tour in France last year.

"This is a piece by Robert Schumann called 'Träumerei,'" I say.

Brian is standing next to the piano holding his violin and bow next to his chest. He joins me after the first section, and we play the rest of the piece together.

Everyone claps when we finish, even the grandchildren. Most of them have had piano lessons and attended concerts with me, so they know how to be polite.

Brian places his violin into its case and sits down.

"The next piece is by Chopin," I say. "This is his *Fantasie-Impromptu*, opus 66. Chopin performed it for me during one of my piano lessons. He wasn't feeling well that day. However, he became instantly invigorated as he began to play."

I remember how difficult the piece is as I begin. I'm grateful to get through it without missing any notes when it's over. The family applauds when I finish, and a few of the men say, "Bravo!"

"I love playing in a small salon setting like this," I say. "It's like the concerts I played in Paris. Brian and I heard the next piece by a composer named Erik Satie when we were in France last year. It's called Gymnopédie number 1."

The simple chords and enchanting Impressionist melody mesmerize my audience. They applaud when I finish.

"Fiona is going to play the piano for a while," I say as I stand up.

Fiona is the best pianist now. She teaches piano at Columbia University in New York.

I sit down in an armchair next to Brian.

"I'm going to play a piece by Claude Debussy," she says. "He played it for me when I was studying with him in Paris. It's called 'Claire de lune,' which means 'moonlight.'"

Fiona faces Brian and me. "I thought this would be appropriate for you, Aunt Elizabeth and Uncle Brian. I love the way you used the moon as a touchstone while you were separated for fourteen years."

We nod and smile. Brian takes my hand.

The music is hauntingly lovely, invoking images of the moon in my mind, and we applaud at the end.

"That was beautiful, Fiona," Brian says.

Everyone chimes in with similar comments.

"Let's move the chairs aside so we can dance," I say after the accolades.

The men move the chairs and sofas against the wall.

Brian takes my hand and smiles. "I'd like to start the dancing with my angel of Innisfree," he says.

Everyone chuckles. They know the story—how I rescued Brian in the Viking meadow next to Lough Gill, and rowed him across the lake to Innisfree.

"This is Chopin's Waltz number 2 in C-sharp Minor," Fiona says.

She begins to play, and Brian waltzes me slowly around the room, matching the rhythm of the music. The refrain picks up speed, and soon my heart and body are soaring. It slows down for the third theme, and most of the adults join us on the dance floor. The kids quickly follow.

THE ANGEL OF INNISFREE

The speedy section comes again, and I'm flying with my feet barely on the floor, my heart pounding in my chest. I'm almost dizzy. Perhaps it's from the wine I drank earlier.

I press close to Brian, gazing deep into his dark eyes as he twirls us in slow circles. I know I can trust him to hold me so I don't fall.

His hair is silver now and he has a few more wrinkles, but his warm smile hasn't changed at all, especially when we dance. People occasionally ask me about the scar on his forehead. I always tell them it's his badge of honor from the Civil War.

I let go, trusting him, and we're one with the music floating around the room. I feel his love shining through his eyes to me, penetrating me, like the bright lights from the lightbulbs Edison invented.

I remember him playing his violin on the Viking rock to comfort the dying then, how he rescued Mary, how he helped Negroes escape on the Underground Railroad, how he helped the wounded soldiers at Antietam, and a hundred other kindnesses over the years, and it occurs to me that *he* may have been the angel of Innisfree all along.

THE END

ABOUT THE AUTHOR

Patrick Francis Rooney, a first generation American with Irish parents, was born and raised in Albuquerque, New Mexico. He lived in Texas and Virginia for several years before he settled down in Colorado. A former software engineer in the computer industry, he now devotes himself full-time to fiction writing, as well as performing and composing music. He plays bass and acoustic guitar with friends in the Denver/Boulder area when he isn't writing or traveling.

Additional information about the author is available here: http://www.savoirpress.com/